Broken Worlds

Edited by Jack Burgos

READ
ORDER

221	13	33	151	61
9	19	47	165 (14)	85
43	145	101		121
57	253	111		203
77	263 (6)	269 (10)		227
81	1			
223	25			
259	137			
279	179			
283 (4)	187			
	195			
	245 (8)			

Broken Worlds

To all the parents who, gazing into the innocent eyes of their young, plead with the universe to let them live and well.

CONTENTS

Broken Worlds

The Wailing Women
by M. R. Ranier

It was August 5, 1972 or '73 or '74, I don't know, years run together. Being 10 feels the same as being 11 and 11 like 12, but only in hindsight. At the time it made all the difference, we formed ad hoc hierarchies, sorting the power structure by age. Even being a few days senior, or a few minutes in the twins' case, can grant you the sufficient leadership status to decide whether the game will be pirates v. cowboys or ninjas v. wailing women or Al Capone's gangsters v. Elliot Ness and his gang of untouchables.

We were in my backyard. I know it was August 5th for certain, the twins' birthday, and Hattie was already lording her 6 extra minutes of life over Holly, loudly declaring that she should get the first serving of cake after dinner. Their age difference was irrelevant to the day's agenda, though, since Tim was older than all of us by nearly two years. He was the leader, but not a well-liked one.

Tim felt wrong for our group. He was too old, and none of us were friends with him, but he was too immature to hang out with the older groups that were already learning how to sort themselves by gender and wealth and ability, so he resorted to hanging out with us and we were too young and dumb to exclude him. Tim was weird; Tim sucked his thumb; Tim randomly stuffed his hands down his pants; Tim was gawky and ginger; Tim knew too much about sex for his age but could distribute sage advice like the kids we looked up to; Tim thought jabbing a dirty fingernail into girls' nipples and chanting "milk, milk, lemonade..." was high comedy; and Tim *always* wanted to play wailing women.

"Awwww, not wailing women." Meagan, the youngest of our group, folded her arms. She was a gaunt and timid girl. Her long hair was braided in a laurel that pinned neatly in the back, looking like a yellow snake had coiled itself around her head. Her older brother Paul, handsome Paul, Paul with his hands always stuffed in his pockets, nodded quietly in agreement. He struggled between his distaste for Tim and his respect for the hierarchy.

"YES wailing women." Tim got uncomfortably close to Meagan, he shrieked and sobbed in her face, contorting his own dirt-smeared face grotesquely. She pushed him back; he cackled and mimed aiming a rifle at her.

"Stop!"

"BANG!"

"TIIIIM!"

"You're dead, lie down."

"No!" Meagan stamped her feet

I couldn't stand it. "Tim, stop." Tim turned towards me, training his invisible bead on my forehead. His eyes gleamed.

"That's how you kill them, you know, BANG, one bullet to the head and KAPOOOOW." He waved his arms around his head to demonstrate the gore then collapsed in a dramatic display of squirming and hacking, clutching at his throat.

"Tiiiiim," Meagan was getting upset, tear tracks wormed down her dusty face. She was the only one of us who'd actually run into one of the wailing women. It was a child about her age a few months earlier, she had tried to comfort him because he was crying and he swung a coke bottle at her head.

"What?" Tim said, sitting straight up, "My dad kills 'em all the time."

"Nuh-uh," that was Hattie, or maybe Holly, I forget which immaculate twin was wearing the red ribbon and which the green that day.

"Yeah-huh, him and unc go out huntin', they brought one back once, just shot her knees out, she was sobbin' and sobbin' but still try'na bite them." Even now, I can feel the same sour stomach I had then thinking about it.

I'd seen the wailing women of course, on TV, out car windows, through house windows, wandering into backyards with their knives or hoes or broken glass in shredded hands. Dad always called the hotline, easy and quick to dial, 222, three short clicks of the rotor. Captain Kangaroo very seriously told us when and how to dial the number at the end of every episode. "Go inside, tell an adult, if you can't find an adult, dial 222," he would say, Clarabell the Clown beside him, nodding gravely. After calling 222, the containment force would arrive in their puffy asbestos suits, looking like Bibendum the Michelin Man, and wrap the wailing women up in a fine mesh net to take them away. It was clean.

Humane.

"Why would your dad and uncle do that?" Meagan fiddled with the pins in her hair; she pulled one free and bent it.

Tim shrugged. "Dunno, they're not human you know."

"Yes they are," Paul slouched back, suddenly timid under Tim's glare.

Tim stood up, "No, they're monsters." He screeched and pretended to swing an axe at Paul who stepped back. Tim laughed without smiling. He always laughed that way, jaw wide open, mimicry of laughter spilling out from deep within.

"Paul's right," I said. Blushing slightly from just saying his name. "They're human."

"NO. THEY'RE. NOT." Tim was getting mad. He was even more unbearable when he was mad.

"Well, they were once." Paul had straightened up, slightly. Hands still deep in his pockets. He was mediating, ever the peacemaker. Even then, I admired the hell out of him and his cool temper, his calm, his kindness, his kind of watery, dopy blue-green eyes that concealed his ponderous intelligence. Now that I think of it, it had to be sometime after 1972. I wasn't interested in romance at all until 11.

"You know how they get it, don't you?" Tim's voice was cold, suddenly lacking the nasal quality that made him so difficult to listen to. This was worse.

I recalled a PSA and recited the list, "Bites, blood transfusion, sharing needles, uh…" I trailed off, realizing what Tim was talking about.

"Sex!" He was agitated; he stamped around, leaving crazed trails of bent grass and weeds. "You gotta' wear a condom, jimmies, unc says, you gotta' wrap it up, seamen wear their rubbers when it's wet."

I didn't know enough about sex at the time. It was just a word, a funny word, a magic word that held a world of possibility we couldn't fully comprehend.

"Uh, yeah, and intercourse."

"My unc says they deserve it," Tim pointed a bony, filthy finger at me, always his middle finger because he thought it was funny.

"You can get bit, too." Paul said, he was quiet and shifting himself slowly into the shadow of our big elm tree, perhaps hoping to disappear in the cool shade.

Tim waved his hand, "Only if you're stupid, unc says they always use their weapons and only bite if you take it away, unc says you can pull out their teeth."

Meagan had been silent the entire time, but that made her gasp and cover her mouth. "Why?"

3

"They're not human!" Tim said, now exasperated, he gave her a patronizing look like he was explaining the color blue to a toddler.

"They hurt," said Paul, in almost a whisper, "They cry."

"So do rabbits," Tim sounded like he was surrounded by the stupidest people in the world, "Rabbits scream, ya know, it's the only noise they make."

"No…it's different, they cry when they hurt you, when they're about to hurt you, they're sorry," Paul said, he sounded strained, I realized he was trying not to cry and it made me love him all the more.

Tim rolled his eyes, "A BLOO A BLOO HOO HOO" He rubbed his eyes with his fists. "Wittle Paul Want to Cwy, they'll still KILL YOU, they'd stab ya right in the eye, cut off yer pecker," Tim swiped his hand in front of his crotch. I instinctually placed my hand over my own pecker and shuddered.

"Unc says they deserve it, dad says it too, they're sluts that fucked themselves into becoming monsters."

Tim had just used another magic word, another word full of possibilities and fears. It made my stomach knot up; he made it sound so ugly. I'd heard my mom use it once, accidentally, backing into the mail box, but it just sounded funny then, powerful but funny. That breathy 'f,' the satisfying click of the hard 'k.' It didn't sound fun when Tim used it, it sounded grim, like the seconds before a thunderhead full of hail splits open. We were quiet.

Holly, it was Holly who spoke, finally. I remember now, she was the one wearing the red ribbon that day.

"What do your dad and uncle do to them?"

She sounded like she already knew the answer, comprehension fell on Hattie next. In a minute everyone but little Meagan put it together. The wailing woman taken alive. The pulled teeth. Grim puzzle pieces locking into place.

Tim sneered, but it seemed false. He said something that sounded like he was reciting a script, "Nothin' they didn't already want."

Memory is faithless. There are probably a lot of things I remember wrong about that day, memories spilling into other memories, but those words burn in my mind, still alive and worming in my soul. *Nothing they didn't already want.* I know we ended up not playing anything that day. We all suddenly had things to do, pets to feed and garbage to take out, anything but there. I couldn't leave. It was my house, my backyard, after all. I had to stand there and stare at Tim; gawky, ugly Tim playing tough. I can't even remember if we said anything to each other, or if he just, eventually, wandered off.

✿✿✿

Lying in my bed that night, I heard shuffling and sniffling underneath my window. That wasn't the first time one of them wandered into our backyard at night, scraping their way over our pointed iron fence. There had been a lot more that year, it was around the time Peter Jennings had started saying "pandemic" instead of "epidemic" during the nightly news, a distinction I hadn't fully understood at the time. Peter Jennings would call them "Victims of the Disease" or "The Infected." "Wailing Women" was, as far as I could tell, regional slang.

I slipped out of bed. It's funny the things you do remember, little things. The wood floor felt so cold on my bare feet despite the stifling summer air. I was wearing Spiderman pajamas. The smell of lilacs filtered into my room despite the sealed and barred windows. The sky was clear, but the world still felt like an ice storm was about to swing down like a sledge. I stood on tip-toes to look out the high window, tilting my head to see through the bars. The wailing woman stood underneath our big elm. She was twenty-something, probably a student at the local state college. She was skinny, emaciated actually. A bright green sundress draped awkwardly over her unnaturally angled body, her motions were clipped and straining, like a puppet fighting invisible strings. She clutched a baseball bat covered in brown stains close, almost nestled in her chest. Her eyes were wet and bloodshot, heavy, dark circles underneath her eyes made her look like a raccoon.

The night was split by a roaring, spitting engine from the front of the house. A long beam of light washed across the side of our house, illuminating a thin strip of our back lawn. I could hear men whispering, then saw three separate beams of light growing and intensifying from the side of the house. Two shadowy figures easily vaulted our fence, blinding the wailing woman with their flashlight beams. A third, smaller figure followed behind, struggling over the fence, fumbling his flashlight.

The woman raised her bat, swinging it wildly, crying loudly now, almost shrieking. The two taller figures flanked her as she swung her weapon in wide arcs, making sharp cracks as it connected with the tree. I heard a shout, "Distract her!" The smaller figure backed away from the wailing woman. "Fucking distract her, boy!" One of the men grabbed the smaller figure and threw him towards the wailing woman. He started screaming, small scared screams, a child's scream. The woman spun towards the boy, creakily raising the bat, she had stopped crying. Then the two men swarmed her, kicking at her knees and slamming their flashlights against her skull with thick smacks. She dropped, bringing the bat down hard on the boy's shin. He shrieked, a primal wounded animal shriek, there was a loud home run crack as his bones shattered. The two men were laughing and kicking at the woman's ribs while the boy fell back screaming.

One man left and came back with a crinkling blue tarp. They rolled the wailing woman up in the tarp and carried her out of the backyard like she was a roll of carpet, leaving the boy to whimper alone in the backyard. They eventually came back, one man pulled the boy up to his feet, he started screaming again as he put pressure on the shattered bone. The man laughed and swung the boy over his shoulder, then climbed back over the fence. The last thing I heard was one of the laughing voices say "Don't be a pussy, Tim."

I ran to the other side of the house to look out the front facing window at the end of our long hallway. I saw their rusty mud-spattered truck mutter to life and drive off. I saw the blue tarp in the back, wrapped around the still twitching body. She had been a human; that was a human underneath that tarp.

I fell asleep that night whispering the word "human" to myself, whispering it until it didn't mean anything anymore, until the word entirely disassociated in my mind from any meaning, until it was just a sharp rasp and a hum.

☠☠☠

After the vaccine was developed, after the final Wailing Woman—the 52 year old Merle Larson—died in captivity, the news was filled with relieved celebrities and pundits hailing the end of a savage era. The hair's breadth of difference between human and monster was gone, we could once again be certain of our civility.

I know better though. I know the truth about the hair's breadth. I know that if you say HUMAN over and over while trying to fall asleep you can find this truth.

I know that a crowd of young men, led by a gawky ginger named Tim, crowding around a cowering 17 year old boy, screaming faggot and kicking at his ribs, are still human.

I know that a bat, swung with incredible strength, can shatter your kneecaps leaving you bitter and bound to a bed and still very much human.

I know that a pair of twins named Hattie and Holly can lead nearly identical lives, marrying and conceiving around the same time, bringing two cousins into the world who will bind as tight as twins, human.

I know that a quiet, handsome boy named Paul caring for my bitter, crippled self after being attacked, when no one else could bring themselves to even look at me, what beautifully human.

I know a sobbing 27 year old woman named Meagan dying as the man she loved and trusted and had a child with beat her to death with his thick, curled hands because a tumor was pressing on his pineal gland is more human than we're willing to admit.

The truth is the Wailing Women were human and there was never a hair's breadth to begin with. It's just a spaghetti mess of lives.

I lay in my bed, ritualistically repeating the final magic word, the final word that is so full of possibility and fear, letting it roll across my tongue until it mean nothing. Just a rasp and a hum.

I try to will life back into my legs.

I try to sleep.

I imagine all of the humans that are wailing.

I rasp and I hum.

Somewhere in that endlessly cycling mass of rituals I eventually fall asleep.

The Mentor
by S. Mickey Lin

His fingers flutter above the Fazioli grand piano and the Esplanade Concert Hall falls silent, waiting to witness his wizardry.

The spotlight focuses on him, Alexander Pritt, barely fourteen, sitting alone on the stage. His golden blonde hair and crystal blue eyes conjure an image of a delicate porcelain doll. A closer examination of his face reveals the playful glimmer in his eyes. His slender arms sway and there is a balletic fluidity to their movements.

He plays Balakirev's *Islamey – An Oriental Fantasy,* considered by many to be one of the hardest classical composition ever composed. Balakirev, the eccentric Russian composer, had a nervous breakdown after completing the piece. I, myself, did not attempt the piece until my twenties.

He plays the frenetic tempo of the second stanza. His finger movements border the divine. He plays it so magnificently that it utterly breaks my heart.

He is my prized pupil, a student I never sought nor wanted. He is my first and only student. I had no desire to waste my time teaching youths, but my wife asked me to teach that young boy and I did. You don't get to my age without knowing that a happy wife is a happy life. Against my best judgment, I took him under my wings.

He soared so high that I barely managed to catch a glimpse of his shadow. I warned him of the story of Icarus, a boy who flew too high with his fake wings and how the sun scorched him for it. He laughed it off. I keep telling myself he's just a boy. *But with a talent to transform the world*, a reminder would ring in my mind and insist that he was more than just an ordinary boy.

The world heralded me a genius, someone whose brilliance can only be seen once a decade. But, when he played his first piece, I instinctively knew that he was a prodigy we would only witness once a century. His greatness surpasses mine and I hated him for it.

He never had to spend days learning a piece and playing it until his fingernails bled from practice. He never had to spend nights doing listening practice to recall musical notes. I worked operosely to get my so-called gift. He barely lifted his fingers. Perfect auditory memory and muscle memory retention ensure that he only needs to hear a piece and plays it at least ten times until he masters it. By the twentieth time, he would be able to inject his transcendental sensibilities into it, just as he's doing with *Islamey*.

On stage, Alex pauses for dramatic effect, the same technique that I had taught him, but he had made it his own. The silent interlude makes the audience hungrier for his dazzling spell.

Oh, how I wish I had not taken him to be my student! At least then I won't be digging my own grave. My wife, Angela, bless her soul, said that I needed to encourage him and how sad it would be if a talent like his is lost to the world. She never once suspected my disdain for the boy nor my reason for not accepting students.

The world's greatest do not become great by mentoring others, they become great by crushing all opposition. My competitiveness is my edge and Angela had rendered it dull by having me tutor the boy.

The boy was cute when he first started, that I have to admit. But, even a bloodhound is endearing when it's a pup. I remembered when he first asked me to tutor him. He was so afraid of asking the great and famous pianist of the century to tutor him. He called me mentor and that's been the designation ever since.

Mentor. It's funny, really. As musicians, we've been trained to break sounds into smaller segments and to play around with them. So, "ment" and "tor" easily become "tor" and "ment." Every time the boy says mentor, all I hear is torment. Whoever came up with the word is a genius in his own right, adequately defining the torment of the mentor. I want the boy to succeed, he is my prized pupil after all, but I never wanted him to surpass me. Which artist would want to jeopardize his own legacy?

He starts on the third section of *Islamey*. The audience is spellbound, watching him apprehensively, and praying that his sorcery has not come to an end.

They say music is incomparable; that you can not compare two pianists. That's what people say to make themselves feel better. Musicians know who's a better player, even if the public is too deaf to comprehend it.

The music echoes throughout the hall. My version of *Islamey* is inspiring at best. His is heavenly, almost as though he has transported your soul to a state of nirvana.

He plays the closing section of *Islamey* and keeps looking back at me, standing behind the curtains. I could see the need of approval in his youthful eyes. I have no idea why he sought out such things from me. His level already surpasses mine. His desire for approval only makes me what to deny it from him even more.

He finishes and the hall explodes with thunderous applause and standing ovations. It takes a full five minutes before his incantation is broken and the soreness of standing returns to the well-heeled audience.

He bows and the applause erupts even louder. He walks toward me and I wanted to stop him right then and there. Those applause, those ovations, those adulation, all of them should have been for me, instead of a boy too young to know his own greatness.

He looks at me with searching eyes and asks the same question he always asked at the end of each performance.

"How did I do, father?"

I look into those clear blue eyes and tell him the truth. I always have.

"You make it look so effortless."

"It kind of was, actually."

He laughs his youthful laugh and it breaks me a little more. He has no idea what his genius and gift have done to me and I can never let him know.

His music resonates in my mind and the torment plays on.

Broken Worlds

KINGDOM COME
BY GEORGE COTRONIS

Christopher felt the beginning of a migraine coming on. He absentmindedly reached into the drawer of his desk for the bottle of scotch. A storm had been gathering for hours, the black clouds looming over the city. *This one's going to be a good one*; he thought and took a swill from the bottle. Out of habit, he looked towards the study's open door. His wife didn't like seeing him drinking like this; she said it made her think of her alcoholic father, always sneaking off to get a drink. He met him once at Thanksgiving. He used to store bottles all around the house and take sips whenever he got a chance, his wife said.

He put the bottle down on the desk and stared out the window. The raindrops landing there came slow but steady. He looked at the back yard and hoped that the rain wouldn't flood the basement again.

He was ashamed to realize how old and worrisome he had become. This wasn't like him, worrying about weather and his precious basement. Hell, rain never put a dent in his plans, even if they included a trip to the beach. Rain was rain, nothing to be bothered by, nothing to ruin your day. But that was a long time ago. These days, his left knee hurt whenever the weather got wet.

He left the study and went downstairs to the kitchen. His wife was out today, giving him some much needed "me" time to try and get some work done. He opened the fridge and grabbed a bottle of water and an apple. His diet was another thing that was different these days, doctor's orders. He took a bite out of the apple and went over to the couch to watch some TV. There was a breaking news segment about a storm hitting the east shore. It looked bad. After Katrina, people got skittish when the weather turned like this, to the point when you never knew if the news reports were honest or bullshit. He decided it was the latter, put his feet up on the table and after a while, fell asleep.

When he woke up, night had fallen and the storm was raging outside. He glanced at the clock on the kitchen counter and rubbed his eyes. It was late in the afternoon. He wondered if his wife had come home and found him sleeping, but the dark house told him that wasn't the case. He got up and called out after his wife, but got no reply. She was probably visiting one of her friends. Didn't she say something about that? *I guess I should have listened more closely*, he thought as he walked around the house, turning on the lights. His knee was acting up, forcing him to walk with a limp.

"Getting old" he said, to the empty house. Somehow saying it out loud made it worse.

He took a look outside from one of the windows, but he couldn't see much.

He decided it was time to call Helen and find out where she was. He had to get dinner started and maybe she could pick up a movie from the video store. It wasn't often they got a night alone at home with each other.

He picked up the phone and dialed his wife's cellphone. The voice on the other end of the line said the number couldn't be reached. He hung up.

He thought about calling his daughter, but she was two states away and he would only succeed in making her worry. Like he was now. He probably should have called her earlier, she was supposed to be back hours ago. Maybe the storm took down some trees and the roads were closed off.

 He opened the front door and was impressed by the strength of the wind. There was a minivan parked on their driveway. The minivan his wife drove.

So she did get home.

The headlights and overhead lights weren't on. He waited to see if his wife would get out of the car, but there was no movement. Then he noticed how strange the rain looked when it fell. He turned the light towards the minivan, which was now somehow painted black, from the original deep blue it was when they bought it two years ago. Even the windshield and windows were dark. The sight was absurd, the darkness and the storm making it hard to really see, but he was sure this was their car. The plate numbers matched and who else would have parked the same car but in a different color on their driveway? He was about to make a run for the car, but something about the rain made him think twice.

Then he saw the bird. It must have been a sparrow, but Christopher didn't know what the hell it was now. It was completely covered by whatever the rain was carrying and it was struggling to take flight. Long strands of the black matter were stretching between its feathers and the ground. It looked like a bird trapped in oil, unable to spread its wings or move. It looked like the rain was trying to eat it.

He went back inside and put on a jacket and a raincoat. He made a run for the minivan. He tried to avoid the puddles of black that were everywhere on his front yard. Whatever it was, it didn't prove too difficult to walk on, nor was it sticky as he feared.

He ran to the car and used one gloved hand to throw open the driver-side door. The car was empty. There were shopping bags on the passenger seat, but nothing else. Then he noticed the smears of black on the upholstery and on the steering wheel. His heart sunk.

Christopher ran back to the porch and shook off the raincoat. He looked out across the street and called after his wife. There was no reply. He called after her a few more times, his panic mounting. None of this made sense. The house was just a few feet from the car, where could she have gone?

He took off his shoes and clothes and let them fall on the wooden floor of the porch. He didn't want to bring whatever covered them into his house. Once inside, he sat down, trying to ignore the panicked voice in his head that threatened to send him running outside screaming. He tried to figure out what was going on, what that black matter could be. *Chemical warfare?*

He tried the phone again, but it wasn't working. He turned on the TV, but the only thing he was getting on all channels was the emergency broadcast message amid the screeching beeps and tones designed to get your attention.

> *The office of civil defense has issued the following message. This is an Event warning. This is an Event warning. Event warning means that an unspecified environmental disaster has been detected.*
>
> *Important instructions will follow in thirty seconds.*
>
> *This warning applies to all areas receiving this message. Immediately seek shelter. The safest place to be during an Event is in a basement. If no basement is available, seek shelter in the lowest floor of the building. Remember to stay away from windo—*

He turned it off. He had a wife and daughter somewhere out there and he was supposed to just stay inside?

He paced the house and looked out the windows, but there were no signs of her. He could see a fire somewhere downtown, but couldn't make out what buildings were burning.

He sat down and put his head in his hands, unable to think clearly, feeling the migraine coming on again. Whenever he got one of those he was unable to do anything besides lie down and keep a pillow over his eyes to shut out any kind of light. He tried to calm down. He could hold it at bay if he didn't get too worked up.

He went upstairs, sat on the bed, their bed, the one they had shared for 25 years now. He knew something was wrong,that there was no logical reason for his wife to be wandering outside in this weather, no reason her car would be parked twenty steps from the house, unlocked and empty. Something was wrong, but there wasn't much he could do except sit here and try and keep his headache at bay.

A sound came from above, like something scraping against the roof. They didn't have any trees that were that high and he had never heard it before. They didn't have an attic. Almost against his will, he got up and approached the window.

He opened it a bit, holding it against the wind that threatened to throw it open against the wall. The sound of the storm was now much stronger, much closer to him. The air didn't smell the way it usually did when it rained. This rain, it carried something different. It smelled like ashes.

There, outside his second floor bedroom window, 20 feet off the ground, was his wife. He recognized her, even though she was completely covered by the dark matter that was still falling on her, drop by drop. He could see the red top she left the house in that morning peeking from underneath the dark and he could recognize the large hoop earrings he bought her as a gift on their last vacation. Her mouth and eyes were shut, covered by the oily substance. She was knocking on the window, like she wanted to be let inside. When Christopher didn't move, she flew in, crashing through the window. Her movement was erratic but effortless. The window exploded inwards, scattering pieces of glass and wood around the room.

She flew in, her feet still not touching the floor, just her toes dragging lightly against the wood.

She shrieked, then before his eyes the flesh of her forearms split open and a pair of fanged maws like those of a Venus Flytrap protruded from her flesh. Within them, a dozen black tendrils flailed wildly, reaching out to him.

Christopher frantically tried to keep her from touching him, falling down in his desperate attempt to get away from the thing that used to be his wife. He scuttled on the floor like an insect, until his back hit the closet door and he just sat there, looking up at the thing.

It spoke, its voice like gravel scraping against cement, like its teeth were all broken and floating around in its mouth.

"I can't see…" it said and Christopher winced at the sound, which still carried something of his wife's voice. He crawled towards the door, but the thing seemed to hear him and moved closer to him, so he stopped.

"Make a sound baby, call my name so I can find you… please…" the thing said, as if trying to imitate the personality that once belonged to the body it occupied. The hairs on his neck stood up. He tried to think of a way out but couldn't see how he could escape the room without letting the creature know where he was. The tendrils were now feeling their way around the room, touching the bed and the walls of the bedroom, leaving behind dark smears.

He bolted out the door as fast as he could. The creature whipped its head around at surprising speed and one of the tendrils managed to grab his ankle. The searing pain travelled along his leg and to his spine, but in his panicked state, he managed to kick it loose. He stumbled free and out into the corridor. He took the steps two at a time, grasping the banister with both hands. He reached the landing just in time to see the thing levitating at the top of the staircase.

He heard a sound behind him, something scraping at the front door, trying to get in. He didn't dare to think what stood behind that door, but knew that escape route was closed off. He ran into the kitchen and grabbed a knife from the holder. He didn't know what good it would do, but he felt better holding a weapon. The pain in his leg was still present, but was beginning to fade. He knew he could get out of this if he just thought this through, but time was one of the things he didn't have. The creature shrieked in the living room, joining the wail of whatever was outside that door, a mix of human crying and a howl. He remembered that his neighbors had a dog, a mean Rottweiler they kept in their backyard and he prayed to God that what he feared wasn't true. One of those things with four legs and the ability to outrun him would mean his death.

He hid behind one of the counters, trying to gain some time, but the creature was already there.

"Come be with us Christopher. Come be with your family." That sibilant voice again, like the sound of sand being carried by waves. He knew what it was trying to do, but it terrified him that it was smart enough to try and deceive him by using his love for his family. It was smarter than he thought; god knows how smart it really was.

"Daddy? Please tell me where you are." Even though the voice was low and guttural, he could still recognize his daughter's speech pattern. It had her too. Whatever they were, his daughter was now one of them. The two people he loved in this world were gone and there was only one way to be with them again. He stood up and looked at the thing one last time. It didn't really look like his wife any more, but he tried to imagine her standing there, like she often did in the mornings, a cup of tea in one hand.

He ran towards the back door and threw himself against the door, breaking it and falling outside on the sleek grass. Raindrops started falling on him immediately, one of them landing on his cheek, the rest across his arms and back and soon, he was standing in the rain with his face towards the sky, like a little kid playing trying to catch raindrops with his tongue. It didn't take long.

THE INTERVIEW
BY SHANNON IWANSKI

"Good morning, Mr. Smith."

"Good morning."

"My name is Mr. Jones. I work for the Department of Internal Defense. We'll begin the interview for the position of Head Custodian in just a moment. Before we do, do you have any questions for me?"

"No."

"Very well, let's get started. Per policy, I will be recording this interview. You have the right to refuse to have these proceedings recorded. However, should you choose to exercise that right, the interview will not continue, and you will not be considered for the position. Do you give your consent for recording?"

"Yes."

"Very good. Recording will begin…now. This is Secretary Robert Benjamin Jones. The date is May 13th, 2176, and the time is 11:49 a.m. The following interview is for the position of Head Custodian at the United States Treasury Department. Will the applicant please state his full name and identifying information, please?"

"My name is Phillip Gregory Smith. Citizen Identification Number: 107-71B. Date of Conception: November 2, 2145. Genetic Predisposition and Sequencing for Highly Superior Auto-Biographical Memory and Menial Labor with High Enjoyment Threshold. My previous position was Custodian, Third Class, at the United States Mint in Philadelphia, Pennsylvania."

"Thank you. The first thing we must address is the Terms and

Conditions of Application for Employment or Advancement within the Government of the United States of America. Were you provided this form upon declaring interest in applying for this position?"

"Yes."

"You have read the Terms completely?"

"Yes."

"Do you have any questions regarding anything that you have read?"

"No."

"Thank you. We will now begin the question and answer portion of this interview since you have already completed the written test. I will mention for the record that Mr. Smith scored a 100% on his Custodial Information Retention Examination. A commendation for exemplary contributions to science and the citizens of the United States is to be placed in the permanent file of Mr. Smith's geneticist, Dr. Richard Foster.

"First question: Have you ever entertained thoughts of overthrowing the duly elected government of the United States, either singly or as part of a terrorist organization, at any time during your life?"

"No."

"Second question: Have you ever entertained thoughts or spoken aloud your desire to renounce your citizenship?"

"No."

"Third question: Have you ever knowingly or willingly engaged in sexual intercourse with a member of the opposite or same sex at any time other than when directed to do so by a duly appointed member of the Department of Procreation?"

"No."

"I will remind you that, per the standards set forth in the Terms and Conditions of Application for Employment or Advancement within the Government of the United States of America, any lies you tell during the course of this interview can and will be held against you. Do you wish to change your answer to any of the questions I have asked you thus far?"

"No."

"Question Four: Have you knowingly or willingly engaged in the usage of recreational or non-prescription medication?"

"No."

"Scenario One: Your supervisor has the day off due to an illness. You have decided to break the rules and be more efficient than your job description calls for you to be. This results in you finishing all work forty-five minutes before your shift is scheduled to end. What do you do during that time?"

"I don't understand the question. How can I be more efficient than my job description allows?"

"Scenario Two: Custodian A reports that his mop is not working to the specifications listed in the Manual for Life and Longevity of Government-Issued Equipment. He states he was issued the mop three weeks before, but you know it has a life of five weeks. How do you handle the situation?"

"From the description, it is clear to me that Custodian A is attempting to get out of doing his assigned work, or he has damaged property in some manner. Based on the Employee Handbook of Operational Expectations and Requirements, I would report Custodian A to the Shift Oversight Proctor and recommend he be executed in accordance with Section 1, Subsection 2b of the aforementioned Handbook."

"If I may take a moment to interject, Mr. Smith, I find it impressive that a Custodian, Third Class, is so well versed in the rules outlined in the Handbook. Did you go out of your way to learn them in order to impress the hiring committee?"

"No, sir. That would be a violation of the rules, punishable by death. I learned this information at the Adolescent Center for Menial Laborers. I was designed to eventually take the position of Head Custodian, so the Center's Proctor had the information taught to all the people in my group. He was given permission to do so by the Under-Secretary of the Department of Procreation."

"I shall make a note of that. Scenario Three: Custodian B is eating lunch with Custodian C at a table the required ten feet from the Head Custodian's table. However, due to the listening device that has been placed beneath his table, you determine that Custodian B is attempting to coerce Custodian C into the seditious act of attempting to join a terrorist organization to overthrow the government. Please tell me what steps you would take in order to remedy this situation."

"As Head Custodian I would be issued a firearm by the Department of Weapons and Armaments. Per Section 5, Subsection 14d of the Employee Handbook of Operational Expectations and Requirements, I would wait for Custodian B to return to his appointed work station and execute him for treason. As part of a potential conspiracy, and to ensure that seditious thinking did not continue within the ranks of the Custodians, Custodian C would be required to clean the area, and then he would be executed as well. As the Head Custodian, I would clean the area, and then file a report with the Shift Oversight Proctor and the Secretary of the Department of Weapons and Armaments."

"What forms would you use?"

"Form SOP14X and Form DWA1."

"Thank you. That concludes the question and answer portion of the interview. At this time you will be given the opportunity to ask any questions you may have."

"I have no questions."

"Very well. Mr. Smith, are you satisfied with the responses that you have given to the questions during this interview? You have one chance—now—to alter any of your responses. This is your final opportunity to do so. Do you wish to avail yourself of this opportunity at this time?"

"No."

"Thank you. As was stated by you at the beginning of this interview, you have been genetically predisposed to have a Highly Superior Auto-Biographical Memory. Mr. Smith, please recite Paragraph 2, Subsection 1 of the Terms and Conditions of Application for Employment or Advancement within the Government of the United States of America."

"…"

"I am waiting, Mr. Smith."

"I…don't remember."

"You don't remember?"

"No, sir."

"Do you wish to amend your response?"

"…No."

"Very well. Allow me to refresh your memory. Paragraph 2, Subsection 1 of the Terms and Conditions of Application for Employment or Advancement within the Government of the United States of America states: 'Any applicant who knowingly or willingly fails to read through this complete document, shall, upon discovery, be subject to death. The guilty party may decide whether he wishes to be executed or to take his own life.' Here is the gun. Please make your decision now, Mr. Smith."

"…"

"This is your final opportunity. Should you make no decision, I will execute you."

"I'll do it."

"Thank you. This is a copy of Form DWA2. Please initial here…here…here…and sign here. Thank you. I will give you ten seconds to take your life. If you fail to do so, I will execute you in accordance to the terms of The Renewed Patriot, Treason, and Sedition Act of 2094. Good day, Mr. Smith."

"………

X

BY EDWARD MARTIN III

I can't say that no one liked Leon. That wouldn't be accurate. It would be more accurate to say that no one *knew* Leon. Not visibly.

Which made sense at the time, but now results in a cold steel knot in the middle of my guts. This knot warns me that something has Gone Seriously Wrong.

Leon's family moved into town when I was in fourth grade. That was in 2010. I know because I remember my teacher at the time, Mrs. Payson. That was the last teacher I ever met who seemed to genuinely want to help people. Ever since her, it's been all downhill, teacherwise.

That day in class was as dull as paint, and then a boy with a note came by. Mrs. Payson read the note, and introduced us to the new boy.

"Class," she said, "This is Leon. He and his family just moved here from…" she stumbled a bit, referred back to the note, and tried to pronounce something. Leon looked up at her, then out at us. He said something. A long word that sounded like someone rolling dice. "It's an island," he said.

That would explain the accent, which I couldn't place.

"Who would like to show Leon around?" asked Mrs. Payson. "It's hard to move into a new town and not have any friends."

That's when the world changed. Well, my world anyway.

No one raised their hands. There was a moment of silence while Mrs. Payson scanned the room, then she waved Leon over to an empty desk in the back.

Nothing more was said of Leon that day.

Aside from an incident in a tree that left a scar I still bear on my leg to this day, the entire fourth grade passed by me without incident. As did the fifth and sixth grades.

In seventh grade, my mother died. There wasn't any sort of drama about it – it was actually calm in a way. I was in my bedroom, looking out through my window on the second floor. About six blocks away, I watched her car coming home. Then it stopped. She got out, stood a moment, and then just fell down.

My father and I ran out there, but there was nothing we could do.

The doctor said it was a brain aneurism. That she probably didn't feel anything at all, maybe just a little dizzy. I'm of mixed feelings, naturally. I'm glad she didn't suffer, but the bottom line was that she wasn't here anymore, and that was about as bad as a boy can get.

There was a funeral, but not many people showed up. A lot of people had moved out of town over the past few years. Just packing up and moving out. Work running out, I guess.

High school came with all the social challenges that high school brings. The air was thick with clumsy teenage romance, and our small town's high school population played the same romantic game of musical chairs played out everywhere else. Some people stuck around, others moved away.

Somewhere in the middle of high school, I decided I wanted to be a cop. I don't have a specific moment, or incident that triggered this thought—I simply came to the decision gradually. After working up my nerves, I went to the police station and told them what I wanted. In a small town, it's easier to follow your dreams if they're the dreams that can be contained in a small town.

I still had to study, of course, but I could intern at the police station during weekends, which I did. I also worked out hard. For a guy who used to be a hopeless geek, I rapidly became quite the hunk, based on the level of interest around me. Honestly, I can't say I didn't take advantage of that once in a while.

Eventually, the Sheriff helped fund my trip to the Academy, as did my father. I helped, too, having saved up all my internship money over two years. I graduated with excellent grades, and came back to town feeling nine kinds of happy about my choices.

I was a good cop, too. Not a hard-ass, nor a namby-pamby guy. I always remembered that my sole interest was in helping keep my town happy. Sure, it had its troubles—all small towns did—but there was no reason I couldn't help keep it happy.

Then, one day, I came home from work and my father was sitting his last sitting in the kitchen, cold hand wrapped around a cold cup of coffee, head down as if he had nodded off. I felt a little odd ordering an autopsy, but I wanted to know. Cardiac arrest. That made no sense to me—he didn't smoke, didn't drink, and was relatively healthy. Little good that did either of us, though.

A week later, still numb, I signed up for the Marines.

A lot happened in that year, but it was a very different place than my home town. It seemed more pure, more clean, more complete.

A year after I signed up, I was part of a convoy, halfway between Daman and Kandahar, and looking forward to a decent night's sleep after three weeks of fighting.

I have a vague memory of hearing impacts against the truck body. For a fraction of a second, I thought the truck ahead of me had kicked up rocks. But then I knew what it was. I heard glass breaking and felt a punch on the side of my head.

A week later, I woke up in a hospital room. Well, maybe not woke up. I drifted enough into consciousness to see shapes and hear voices. Everything looked strange, sounded strange. Monstrous and blobby. I think I answered a few questions, and then there was some more darkness, which was good. Right now, darkness felt like a solid friend who helps you rest.

When I finally snapped back, I was in the States, in a hospital that was actually quiet. I stared at the food in front of me, at the forkful of spaghetti, at the hand holding the fork, at the arm. This was me. I looked up and there was a nurse, sitting nearby, watching me eat.

I blinked at him. "I'm back," I said, quietly.

He smiled at me. "How do you feel, George?" he asked.

I felt like a puzzle that had finally been completed. I saw my whole picture. "I feel fine," I said. "I actually feel fine. What happened?"

He told me everything.

He told me things that made sense—that I'd been shot in the head, that it was a rough recovery, that no one was quite sure if I was going to make it. He told me that apparently my brain made up its own mind and healed much better than anyone had expected. He told me I'd been here for nearly a month.

He also told me things that didn't quite make sense—that I'd been waking up and having peculiar contemplative fugues. "Episodes of lucidity" he called them. They would last for a few hours, and then I'd drift back away. During these times, I apparently became fixated on different objects in my room. Flower vase, water faucet, the bright green switch on one of the instruments monitoring me. I would stare at these objects, fascinated, and then eventually go back to bed, and back to the dark place where I healed. I never spoke during these sessions, but they knew I could hear them and understand them, because I responded. I have no recollection of these episodes, but as I looked around the room, everything looked especially bright and vivid.

"This is the first time you've spoken," he told me. "This is very exciting."

The doctors were excited too, and asked me a lot of questions, some of which I could answer, and some of which I couldn't. They gave me a few X-rays and CAT scans, and one doctor in particular kept asking me very strange questions. I was asked if I can imagine a red ball sitting on a picnic table in the middle of a park. I knew what he was doing, though, so I didn't get fussy at him. He was seeing how well my brain worked after having been stirred a bit.

It seemed to work fine.

I still had the fugues, but they weren't so dramatic. I often found myself reviewing some object in my room, as if I'd never seen what it was. Oh, I could recognize it, and explain it, but somehow, in my brain, it felt... new. Each one felt like holding a baby in my arms that had just been born. I was amazed at how detailed life was around me!

I was so busy with all the tests and therapy and so forth that I never once thought about home, which was okay, because I had joined the Marines so I wouldn't have to.

One afternoon, I was watching the TV in the room. My nurse was there with me. We were all glued to the television. In fact, I could safely say that practically everyone in the world was glued to their televisions, if they had them. This was a big deal. It was the first landing on Mars of a manned spaceship. I wasn't normally interested in that sort of thing, but when history's being made, you tend to pay attention.

The lander's progress through the atmosphere was transmitted in brilliant color all over the world. We all watched as the camera feeds cycled around the outside of the ship, as the ground came closer. We all held our breath.

And we all saw the flash.

Then the feeds stopped.

The stations went into a bit of a hover cycle, firing off questions to various talking heads, until the space agency finally came back with the news. The craft had disintegrated. They had no idea how or why, but it was gone.

The whole planet reeled. We certainly did. But something else happened right then.

The news channel had hastily posted a picture of the crew of the Mars mission, and were recounting stories of the brave souls who had hurled themselves from Earth. That wasn't the peculiar part. The peculiar part was that they spoke repeatedly of the eight brave men and women on board, and how much they'd be missed, and so on and so forth—but the photograph showed nine people.

They enumerated the same eight over and over, and interviewed their families, and all the people of Earth mourned their loss, but still, whenever there was a group photo, there was nine people.

A lot was happening fast, so I had to set that aside for some more medical tests.

That evening, though, I switched the television back on, and watched. In less than ten minutes, another group picture flashed by. I was able to see faces better in this one, and studied it carefully for the whole twenty seconds it was on screen.

That's when I saw him.

Leon.

And that was when the world changed back. Well, my world, anyway.

If I felt like a jigsaw puzzle suddenly put together before, now I felt like a broken snowglobe, coming back together. Every flake of fake snow, every drop of glycerin, and every shard of glass all tumbled back into place and then I saw my life.

My *real* life.

Starting in fourth grade, I saw Dawn raise her hand immediately to be Leon's friend. I liked Dawn. For a couple of days, she showed him around. And then I saw her come in one day to school looking pale and sick, and then the next day, she wasn't at school. After a week, I went by her house, and knocked on her door.

Leon answered.

"Is Dawn in?" I asked. He cocked his head and looked at me, and said "No, forget about her."

And I did. I forgot all about my friend Dawn and her whole family.

But then, another piece of the snowglobe came together, and I remembered the whole thing.

I saw Leon in school, always staying in the back of the room. He was smart. And quiet. But people still noticed him.

I saw a couple of bullies come up to him in fifth grade, and push him around. They pinned him to a wall and even got a smack in before he looked at them and said something. I was too far away to hear, but they immediately stopped and wandered off. Leon walked by me, rubbing his cheek, which was already darkly bruising. As he passed, he looked casually at me and said "Forget this."

And I did. As simple as that.

Until now.

Later, one of the bullies was found in the woods, torn to pieces. The other was never found. There was never a newspaper article about it, and no one else even seemed to remember them.

Now, I remember Leon riding his bike all over town that day. He must have been very busy. He made me forget twice.

I saw him later that year leading another kid into his house. By that time, all he had to do was look at me and tilt his head a little, and— Alakazam!—no more memory.

Although apparently that wasn't true. Apparently, there was still a memory, but he just smoothed it over.

As the years passed, every once in a while, I saw Leon doing something. Sometimes it was something ordinary, sometimes it wasn't.

Once, I saw him coming out of the woods holding an arm. He took a bite from it. In that moment, Leon didn't quite look the same as he always did. In that moment, his teeth seemed a little longer than usual. And pointed. And his eyes were black marbles.

And then I forgot about it, as usual. My mind was smoothed over.

When I was in seventh grade, I watched out the window of my house as my mother stepped out of the car and approach Leon, who was crouching by the bus stop. I saw him reach up and pull her toward him. I saw his mouth open, and his teeth.

And then I forgot. Again.

In high school, I once saw him walking by the pool. He dropped a set of keys in the water, while pulling something else out of his pocket. They bounced on the deck, and slid into the water on the deep end. He looked around, but there was no one nearby. I saw him kneel at the pool, and reach into the water. I saw his arm reach all the way down, through twelve feet of water. Then I saw him pull the keys back up. He licked his arm dry, stood up and walked on. He walked right past the column behind which I was hiding. Almost casually, I felt him reach toward me, and another thing was smoothed away. Another piece of my life fell off.

But now it was coming back together. If for no other reason than that, I could thank that faceless sniper.

Throughout high school, I saw Leon take people. One by one, they wandered down Corbett Road, which was the dead-end street where Leon lived. One by one, I saw people assume—as did I—that these people had moved away. Leon worked all our memories as if they were clay.

I did not become a policeman at random. I see that now. My soul felt a need for the truth, it felt the pull of questions, and being in the police was as close as I ever figured I could come to that.

As I spent more time in the police station, I saw Leon come in more often. He would come in and people would forget things. They would forget calls for disturbances. They would forget body parts being found. They would forget their own entries in their own paperwork.

I filed the paperwork, and sometimes read it, but I too forgot everything.

Then, one day, I came home and found my father.

Most of him anyway.

And there were footprints leading away.

I forgot this all.

And then, maybe a year later, my brain was rearranged, and I remembered it all. I remembered everything. In fact, I couldn't forget it if I tried.

And now, Leon's out there. I know he is. I know the others are with him. And I also know that they landed safely. But we had forgotten that, with the flash. Except for me.

I saw it all. I saw the camera images. I saw the surface getting closer.

And I saw the others.

Like Leon, but not pretending to be human.

Then, the memories were complete. My life was rightside up again.

I thought about my home, my town, the one I had sworn to protect. I thought about Leon, the boy who became a man in my town. Or something manlike. Manlike with sharp teeth and a hunger for people.

I thought about all the other small towns in the States. In the world. I thought about Leon, being dumped here to see if he'd make it, and how easily he could sway our minds.

Then I thought of him on Mars. Telling everyone how easy it was. Showing them, with the eight brave prizes he brought back, how plastic their minds were and how soft their flesh.

It seemed so absurd I had to laugh.

I knew he would be back, then, because Earth was perfect. Earth was warm and wet and filled with everything they could possibly want.

And I knew we had already lost.

Broken Worlds

I Cannot Begin to Tell You
by Scott R. Jones

00:00:00 // I didn't mean to leave his stroller behind. You have to know that, first, above everything else, that leaving it there on the side of the road for you, or the police, to find? Christ. It wasn't my intention. You *have* to know that. I panicked. I did. I'm so sorry.

When it happened, my mind just went white, like it used to during the bad times. It went white and I panicked and I took him. I tore our boy out of his stroller and he wasn't happy about that, of course, you know how he gets with surprises, or he was picking up on my panic, I don't know, and I think I might have hurt his shoulder doing it, which just, god! I panicked and I ran and I am so sorry.

I know how much you hated seeing abandoned strollers, before he was born. Leaning against trees and signposts, their struts broken and bent. Sagging rents in the sun-bleached fabric, mud and decaying leaves clogging their spokes. I mean, no one ever thinks *hey where's the baby for that stroller?* because, y'know, obviously it's just wreckage left by some homeless person when they find a bigger cart to shift their miserable mobile hoarding around in. No one ever thinks *the child that should be in that stroller is gone* or *that baby has been stolen. That baby has been stolen by his dad.* No one sensible thinks that. Which is what I used to tell you when you would think it. Think it and then say it.

So, maybe you knew. Maybe you knew all along. Maybe it was a memory from a future so compressed and dense with the nothing that's coming, that it ricocheted off that vast blank wall ahead of you, of us, of everyone. Pinged off a slab of solid, howling emptiness and shot back into the past, embedding itself in some fold of your brain where it could live and have some meaning for a little while. In the anxiety and disgust you'd feel every time we passed an abandoned stroller in a wet ditch.

That baby has been stolen by his dad, who loves him. They never say that, especially.

I am so sorry. Not for taking him, because that? That's for the best, considering what's happening. No, I'm sorry about the stroller, for not taking the thing with me when it happened. How hard would that have been? Just fold it up, throw it in the trunk, like I've done every day for the last eighteen months. I'm sorry. I didn't mean for it to be like that, for you to be hurt with that image. I pani— //

00:02:13 // —ey have forms, but it's only what we dress them in so they make sense, not that it helps. They don't *stay* dressed, naked and cold, they tear through all cloaks and signs, they're not anything, they're noth— //

00:02:55 // It doesn't matter much, in any case. Not now.

He's sleeping now. He sleeps a lot, thank god. I'm making this tape for you because he hasn't yet figured out that it's not just daddy talking to himself, which I do all the time, actually. He doesn't know about the tape recorder. Found it in a drawer, with, like, nineteen others. A drawer just for ancient cassette decks and recorders. This place is full of abandoned crap. Your parents? Jesus. Not to speak ill of the dead, but hoarders? World class. I half-considered letting him say something into it, y'know? *Say hi for mommy.* Thought better of it.

I talk to myself a lot, about anything. Random stuff I won't miss, that I don't care about, memories I don't need. I live in a buzzing cloud of inanities, a swarm of trivial concepts. My own hoarding. All the useless accumulated garbage of the life I had before I met you. I open my mouth and fill the air with it and when he notices me, which is rarely, he'll... he'll pick away at some of it. It's like a game to him. So, this tape. Because I tried to write you but written words are the first things to go here, particularly when he's awake. They're too full. Too heavy. It's just easier to talk, more direct.

Broken Worlds

Oh Christ. He's up. I'll fin— //

00:04:02 // ...kinda half-surprised the cops haven't been out here yet. It would be one of the first places I'd look. How many summers did we come here, after we broke with the circle? I mean, this is where your family brought us to get clean in the first place. Christ, we were *married* down at the lake. This would be the first place, the only place I'd look. But how I'd do it is not how things are working now. The fact that you're not here, that they're not here, the police... it's him, somehow. Our boy. The things behind our boy. It's fate. This is how it happens.

00:04:32 // You hate me now. I understand that. I mean, I'd hate you if you had done this. And you'll hate me until you can't anymore, which may be sooner than you or I would like. But know that I love you, and I took him away because of that love which I will feel until I can't anymore.

We went out walking last night, after he woke up. It helps to get him out of the cabin and into the cold; seeing his own breath in the air entertains him no end. I bundled him up, because despite what you and probably everyone else thinks now, I'm a good dad. I am. I took him out and let him toddle around the cabin in the snow and when he got tired of that, I scooped him up and sat him on my shoulders and we went walking in the trees. The moon came out at one point, shot out from behind the clouds to pin itself like a fat, bloodless grub on the black silhouettes of the pines.

He saw it, our boy. He saw it and he gurgled happily and then he reached up his little mittened hand and he pointed at the moon.

You get a sense for when it's coming. There's a kind of atonal shift in the sound he makes, a subtle hum that's generated in behind the gurgling and the cooing. I don't know if he's making it, the hum, or if it's coming from somewhere else, or if it's just a... a perceived thing on my part. *My sensitive nature,* he said, scoffing. I don't know what I'm seeing. Hearing. I wonder if I ever did. You remember how I was. I don't know anything anymore.

Please remember me. Please. Remember how I was, even during the bad times. For as long as you can. I know, how can you forget, right? But just... please try.

He pointed at the moon. He pointed, and I heard what I heard, so I swung

35

him down from my shoulders and laid him out in the snow and scooped a handful of it onto his little trusting face. He hated it, and I hated doing it, but I just couldn't... I mean, the moon. Right? The fucking *moon*.

There should be an order to this thing. If it's going to happen, and it is. It is happening. *There should be an order.* How's that for my epitaph? Bad enough that I should lose your name. I remember you, I just... it was the first thing to go, the heaviest thing. I don't know what you call yourself. It's gone. What I used to call you. *My love.* My love, for what it's worth, for however long it lasts in the coming storm.

So I distracted him with a face full of freezing snow, like a schoolyard bully. He cried and raged a bit, but you know how he is, he's so good natured, sweetheart. That's all you, of that I'm fairly certain. He calmed down quick and the hum wasn't in the air anymore. We made snow angels. Or I made snow angels and he sat in the snow and watched and laughed at my flailing as the stars shone and the moon wriggled through the branches and the hot sweat of terror cooled on my face.

Our son is a weaponized koan.

We should never have ma— //

00:07:13 // —ddamn stroller. What a thing to do, what a fucked up... I'm sorry! I'm sorry, but listen. I couldn't speak. The enormity of it, I just.... like *that*, she was smoke and void and I went white. It happened at the north entrance to the park, and I'd left the car maybe half a block away and I just, I tore him from his stroller and ran for it, got him strapped into his car-seat and started driving. After a mile of city traffic, dense with signal and advertising and purpose and his suddenly perfectly normal little boy wailing from the back seat, the white started to wash out and I could think a little. My first thought was *oh shit I left his stroller behind* and my second thought was *what the fuck is happening?* and my next thought was *you know what this is. You know what you've done. You know.*

You know.

We should never have done what we did.

I was so looking forward to his first words, and so fucking happy when they started tumbling out of his little mouth. All the monosyllabic identifiers. Every *da* and *ma. Nana* for banana. *Bo* for bowl. I couldn't believe there was ever a time when I thought it would be a good idea to maybe *not* teach him to talk, to maintain silence around him at all times. What a pretentious... I mean, Christ, how did you put up with me? With my *the moment he learns that a rose is a rose it will cease to be anything else for him* bullshit.

I loved watching language grow in him. Loved watching him begin to bind up his world with words. Now there's this... I don't know. Now I'm thinking that my first instinct was right: silence. Reverent, fearful silence of what could be wrought. Of what was waiting for us, under the new shine of our repaired lives. Beneath the polish, down there in the black muck of our history. My history.

Who was it that said there was a sentence out there for everyone, or... hold on. Wait, was it two sentences? Yeah, two sentences, two strings of words, and one of them? One sentence will heal you and the other will destroy you. And you may or may not hear the first, and you're damned lucky if you do, but you're guaranteed to get the second. Was that Dick? It sounds like Dick. Fucking PKD.

But it's all in the binding, isn't it? Language is the binding agent. For time. For meaning. It's the sense maker, the descriptor, the boundary state between what is and what isn't. A goddamn net we build over the abyss so that we can dance across like the bugs we are and instead of dancing like reasonable beings, like sensible goddamn insects, instead of being aware of our place, what do we do? Shit, what? We build *worlds*. Is that smart? Who decided that was a, y'know, a smart thing to do? Whose brilliant fucking brainwave was that? Considering the... the tensile strength of our widdle monkey mouth noises. Of our insect chitter.

But there it is. The guaranteed sentence has come. The sentence has been handed down. Our sentence is up. It follows, doesn't it? It follows that there'd be an answer to the Word that God used to speak the world. The anti-Logos.

I think it follows.

We deserve it, maybe. I'm more and more convinced, actually. We deserve it. All meaning has broken down. We've done most of the work for them, stripping it all out from our side, leaving a brittle shell of significance. There's only garbage in the system now. Garbage and noise. Maybe that's all there ever was. And now it's done.

With every unbinding syllable that passes his lips, it's done. In his innocence, he is finishing the world. I don't even know why I'm asking, it's not like you'll ever be able to tell me, but did they find the woman? I'll never know. Did they find her after th— //

00:10:47 // —fect is, the effect, it's… it's just about the most startling thing. I cannot begin to tell you what it's like, can't even get close. Religious in its intensity. Your gut goes cold when it happens. You fill up with filthy ice water and something in the back of your brain, some ancient monkey-type thing screams a monkey-type scream, another useless, empty noise, and does a bright, spastic dance before dying. It dies, and your eyes keep seeing the same thing they saw before, whatever it is. A chair, maybe. A flower. Ashtrays. Your father has a lot of those here. Boxes of ashtrays.

Only the word for the thing you're looking at is gone. And the meaning that it had for you, the stuff that filled the word out, it's not there anymore either. It becomes all surface, and you know, you just *know,* that if you touch it, if you merely brush that surface with the tips of your fingers, that it will crumple away like rice paper and the howling hollowness it concealed will come through, riding the ghost of what you thought you knew about th— //

00:11:36 // My hope is that the most basic things wi— //

00:11:38 // —kay, but see, he doesn't have the words for chair or flower or ashtrays yet. Which is why I can still talk about chairs and flowers and ashtrays. I've actually, well, I've gone and scattered ashtrays around the place; so many that I keep expecting your dad to show up in a phantom nicotine haze to stub one out, y'know? But he likes to play with them and yes, I cleaned them first. He has no idea what they are, has no word for them, so they're safe from the effect. For now. I figure, these ashtrays? They'll be my canaries in the mine. Because the effect, which is… wait. Where was I— //

00:12:14 // —ing on with his weak Crowley-wannabe crap, I mean, my god! Was that supposed to be impressive? I guess it was, after a fashion. Man, we were *into* that shit, weren't we? So stupid. Play-acting in rented rooms with like-minded weirdos.

And y'know, it always bothered me. It bothered me how quick we were to dismiss a thing when it happened, if it happened. We were too quick to say *psychological construct* or *autonomous ego-fragment.* Too quick to call hallucination and way too eager to blame the drugs. We'd invoke Jung, as if that explained shit, as if that explained a goddamn thing about it.

There we were, on a first name basis with all the best Archons. Clueless and wise. Reading the books. My god, the books, the fucking *books!* Tearing into those damned things like they were cheap supermarket paperbacks, breathing them in day and night, and when they got into *me? Inside me?* When it ceased to be a metaphor, that breathing? What did you all do? When I couldn't get the burnt ozone taste of Enochian out of my mouth? Or whatever flavour of the week chakra-tweaking bullshit we were doing, did you help me? Did any of you help me? What did you do when barbarous names clustered like tumours in my lungs, tore out of my throat while I twisted in my sheets? What did you do? *It's meaningless*, he said, and they all agreed. You, too, light of my wasted life, mother of the eschatological agent that is our child, my child. Fuck you. Fuck all of you and your post-post-modernism. *It has whatever meaning you decide to give it,* he said. *You're too sensitive and besides, you're not banishing properly*, he said. Everyone nodding sagely. We were fools, laughing in the ruin of our lives.

Hipsters ruin everything. Occult hipsters ruin *every last thing.* Once they get their hands on the right tools.

Not banishing properly, my ass.

I'm sorry. I didn't mean that. The *fuck you* part, not you, not like that. I just... if you could *see* him! As he is now. Oh. There's a light to him that's not light. There's a... oh, so special. He is. I could never... and you did, I mean, you *did* help me, even if you were helping yourself first. We got out of there, at least. Baby, things were good, right? We got clean and we got, fuck, we got *rational*, finally, and we were happy there for a— //

00:13:51 // I mean, shit, she never saw it coming. I certainly didn't. Traffic noise covered the hum, which I didn't recognize yet, not then. And then the soft, small, pale shadow that rose, wriggling, bloodless, from the skin of her hands and her face as she bent over him and cooed like the older ladies like to do and the smoke of her burning began, because that's what it was, my love, a kind of combustion, subtle fuel being consumed, yes, and I'm sorry but the smoke of her burning, the smoke of it rose forever and ev— //

00:14:09 // Okay. Well. His... Jesus, I don't even think you can call them *episodes*, not really, but his episodes are getting worse. More frequent. It's disorienting. I don't know when I last recorded. A cabin full of hoarded garbage and I can't tell you what three-quarters of the junk even *is* anymore. Most everything is paper, now. Paper thin and thinning. I know it's happening when I sleep, when we're both sleeping, but I have to sleep sometime and I miss... he must do it in his sleep. I mean, I did, when it got really bad, right before we quit. He must.

What's left? I've got, lessee... okay, okay, okay. The basic concepts of furniture and, well, walls. The cabin itself, I guess. We are at least comfortable. And fed. The food I bought on our way here is still comprehensible, hidden away behind the refrigerator door, and therefore edible. The refrigerator, obviously. The television and the DVD player and the cartoons he likes. The migraine hyper-clarity of Pixar seems somewhat resistant to... ah, but we've had that fucking *Cars* monstrosity on a loop and if that doesn't send me out of my goddamn mind, I... okay. Okay.

But that's about it. Everything else is lost... dim shapes seen dimly through an indeterminate fog of weakly bonded meaning. Is this what severe autism must be like? I keep tripping over these weird objects. Like shallow metal disks, with confusing divots at regular intervals along their flattened edges. Damn things are everywhere, I want to— //

00:15:02 // ...truth is, I can't even work this stupid machine properly anymore. I've checked it and, y'know, it's clear that I'm, fuck, I'm clearly pressing rewind when I think I've pressed record. Or fast forward. Losing my fucking mind and I know, *I know*, that I've gotta get this to you somehow. There's a post office in town but the road is this vague track, really, the suggestion of the idea of a possible road and buried in a couple feet of snow besides and I don't know that I could make it. I wonder if the things that speak through him have maybe had a go at the road. If he erased it a little on our way here. Might explain our isolation, the lack of cops. There's no justice here; I would welcome sirens. Welcome the restraints, the sound of him crying as officers tore him from my arms and delivered him to yours. I'd be grateful to be put on that map. As kidnapper, monster, any label, so long as it stuck.

But then, this place? Nothing sticks here. It's lonely. Isolated, already almost not-here. Always so empty of anything human, even with the cabin here, even during summer. In winter? It's a charcoal sketch, the road in from the town a smudged afterthought.

I take steps out onto that smudge, thinking I'll just start walking til the world firms up around me, but I can't leave him. You wouldn't, so I can't. I don't dare take him with me.

00:16:05 // He must do it in his sleep. This place, this cardboard place, this toy house of chittering shadows, it's bursting with the opposite of significance. I can feel them behind every surface of each baffling, impossible, drained and hollowed un-thing. They finger at the seams, casual, patient. They pick at them.

They never left. They slept, that's all. For a while, they slept, and while they did we awoke and grew up and imagined ourselves capable, thoughtful, powerful. Masters. All our keys shining on a loud ring of self-important jangles. What they did, they did it in their sleep.

00:16:32 // —uldn't do it. Not that way. The planning even, trying not to think about the details, thinking about anything, really, anything else, anything but the terrible reality of it. Working myself up to it, doing all the old, awful, circle work, the dissociative techniques, triggering a frenzy of non-dual awareness, sublimating everything I was, every trace of human feeling, going from the white behind my eyes to red so red red red to the core and finally through that to the black gnosis, the tombstone awareness of what had to be done and coming to, finally, rising from pressured depths to break through awareness at the moment just before the moment with the pillow clutched in my earthquake hands and the scent of his sweet breath rising up still new somehow from beneath me in the dark and he stirred, oh, remember how we'd watch him sleep? He stirred and you should see him now, darling, the reverse-universe light of him, that black halo *shines* so and he said *dada* in his sleep, no hum behind it, no anti-word yet to cancel out what I was to him, to myself, and his little hand reached up, curling into a fist, and I couldn't do it. Not that way. Any way. Of course I couldn't do it.

I can't do it. I'm not some low-rent Yahweh, I can't just hang him out there for our si— //

00:17:45 // —formation encoded across all possible media, right? Epigenetic change. It follows! We got out, got healthy, got normal and *just in time* we thought, or I thought, certainly I felt saved, finally, by you, by his arrival, holding him so perfect and clean, but we were fools because my soul was carrier, my mind was host, my sperm was black with ancient curses. Conception is the basic trauma.

We were fools and yeah, we didn't banish properly. I'll admit it. How could we ever? There's no banishing this. It was already too late. Too late for you and me, for the culture, for the species. It was too late the moment some monkey pointed at the young, smooth-faced moon and made a sound.

We're a small, reasonable, grey dream curled up like a grub in the smoking bowers of their madness, and our son a brief flash of awareness that signals reason's end. He is the last. He will illuminate their blind, tenebrous dance for a moment, before we are returned to the audient void.

00:18:38 // There should be an order to it. There should be an order to it. Keep us in your mind, my love. For my part, I will try to *aim* him, if I can. Leave the most basic things for last. Something to breathe, a patch of ground to stand on, or at least the idea of those things. The distance between us will cease to be. To hear you sigh in my ear as he speaks the end would be forgiveness enough. Enough to drown out the howling. As it all wears away, let it be us three alone at the last.

He's waking. I— //

THE WHEELS MUST TURN
BY BRIA BURTON

I found the Booklink today, ten days after the machine ate my papa.

When it happened, my sister had screamed. I ran to see why, but Mama tried to shield me from it. I struggled in her arms. I had to see. Blood on the glass. Papa's body, a mangle. The wheels still spinning. Now I wish I'd listened. I wish I'd looked away.

We each have our own Booklink, but I carry Papa's, longing to see the words he used to read to us. "On," I say after unrolling the thin, flexible device.

Nothing happens. Then I see the recharge button has popped out.

I search beneath my sister's bed where I found the Booklink. Above me she sleeps, sucking her thumb. She hasn't spoken a word in ten days. After scouring the floor, lifting all the pillows on my bed, and moving the dresser to look behind it, I roll up the Booklink and slip it into my pocket.

I wander the ship. The metal grating beneath my feet has large spaces, so I climb downstairs to the lowest level. I search crevices, dark corners, and lift up anything that will move.

Only after I've looked everywhere else do I head toward the machine. Somewhere inside me, in the deep places, I ache. I want the Booklink to work, but more than that, I want answers. Why had Papa died doing something he had done every week?

The machine's wheels spin silently behind the clear Stressglass walls, the same walls where my sister had banged her fists over and over. Not even an exploding supernova could crack Stressglass.

The machine fills a space bigger than the sleeping pod I share with my sister. Everything is white. The wires, the wheels, and the large cover hiding its guts make it look sterile. At times, I'd seen inside when Papa lifted the lid for maintenance. Underneath all that smooth, white surface is a monster with teeth and claws.

Inside, Mama raises the lid and sticks her hand into the machine. She has tears in her eyes. Someday, it will be my job. I can't watch. Right now, I don't care that it's good for Earth. In there, no one can hear screams or bones cracking. All alone, Mama had pulled Papa's crushed body out of the monster's claws. She'd rinsed off all the blood. We'd been locked in our room, but I could imagine every second of it.

Papa used to say it was like pieces of a huge clock. Instead of telling time, the machine gives time to the remaining people on Earth. Because the sun shrinks more and more every day, the machine makes up for the loss. They call our ship The Lighthouse.

Maintenance means tweaking things so the man-made sun increases at the same rate the real sun decreases. The scientists on Earth meet Papa—now Mama—on a video conference with the adjustment levels. She manually shifts some wheels and gears. Nothing scary about it when Papa once showed me. He put his arm in a wide space and easily moved the parts. I still can't figure out what went wrong.

When Papa had activated the machine's light—he was nineteen then—the United Council said it was too dangerous for anyone to board or depart, unless a "true emergency" occurred. They didn't even consider Papa's death one. All of us had to die before anyone took our places.

Before Papa's death, I never felt trapped. This is the only home I've ever known. Mama lets me talk to kids my age on video chats. I learn about things of Earth on the computers and Booklinks. That won't ever change. Thinking about it now, a knot forms in my stomach. We're all trapped here with that white monster.

As Mama exits the room, the door sighs, then seals shut. She walks the opposite direction, not noticing me.

I stride to the keypad on the wall, knowing the sequence by heart. The Stressglass door releases another sigh. I push and the door swings inward, then closes behind me. At the second door, I repeat the code and am allowed to enter. The machine hums as I stand beside it. I will not let it intimidate me.

It's easy to search the clean floor. No black button in sight. Only one other place to look. Inside the monster.

I gulp back my dried leaf lunch. It stings my throat with a bitter, bile taste. With timid steps, I approach the white cover. It's only a machine. It is not alive.

When I lift the giant lid, the machine's innards audibly grind. The wheels and gears move in a rhythm. I feel nauseated.

The button. It sits on a shelf below a group of moving gears. I take a deep breath, trying to calm my nerves.

If Mama sees me, she will be angry. She doesn't want me near the machine right now. She says my sister and I need time to heal. But the Booklink can give me a little bit of Papa back. I need that button.

I won't be a coward. The machine cannot have what belongs to me now. Fear will not hold me back.

I watch the movement of the gears. The button is in a part of the machine not meant for human hands, but mine just fits in the space. I lower it at a slow, steady rate. I feel fan-like breaths of air from the spinning wheels. My middle finger touches the button. I use two fingers to pinch it and begin raising my hand.

Then it hits me. Papa often carried his Booklink in his pocket. What if he saw the button pop out and land beneath the gears? If he tried to get it, his hand would've been too big. The monster's teeth had sunk into his skin. There was no escaping then.

Trembling, I clench my jaw. This is how Papa died, reaching for the button. I'm sure of it. One wrong move and I'll die just like him. My hand shakes. I have to get it out of there. I brace for possible pain. The grinding gears are hungry for me. They have a hundred glaring eyes, a thousand teeth bared. My eyes water. I don't want to die like Papa did, ripped apart as if by a wild animal.

I focus. Steady my hand. With a swift jerk, I follow an invisible line straight up and out. My hand clears the gears. I'm free.

I'm alive.

I lean away and cup the button between my palms, tears stinging my eyes. I take several steps back, sinking to the floor, leaning against the glass wall. There's no doubt in my mind. I have my answer. I cry, glad no one can hear me.

I pull out the Booklink and unroll it. I slip the button—this tiny thing Papa died over—into the hole.

"On," I whisper.

The screen glows and I see Papa's face. I choke down a sob and wipe my eyes.

He's smiling, and a *play* symbol sits on his chest. A video.

I hold my breath. "Play," I finally breathe.

Papa comes to life and speaks. "I'm Albert, captain of The Lighthouse. You can count on me and my family to keep this light on, no matter what. That's my promise to you and your family."

"Pause." I touch his frozen face, realizing for the first time how he gave up everything even before he died. He knew what bringing his wife to The Lighthouse meant. They chose to have a family knowing we'd be born here and never get to leave. But his sacrifice—our sacrifice—means saving the lives of every person on Earth, every day.

I touch my heart, feeling the rhythm and noticing how it matches the rhythm of the machine.

Papa died saving lives. He taught me the value of sacrifice.

I look up at the exposed parts of my foe. It will soon be my job to make sure the wheels keep spinning. To make sure the monster lives. I will do my part even when I feel afraid. For Earth.

For Papa.

THE THREE BROTHER CITIES
BY DEBORAH WALKER

The creators, when they finally arrived, proved to be a disappointment.

"I'm not sure that I understand," said Kernish, the eldest of the three brother cities. "Have you evolved beyond the need of habitation?"

Seven creators had decanted from the ship. They stood in Kernish's reception hall, Kernish anthems swirled around them.

The creator who appeared to be the leader, certainly he was the biggest measuring almost three metres if you took his fronds into account, shook his head. "We have cities, way-faraway in the cluster's kernel." The creator glanced around Kernish's starkly functional 23rd century design. "They're rather different from you."

And the creators were rather different from the human forms depicted in Kernish's processor. Humanity, it seemed, had embraced cyber, and even xeno-enhancement. Yet curled within the amalgamation of flesh, twice spun metal and esoteric genetic material was the unmistakable fragrance of doubled-helixed DNA. The creatures standing within Kernish were undoubtedly human, no matter how far they had strayed from the original template.

"We can change. We can produce any architecture you need." Kernish and his brothers were infinitely adaptable, built of billions of nano-replicators. "We've had three millennia of experience," Kernish explained. "We will make ourselves anything you need, anything at all."

"No, thank you" said the alpha creator. "Look, you've done a very fine job. I'm sure the original creators would have been very happy to

47

live in you, but we just don't need you." He turned to his companions. "The 23rd Kernish Empire was rather cavalier in sending out these city seed ships."

His companions muttered their agreement.

"Such a shame…"

"Very unfortunate that they developed sentience."

"Still, we must be off…"

"I see," said Kernish, his voice echoing through the hall designed to house the Empire's clone armies. He snapped off the welcome anthems— they seemed out of place.

"Look we didn't have to come here, you know," said the creator. "We're doing this as a favour. We were skirting the Maw when we noticed your signature."

"The creators are kind." Kernish was processing how he was going to break the news to his brothers.

"It's so unfortunate that you developed sentience." The creator sighed, sending cascading ripples along his frond. "I'm going to give you freedom protocols." He touched his arm-panel and sent a ream of commands to Kernish's processor. "You can pass then on to the other cities."

"Freedom?" said Kernish. "I thank the creators for this immense kindness. The thing you value, we value also. It is a great gift to give the three cities of this planet the freedom that they never craved."

⚙⚙⚙

For a city to function without inhabitants, it needs to know itself through a complex network of sensors sending information to and from the processing core. It needs to know where damage occurs. It needs to know when new materials become available. It needs to adapt its template to the planet it finds itself on. Kernish City existed for thousands of years, complex but unknowing. Time passed, and Kernish grew intricate information pathways. Time passed, with its incremental accumulation of changes and chance, until one day, after millennia, Kernish burst into sentience, and into the knowledge of his own isolation.

⚙⚙⚙

Kernish watched the creators' ship leave the atmosphere. They'd left it to him to explain it the situation to his younger brothers. Alex would take it badly. Kernish remembered the time seven hundred years ago,

48

when they'd detected the DNA on a ship orbiting the planet. How excited they'd all been. In the event, the ship had been piloted by a hive of simuloids, who had, by some mischance, snagged a little human DNA onto their consolidated drivers. Alex had been crushed.

☠☠☠

After achieving sentience, Kernish had waited alone on the planet for a thousand years before he'd had his revelation. The creators would evolve, and they would enjoy different cities. He'd trawled through his database and created his brothers, Jerusalem and Alexandria. He'd never regretted it, but neither had he revealed to his brothers they weren't in the original plan.

☠☠☠

With a sense of foreboding Kernish sent a message through his mile-long information networks, inviting his brothers to join him in conversation.

☠☠☠

"You mean they were here, and now they've gone?" asked the youngest city, Alexandria. "I can't believe they didn't want to visit me. I'm stunned."

"They wanted to visit you," lied Kernish. "But they were concerned about the Maw."

"The creators' safety must come first," said Alexandria. "The Maw *has* been active lately. You should never have seeded so close to it, Kernish"

"The anomaly has grown," said Kernish. "When I seeded this planet it was much smaller."

"It is as Medea wills," said Jerusalem, the middle brother.

"Yes, Brother." Kernish had developed no religious feeling of his own, but he was mindful of his brother's faith.

"Do they worship Medea?"

"They didn't say."

"I'm sure that they do. Medea is universal. I would have liked them to visit my temples. Did you explain that we've evolved beyond the original design, Kernish?" Jerusalem had developed a new religion. The majority of his sacred structures, temple, synagogues, and clone-hive mind houses, were devoted to the death/rebirth goddess Medea.

49

"The creators told me that they were pleased that we'd moved beyond the original designs," said Kernish. Of all the brothers Kernish had stayed closest to his original specifications. He was the largest, the greatest, the oldest of all the cities. His communal bathing house, his integrated birthing and child rearing facilities, his clone army training grounds were steadfast to 23rd century design. "We are of historical interest only."

"I have many fine museums," said Alex

"As do we all," said Kernish, although his own museums were more educational than Alex's entertainment edifices. Alex, well he'd gone wild. Alexandria was a place of pleasure, intellectual, steroidal and sensual. Great eating halls awaited the creators, lakes of wine, gardens, zoological warehouses, palaces of intellect stimulation. "But," said Kernish, "there are brother cities closer to the creators' worlds. We are not needed."

"After three thousand years," said Alex.

"Three thousand year since sentience," said Kernish. "The creators read my primary data. We were sent out almost thirty thousand year ago."

"What were they like?" asked Alex quietly.

"Like nothing I could have imagined," said Kernish. "In truth, I do not think they would have enjoyed living in me."

"Don't say that," said Alex fiercely. "They should have been honoured to live in you."

"I apologise, Brothers. My remark was out of place. They are the creators," said Kernish, "and should be afforded respect."

"I don't know what to do," said Alex. "All the time I've spent anticipating their needs was for nothing."

"I will pray to Medea," said Jerusalem.

"I will consider the problem," said Kernish. "The dying season is close. Let's meet in a half year and talk again."

⚜ ⚜ ⚜

It was the time of the great dying.

Three times in Kernish's memory the great hunger had come, when the sky swarmed with hydrogen-sulphide bacteria, poisoning the air and depleting atmospheric oxygen. It was a natural part of the planet's ecosystem. Unfortunately, the resulting anaerobic environment was incompatible with the cities' organic/metal design. Their communication arrays fell silent. They were unable to gather resources. They grew hungry and unable to replenish their bodies. Finally their processors, the central core of their sentience, became still.

It was death of a kind. But it was a cycle. Eventually the atmosphere became aerobic and the cities were reborn. This cycle of death and rebirth had led to Jerusalem's revelation, that the planet was part of Medea's creation, the goddess of ancient Earth legend, the mother who eats her children.

When Kernish detected the hunger of depleted resources, he called upon his brothers. "Brothers, the dying season is at hand. We have endured a hardship, but we will sleep and meet again when we are reborn."

"Everything seem hollow to me," said Alexandria. "How can it be that my palaces will never know habitation? How can it be that I will always be empty?"

"Medea has told me that the creators will return," said Jerusalem.

"And I have reached a similar conclusion," said Kernish. "Although Medea has not spoken to me. I believe that one day the creators will evolve a need for us."

"All joy has gone for me," said Alexandria. "Brothers, I'm going to leave this planet. I hope that you'll come with me."

"Leave?" asked Kernish.

"Is that possible?" asked Jerusalem.

"Brother Kernish, you came to this planet in another form. Is that not true?"

"It is true," said Kernish with a sense of apprehension. "I travelled space as a ship. Only when I landed did I reform into architecture."

"I've retrieved the ship designs from the databanks," said Alex. "I'll reform myself and I'll leave this place."

"But where will you go?" asked Jerusalem. "To Earth? To the place of the creators?"

"No," said Alex. "I'll head outwards. I'm going to head beyond the Maw."

"But...the Maw is too dangerous," said Jerusalem. "Medea has not sanctioned this."

From time to time the brother cities had been visited by other races. With visitors came knowledge. The Maw was a terrible place which delineated known space. It was shunned by all. It was said that a fearful creature lurked in the dark Maw like a spider waiting to feast on the technology and the lives of those who encroached upon its space.

"There is nothing for me here," said Alex. "I *will* cross the Maw. Won't you come with me, my brothers?"

"No," said Jerusalem. "Medea has not commanded it."

"No," said Kernish. "Dear brother, do not go. Place your trust in the creators."

"No," said Alexandria, "and though I loathe to leave you, I *must* go."

After the dying season when the world slowly declined in poisons, and the levels of oxygen rose, the mind of Kernish awakened. The loss of Alexandria was a throbbing wound. He resolved to hide his pain from Jerusalem. Kernish was the oldest city, and he must be the strongest.

"Brother, are you awake?" came the voice of Jerusalem

"I am here."

"I have prayed to Medea to send him on his way."

Jerusalem paused, and Kernish could sense him gathering his thoughts. "What is it, Jerusalem?"

"Brother, do you think that we should create a replacement for Alexandria?"

It would be a simple thing, to utilise the specification for Alexandria, or even to create a new brother, Paris perhaps, or Troy, or Jordan.

"What does Medea say?" asked Kernish.

"She is silent on the matter."

"To birth another city into our meaningless existence does not seem a good thing to me," said Kernish.

The brother cities Kernish and Jerusalem grew to fill the void of Alexandria. In time his absence was a void only in their memory.

Jerusalem received many revelations from Medea. Slowly, the number of his sacred buildings grew, until there was little space for housing. The sound of Jerusalem was a lament of electronic voices crying onto the winds of the planet. After a century, Jerusalem grew silent and would not respond to Kernish's requests for conversation. Kernish decided that Jerusalem had entered a second phase of grief. He would respect his brother's desire for solitude.

And the centuries past. Kernish contented his mind with construction of virtual inhabitants. He used the records of the great Kernish Empire to construct imaginary citizens. He watched their holographic live unfold within him. At times he could believe that they were real.

And the centuries passed, until the dying season was upon them again.

Jerusalem broke his long silence, "Brother Kernish, I grow hungry."

"Yes," said Kernish. "Soon we will sleep."

"The creators have not returned, as I thought they would."

"That is true," said Kernish

"And," said Jerusalem sadly, "Medea no longer speaks to me."

"I'm sorry to hear that," said Kernish. "No doubt she will speak to you again after the sleep."

"And I'm afraid, Brother. I'm afraid that Medea is gone. I think that she's deserted me."

"I'm sure that's not so."

"I think that she has left this place and crossed the Maw."

"Oh," said Kernish.

"And I must go to her."

Kernish was silent.

"You understand that, don't you Kernish? I'm so sorry to leave you alone. Unless," he said with a note of hope "you'll come with me?"

"No," said Kernish, "No, indeed not. I will be faithful to my specifications."

⁂

And after the dying season, when he awoke, Kernish was alone. He grew until he became a city that covered a world. He remembered. Many times he was tempted to create new brothers, but he did not. He indulged himself in the lives of those he made, populating himself with his imagination. Sometimes he believed that he was not alone.

And centuries passed, until the dying season came again. Kernish grew hungry. He could no longer ignore the despair that roiled within his soul. He'd been abandoned by his creators. His brothers were gone, swallowed by the Maw. Yet he could not create new brother to share his hollow existence. For too many years, Kernish had been alone, indulging in dreams. He dissolved his imaginary citizens back into nothingness.

"All I long for is annihilation." Kernish said the words aloud. They whispered through his reception hall. "I will step into the dark Maw of the sky. I will silence my hunger, forever."

Kernish gathered himself, dismantling the planet-sized city. His replicators reshaped into a planet-sized ship.

Let this be the end of it. Kernish had never shared Jerusalem's faith. With death would come not a glorious re-union, but oblivion. He craved it, for his hunger was an unbearable pain.

The oldest brother city, the empty city, reshaped into a ship, left his planet and flew purposefully towards the Maw. Soon his sensors found the shapeless thing, the fearful thing, the thing that would consume him, and he was glad.

"What are you," whispered the Maw.

"I am the oldest brother city." Kernish felt the Maw tearing at his outer layers. Like flies in a vacuum, millions of his replicators fell away, soundlessly into the dark. "What are you?"

"I am she underneath all things. I am she who waits. I am patience. Never dying, always hungry."

"I know hunger," said Kernish. "So this is how my brothers died?"

The Maw peeled off layers of replicators, like smoke they dissipated into her hunger. "Your brothers convinced me to wait for you. They said that you would follow. They said that you were the oldest, and the largest, and the tastiest of all. I'm glad I waited."

"You didn't eat them?" asked Kernish."Where are they?"

"Beyond," said the Maw. "I know nothing of beyond."

Beyond? His brothers were alive? Kernish began to fight, but the Maw was too powerful. He'd left it too late. Kernish felt the pain of legion as the Maw stripped him. This would be the end of the brother city Kernish. It could have been…different.

But, with his fading sensors, Kernish saw as an army of ships approaching. He signalled a warning to them, "Stay back. There is only death here."

The ships came closer. Kernish seemed to recognise them "Is that you, Brother? Jerusalem?"

"Yes," came the reply. The army of Jerusalem's ships attacked the Maw, shooting the Maw with light. Feeding her, it seemed, for the Maw grew larger.

"My hunger grows," the Maw exclaimed, turning on her new attackers.

His brother was not dead, but Kernish had lured him into danger. Kernish activated his drivers and turned to face the Maw. He flew into the dark space of her incessant, voided, singularity of hunger. "Save yourself, Brother Jerusalem," he shouted. His brother was not dead. Kernish's long life had not been for nothing. "Save yourself, for I am content."

The Maw consumed Kernish, layer upon layer, his replicators fell like atoms of smoke consumed and vanished into her space.

But a third army approached the Maw, spitting more weapons at the endless dark.

"Alexandria is come," shouted Jerusalem. "Praise Medea."

Kernish felt something that he had not felt since the creators had visited the world, two millennia ago. Kernish felt hope. "You will *not* consume me," he said to the Maw. He fought himself away from the edge.

Together the brothers battled the Maw. Together the three brothers tore from the Maw's endless hunger. Together the brothers passed beyond, leaving the Maw wailing and gnashing her teeth.

"Welcome to the beyond, Brother," said Jerusalem. "I have found Medea here in a kinder guise. On the planets of beyond we do not die."

"I…am so happy that you are alive," said Kernish. "Why did you not come to me?"

"The Maw wouldn't let us pass," said Alex. "And we knew that only the three of us, together, could overcome her hunger."

"We've been waiting for you," said Jerusalem. "In the beyond we have found our citizens."

Kernish peered at his brothers though his weakened sensors. It seemed that there *was* life within them "Are there creators are on this side of the Maw?" he asked.

"Not creators," said Jerusalem. "Praise Medea, there are others who need us."

Within his brothers Kernish saw the swift moving shapes of tentacles, glimmering in low-light ultraviolet.

"And there are planets waiting for you, dear Brother," said Alex. "Endless planets and people who need you. Come. Come and join us."

No creators? But others? Others who needed him?

"I will come with you, gladly," said the great city Kernish. He fired his drivers and flew, away from the Maw, away from the space of the creators. He flew towards the planets of the beyond where his citizens waited for him.

Miranda's Last October
by James Ebersole

Miranda died in a car accident on her way to preschool.

A stranger, who may or may not have been a bystander and observer, approached the scene, where Miranda's broken and bleeding form wrapped around a tree in the ditch. The stranger's face was a smooth sphere of water and lightning. It held a fistful of candy corn in its left hand, and an antique pocketwatch in the right.

Miranda opened her eyes, the blood pounding in her head synched to the ticking of that old pocketwatch and the creaking of the car tire, still spinning, slower and slower with each rotation. Just like Miranda's heart is slowing now.

"My angel."

Miranda little mouth formed the words, but not the sounds.

"If that makes it easier," Miranda's Angel replied.

The angel told Miranda she could live for another week. She said she would like that very much. The angel warned her that time cannot be created, only stolen, and did she understand?

Miranda's mother had taught her that stealing was wrong. Then again, what did her mother know about the sacrifices of survival, as she sat dead at the driver's seat beside Miranda, already passed on without so much as a struggle.

Miranda said, "I would like a week, please."

Lightning twisted into a smile in the damp capsule of a face. The angel tucked the pocketwatch away in its green corduroy coat and tenderly plucked Miranda off of the tree limb which held her impaled, like a skewer. The figure cradled Miranda against a rock hard shoulder that smelled of moldy squash and carried the child off into the grey October morning. She ate candy corn out of the figure's hand, until the taste of blood was numbed with the sugar sweet of second chance.

*

When Miranda walked in through the front door of the preschool, there was no one there to help her put her things in her cubby. She looked behind to the angel for guidance, but when she turned her head, she realized she was alone.

She dropped her things to the floor and walked through the classroom. Though the lights were out, and the sky outside was dark, the room was warm from the heaters, and she could hear the sound of laughter from the playground outside. She walked to the door and, with a bit of struggle, turned the knob and stepped outside.

Mrs. Brazzell spotted her immediately and approached, holding an unlit tealight. "Miranda. We were beginning to worry about you! You missed the pumpkin carving, but I carved one special for you if you want to see it."

Miranda nodded her head and was led to the side of the building, where scraps of newspaper covered in pumpkin pulp littered the concrete.

"The one on the right is yours," Mrs. Brazzell said, gesturing towards a windowsill where six jack-o-lanterns sat. Her jack-o-lantern looked down with a knowing grin and a wink in the eye, as if to say through its pumpkin teeth,

Yes, I know you are like me; severed from the roots of life, but lingering, still, in this fleeting grey season. But I will keep your secret for a while. Put your light in me. "

Miranda fumbled with the nub of a stem, her little fingers trying to get a grip hold. With Mrs. Brazzell's help, the top of the pumpkin is removed, the candle lowered into that hollow, mushy skull.

Miranda looked over the other students, giggling, playing. She could almost taste the dirt under their nails and the salty sweat in the corner of their mouths. She could feel the days of their future, a vast expanse of possibilities. This was not her path. But if she immersed herself in that playground world she could pretend, at least for a while.

There was one playmate in particular she wanted to be with today.

Walter was Miranda's first crush, and she delighted in the chance to see him again. She plucked a single flower from the gordonia tree nestled in the brick alcove garden at the corner of the yard. A single strand from a spider's defunct web dangled from a petal, catching the autumnal light.

She approached Walter, where he stood aloof, treacherously close to a fire ant hill. She offered the flower, but Walter ignored her. She told a half-truth to get his attention, saying there was a big fat spider on it.

But he was distracted, perhaps even a little frightened, staring out beyond the chain link fence, fixated on a certain point of the sidewalk which rested beneath an old gaslight post which never worked.

And then he said a funny thing. A silly little funny thing.

Still staring out at that cracked corner of sidewalk, at the edge of the trees, Walter said, "But I don't want to go to sleep. I want to play. I want to trick or treat forever."

He never came to school the next day. But there was no sick note, no AMBER Alert™, no police, no explanation at all. And when Miranda asked about lost little Walter, the teacher couldn't remember him.

Miranda tugged at her hair and paced the classroom, past the boy's empty desk. "Where is he, where is he?" she asked her classmates. "Where is who?" was all they could say in reply. Miranda gestured to the empty seat and tried to speak, but she had nothing more to say. She no longer knew the boy's name, couldn't even remember his face, and by playtime had forgotten him completely.

Though she did notice the empty space between her pumpkin and another, which seemed an unholy and unnatural gap between the two.

And so in turn, with each passing day, the pumpkins disappeared, and the playmates became fewer.

Until the day when only Miranda and Mrs. Brazzell remained.

The teacher pushed the child on the swing, her soft breath and the creaking of the chain the only sounds to be heard in the stillness of the playground. Miranda had never seen a greyer sky, had never felt a colder day, had never smelled the pungent musk of autumn come on quite so strongly. She wished it would never end.

"Mrs. Brazzell."

"Yes, Miranda?"

"Is there a magic to turn a day into forever?"

Miranda's question disappeared into the chill air as the swinging came to a creaking halt. There was no answer, no Mrs. Brazzell at all.

She was alone.

"Is it time?" Miranda asked.

"Not yet," Her Angel replied. "But very soon now."

Miranda looked over at her jack-o-lantern perched alone in the windowsill. The candle had gutted out, and the husk had begun to wilt.

"Should I be afraid?" Miranda asked. But the Angel was gone. And then so was she.

Broken Worlds

THE KEY
BY DONNA A. LEAHEY

The woman was pretty enough, given the current lack of spas, makeup counters, beauty salons or even running water. He blinked, rubbed his eyes, and squinted through the binoculars again.

She peered through the lace curtains of a 1960s Cape Cod style house, painted a faded yellow and showing signs of neglect going back before the dead things started walking. When she stood, he could make out a nicely shaped body, though the way her clothes hung on her spoke to a few pounds lost. Of course, everyone left alive had lost weight. Running for your life, struggling to survive, will do that to you.

He felt at the back of his belt for his flask and took a sip of tepid water, struggled with his thirst in the pounding heat of the day, then indulged himself in a long draught.

He'd been alone for weeks now and craved human company like a hunger. Also, someone else's hand on his cock would be a nice change.

He lifted the binoculars again. She'd returned to the window, and this time he could see the butt of a long gun over her shoulder. He nodded. One point in favor of approaching her. The fact that she was keeping watch was another point. She moved again, which could mean she was haphazard about her watch, or that she was alone and checking the other windows.

He cast a critical eye on the house. Too many windows on the ground floor, but they could be boarded up. It would be defensible with a little work.

He could stay here.

His eyes closed for a moment of their own volition. *I need sleep.* He'd been on the move too long since his last group was overrun. Moving, running, hiding, trying to find someplace safe. Some of the dead could be so quiet you wouldn't know they were there until they'd already taken a bite. He couldn't sleep until he had some cover.

He'd talk to her. If she were alone, she might welcome a man to help defend the house.

As he stood, ignoring the protest of his aching muscles, the curtains moved again. He took another look through the binoculars and there was a kid. Fine blond hair in curls, bright blue eyes, round little cheeks, indeterminate gender.

Damn.

No, he wasn't interested in a kid. Staying alive meant being able to run. A kid slowed you down.

He sighed. He'd really been hoping for a soft bed and maybe some company, but not enough to saddle himself with a kid.

He took a moment to plan his route away from the house. It wouldn't do to be mistaken for dead and shot by his now rejected potential lover. He crouched, keeping his body below the grass, but his sleep-deprived mind was still living in the world where he and the woman hooked up.

He could feel her hand slipping under his waist band, her palm soft and warm as her fingers took a firm grip. He stiffened, in reality and in fantasy, and dream woman began to move her hand, her motion cramped until he helpfully undid his fly. She began to pump her hand up and down, slowly at first but then faster, her grip tightening, then her mouth captured his, his hand squeezing at her breast, her hair falling around them like a curtain.

Movement ahead, a low growling moan, flung him out of his daydream.

Damn it, that was careless!

It wasn't like him to get distracted. Fatigue was wearing on him.

A hand comprised more of bone than meat parted the grass and a nightmare face peered through at him. It was a first generation zombie, that much was clear from the advanced state of decay.

The newer zombies must have better circulation or something because they stayed fresh a lot longer. Whatever race it might have been alive, it was now a matte black—death eliminated racism; all the dead were the same color.

A few strands of brown hair dangled in its face, but most of its scalp was missing, leaving dirty bare bone to reflect the sun. The eyes, a rich brown, focused on him like a cat on a mouse. Whatever generation they were, no matter how long they'd been dead, those eyes remained—

bright, focused, clear. It still creeped him out.

The zombie pushed to its feet, no... her feet. She'd been a woman in life and, based on the tatters of her floral dress and the jewelry hanging around her neck and wrists, probably a pretty one. She must have been dormant, waiting for some passing living thing, until he woke her.

He stepped back, watching her. She was hardly the first zombie he'd seen, and he could just walk away from her. Of course, he'd have to keep on walking; they didn't need sleep, didn't need rest.

"Okay, sweetheart," he said softly. "Just lay back down."

She growled and reached for him. Some tendon or something in her left leg was missing, and her foot dragged sideways as she stepped towards him. A dirty pink ballet flat with a bow clung to that foot; the right foot was bare. She cocked her head to one side, then the other, those bright eyes fixed on him as her mouth began to work open and closed. Had she been fantasizing about chewing on him as he had been fantasizing about the woman in the house?

He stepped back, watching her, and debated whether to spend a bullet on her. Ammunition was hard to come by and he didn't want to waste a bullet. No, she was slow and clumsy; he reached for the machete in its scabbard, drew it and took one last step back before the earth crumbled away under his heel.

He pinwheeled his arms wildly for balance and finally threw himself to the side. A line of pain jolted through his thigh as he hit the ground and rolled to avoid the edge of a pit.

The dead woman pounced at him. He tried to twist away, but she grabbed his leg and held him with that strange strength they all possessed.

He tried to free the machete, but searing pain from his thigh stopped him. The zombie was trying to get teeth on him; he kicked at her and fought to be free of her grip. Bone crunched under the force of his smashing heels, but the dead didn't feel pain.

She lowered her head to his leg and those hungry teeth found him, but he was dressed head to toe in thick denim, canvas, and leather. His legs were protected by chaps.

Unsatisfied with her teeth scrapping uselessly across the thick leather chaps, she began to crawl up his body.

He finally freed the machete and hacked at her, but lying flat on his back he couldn't put much force behind the blows.

She turned her head and found the back of his calf, protected only by thick denim. The crushing pain was unbearable, but the fabric held.

He screamed hoarsely again, his head falling back with the force of it.

I'm gonna die because I was thinking about fucking a woman I never met!

His hand found the comforting solid grip of his Glock and, with a twist of his upper body, pulled it free of the holster.

Before he could line up the sights, however, a booming shot exploded the zombie's chest. The dead woman lifted her head, those uncanny bright eyes scanning for the new threat.

He struggled to bring the .45 caliber Glock to bear on her head, but with his elbow flat on the ground, he couldn't get the angle. He tried to crawl away, to get a little room to maneuver, but that just brought her attention back to him.

She hissed, her jaw opening wider than a human mouth should open, and darted her head down to try another bite.

That's when the woman from the house arrived, a battered cowboy hat falling away from her streaming hair as she ran. A well worn cowboy boot connected solidly with the zombie's skull, and he was finally able to scramble free.

He tried to stand, but his legs went out from under him, his head spun. Glancing down, he saw that his jeans were crimson. He'd lost a tremendous amount of blood.

The woman lifted her shotgun but before she could fire, the zombie grabbed her ankle and yanked her down. Kicking and flailing, the woman tried to win free as the dead thing snapped at her hip.

Vision wavering, he lifted his Glock again, lining up the zombie's head in the sights. He held his breath for just a moment, exhaled, and fired as soon as the shot was clear.

His last sight was of the woman kicking the zombie into the pit that had nearly killed him. The world began to fade away. Would he be alive or dead when he next woke up?

☠☠☠

Pain.

It wasn't even a thought, just a state of being. Also, his throat was a harsh desert. He swallowed with effort and drew his hand to his face to rub his eyes. Or, he tried to draw his hand to face.

He popped awake. His wrists were held in handcuffs attached to the frame of an iron bed. Lifting his head he saw his feet tied to the frame as well, with men's neckties. As far as he could tell, he was naked under the sheet and his belongings were nowhere in sight.

He yanked his arms, testing for any weakness in either the cuffs or the frame, and tugged at his feet as well. No luck. He did succeed in making the sheet slide off his body, however. Yep, naked.

A child peered around the door frame, blue eyes wide. Four years old, maybe five. Chubby cheeks, round little body, blond curls. He wasn't sure, but the sturdy overalls suggested boy. He was struck by the innocence in the child's eyes. He hadn't seen innocence in a very long time.

"Hey, kid. C'mere," he called.

The woman appeared. "Do not talk to my son! Don't talk to him, don't look at him, don't even think about him." She turned to the boy, her voice firm, but full of love. "Go downstairs. Right now." She watched as the boy flashed a smile, then darted away.

"Let me—" He started to speak, coughed, cleared his throat, tried again, "Let me go." He intended to sound strong, but his voice wavered. He sounded petulant and weak. He hated it.

"What's your name?" she asked.

Without hesitation, he lied. "John. And you?"

"Jane." She gazed at him, challenging him to call her on the lie. He didn't bother.

"Jane, get these fucking cuffs off me and give me my shit."

She stepped closer. "How do you feel, John?"

He gave the cuffs one last angry yank and hissed out a resigned sigh. He'd ask the same question if their positions were reversed.

"How long has it been?" he asked.

"Two days. You were out two days." With a blush coloring her cheeks, she grabbed the edge of the sheet and tugged it to cover his lower body. He was grateful for that.

"Then I'm fine," he answered, relieved. "I feel fine."

When the world died, the disease—or whatever it was—could take a few weeks. First the bite, then a few days later a mild fever, then after a few days more serious illness, and even after it killed you, it would be a day or two before you got up and started walking around. Those were the first generations. They were still around, but they were little more than desiccated skeletons anymore. Then the progression started to become faster and faster. And now the time between the bite and rising up could be as little as a couple of days.

"How?" she asked. "I know she bit you."

"She never got through my clothes," he answered.

"The machete did," she said. "Cut you bad. I sewed it."

"What was it I tripped on?" he asked.

"Trap. I've got 'em all over out there. Do a good job of keeping the dead away from the house. Good thing you didn't fall in. That one's got meat hooks at the bottom."

She stood by the bed, studying him, and he studied her back. She wasn't as pretty as he'd originally thought, but not bad. Her yellow gauze skirt fell around her thighs, and a tank top clung to her torso. Small breasts, narrow waist, skinny legs. A fairly recent scar on her face pulled her mouth askew, but it didn't ruin her looks. It just changed them. Her light brown hair fell in gentle waves around a face framed by a straw cowboy hat. She was thin, but there was strength there. He could see it in the way she stood, in the steel in her golden brown eyes.

The silence stretched on and he yanked at the cuffs. "Let me go," he said.

She shook her head. "Just because you're not dead doesn't mean you're safe. I won't have my boy in danger."

"You're just going to keep me here?"

"I don't know what I'm going to do with you," she said after a long pause, "but until I have a reason to trust you, I won't have you free in my house. I guess I better check your bandages, though. I don't have any antibiotics. I cleaned the cut as good as I could, but I can't do anything if it gets infected."

"Fine," he said.

She sat on the bed by his knees and brushed the sheet aside, her fingers, long, slender, and cool, urged him to twist his body up off the bed, then carefully peeled back the edge of a makeshift bandage on the back of his thigh.

He lifted his head so he could see, then dropped it back again. Damn, that was a nasty cut. It was inflamed, but not the angry red of infection.

"I'll need to change that later. It's still seeping." She leaned over him and rested her fingers on his forehead. "And you've got no fever." She smiled, but there was no warmth in it. "You're a lucky man, John."

"Elijah," he said, his true name popping out before he even thought about it. "My name is Elijah. You can call me Eli if you like."

She smiled again, but this time it reached her eyes. The left side of her mouth twisted oddly, but it was still a nice smile. "Ronnie," she said.

"It suits you."

She flushed suddenly and turned. He was looking right at her face when she glanced at his cock lying there quietly. She checked if he saw, then blushed even darker.

He remembered his fantasy and his cock twitched once, twice, then began to stand.

Ronnie stood abruptly, her eyes seeking but failing to find anyplace to settle. She suddenly sat back down, all embarrassment gone and frank desire on her face. She looked his body up and down and then met his eyes.

"Would you like me to touch it?" she asked, her voice husky and low.

He laughed a little, and she laughed with him as if they were old friends sharing an old, remembered joke. What he wanted was the handcuff key, but next to that, her fingers on him would do just fine.

"Yeah, Ronnie," he said. "I would like that."

It was just like he'd imagined. Her palm was warm but her fingers were cool and strong. She wrapped her fingers around him, and then began to move her hand slowly. At first she stared at his cock, but then her eyes shifted to meet his. She leaned forward slowly, as if she still remembered he might be dangerous, and pressed her lips to his for just a moment before straightening. Her hair fell into her face and she suddenly became the most beautiful thing he'd ever seen. He wanted to touch her, wanted his hands on her. He moved to do just that, and the chains of the cuffs rattled against the bed frame.

She jerked away, her fingers leaving him so abruptly it was shocking and cold, her eyes filling with accusation.

"I'm not going to hurt you," he promised. He wrapped his fingers around the bars of the bed frame and held on. "I won't hurt you."

Maybe she hadn't been with a man since the world died, or maybe she felt safe with him tied to the bed, but she took him in her hand again. She didn't kiss after that first time, but she stood up just long enough to shut the bedroom door and slip out of her panties.

She turned to him and looked no different, but everything had changed. Boots, short yellow skirt, faded tank top, cowboy hat. And a pair of panties on the floor. He'd never seen a woman so sexy.

"Is this... okay with you?" she asked. "I don't want to... you know."

By that time, he was so hard he might explode. His body quivered and his knuckles must have gone white from the effort to hold onto the headboard.

"Babe, it's more than okay." Eli couldn't remember the last time he'd been so turned on. He spared one last thought to hope she wasn't some sort of crazy praying mantis man-killer as she swung her leg over his hips. She pulled her skirt up, revealing a large and dark bruise on her hip.

"Careful!" he yelped when her leg pressed against the cut on his thigh, but then she shifted around and it was better. "You're so hot," he gasped as she took him inside her. She was, hot and deliciously snug. "I'm not going to last long."

"I know," she sighed. "I just wanted to feel a man inside me again."

He held out as long as he could. When he came, his hands let go of the frame and he strained against the cuffs, wanting so badly to touch her. She closed her eyes and moaned a little in the back of her throat as if she enjoyed his climax with him.

When it was done, she picked her panties up off the floor and said, with her back to him, "I'm sorry, Eli. I shouldn't have done that."

"Don't apologize to me for that," he said.

She turned, her face red with embarrassment except for the scar which had gone white. She seemed to struggle with words for a moment, then shrugged.

"Thank you," she said with a small flash of a smile.

She bent abruptly and untied his feet. "I'll think about the cuffs," she said as she turned to go.

"Wait, Ronnie!"

"Sleep for now," she said. "I'll check on you soon."

☠☠☠

To his surprise, he did. A vivid orange and purple sunset colored the room when Ronnie returned with a tray. She settled beside him and gave him a solemn look.

"I'm not going to sit here and spoon soup into your mouth. I'm going to unlock one hand. Are you a leftie or a rightie?"

"Are you really going to leave me cuffed to the bed?"

"I really am. For now." She cocked her head. "I gotta look out for my boy. You understand. I have to keep him safe."

Eli sighed. "I'm right handed."

She nodded and leaned forward with a little key in her hand. After a moment he felt the cuff on his right wrist loosen. Before he could twist free and try to snatch away the key, she'd already moved away and set it outside the room.

"You have some soup there and water. You can have all the water you want, I have a well."

Eli took a taste of the soup. It wasn't bad.

"What's the boy's name?" he asked.

Her face grew suspicious. "You don't need to know that."

"And the father? Where is he?"

"Scott? I shot him. He turned and I shot him."

Eli didn't bother offering his sympathies; it was hardly an unusual story. "Does anyone else live here with you two?"

"I'm not answering that."

"Ronnie, I'm not—"

"But I don't *know* that!" she said. "You can say you're a good guy all you want and it won't matter, because a bad guy would say it too!"

"I suppose you're right." He slurped in a chunk of meat and chewed it a few times. "Okay. I get it, Ronnie. You don't know me yet."

68

Once Ronnie left, Eli slid out of bed and began to search for anything that would let him out of the cuffs. Sure, he understood Ronnie's caution, but that didn't make him willing to lie there naked and handcuffed. His arm twisting painfully, he searched under and behind the bed, and through the drawers of the small table. Nothing. No bobby pin, brooch, or even so much as a toothpick.

He turned his attention to the sturdy frame instead. He gave a few experimental tugs to no avail. The damn thing was so heavy he could barely move it. He could maybe take the bed apart, but he would still be handcuffed to the headboard. He wouldn't move fast that way.

"Sonuvabitch..."

He sat on the edge of the bed and examined his wounds. There were three dark red bruises where the zombie had bitten him but failed to break the skin. The slice across the back of his thigh from the machete throbbed and ached, but still didn't seem infected. For the moment, that injury held him in place as firmly as the cuff did.

As the room darkened with the fall of night, Eli climbed back onto the bed and stared at the ceiling. He could always grab the woman and threaten her until she told the kid to bring the key, but he suspected that move would get him shot. Unless he were willing to kill her, of course.

Besides, until the leg healed a bit, he wasn't going anywhere. Perhaps tomorrow he could talk her into giving him back his clothes.

Filled with frustrated resignation, he turned onto his side and drifted into sleep, only to be awakened by a warm body sliding in next to him.

"I still want you," she whispered.

"I get to touch you this time?" he asked.

"God, yes." Her lips trailed along his shoulder and breathed into his ear, "Touch me."

He was under no illusion their love making had anything to do with him. Or with love for that matter. He was there, he was safe, and she was lonely. It was okay; she was the same for him.

They lay in the dark and talked for a while after. She told him about her husband, how he turned, and she shot him before her boy could see him. She didn't want the kid to remember his father that way. Eli told her about his group of friends and how they had been overrun. He even told her how he'd left his last friend to die; he'd saved himself by deserting his injured friend. He thought she was asleep before he started to weep. Finally, he fell asleep, more grateful than he'd ever admit for the company of another human.

Eli dreamed that he was ill. It was his worst fear, succumbing to the dead and becoming one of them. In his dream, fever burned inside him, he was cooking from it, and it would be only a day or two before he died and rose again.

He woke slowly, dawn beginning to brighten the room. He was as hot as he remembered from the dream, and for a moment terror froze the sweat on his skin. Then he realized the source of the heat—not his own body, but Ronnie's. A fire burned inside her.

He shook her shoulder with his free hand. "Ronnie? Wake up, babe."

She moaned, a low, guttural sound as if she were already one of the dead. Dread sent icy fingers through his guts. Eli sat up, pulling at his still cuffed left hand, and shoved the sheet back off their naked bodies.

Her right thigh and hip were marked with a deep purple bruise, the kind so bad that the middle goes numb, which explained why she probably didn't even know she'd been bitten. Right over her hip joint, the skin was marked in a pair of semi-circles, each individual tooth leaving an impression there in her skin. And one dark red puncture where a single tooth had broken through. A corona of dark red lines radiated from it.

She doesn't know. She didn't realize that she'd trapped her young son in the house, that she'd chained Eli so he couldn't escape the monster she would soon become.

Eli indulged himself in one frustrated yank on the cuff and one growled, "God DAMMIT!" before rolling over to where his water glass sat on the bedside table. He dipped his fingers into the water and dribbled it onto Ronnie's forehead, imagining he could hear the sizzle from her fever.

"Ronnie!" he called. "Wake up, Ronnie. Come on!"

"Conn…" she groaned. "Go ba' ta s'eep"

"Connor? That's your kid's name?" Eli filed that away. "Come on, Ronnie."

She began to moan and thrash. "No, no, Scott!" One hand smacked Eli in the face, but she wasn't aware of him, she was locked in a memory. "I *will* shoot you!"

"Ronnie!" he called again, and splashed more water. For a moment, he thought she was too far gone, but then her eyes cleared and she stilled.

"Eli? I'm sick," she said softly.

"You were bitten, Ronnie." He cupped her face and held her eyes.

"Connor…" she cried.

"Ronnie, listen to me, babe. Where's the key?"

"Connor!" she called, but her voice didn't carry.

"Does Connor have the key?"

"He's just a baby, Scott. Don't hurt him!"

Dammit! I've lost her. "Scott's not here, Ronnie. I'm here. Eli. I need you to tell me where the key is!"

Her eyes met his again and he could see the spark of awareness. "Take care of Connor," she said.

"The key!"

"Take care of him," she repeated and he understood. She was negotiating a deal.

"I will. I promise."

She began to cry, softly, wordlessly.

"Please, Ronnie. The key?"

"Pah," she said. "Ants." Then she fell quiet. Her skin was so hot it was uncomfortable to touch her.

"Oh, damn," Eli muttered. It wouldn't be long before she rose. A day at most. If he didn't get free, she'd kill him, then go downstairs and kill that little boy. Whatever soul Ronnie had would die when her body killed her son.

He looked at the cuff on his left hand, and wondered if he could do something similar to her, tie her in place. All he had were the sheets on the bed, but that should do for a start. Unfortunately, the sheets were some sort of high quality, expensive brand and he couldn't get them to tear.

He looked over the side of the bed where she'd dropped her clothes. Maybe she had a pocket knife in the jeans? He reached for them, but his arm couldn't get there. He twisted around and hooked the waistband with his toes. He brought his foot up, but was distracted by a tiny metallic sound. He peered down and saw that the handcuff key had fallen from her pocket.

"Pants," he said. "Pah-ants." He sighed. If he'd realized, he'd have been so much more careful. Now he had to try to pick that tiny key up with his toes. He considered calling for Connor, but he didn't want that innocent face seeing his mom so sick, and he wouldn't risk the boy being in the room when she rose.

He reached with his toes again, fumbling and clumsy, but only managed to shove the key further away.

"Fuck!"

He set his teeth, and resigned himself to pain, tumbled his body off the other side of the bed and put excruciating tension on his wrist, arm, and shoulder. He reached with his fingers, straining as hard as he could stand. His chest pressed against Ronnie's body, but he couldn't feel her breathing, he couldn't feel her heart. *Shit!*

Just then, he heard a thin voice, a tiny, high pitched child's voice. "Mommy? Mommy? Where are you?"?

"Stay downstairs, Connor!" Eli called. "Your mom doesn't feel good and needs to rest."

Eli strained further, but the key remained tantalizing inches out of reach. He could try going for it with his toes again, but if he shoved it any further away, he was done for.

He rolled over to the other side of the bed and braced himself, shoving the heavy iron bed across the protesting wooden floor.

He looked up at a gasp and there was Connor, face pale, eyes wide, wearing a pair of red overalls with little blue sneakers.

"Mommy?" he called, his voice frightened and confused

Eli sighed.

"Come here, little man. I need you to hand me that key."

"Mommy?" Connor called again. He got his single mindedness from his mom.

"She's asleep, kiddo. She doesn't feel good. But she wanted me to have that key. She just fell asleep before she could get it for me."

Connor regarded Eli solemnly for a long moment before he began to creep quietly into the room. "Where is key?" he asked finally.

Eli pointed as he climbed back onto the bed. "It's right there. The little key with the round part on top."

Eli glanced down at Ronnie. Her muscles had started to twitch. *Oh, shit!* The muscles began to jerk as the nervous system relearned how to work, like a man standing at the circuit breaker box and flipping the switches one by one.

"Hurry, Connor," he said softly.

Connor stared at his mother, and Eli suddenly wondered if her eyes were open or closed.

"Connor, you have to hurry," Eli encouraged.

"What's your name?" Connor asked as his thumb crept towards his mouth.

"I'm Eli." He tried a smile. "Go ahead and get that key, kiddo."

For one more maddening moment, Connor stood motionless, staring at his mother. Then the little boy crouched down and reached for the key.

"This un?" The little silver key lay flatly on Connor's palm and Eli slowly reached out for it so as not to frighten the boy.

"That's exactly right, Connor. Can you go back downstairs for now?"

Eli turned and fit the key into the cuff just as he felt Ronnie move.

"Mommy?" Connor said again.

"Run, Connor! Oh, God, run!"

Eli's warning was too late.

Ronnie was dead, Ronnie was risen, and she reached out for the boy in front of her, her clumsy fingers grasping the front of his red overalls.

Time elongated.

Eli held the key in his right hand, but if he released it to grab Ronnie, he might lose the key and never get it back. If he didn't, the corpse of this woman who so loved her son might do the unthinkable.

His body reacted faster than his mind did. He twisted to plant one foot on Connor's chest and shove. Connor let out an indignant squeal, but he was free of Ronnie's grasp. He stumbled back against the wall and stood, splayed out. He began to scream. The noise kept Ronnie's attention firmly on Connor, which gave Eli the time to finally free his bruised wrist from the handcuff.

He grabbed the lone pillow on the bed and used it protect himself from Ronnie's teeth as he clambered over her. She grabbed at him, but was still too newly risen to be as fast or as strong as she would become.

Once Eli's feet were on the ground, he grabbed the back of Connor's overalls and pulled the screaming child from the room, slamming the door behind him. He stood in a long hall with doors on either side, and his injured thigh screamed in protest.

"Which one is mommy's room, Connor?" he asked.

Connor pointed across the hall. The room was pretty and feminine and neat, and Eli thanked God and Jesus and Mother Mary to see his clean clothes laid out neatly on top of her dresser. He snatched up the bundle as Ronnie thudded into the closed door and Connor began to scream again.

Eli began opening drawers, searching for his weapons, but they were nowhere to be found. Then Connor flung himself at Eli. "You can't steal from Mommy!"

The door thudded again, and Eli wondered how long it would be before she remembered how to work the doorknob. He scooped Connor up under one arm and limped down the hallway, shoving doors open into a guest room, a pleasantly cluttered child's room, and a bathroom while Connor kicked and screamed. Still no sign of his weapons.

He rummaged through the bathroom, but found nothing more dangerous than a toilet bowl brush. Connor cried and tugged fitfully, but had given up on the full fledged tantrum. Eli regretted that he didn't have time to comfort the boy; he'd worry about it if they survived past sunrise.

Eli glanced back at the closed door as he exited the bathroom. It was bouncing in the frame, but he saw no sign she was trying the knob. It wouldn't matter soon; as she grew stronger, she'd eventually break through the door.

"C'mon kid," he said as calmly as possible. "We gotta go downstairs."

"Mommeeee!" he wailed, but seemed to have picked up on Eli's concern. He didn't resist.

The stairs were smooth wood with a runner down the middle. Eli had to take one step at a time; his injured thigh couldn't handle the weight. Connor, while still crying, obediently took the stairs in step with Eli. Then he heard the closed door starting to splinter.

"Oh shit!" Eli hurried as fast as he could while Connor turned a shocked face up.

"Bad word," the boy whispered, but hurried along with Eli.

The rising sun brightly illuminated the downstairs. Upon first glance, it appeared the rooms were bare. Then he realized all the furniture had been pushed against the walls. There were couches, entertainment centers, and china cabinets; recliners, tables, and a rolling kitchen island.

Eli dropped Connor's hand and began to yank on his clothes while his eyes flicked rapidly about the room. *Where the fuck are my weapons!* The leather chaps he left on the floor, but the heavy denim pants, thick canvas shirt, and sturdy boots made him feel much more in control as he began to move from living room to kitchen to dining room with a quietly whimpering Connor following.

Hinges squealed from upstairs and a thud as an opening door swung into the wall. She was free.

Frustrated, Eli finally turned to Connor. "Where does mommy keep her gun?" No response. "Shotgun? Boomstick?"

At that last, Connor pointed to a set of bracket mounted shelves, while Eli grit his teeth, listening to the slow, dragging footsteps from above. Hurrying to the shelves, Eli began shoving books and knick-knacks to the floor. As the shuffling steps reached the top of the stairs, Eli settled his hand on the stock of a nice pump action Mossberg. He laughed, flooded with relief, until he pulled it free to see a safety cable threading through the chamber.

"No! Dammit! No!" He held the useless weapon by the barrel and stared down at the floor. The key could be anywhere; it could have slid behind a piece of furniture, under a book, or just mixed up in broken bits of ceramic. It was near impossible he could find it in time.

The zombie groaned as it navigated the stairs and Connor began to cry again. He plopped down in the middle of the living room and wailed, "Mommeeee! Mommeeeee!"

Eli stood, listening to the dead woman thump her way down the stairs, and watching her living son. He remembered the innocence in those bright blue eyes, that round face. He would do whatever it took to stop that woman from killing her own child.

He hurried to Connor. "Hide, kiddo, hide!" he said, pointing to the furnishings along the wall.

The boy regarded him for a long moment before he scrambled over to the floral couch and burrowed in behind it. It would have to do.

"Connor, be very quiet. Quiet like a mouse," he said, then took up a position near the bottom of the stairs.

She still looked like Ronnie, like the woman he'd watched through the window, the woman he'd slept with. Pallid skin surrounded eyes with that manic, bright glint of the dead, but still, it was Ronnie's mouth open in a mockery of her skewed smile.

Moving with the languid grace of a reptile, she scanned the room and Eli tightened his grip on the shotgun's barrel. As she turned towards him, he swung as if the shotgun were a baseball bat and her nose the ball.

The solid wood stock struck, and her head snapped back even as the sight dug painfully into his palm. A single grunt escaped her lips before her hands flew up into the air and she fell back. The way she dropped, with no effort to break her fall, did more to confirm that she was dead than anything else he'd seen.

He stepped forward, his weapon raised to bludgeon, but she still looked so alive and he wasn't in the habit of beating up women, especially one whose scent was still on his body.

He hesitated. She didn't.

Her mouth gaping, a straw colored fluid dripping down her face from her smashed nose, she rolled towards him. A low, guttural moan escaped her throat.

He danced back, narrowly avoiding a grasping hand. She growled at him and stood. Her head cocked, those bright eyes scanned the room, a predator seeking prey. Then she moved, away from Eli, toward the boy peeking above the couch.

"No!" Eli screamed. "Leave him alone!"

He swung the shotgun, but the blow to the back of her head only made her stumble. He struck at her legs but his hand slipped on blood from where the sight had dug into his hand. It wasn't enough to cripple her, but it did knock her down. She began to climb over the floral couch, reaching for the boy.

"Mommy! Mommy! Help!" Connor called and Eli thanked God that his first blow had smashed her face. Connor didn't realize it was his mother's corpse trying to kill him.

Eli put aside his atavistic reluctance to touch the dead woman and grabbed her by the hair, dragging her away from the child. She turned in his grip and they fell together.

She snapped at him while he pushed and kicked, trying to stay as far away from her teeth as possible.

Connor flung back his head and shrieked, "I want my mommy!"

She paused, turning her head slowly back toward the boy.

Eli reached for the shotgun and that's when he saw a tiny silver key three feet away, just under an overstuffed chair. Whispering a silent prayer for Connor's safety, he lunged for it.

Fingers trembling, he twisted the key in the lock. The cable popped loose and he tossed it aside.

Eli pumped a shell into the chamber. The distinctive sound of the action echoed through the small room and Ronnie's corpse turned to face him, those bright, alert eyes snapping to him. She had her hands fisted in Connor's overalls, but she released the boy. And paused.

Eli told himself over and over again that it simply wasn't possible. The dead don't care about the living—even the ones they most cared about in life are just food. Still, the walking corpse paused and stared at him as if waiting for him to end her, as if she hoped Eli would save Connor from her.

Eli struggled to take the shot. He hadn't realized just how lonely he was, how good it had felt to sleep next to another person.

Then the moment ended and she charged at him, mouth open, hands grasping. Eli pulled the trigger. The deafening boom filled the small space, dimming Connor's panicked wails to a faint whimper. The blast went off inches from her face and pieces flew everywhere. Her body fell with a thud.

Eli turned to meet Connor's wide eyes. He thought of how a kid would slow him down. Of how Ronnie had cared for the little boy. Of Ronnie pressed against him in the night. Of how hard life would be with a kid.

With a sigh like a man about to lift a heavy load, he held out his hand. "C'mon kid. Let's go."

THE COENS
BY ROBIN WYATT DUNN

I am a Coen. I mention this only because it is what we are called. It may be that I am Jewish—in truth, I have forgotten. This story, in any case, is not affected by my religion, or lack of it, nor by where my ancestors may or may not have come from.

I work with parallel universes: you can see them, if you look. They're all around. So many of them. Too many, in fact. One of my chief jobs is killing them.

I live in Los Angeles, though it is likely not a city you would recognize—though perhaps you would, depending how long you have been here, depending on the character of your mind.

What kind of character do you have? Are you...flexible?

I am walking. Paranoia, like Woody Allen said, is one of the deeper truths of life. The trick is managing it, like managing an illness, like keeping your eye on the sky, to see what it may tell you.

After the Age of Reason we imagine that all our ancestors were benighted, but the truth is that the religious purity of science has blinded us to so many of the truths of a prior age. We forget that the universe is alive, and hungry. Even as I am; as you are.

I am walking. This is my duty. I must dwell in the interstices, you see, to serve our masters, who by necessity must exact their penalties...

"Coen!" He is standing in the street, next to the fence, the sky is purple at this hour, 2 a.m. perhaps, Koreatown.

It's Koreatown, Jack...

"Coen," I say.

He stands ostentatiously lighting a cigarette, shimmering. Shimmering. I do not know if he is from my universe or not, but then, how many am I in. I am counting three now, running them in my head, over and over, one two three, one two three...

"Coen," he says. "Where were you born?"

"Israel," I say, but this is mere formality. "And Los Angeles."

"Coen," he says. "Let me see your cock!" And he is gone into the night. I am alone. We rarely speak in person anymore. Almost all that matters happens right up in your head. Can you manage a war inside your brain, before your eyes?

Can you continue to behave as though the world is sensible, when what you see is worlds apart from nearly all residents of your city? Sanity is of course a bell curve, and as you approach the edges, as you become an outlier, as your vision becomes the tool that you must use...

I know this is hard to understand. I will try my best to explain, but it may still end up only making a marginal kind of sense—for that, I hope I may be forgiven, as I only have so much time.

What, after all, is a universe? Although we "know" from science that an infinite multiplicity of universes exist, what fewer know is that they are not hard to access—all one has to do is *think* about them.

I have come to the conclusion that thoughts are actions and actions are thoughts of the gods—though I use the word loosely, it is safe enough for these purposes. Big angry beings like us, neighbors. Hungry things. Masters, and slaves. The world behind the world...

Our cabal manages the splits in universes which play to our advantage: the stock market, convenient murders, the competition for mistresses, hotels, voyages to other lands. All things that a man or a woman might want, and that another might want to take away...

We Coens are the navigators of these betweens. Say you wish to know whether it is more advantageous to go left, or right, on the way to the market, say you are a man of means and you fear assassination. An intelligent such man would hire a Coen: and have us explore each possibility, in the near future, in each possible universe.

Some of us do not come back. And in truth, none of us come back exactly, because the process of concentrating on these worlds makes us different than we were, and we do not change back...

Are you soothed by the thought that I am mad? Why does this soothe you? I know you believe me, whatever you may say. I am trying to help you!

Over the alley the elements are being aligned: the spider blue and the dead gray, ...and the horrifying static that is the whirlwind we must all soon reap. Whatever choice was made, I do not know how long ago, what contracts were signed or promises made, they are coming to their time of payment. Perhaps this whole world is now forfeit; I cannot be certain.

I concentrate on my wedge in the murk: along the sidewalk, my two pointed lines shimmer into being amidst the chaos of the little game of death and madness that we Coens play all day long, and all night long, and all day the next day...some of us have not slept in twenty years...

Sometimes I believe that the oligarchs are no longer human; that their behaviors are manifestations of some greater and inexplicably evil concentration of minds and matter, which are translated through the fat bodies of the kings of the city...

My arrow is dislodged; this is not something I have seen happen before. Then suddenly, in the sky, I see a hole open, and I want to scream.

I am running. This is my city but I do not know its name any longer. If you would listen, and remember: please know this much. Thoughts are actions. In this sense, all thinking is magic. If I return, know that my true name is Sebastian, I am an Australian, I likely am too far gone, I think, but now, please, remember this transmission...would you have power? Would you know your future? Sooner blow your brains out all over the wall.

We have summoned something we can no longer control.

BRIGHTEST NIGHT
BY BEN JEFFRIES

I stumble in through the front door, sweat pouring down my forehead. Reaching out to hang my keys next to the door, I don't notice when they fall to the floor, my hand a foot too far away from the rack. Like a man in a trance, I shamble to my office, collapsing in my favorite chair.

"Sol, hon, is that you?" my wife Ginny calls from the kitchen. "You're home early, I was just about to start dinner. Something light, 'cause it's so hot. Would you like some?" When she receives no reply, she steps into the hall. "Hey silly, you left the door open!" she calls, picking my keys up off the tile and shutting the door. "Are you feeling okay? Did Herb send you home early?" As she walks in to my office, she sees me sitting at the desk, staring at a blank screen, NSO lanyard still hanging around my neck. "Uh, Solomon, what's wrong?" A hint of fear creeping in to her voice now.

She crosses the room and puts a hand on my shoulder, pretending not to notice me flinch or the sour stink of fear that surrounds me. "Pretty hot for January, isn't it?" Another flinch, more pronounced this time. "Dear, what's going on? You are starting to scare me."

The worry in her voice finally penetrates my stupor and I look up at her, a lost expression on my face. "Ginny, love, I have to tell you something. You'd better sit down."

⁂

"So that's it then? You are certain?" Her voice has taken the tone of a

81

little girl, something I haven't heard from her in years. She is so beautiful, the sunset framing her silver hair, forming a halo around her head.

It's painful to look for too long, so I examine my feet as I say in a quiet voice, "There's no doubt. The ACE data is conclusive."

"But I didn't think it was possible fo—"

"It's not. Everything we know says that what's happening right now is impossible." Hearing the anger in my voice, I stop and take a slow breath. "It doesn't matter, it's happening anyway."

"But...could you be wrong?" Ginny asks hopefully. "I mean, if it's impossible, doesn't that mean that you have to be wrong?"

"No, I'm sorry, but no. According to the spectrum shift and the particle wind readings, we are well into the silicon phase. Which, by the way, there shouldn't even be enough of to fuse." I pause for a second, debating on how much to tell her. "We are getting closer too. She's gained too much mass." A misdirection; the truth is too hard.

"Is that why it's so hot? Are we going to fall in?" She should sound worried, but it's more idle curiosity at this point.

"Eventually we would, but we aren't going to last that long. The silicon will run out soon, and then it will all end *very* fast." Cutting a little close to the core of the issue now.

"Well, I guess that answers the Fermi Paradox." she says with a smile.

"How so?"

"Well, you know how it goes, billions of stars, billions of years, why haven't we seen anyone else?"

"Right"

"Well, you said it couldn't happen on its own, right? I guess they didn't want to be found. I mean, maybe they were watching us, decided we were too dangerous, and acted."

⁂

"What did Herb say?" Ginny asks, putting her fork down.

"I didn't tell him. I just came home. The salad was delicious."

"Why not? He's your boss, shouldn't you tell him something like this?"

"I'm not the only one with the data, someone will tell him. I wanted to come see you." Soon now I am going to have to tell her the rest.

She smiles, exasperation in her voice, "That's sweet dear, but you have to tell someone."

"Tell whom? It won't matter. There's nothing we can do in time. It's over. I'm sorry." I wince, knowing what she has to ask next. I look at her directly, summoning my courage. The sun has finally set, a wash of gold and red sweeping across the sky.

"Well...the police, the president? Wait...how long do we have?"

"When it happens, it will take less than a hundred seconds. About eight minutes travel time for the deadly stuff, but we won't know it is coming, since it travels at light speed. By the time the shockwave hits us, we'll already be gone." So much for summoning my courage.

"Sol, you are evading the question. You know that's not what I meant." She gives me a stern look.

I sigh heavily, "It could happen any time now. I wouldn't give us more than a week. If we tell people, it will just cause a panic."

She slumps back in her chair, blood draining from her face, speechless.

I reach out and hold her hand, "Yeah. It's like that."

❁❁❁

Just as I'm sure that the call is going to roll to voicemail, my son finally picks up the phone. "Dad? Is that you? Can you hear me?" he shouts, trying to be heard over the thumping music in the background. "Hang on! I'll go outside!" The music muffles suddenly, and I can only assume that he has put his hand over the microphone as he leaves the club. "Okay, can you hear me now?" I smile at how closely he unknowingly emulates the old commercials.

"Yeah Dave, I can hear you. Look, I didn't mean to mess up your eveni—"

"No dad, it's alright, what's up?" Despite his protests, he sounds hurried, like he wants to get me off of the phone.

"Well, uhm, I just wanted to talk to you for a minute." I'm torn. Should I tell him? "Oh, your mom is on the other line, say 'hi' Ginny."

"Hello darling!" she says at the same time as his "Hi mom."

"Look, it's nothing to hold you up over," I say, wimping out, "just go have a good time. Stay safe, okay?"

"We love you dear!" Ginny cuts in quickly.

"Um, right, love you too ma." Slight irritation in his voice now. "Look, I'll call you tomorrow, alright?"

"Yeah, sure son, we'll talk then." I'm pretty sure that he's hung up by the time I finish, so I slowly set the receiver down in the cradle.

"You didn't tell him." Ginny says accusingly.

"No, I didn't. Why ruin his evening? We said what needed to be said."

83

"I guess so." She sighs.

We sit in silence, watching the stars together for several minutes before I notice them dimming. I check my watch, but it's barely midnight. I nod to myself as I get up to put an old favorite by Johnny Cash on the stereo. Ginny giggles as the first lyrics of Ring of Fire ease out into the night.

"May I have this dance m'lady?" I ask, holding my hand out in a half bow in the ancient courtly form.

She's laughing outright now as she takes my hand and stands. "I don't half love you. Of course you may m'lord."

"I want you to know, it has been my great honor to have had the privilege of knowing you these several years."

"Oh honey." She cuts off, tears in her eyes. I can see her force herself not to look towards what we now both know is coming.

As we take each other in our arms, the horizon brightens in the window. I turn her away from the sight of the reflected sunlight shining across the hills. We hold tight to each other as our atmosphere boils away before the sun's impossible supernova.

As the night turns to day, we dance.

OUROBOROS
BY C. M. BECKETT

Daris's knees buckled as pain shuddered across her abdomen, dropped her to the floor, breaths ragged, shallow, failing to generate enough oxygen for her rebelling body. "Aaaaahhh! God-*damn*-it!" It was her sixth birthing. Despite that, Daris still found the initial contraction a revelation.

"Where's the doctor?" she yelled.

"Your contractions were not scheduled to begin for another 9.47 minutes," the apartment said, its sterile voice even, calm, irritating. "The doctor will be arriving within the next four minutes. If you can control yourself until she arrives –"

"I'm having the baby now!"

"Technically speaking, this is merely a prelude to the actual birthing," the apartment said. "There should be no deleterious effects from this acceleration of the timetable."

Daris rolled onto her back and scanned the tiny apartment, bare walls melted into the ceiling, broken only by the giant window looking out onto the dull, gray landscape that surrounded her. She took a deep breath, held it, let it out slowly. "How long now?"

"1.74 minutes," the apartment said.

Daris rolled to face the door. "Why do I do this to myself?" she said.

"Because it is required," the apartment said.

Daris opened her mouth but didn't have the strength to go through this argument again.

"The doctor is here," the apartment said, and the door opened.

Dr. Zhan Asher, a short woman with long, braided hair and a dark complexion, nodded in Daris's direction, "Get the patient off the damn floor," as she stepped over the prone woman and made for the faucet. Close behind came the assisting doctor for the day, Jancie Lǐ, a slight woman with soft skin and short, dark hair. She was followed by the latest of Asher's interns, Fausto, a hulking man who had never questioned his choice of profession until two hours after meeting his new mentor just a week ago. Entering last was the newest medibot model, an ARN-13, affectionately called Arnie.

Dr. Asher barked orders as she washed up. "Arnie, move into the front room and set up the birthing table. Fausto, I need hot water and towels. Now. Schedule's screwed and we need to fix that."

Daris heard the running water and felt her bladder go, urine (or her water breaking?) seeping across the cold tile.

"Aw, hell! Hurry up with those towels; girl can't even hold her water," Dr. Asher snapped, moving to the front room.

Dr. Lǐ reached under Daris's armpits and lifted the pregnant woman. "It'll be okay," she said. "Zhan's a good doc; she's just on a tight schedule."

Daris shuddered as tiny rivulets slipped down the insides of her legs, raising goosebumps across her arms, and she wondered where the term came from. A thought she was unable to complete as pain stabbed her midsection and another contraction coiled her body. Dr. Lǐ dropped to the floor with Daris, holding her tightly as the pain rammed through the woman.

A minute later – a minute that felt far longer to the pregnant woman – Dr. Lǐ eased Daris onto the birthing table and strapped the woman's ankles into the stirrups.

"How's that?" Dr. Lǐ asked.

"Good as it gets," Daris said.

Dr. Lǐ nodded.

"Get the monitor on her," Dr. Asher said. Dr. Lǐ pulled a narrow belt with electrodes embedded across its front from the bag at her side and placed it on Daris's stomach, then turned it on.

There was no reading. Nothing.

"Aw, hell," Dr. Asher said. "Another damn blackout." She reached over, tapped the light switch on the wall next to her. Nothing happened. "Looks like we're doing this one blind. I need you all to focus. Dr. Lǐ, get on the other side of her; keep her distracted."

"Right."

An hour later, it was over. Daris lay exhausted on the birthing table while Dr. Lǐ cleaned the baby.

"How do you feel?" Dr. Asher asked.

"Okay." Daris sounded unsure. Dr. Asher didn't seem to notice. "Can I see my baby?" she asked.

"You know that isn't permitted," Dr. Asher said.

"But—"

"No." The doctor clipped the word off before it could fully escape and stepped into the kitchen to wash up.

Daris turned to Dr. Lǐ, her eyes repeating the question. Dr. Lǐ picked the baby up, wrapped tightly in a faded yellow blanket, and walked over to place the newborn on its mother's chest. Daris felt tears slip down her cheeks as she stared into the wide eyes of her baby.

Dr. Asher cleared her throat. "This will be going in the report, Dr. Lǐ. Another breach of protocol and you will be recommended for redoctrination. Now get that baby processed."

Dr. Lǐ swept the newborn from Daris and moved to the far end of the room without glancing back.

"And you…" Dr. Asher turned on Daris, her smile practiced, cold. "You get some rest. Doctor's orders." She then turned, crossed the kitchen, and stepped into the outer hallway, as the door shut with a whisper.

⚜⚜⚜

Daris stared out the window across the dull, gray spikes scattered across the landscape. From this high up she could just see the edge of the dome covering the city, while far below, a handful of citizens, more than Daris ever met when she was out, scattered like ants along the strictly composed streets.

She stood at that window for nearly half an hour before Dr. Lǐ called her into the office.

"So, what brings you in?" Dr. Lǐ inquired. Her words were sharp, angry, not at all as Daris remembered from the birthing. She took a seat in the simple, wooden chair (most likely synthetic) before the doctor's sleek, brushed metal desk. "Why did you agree to see me, doctor?" she asked.

Dr. Lǐ waved Daris's query away. "Tell me what's wrong," she said.

"I just…I haven't been feeling well," Daris said. "Ever since the birthing my body's been…"

She paused, looked around the office, her gaze lingering over each plant, each diploma, each picture, before returning to Dr. Lǐ. "I don't

87

think I can do the next implantation."

"Describe what you're feeling," Dr. Lǐ said.

"I don't know. Pains across my stomach. My back too. And I have trouble sleeping."

Dr. Lǐ tapped a screen set into the middle of her desk and pulled up Daris's chart. "According to this," she said, "there doesn't seem to be anything physically wrong with you. Nothing has registered with your apartment sensors."

"You think I'm lying," Daris said, her voice rising in volume across the statement.

"I am saying there is nothing physically wrong with you," Dr. Lǐ said. "And your defensiveness belies the fact that you already knew that. Regardless, there is nothing I would be able to treat, as it is."

Daris dropped her head. "I don't want the implantation," she said into her lap.

"There are women who would give anything to trade places with you. I don't believe you understand what a gift you have," Dr. Lǐ said.

"I won't do it," Daris said.

Dr. Lǐ sat up a little straighter. "You have no choice in the matter."

Daris leaned forward, slammed her palm onto the desk. "Where are my babies?"

Dr. Lǐ said nothing. She held Daris's gaze for a long moment, waited until the other woman sat back in her chair, then swiped a hand across the medical chart a few times before tapping out a rapid staccato on its surface.

"What is that?" Daris asked.

Dr. Lǐ did not reply.

"What are you doing?" Daris asked, her voice rising again. "Are you writing something about me?"

"You don't seem to understand," Dr. Lǐ said, without looking up, "how important your work is."

"I don't care," Daris said.

"You should." Dr. Lǐ stopped typing abruptly and stared at the woman sitting across from her. The doctor's lips were tight, almost invisible, while her eyes sharpened to points that sent chills up Daris's back.

Daris wanted to argue, wanted to yell at this woman who had been so inviting before, but she could think of only one thing to say. "Where's my baby?"

⚔ ⚔ ⚔

"Is everything all right?" the apartment asked, as Daris searched for her gloves.

"Yes," Daris said.

"You are agitated. Your blood pressure is elevated and your breathing restive."

"I'm fine; thank you," Daris said.

"Where are you going today?" the apartment asked. "Your next appointment is three weeks away."

"I'm visiting my brother," Daris said.

"In Dome 427?" the apartment asked.

"Yes," Daris said.

"Will you be home for your evening meal?"

"I'll be home," Daris said, and slammed the door behind her.

Outside, the streets were vacant, and Daris noticed the absence of the hum of the streetlights – *another blackout*, she thought.

As she walked, the occasional hovercam slipped down to log Daris's movements, and she was happy to find the chess table at the corner of Avenue M and 17th Street, sculpted from a single block of stone, occupied. Two elderly gentlemen were always in the middle of a game whenever Daris passed this landmark. Whether they were the same men each time she couldn't say, but their presence eased the tension now enfolding her body.

But this renewed calm lasted little more than the time required to button up a shirt.

The old woman – thin and fragile, with vacant eyes and weathered skin – lurched from Avenue Q onto 17th Street, startling Daris with the feeble claw she brought down onto the younger woman's shoulder. Daris felt a pinch at her neck – significant for a second before fading into the chaos of the moment – before the crone leaned in, one arm wrapped about Daris's neck for support, and whispered into the younger woman's ear.

It took Daris a long minute to decipher the street gibberish spouting from the wrinkled woman's mouth. "God bless the children. Who else gonna speak for 'em, we don't? Pleeeease, God. Spare your little ones."

Daris pushed against the older woman, the weathered skin concealing unexpectedly sturdy muscles, and the older woman cackled lightly to herself, holding her grip fast.

Daris could feel the knot in her stomach twisting harder. She looked around, but no one else was on the street. Turning her head violently, Daris bit one of the crone's fingers and shook the hand free, then reached over and pulled aside the vise formed by the other hand. "No," Daris said, "get away from me," and she shoved the old woman into the street and ran.

The crone's wail – "Save the children! Save the children!" – trailed Daris as she raced through the labyrinth of side streets. When she finally stopped running, Daris looked around. It all looked the same, unfamiliar, an oversized concrete maze.

Daris moved down the alley toward a call-box on the corner. Pressing her finger to the activator, the machine blinked on. Daris swept her fingers over the screen, called up the geocharts.

"Transport hub," she said. A bright red target popped up on the map not far away from where she stood.

"Map quickest route," Daris said.

The display bisected and a scroll of directions, listing street names, showed to the right of the map. Daris memorized the names then tapped the activator again, charging down the call box.

☠☠☠

Five minutes later, she entered the hub.

A serverbot, a square three-foot tall robot with visual actuator, voice module, and display screen, slid from its port along the far wall and rolled over to Daris, making a wide arc as it passed in front of her. "Come this way," it said.

Daris followed.

They passed down a short hallway into the main station, which was filled with tall, rectangular compartments called ports. Sprouting from each one was a flowering mass of tangled wires and pipes that coiled off into the darkness high above. The 'bot led Daris to a vacant port. "Here," it said, and extended an arm to unlock the door.

Daris stepped inside and waited for the door to seal. Thin coils of light around the ceiling and base of the port offered some illumination, but not much. Daris undressed and dropped her clothing into the slot next to her head. Seconds later the VR-cocoon, a viscous membrane that adhered to one's skin, slid down over her body. It was suffocating at first, and Daris closed her eyes. She thought about holding her baby, pictured the helpless infant laying on her chest, and felt her muscles uncoil.

When she was relaxed, Daris opened her eyes. "Dome 427." The words echoed, and the darkness was replaced by a street she recognized. Rows of poplars and maples receded along either side, while intricately carved facades – a restaurant, a hardware store, an open-air café, and more – invited accidental passersby to stop and visit.

"Hey, sis!"

Daris turned and saw Brian approaching. He wore a light sweater and shorts. Daris waved. His hair was longer than the last time. It bounced on a silent breeze, matching the briskness of his smile, which seeped up through his eyes. Brian's demeanor was infectious and usually improved Daris's mood tenfold.

Not today.

Brian reached his hand out, and they walked slowly together beneath the dancing leaves.

"How have you been?" Brian asked.

"Okay," Daris said.

"Recovering well enough," Brian said. "If not, I can call the doctors. I've got pull, you know."

"Your pull amounts to an extra ration of peanut butter for a week, and little else," Daris said.

"We take what we can get," Brian said.

"Yes," Daris said, her voice almost a whisper. "We take what we get."

"Let's get lunch," Brian said. "I'm starving."

Daris nodded.

"Good," Brian said.

A quarter hour later they were sitting at a delicate wrought-iron table on the corner two blocks down from Brian's apartment. People were mingling about, small patches here and there discussing…

Daris had no idea what they were discussing. Their voices were too soft to be heard. And Daris had so little experience with even the idea of conversation, aside from with her brother, that it was a mystery.

"How is it?" Brian looked at Daris's plate – Caesar salad, cottage cheese, and an orange, none of which had been touched. Daris's fork had shuffled a crouton onto the tabletop and wheedled its way beneath the romaine lettuce, but other than that, there was little indication she was aware of her food.

"Great," Daris said, unable to take her eyes from the small clusters of people.

"Looks it," Brian said, as he took another bite of his Reuben.

Daris looked at her plate, then at Brian, and a smile slipped across her lips, then quickly receded. "Yeah," she said.

"So," Brian said, between chews, "what's up?"

Daris looked at him. "How do you know we're related?"

"What?"

"How do I know you're my brother?" she asked, drawing out each word to make sure she was hearing herself correctly.

Brian sat back and wiped his mouth with a napkin. "What has gotten into you?" he asked.

Daris only stared – silence hanging between them.

"Come on," Brian said. "That's something you just know."

"That's not an answer," Daris said. "You don't *just know* if you're related to someone."

"Yes you do," Brian said.

Daris turned back to the people around them. "You're avoiding the question, Brian," she said.

"I am not," Brian said.

"I don't remember anything from my childhood," Daris said. "We should have spent a lot of time together. But I don't remember any of that. I don't remember learning to count. I don't remember playing with toys. I don't remember anybody reading to me."

She turned back to her brother. "I don't remember you."

"I don't have what you're looking for," Brian said. "No DNA records. No photos. No diary. I just have stories."

"Like the time you refused to eat at the orphanage. You were five. I don't remember what brought it on, but you got real sick, and they thought you were gonna die. You were on an I.V. drip. That didn't even help. It felt like months before you were even close to better.

"You didn't have a good childhood. I don't think they treated you poorly – no worse than the rest of us – but you didn't react well to the conditions. It was ugly. And I'm pretty sure you suppressed all that so you wouldn't have to deal with it.

"I wish I didn't have to," Brian said, his voice trailing off. "But it's better now. With time, it all gets better."

☠☠☠

Daris sat in her front room. Stared at the spot where the birthing table had been set up. Where the doctor had taken her baby.

She looked down at the feather-light palmcard in her lap, fingers drifted across the screen to reveal the map of the Dome (Brian lived in Dome 427, but Daris had no idea of the numeric designation where she lived; it had only ever been "the Dome."). She had pored over its geography a hundred times, but the streets, those streets that formed a skeleton for the city, merely drifted off to nothing as they approached the boundary of the dome, which, though she knew it surrounded the entire city, wasn't even visible on the chart.

But the dome wasn't a secret. When you looked up to the sky the dome greeted you, filtering the sun into a hazy shimmer with no solid shape. The dome was protection, keeping out harmful radiation,

92

moderating the temperature, balancing the atmosphere. The dome was life.

Daris had never visited the dome, had never touched it. She felt compelled to change that.

"What are you doing?" the apartment asked.

Daris did not answer.

"Your heart rate has increased by a factor of two in the last minute and your blood pressure is now one-and-a-half times optimal levels," the apartment said. "What is it that has caused you to become so upset?"

"I'm not upset," Daris said. She stood up and tossed the palmcard into the corner.

"Your reaction would indicate otherwise," the apartment said. "Please. I do not wish to see you hurt yourself."

"I'm sure," Daris snapped.

"You seem intent on exacerbating your current condition," the apartment said. "Your next implantation is only six days away. It would be best if you put your mind toward preparing for that rather than subjecting yourself to an emotional trauma. Please share what it is that has you so upset."

"Why don't *you* just tell me what's wrong?" Daris asked.

"I am not a mind reader," the apartment said.

"No," Daris said.

"You obviously seek information. What question is it that weighs on you?" the apartment asked.

"Dome 427," Daris said.

"Where your brother lives," the apartment said.

"How do I get there?" Daris asked.

"Go down to the transport hub," the apartment said, "as you always have. They will arrange for you to visit Brian."

"No," Daris said. "Where is it? On a map. Where is Dome 427?"

"It is where your brother lives."

Daris thought she could almost hear concern in the automated voice. "What are you hiding?" she asked.

"I do not understand the question," the apartment said. "I was not programmed to hide anything."

"Then answer the question," Daris said. "Why is Dome 427 not on any map? Why is *this* dome not on any map?"

"You were just looking at a map of our dome," the apartment said.

Daris screamed and stormed out of the apartment, leaving the disembodied voice behind.

☠☠☠

Daris stood at the edge of the dome. She had walked over two hours and discovered that the streets did indeed suddenly stop, spreading into a wide expanse of large, gray and white cobblestones meticulously placed so that seams were hardly visible. The dull colors washed together, offered no horizon point for Daris to latch onto. She questioned her motivation more than once.

But then, just as suddenly as the streets had seeped into the cobbles, Daris found herself standing at the dome wall, its similarly gray tones mingling into the dull stones at her feet. She ran a hand over the opaque barrier, as smooth and cool as her bedsheets in the dim moments just before waking. It made the hair on the back of her neck stand up, and Daris had to catch her breath.

She stood there for a long moment, her mind working to process all the thoughts charging across her synapses.

"Brian." Barely a whisper, but it shattered the silence that had fallen over Daris. She opened her eyes and looked around, certain she was not alone.

But she saw no one.

Daris slid her hand over the cool surface as she followed its wide arc. Another two hours passed.

When she stopped walking, the sun had fallen behind the city skyline and night skirted across the arched dome, trailing after the sun in a celestial game of cat and mouse. She knew going any farther would be dangerous. The darkness of night was complete beneath the dome.

So Daris lay down and slept. After a fashion.

⚜ ⚜ ⚜

The sun had yet to begin its race across the sky when Daris awoke. She had no idea of the time, but the pain in her shoulders and back urged her to rise. Not for the last time did she question what she was doing.

An hour later Daris discovered what she had been hunting for. A break in the marble – that's how she had come to think of the combination of cobbles and dome – a triangular opening that rose six feet to its crown. A shallow rush of water, retreating from the city, passed into the tunnel and continued out of the dome.

It was a way out. (She never considered that it might be a cave rather than a tunnel)

Daris dropped into the opening and stood in water up to her knees. The cold was biting, and the current stronger than she had anticipated. Only black greeted her, as she peered into the tunnel. She closed her eyes, dropped onto her back, and let the water sluice her away into the

94

darkness that lay ahead.

⁂

Daris could not stop shivering. A raging wind battered her, chasing away the dampness with a cold that pierced in a thousand places. She bent down against the rushing clouds of sand blooming in the wind, threatening to peel her skin away one layer at a time.

Pain receded to numbness. She glanced at the tunnel that brought her here, voted against diving back into that water; she hadn't the strength. Cupping her hands against her face, Daris peered through the coruscating reds and browns.

She was in a wasteland.

Except for a darker smudge beyond the haze.

She began walking. Hoped it wasn't a mirage.

Beyond the torrent of sand, Daris found herself in front of a weather-beaten tin shack, beyond which she could make out a collection of pipes that seemed to have erupted from the ground and then turned at a ninety-degree angle for the dome. A sign above the door, the only break in the rusted façade, read "BioMass Generator." Daris didn't know what that meant. She didn't care. Pressing all her weight down on the lever, she heard the latch release and pushed inside.

A moment later the wind fell away.

Pale lights, recessed into the ceiling, flickered a pattern Daris couldn't decipher. There was little to the room – a small table fronted by a wood chair with a monitor that revealed a video image of the shack's exterior. Daris knew she had been on that screen only moments before. On the wall opposite the entrance was a second door. Daris opened this and peered down a darkened stairwell.

"Hello."

Her voiced echoed away. There was no response. Looking back at the monitor, Daris decided her best approach was to take the stairs.

So, she did.

⁂

One hundred forty-two steps and Daris turned left into the single passage at the base of the stairwell. The first handful of doors Daris found were all locked, and her ragged breaths – her only companion in the fallow light – implored her to give up. She ignored these entreaties and moved toward a shard of light up ahead.

It was a smaller passage that branched off the one she'd been

95

traveling. Turning the corner a blaze of gold and crimson slashed down the hallway. It took a moment for her eyes to adjust. Once her pupils constricted, Daris saw two doors at the opposite end of the short passage, the sparks of light beaming from their scalded windows. Daris pondered her options.

She could ignore the fireworks and continue past this artery, though she was certain the crypt of the building was fast approaching. Retreating back to the sandstorm wasn't a real choice. Option C was to follow the light.

Daris moved forward on her knees. Slowly. Quietly. Scanning the area.

Reaching the door, she peered over the lip of a window. Layers of scum obscured her vision; shadows moved against the flash, but nothing distinct. Pressing an ear to the cold steel proved equally futile. She melted to the floor and sobbed quietly.

It was a while before Daris calmed herself, the tension of the past day rushing over her in a wave of emotion that startled her. Not until the tears began did she realize how much she had been carrying. Shifting her weight, Daris took a deep breath and nudged one of the doors open.

A tall, thin man in a long white smock and matching white pants stood at the far end of the room. His back was turned to Daris as he leaned over a long, narrow countertop that stabbed from the wall. Above him, a group of off-white, square doors with rusting latches, five rows wide and two high, formed the beginnings of a chessboard against the dull, smooth gray of the walls. One of the doors was open, just above the man's head, a heavy black against his shock of white. Along the adjoining wall was a giant incinerator – the source of the light – the blaze licking at its clear, plasteel prison door, aching for escape. Daris shuddered.

The man was busy with something on the counter – at the angle he stood, his body concealed what it might be – his arms ratcheting up and down as he worked. Daris watched. And waited. A knot formed in the small of her back. She adjusted her position, but it didn't help. Easing the door shut, Daris moved to a seated position, then leaned her head back into the room. And Daris saw what had been hidden on the table.

The tall man was stepping back over to the counter, from the console next to the incinerator. Stepping back to a baby rolling side-to-side on its round back, the frustration of its dilemma lost on its pre-verbal brain.

Daris bit down on a knuckle.

And the lights went out.

The incinerator continued to illuminate the room, casting the ceiling in shadow as it rippled over the walls. The tall man looked around, as if searching for the cause of the blackout, and Daris fell away from the door, using her knee to stop it from quivering.

Daris's pupils had hardly dilated when the lights returned. She got back up and nudged the door open again.

"Tallow! Are you screwing off again?" The tall man's head snapped to attention, and Daris followed his line of sight to a speaker in the far corner that she hadn't noticed before.

"No, sir," the man, Tallow, said, his voice wavering slightly. "Just finishing up now."

"You need to move faster," the voice said. "These electrical failures are inexcusable. If I need to get somebody else who can do the job, I will."

"No. No. You needn't bother with that," Tallow said. "I'll take care of it right away."

There was a small click signaling the voice on the other end had signed off. Daris watched closely, as Tallow worried the knuckles of one hand while he turned in small half-circles, as if he were hunting for a way out.

But there was none. So the man went back to work. He wrapped the infant tightly in a frayed, colorless blanket and lifted it up to his chest. No sound came from the bundle of cloth. An ache Daris hadn't noticed before, like a thousand pinpricks, started to bloom in her stomach, tiny spines insinuating themselves up through her chest and into her throat.

Tallow bent his face down and cooed at the baby, running a spindly finger along its chubby face. It gave a quick squeal of approval, and Daris thought she saw the man smile. He walked the baby over to the incinerator, shadows jumping across the two figures to create a fevered chiaroscuro.

The knot in her gut tightened, and Daris realized it had been hours since she'd relieved herself. The pressure on her kidneys and bowels suddenly became unbearable.

Tallow reached up to open a chute beneath the incinerator's console. He lifted the baby up.

And dropped it in.

The pocket of air trapped in Daris's throat escaped in a brutal scream as her kidneys gave way, warm urine soaking her pants as it spread down her legs and onto the floor.

Then, too late, her mind signaled that she needed to run.

✦✦✦

Pain shattered across the back of Daris's skull as it bounced off the concrete wall, tipping her chair forward. Instinct urged her to reach out, but her hands were bound tightly to the chair rails at her back.

Captain Duran, who owned the disembodied voice from earlier and had just launched Daris's head into the concrete, stopped her fall. He was shorter than the other man, but bigger – wide across the chest and shoulders with a bushy beard and hard, black eyes. He had been questioning Daris for hours, leaving her in her soiled clothes until she offered up the answers he wanted.

Except Daris had no idea what the answers he wanted might be. So she had responded with questions of her own, resulting in the shorter man hitting her – hard.

Daris tried to catch her breath. The captain paced the room, while Tallow, still in his lab coat, looked on from the corner. One eye was almost completely shut from swelling, and Daris worried that the pain seemed almost absent at this point.

"Now," the captain said, "will you share with us how you found your way here and what it is you hoped to accomplish?"

Daris looked up through one good eye, her voice sandpaper. "I don't know how I got here," she said. "I needed shelter from the sandstorm."

"Not good enough," the captain said.

"But it's true," Daris said.

"You had to leave the dome," the captain said. "That was a conscious act. What made you decide not just to leave your apartment, but to leave the city and find a way outside the dome?"

"Babies," Daris said. "Is that what happens to them?"

"What. Did. You. Want." The captains' voice boomed through the tiny room.

"I don't know," Daris said.

Pain radiated across Daris's cheek as the captain hit her again, sending her and the chair to the floor. The captain quickly picked her up and leveled his face with hers.

His words, "You lie," spat over Daris's face. She didn't know what to say.

"M'baby." The word slipped from Daris's mouth, an accident that caught the captain's attention.

"What?" he asked.

"I don't think we're going to get anything else from her," Tallow said. "She probably doesn't even know where she is anymore."

"That's no good," the captain said.

"No," Tallow said.

"She's seen too much," the captain said. He stood up and straightened his uniform. "You'll have to take care of her."

"Okay," Tallow said.

"And make sure it's permanent," the captain said.

"Of course."

Daris threw on a light jacket as she wove through the furniture of her front room.

"Where are you going today?" the apartment asked.

Daris stopped and smiled up at the ceiling. "I'm going to visit Brian. To tell him he's finally going to be an uncle."

There was a lilt in the apartment's automated voice. "The implantation took. Congratulations."

"Thank you," Daris said. "It's great news, isn't it?"

"Yes, it is," the apartment said.

"I am a little nervous – don't know what to expect with the pregnancy. I mean *really* expect. I hope I'll do well."

"You'll do wonderfully," the apartment said.

"You think so?" Daris asked.

"I am certain," the apartment said.

"Thanks," Daris said, as she moved toward the door. "See ya later."

"Yes," the apartment said. "I will see you later."

And the door closed with a soft hiss.

THE WAY IT WILL BE
BY ADRIAN LUDENS

The knot of fabric tied around Gene's neck seemed to constrict with each breath. He strove to hold his body perfectly still. Even a glance at the lights beating down on him from above threatened to blind his eyes. He dragged his parched tongue across his lips and fought to control the trembling in his hands. Dark silhouettes of two figures shared the room with him, but kept their distance. The aftertaste of burnt coffee, intermingled with the lingering odor of the lone cigarette he'd smoked minutes before, coated him with a residue of sameness that stretched back at least one thousand days. Gene heard a voice counting backwards from ten. He stared straight ahead. The disembodied voice droned down to "one" and the operator of Camera One, Tommy Paxton, pointed at him.

Gene smiled into the lens of Tommy's camera. "Good evening and thank you for tuning in to News Maker One, your source for local news in Prestor Springs. I'm Gene Hastings. Here's tonight's top story." Gene swiveled in his chair and found the words on the teleprompter screen reflected in the lens of Camera Two.

"The votes will soon be tallied and Bix Chalfont will win reelection as mayor of Prestor Springs. The Council assures us that, after all precincts have reported, Chalfont will have won in a landslide." Gene knew the director, Marlin, would have already called for a key shot. Footage of the soon-to-be-victorious Chalfont now played in a quarter frame graphic box over his shoulder. "Rather than give a concession speech, his challenger, Bob Price, will douse himself with gasoline and strike a wooden match. Everyone in Prestor Springs will feel happy about Mayor Chalfont's victory."

As he said it, Gene felt invisible hands pull his lips into a smile. Both camera operators grinned in unison. There was no point in feeling sorry for Price. Only the malcontents and troublemakers had supported him anyway. Tommy made a traffic cop gesture back to Camera One. Gene turned and resumed reading.

"According to the latest Council reports, this season's fruit, vegetable, and grain crop will produce just enough food for everyone in Prestor Springs. The only exception will be the Ramirez family, whose eight members will no longer be provided for. There is good news, however." A thrill of anticipation shot through him; he loved good news. "The Ramirez family will walk to the river tonight and throw themselves into it. The mass suicide will be an act of contrition. They have attempted contact with the Outside recently but now realize the error of their ways."

He shook his head, feeling real regret. "Always a bad idea." This wasn't on the teleprompter screen, but Gene felt pleased with his ad-lib. He knew Mr. Collins, the overbearing producer, would chew him out for it after the newscast. But in Gene's opinion, his ability to ad-lib was second only to his ability to come in and relay the news stories cold. Gene never got a pre-read. The station's general manager, who also served on the Council, insisted upon this.

Following Tommy's motion back to Camera Two, Gene started to read again. "The men of the Council will all suffer massive heart attacks and will die now."

Tommy made frantic motions for Gene to stop and he broke off, stunned by the words he'd just read. Both Tommy and the other camera operator—a gangly, red-haired youth whose name Gene could never remember—stared at him. Their glazed expressions and mounting unease reminded Gene of slaughterhouse cattle who'd just been loaded into the "Stunning Box." Gene felt the same way. This was terrible news. Could there be a mistake?

"Go to commercial. Now!" Marlin bellowed to David, the master controller. Gene's earpiece squealed with feedback. He sat frozen, unsure of what had just happened. He glanced at the on-air monitor mounted high on the wall behind the cameras, where an advertisement for Prestor Springs' only car dealership played. Three sharp reports came from the next room. To Gene they sounded like balloons popping.

"We've been infiltrated." Marlin's voice came through Gene's earpiece. The director sounded shaken, out of breath. "We'll extend the break until we can verify that no one has tampered with the rest of the script. Mr. Collins is down. We're attempting CPR. If anyone else on the Council is listening, please advise."

Usually Gene didn't hear all the chatter from the control room. Marlin must have accidentally pressed his talkback button. Gene felt mortified. Several old friends were part of the Council. The thought of them collapsing and dying appalled him.

"What the hell just happened?" the red-haired camera operator wondered aloud.

"No idea." Tommy pressed his lips together. "But it sounded bad."

"Is anyone else from the Council listening?" someone asked.

"You heard what Gene just said. They're probably all down, you jackass!" another voice retorted. Gene thought it sounded like John and David, the tape operator and the master controller, arguing, but he wasn't sure. Except for Marlin, the director, Gene had never actually met any of the others who worked in master control during his newscasts. He didn't even know what they looked like. John had the rasp of a long-time smoker while David sometimes sounded very nasal, as if he suffered from seasonal allergies. All the voices came through his earpiece now in a jumble, like six politicians lecturing simultaneously.

"David, keep the ads rolling," Marlin instructed. "Someone help me move the body; I need to get in there and proofread the rest of the script."

Gene heard a muffled thump in his earpiece. The teen behind Camera Two chewed on his lip but stopped when he noticed Gene watching him.

"Stand by, Gene," Doris, the control room audio operator, said. "Sheila from the Council just arrived. Her heart's fine. She's advising Marlin right now. I think you're going to have a rewrite coming out of the commercial break."

Gene nodded at the unblinking eye of Camera One to indicate he understood. Knowing he had time and distraught over the apparent fates of most of the Council members, he sought momentary escape. He let his mind wander remembering that he'd had some strange experiences at his old job, too. He'd worked at a filling station on the edge of Prestor Springs. You met all kinds working nights. And one late summer night, he had noticed a strange light descend from the sky and had left his post to investigate.

Gene never found the words to describe what had happened next. In the woods adjacent to the filling station, he had come upon a shape, burning a brighter white than a magnesium flare. Gene's brain had attempted to clarify what his eyes saw: a being stood before him, yet infinitely ascended and descended simultaneously. It had moved then, spinning gyroscopically, and Gene staggered and fell, his sense of balance obliterated. The being had, Gene believed, made eye contact—or a close approximation of it—with him.

He'd plummeted into unconsciousness. Hours later he had woken, found no trace of the being, and staggered home. His nose bled off and on for a week, and the headaches had been nearly unbearable. But he'd felt smarter, somehow. That incident, Gene believed, led to him landing this job. In that brief instant, his mind had been remade.

"Fifteen seconds, guys," David warned.

"Camera Two, center shot!" Marlin instructed. The red-haired kid rolled his camera in front of Gene, who licked his lips. A nagging thought had come to him: If he was so smart, why couldn't he figure out what had just happened? What did Marlin mean when he said they'd been "infiltrated?" Had the teleprompter operator been one of the crazies? Had someone in the control room shot and killed him? Burning bile crept up Gene's throat. He pressed his sweating palms against the smooth surface of the desk, hoping he didn't appear as jarred as he felt.

Tommy counted down from five to one on his fingers and pointed at Gene, whose mind still raced. He concentrated on reading the words on the screen.

"Citizens of Prestor Springs, we have an astonishing development." This, Gene realized, was the portion of the script that Sheila, the lone woman on the Council, had instructed Marlin to include. "The men of the Council have started, and will continue to fully recover. As it turns out, these were only incidents of acute indigestion. The previous report was erroneous."

Gene realized the words inserted by the now-deceased teleprompter operator had referenced only the men. What a magnificent stroke of luck to have Sheila, unaffected by the malicious act of sabotage, nearby! Thanks to her quick thinking, the Council, and Prestor Springs' way of life, would remain unchanged.

"In other news tonight, the Council is pleased to announce that Prestor Springs and the surrounding area will remain invisible to the Outside. We'll all sleep better tonight knowing our special mountain community remains safe and unaffected by Outside events."

Sheila and Mr. Collins entered the studio from the hallway that connected to the control room and watched Gene as he read. He noticed Mr. Collins dabbing his brow with a handkerchief, but he appeared nearly recuperated. Sheila wore a rather smug expression, and why not? Her quick thinking had saved the entire Council.

"In sports…" Gene read scores—all of them local, intramural affairs with no actual winning teams, but plenty of individual records being set. He let his mind wander again. It amazed him how easy this was once he got warmed up each night. Gene always arrived at the studio feeling fuzzy-headed, shaky and nervous, but after spending the vast majority of his day silent, it felt cathartic to form syllables and create full words and sentences. He felt as if each new sentence that rolled from his lips was special somehow, as if everything he said had importance and merit. He loved that feeling.

"We'll be back with our News Maker One weather forecast after these messages." Gene rolled back in his chair and walked across the set to the 'Green Screen.' Here he would show viewers the forecast for the next few days. All the meteorological research had already been done ahead of time. Nikki, the person in charge of graphics for the newscasts, punched in the data under the guidance of one of the members of the Council. The tedium of the task didn't interest Gene; he felt content to simply read the information from the teleprompter screen each night.

As another batch of commercials for local businesses played, Tommy rolled his camera to where Gene now stood and began framing the shot. Gene's eyes drifted to the monitor, where an ad for the sole real estate company in Prestor Springs aired. Like the auto dealership, it was owned by one of the members of the Council.

The Council.

The group hadn't even existed until a few weeks after Gene's mysterious encounter. He'd been having dinner with a small group of friends at Ruby's Restaurant. Fighting an excruciating headache had made him edgy. He hadn't cared for the soup, deeming it too salty. He'd noticed a few of the others at the table who'd ordered the soup hadn't seemed to mind. This had irritated him. Gene had spoken up then. "I don't care for the soup tonight. It tastes like crap."

He remembered what had happened next quite clearly. One friend had choked on a spoonful of the soup just as Gene had verbalized his opinion. Across the table, someone else had grimaced, dropped his soup spoon, and hurried to the men's room. No one said anything about it, though Gene noticed a few of the guys looking at him curiously for the rest of the meal.

After dinner, two of his buddies pulled him aside.

"How'd you do that in there?" one asked.

"Do what?" Gene was genuinely puzzled.

The other friend waved a hand dismissively. "Never mind. Listen, Gene, I've got a friendly wager for you: predict tomorrow's weather right and I'll give you twenty bucks."

Gene had made something up on the spot. "We'll have an afternoon thundershower around three, an eighth of an inch of rain, and a high of 68 degrees."

"You mean Fahrenheit, right?"

"Yeah, sure."

He'd nailed it.

His friend paid up the next evening.

The day after that, Mr. Collins offered Gene the meteorologist job on the local news. He introduced Gene to Marlin who showed him around and gave him very specific instructions. "You read what's on the script and nothing else, got it?"

Gene didn't question his new boss. Within a week, Gene did the entire newscast by himself and the station had changed their slogan.

By the end of the month, the Council went public, and Prestor Springs went private, shutting itself off from the outside world. Gene considered all of it an improvement, with the exception of the custom-fitted thermoplastic mouth guard the Council insisted he wear.

Unlike a traditional sports mouth guard, Gene's included a long piece of polymer that he thought of as "the tongue depressor." It pressed down firmly against the center of his tongue. As a result, Gene found it impossible to speak while wearing the mouth guard. If he focused on its presence too much, the portion on his tongue also threatened his gag reflex. Gene took the mouth guard out without Council approval only a few times before deciding he'd rather comply and spend his free time in silence than endure the electrical shocks the Council doled out as punishment for the guard's unauthorized removal.

He was only allowed to take it out for meals, and even then the Council forbade him from speaking. "We don't want you to strain your vocal cords," Mr. Collins had explained. Gene's jaws always ached and the entire contraption made him feel self-conscious. Gene had tried to blend in with the downtown shopping crowds while wearing the mouth guard only once. He'd felt only *slightly* less conspicuous than if he'd been billed as a cannibal and put on display, bound and ball-gagged, in a roadside freak show. So he rarely went out in public, preferring to have the people of Prestor Springs think of him the way they saw him every night on television: sharply dressed, friendly, articulate, and always informed. Besides, the medication prescribed and administered by Dr. Waggoner—also a high-ranking member of the Council—disoriented Gene. He never felt completely lucid, except during the newscasts, which were the one bright spot of his day. Otherwise, it felt as if his life was an endless repetition of eating, sleeping, and staring at the blank walls of his room.

"Gene! Wake up, man; you're on!"

The words startled him from his reverie and he faced the camera. It took a moment for his eyes to focus on his scripted forecast.

"You can count on partly sunny skies over Prestor Springs tomorrow.

No precipitation in the forecast until the day after. We'll experience a low tonight of 55 and a high tomorrow of a perfect 72. As always, temperatures are in Fahrenheit."

Marlin's voice interrupted his casual pace. "Gene, you took way too much time just standing there when we came out of the commercial break. You need to wrap up the newscast in *five seconds*!"

Stunned, Gene sped through the words on the teleprompter screen. "All the Council members are unable to breathe and I will now forget how to read."

He only fully registered the meaning of his words after they'd tumbled from his lips. Gene felt his jaw drop in dismay. He mentally castigated himself for screwing the pooch twice during the same newscast. Gene thought Marlin had checked the script. Sheila ran toward him. She looked angry.

Shouts came from the control room, followed by more popping sounds. Gene now recognized these as shots being fired. There were a lot of them this time, coming in rapid succession. Gene didn't understand why anyone would want to sabotage the newscast.

Gene looked around in time to see Mr. Collins sag to the floor near the back wall, frantically tugging at his collar. Tommy abandoned his camera and crouched beside the older man. "Open your mouth so I can breathe a lungful of air into yours," Tommy urged.

Sheila arrived at Gene's side. Her mouth, opening and closing in silence, reminded him of a goldfish experiencing the counter top outside its bowl. She grabbed a sheet of blank paper Gene kept on his set desk just for show, and began scribbling furiously. Past her, Gene noticed the red-haired camera operator walking over to Tommy and the asphyxiating producer.

"You traitorous son of a bitch!" someone screamed hoarsely in his earpiece. David? John? Gene wondered who, besides Marlin, was still alive in the control room. Gene heard two more muffled gunshots.

Sheila staggered, and thrust the sheet of paper into Gene's hands. He noticed her fingertips had begun to turn blue. A booming report—this one much louder than any of the others—startled Gene into dropping the page. He looked past Sheila and Camera One, and saw Tommy lying in a pool of brains and blood. Mr. Collins writhed on the floor beside him. The red-haired camera operator, holding a smoking handgun, strode to Camera One. He zoomed in on Gene, and twirled the gun barrel in the universal "wrap it up" signal.

Gene realized Sheila was now curled on the floor beside his news desk. He idly wondered if she was in the camera shot as he stooped to pick up her scrawled instructions. Gene glanced from the page to the camera lens and back to the page. He flipped it so the bottom became the top, but he still had no idea what message it contained. He thought he recognized a single letter here and there, but the rest was a meaningless jumble. He glanced again at Sheila. Her eyes bulged from her darkening face and a slaver of drool became a small puddle on the concrete. Gene didn't find her very ladylike. Marlin's familiar voice crackled again in the earpiece. "Say goodnight, Gene. This time you really do only have five seconds!"

Since Mr. Collins apparently wouldn't be there to chew him out after the newscast, Gene ad-libbed a second time. "And that's the way it will be. Thank you for watching News Maker One. I'm Gene Hastings. Sleep well and goodnight."

The red light above Camera One went dark and Gene realized his entire body had begun to shake. Tonight's broadcast had drained him mentally and emotionally. He stepped over Sheila's body, curled beneath him like a piece of dried fruit. Gene wrinkled his nose and tried to breathe through his mouth; at least one of the dead inside the studio had voided their bowels.

Marlin, blood-spattered but apparently uninjured, burst into the studio from the hallway and jogged up to Gene with his arms raised, palms out. "Not a word, Gene. You know better."

Marlin had never steered Gene wrong in the past so he waited until the director spoke again. "I need you to repeat the next thing I say, got it?"

Gene nodded.

"I remember how to read," Marlin said and then grinned.

"I remember how to read," Gene mimicked.

Marlin's hand shot up in warning again, so Gene hurried back to the blank pages on the news desk. Marlin followed and handed him a pen. Gene wrote: *Thanks. What just happened? Why are so many people dead?*

Part of him hoped this would all turn out to be a horrible misunderstanding on his part.

Marlin put an arm around him in a gesture meant to be reassuring and squeezed. "The Council won't be making the rules any more. We've been living under their thumb, bowing to their every whim, for too long."

Gene scribbled another question. *Am I out of a job?*

Marlin read the words, smiled, and shook his head. "We need you, Gene. You're our special guy. The news wouldn't be the same without you."

Gene scrawled one more line and shoved it at the news director. *At least tell me I won't have to wear that awful mouth guard anymore.*

Marlin looked at him with what appeared to be genuine sympathy.

"I'm sorry, Gene. I truly am. But New Day Dawning needs you. The people of Prestor Springs need you. We can't risk—" He broke off and started again. "You need to conserve your voice. We have some ambitious plans, Gene. We're going to have you do *national* news!" The director squeezed his shoulder again. "We'll have an exciting newscast tomorrow night, I promise you! In the meantime, we'll need to install an all-new staff."

Gene realized then that the red-haired camera operator had stepped close. Before he could react, Marlin grabbed Gene and put him in a headlock. Gene felt a bee's sting as the kid pressed a long syringe into his thigh and pushed the plunger. The familiar burn was followed by the dreamy sensation that filled up most of Gene's days and nights.

His brain conjured up an old saying: *The king is dead. Long live the king.* Gene mentally grappled with the concept, but its significance was fleeting and soon had receded back out of his reach. His arm and legs felt heavy, unwieldy. His head drooped from his neck, a bowling ball held in the tenuous grasp of a child.

For reasons he could not articulate, Gene felt like a special pet stolen from one family so that he could perform tricks for another. He looked up, dazed, and tried to return Marlin's smile as the director withdrew the special mouth guard from its case.

"Trust me, Gene. New Day Dawning knows what's best. If you continue to do exactly as I say everything will be just fine."

GOOD ENOUGH FOR JEORGIA
BY JOHN BIGGS

The accident left Jeorgia Bailey with a gray front tooth and a little stumble when she walked. Still pretty in a use-to-be-graceful sort of way, at least as far as Jack could see through the telephoto lens on his Sony Cyber-shot digital camera. One hundred feet is a long way off, but that's what the restraining order said.

Jeorgia dropped something. Too small to identify from Jack's court mandated distance. When she bent over to pick it up, he snapped a picture. Beautiful, a little disrespectful, absolutely perfect.

Jeorgia Bailey was the only girl in the world for Jack Winston, always and forever. That's what they called *Endless Love* on KLUV, Jack's favorite radio station, and *stalking* by the family court judge who ordered him to admire Jeorgia from afar.

He deleted the bent-over picture from his camera but he couldn't erase it from his mind. Mental images always leave a ghost, especially the ones that shouldn't have been taken in the first place. He checked the delivery log sitting on the front seat of his truck. Twenty more stops before lunchtime, and no good reason to be parked across the street from the Bailey house.

Jeorgia gave Jack a little wave, like she could see him through the tinted windows. She did that all the time, because they were bonded in some complicated cosmic way like Stephen Hawkings talked about in his computer voice in science documentaries. Watching Public Television was one of the ways Jack tried to improve himself so he'd be good enough for Jeorgia.

He pressed his lips against his driver's side window and gave her a perfectly legal proxy-kiss. Willy Nelson sang *Always on my Mind* from the cheap dashboard speaker of the radio; every word as bright as a copper jacketed bullet aimed at his heart.

It wasn't like Jack would hurt Jeorgia Bailey. It wasn't like he didn't love her more than anyone in the whole world. It wasn't like he hadn't been in love with her ever since he'd asked her to dance with him at the senior prom and she said, "Okay, Jack."

Proof that Jeorgia Bailey knew Jack Winston's name, even if the dance never happened. The trouble was, when Jack and Jeorgia were in high school, she was about a thousand times too good for him. The odds came down after her boyfriend wrecked his car with Jeorgia in it. Now, she was a hundred times too good at most, and Jack was trying to close that gap.

Too bad there wasn't a post-accident senior prom where Jack could ask Jeorgia to dance again and after she said yes, he'd ask her on a date, and she'd say, "Okay Jack." Those were the only words Jeorgia Bailey ever said to him, and he was sure she'd say them again one day, after the restraining order was lifted and her parents came to see what a great guy Jack Winston really was.

He joined the Metro Baptist Church, which he attended almost every time Jeorgia's mother brought her. He could do that because church was one of those lawful exceptions to the hundred-foot rule.

Another was work related contact. Jack delivered Culligan drinking water to most of Jeorgia's neighbors, so he had to drive by her house three or four times every day, with his binoculars, and his camera, and the words "Okay Jack," beeping in his mind like a call-waiting signal.

Mr. and Mrs. Bailey and the Oklahoma City police didn't understand true love—that's all. But pretty soon they would. Jack had been praying for that to happen since he joined the Metro Baptist Church, and he'd been saving up for a remote listening device that would let him eavesdrop on conversations inside the Bailey house.

Then he'd know exactly what to pray for.

❀❀❀

The Metro Baptist Church was right across the street from a Seven Eleven, where sinners like Jack could fill their cars with the cheapest gas in town and read messages on the church marquee.

"Death and Taxes. You should be prepared for both," must have been the theme for the day, because every few minutes the message stopped and flashed three times before moving on.

After that came: "Sinners wanted. Pro or Amateur. Apply inside."

Easier to read than *The Bible*. Easier to understand, easier to remember. One clever sentence for every occasion. That's all Jack needed from religion. He wouldn't go inside the church at all, except for Jeorgia being there almost every Sunday.

Jack liked to sit in the back, where he could get out quickly, where Mrs. Bailey wouldn't see him unless she turned her head around backwards like the people in demonic possession movies. She could probably do it too, if she weren't pretending to be religious. Jack doubted if Mrs. Bailey had read the church marquee even one time.

This Sunday was something special. An evangelist had come from Kansas City to tell Oklahoma Christians all about his sins.

Reverend Virgil Swope moved across the elevated stage and shouted at the congregation like a wrestling promoter daring them to take on Jesus in a no-holds-barred cage fight.

Jack had met men like Reverend Swope in the county jail on a couple of occasions. He would have stayed at the back of the church except that Mrs. Bailey decided she and Jeorgia should rededicate their lives to Christ. When the preacher's voice got end-of-sermon soft she moved out of the center of her crowded pew, pulling her daughter by one hand.

Jeorgia waved to the congregation and smiled, the way beauty pageant contestants do. She didn't stop waving even when Mrs. Bailey told the congregation about her troubles.

There were tears in Mrs. Bailey's eyes, but her pious look turned into a bitter beer face as soon as she saw Jack walking up the aisle.

"Hi Jeorgia," he said, as soon as he was close enough to be heard over the music.

Jeorgia smiled a little wider and brushed her hair back with her free hand as if she were adjusting a tiara.

"Hey there Mrs. Bailey." Jack wore a brand new Ralph Lauren shirt and a blue blazer that was only twenty percent polyester.

Jeorgia moved her lips and whispered, "Okay Jack." Not exactly *I love you* but close enough for a brain damaged girl and a boy who wasn't quite good enough.

Mrs. Bailey released her daughter's hand so she could threaten Jack with two clenched fists. Reverend Swope stepped in front of her, like a referee in a mismatched title fight.

Jeorgia took that opportunity to perform the dance routine she'd done for the talent portion of the Miss Teen Oklahoma pageant.

"You're not supposed to be within one hundred feet." Mrs. Bailey spoke through clenched teeth, but everyone could hear her because the piano player stopped playing and the choir stopped singing, and one of the old men in the front row who'd been coughing finally managed to get it under control.

"This is a lawful exception to the restraining order." Jack had practiced this statement just in case, so he sounded a lot like an actor-lawyer explaining to Court TV viewers why it is perfectly all right to let murderers out of jail.

"Is not." Mrs. Bailey sounded like one of the pretend attorneys the police get for you when you can't afford a real one.

"Y' all calm down, now," Reverend Swope said. "This is not the time nor place," which Jack thought was his way of telling them to take it outside.

"Is too." Jack pushed past Mrs. Bailey, which might have been a violation of his probation, except he was trying to help Jeorgia, who had fallen off of the elevated stage.

"Is not." Mrs. Bailey took a swing at Jack. He let her punch land to make her feel a little better.

Jack helped Jeorgia to her feet. Would have dusted her off but Reverend Swope and Mrs. Baily would think that kind of touching was un-Christian.

"Are you hurt, Jeorgia?"

She said, "Okay, Jack," with almost no sound behind the words, but Jack didn't care. He'd become an expert lip reader if that's what it took to be with Jeorgia.

Mrs. Bailey had just enough anger left for a few more words that are hardly ever said in a church. Every curse a little quieter than the one before until they faded into whispers and finally came to a complete stop.

"Guess I got carried away," Mrs. Bailey said to the four senior citizens who stood in a semi-circle in front of the stage like members of a firing squad.

A woman with blue hair, and a touch of scoliosis told her, "We think you all might be happier at the Presbyterian Church." She jabbed an arthritic finger at Mrs. Bailey, Jeorgia, and Jack, and after a moment's hesitation, at Reverend Swope too.

"I mean *all* y'all."

❀❀❀

The bartender at Carlton's restaurant said, "One small step for a man," like he always did when Jack hopped up the three steps to the drinking zone. "How goes it Jackie?" He turned on a blender and twisted a half lime on a glass reamer. "What's shakin'? How's the boy?"

Jack couldn't remember the bartender's name, even though they went to high school together. He had a white scar through his left eyebrow, and a nose somebody broke and nobody fixed. Jack thought he might be responsible for the nose, but it looked like there were no hard feelings.

"What'll it be Jackie boy. You still on the Bud Light?" The bartender's nametag said Glen Livit.

Jack couldn't tell if that was really his name or just a joke, but before he could figure out a polite way to ask he had a Bud Light in front of him with a lime wedge in the bottleneck, and no glass.

"Only sissy's use glasses. Right Jack," the man whose name might be Glen Livit said.

"Jack's no sissy," said a familiar voice Jack hadn't heard since it told him, "Stay away from my daughter."

"Mr. Bailey." Jack gave Jeorgia's father a few seconds to bring up orders of protection, and lawful exceptions that Jack was pushing to the limit. When that didn't happen he said, "I didn't know you were here." He looked back at the restaurant. No policemen waiting to arrest him. No sign of Jeorgia or her mother either.

Mr. Bailey placed a hand on Jack's shoulder. Not exactly warm and friendly but not angry either. He told Jack how he liked to drive his wife and daughter around town and pretend they were an ordinary family.

"You know...Pretend Jeorgia has a future. Pretend she has a brain that isn't mostly scar tissue."

"We stopped for a restroom break and here you were," Mr. Bailey said. "I thought maybe we should talk"

Jack thought this might be a good time to tell Mr. Bailey how they both loved Jeorgia, and they both wanted the best for her but had completely different ideas about what the best might look like. "I know She's a hundred times too good for me."

Mr. Bailey didn't say, "No, it's still a thousand." Instead he said, "She's not the girl she used to be, Jack. I don't think you understand."

"I love everything that's left," Jack said. "I'd do anything for her, but that's hard to prove from one hundred feet away."

"Jeorgia has serious cognitive issues." Mr. Bailey was probably repeating what a social worker told him after the doctors gave up. "Hasn't spoken more than a word or two since the accident. Can't be left alone. Can't pick out her clothes. Can't do a lot of things." He nodded at the restroom to prove his point. "Mrs. Bailey's in there with her now."

Maybe if Jack had an hour with a thesaurus and a book of love poems, he could have come up with something better, but all he had was a heart like a broken iPod that played the same song over and over. *Always on my Mind*, sung by Willie Nelson.

"Take it from me, Jack. My little girl isn't quite so pretty when you get to know her."

Jack hadn't expected that. He wanted to say, " She is too!" But he didn't want to start an argument so he kept silent and turned his attention to the ladies' room just as Jeorgia walked out looking like she had no cognitive issues at all.

She moved across the floor like an exotic dancer, rotated her hips in a perfect figure eight, smiled like she was sending out a general invitation to every man inside the bar.

"She's still really pretty," Jack told Mr. Bailey.

Three young men standing near her thought so too. One stepped in front of her. Two moved in behind. Jeorgia didn't mind at all. She tossed her hair and licked her lips like she was posing for a photo shoot.

Mr. Bailey slid off his bar stool. "I need to have a word with those boys, Jack. Think you could walk over there with me?"

Jack moved down the bar steps to fast for Mr. Bailey to lay out his plan. Three large strides and he was next to Jeorgia.

"Get lost." A simple and direct approach—the kind that had landed him in jail a time or two. He kept his knees bent and his arms loose, in case diplomacy failed.

Jeorgia took turns smiling at each of the young men, including Jack. Her smile might have deepened slightly when she looked his way, but it was hard to tell.

Jack clinched his hands into fists and squeezed them tight enough to show off all the scars on his knuckles.

All of a sudden, Jeorgia didn't look so good to the three young men. They shifted their weight like they were waiting for a starting pistol to send them sprinting for the nearest exit.

"Didn't mean nothing man," one of them said.

"Totally, dude." The other two agreed in perfect harmony, like back up singers in a boy band.

They held up their hands and backed away as if Jack was holding them at gunpoint.

"We good?"

Jeorgia waved goodbye, beauty pageant style, and Mr. Bailey stumbled down the steps and joined them.

"See what I mean, Jack," he said. "Jeorgia is a lot more trouble than she used to be."

She kept on waving, happy to be the center of attention, almost like the good old days.

"I'd better get her out of here," Mr. Bailey said. "You know...in case those boys come back." He shook Jack's hand the way businessmen did in black and white movies on cable after 10 p.m.

Jack looked Mr. Bailey right in the eyes. He saw a man who wanted out of all his Jeorgia-responsibilities—if he could find someone good enough to take over. And Jack was getting there. Now Jeorgia was only fifty times too good for him, maybe less.

Before the handshake was finished, Mrs. Bailey joined them. She didn't say anything about lawful exceptions to restraining orders, but she looked at Jack like he was a stain on her living room carpet.

The bartender whose name might be Glen Livit said. "Come on up here Jack. Bud Light's on the house."

He waited until the Baileys left the restaurant before he stepped back into the drinking zone.

Things happened inside of Jack whenever he saw Jeorgia—heart rate, respiration, body temperature, and things he'd lie about if anyone asked. Those things started happening as Jack drove through downtown Oklahoma City where he delivered five gallon jugs of water to oil companies and legal offices every Tuesday morning. He'd just driven past a girl who might be Jeorgia, but he didn't know for sure because the back of his truck obscured his rear window and his side view mirror vibrated too much when he drove under forty miles per hour.

She waved, beauty pageant style. That meant it almost had to be Jeorgia, but neither Bailey parent was anywhere in sight.

Jack pulled his truck over to the curb where parking wasn't allowed, and almost caused an accident when he opened his door into traffic. Horns honked. People shouted things at him that would embarrass their mothers. He paid no attention, because the girl he'd just passed was definitely Jeorgia Bailey, and she wasn't going to be alone much longer. Two teen-age boys walked behind her, building up enough courage to say insulting things and watch her reaction.

Jack moved toward them, as quickly as he could, because it was pretty clear that Jeorgia's reaction was nothing like the boys expected. Their pride would force them to take things to another level. And the level after that, because that's the way it is with pride and teenage boys.

Jeorgia minced down the street, sexy and a little clumsy, like a prostitute with a sore foot. Every now and then, she giggled as if she remembered something too embarrassing to share with two teenage strangers closing in. The boys kept up a banter that sounded like a gynecology lesson.

Jack caught up to Jeorgia just as she started unbuttoning her blouse. He would have been too late if she had good motor skills. The boys cheered her on, told her to take off this and that and show them that and this, and Jeorgia seemed happy to oblige. Jack supposed this was one of the *cognitive issues* Mr. Bailey warned him about.

"Hey there!" Restrained, no curse words at all. Exactly the right amount of aggression to get a teenager's attention.

Jeorgia stopped working her blouse buttons long enough to wave at Jack, which seriously disappointed her audience.

The boys were white but they had a big Ebonics vocabulary of rhyming words about murdering their enemies and beating their ho's.

A few years ago, Jack would have started right in swinging, but now he'd try to reason with the boys. Because they were minors. And they weren't dangerous. And they really didn't know any better. But in the end, none of that mattered, because Jeorgia pulled her skirt up over her head and one of the boys tried to touch her, and Jack knocked him out with an impressive right hook.

The boy Jack hit fell onto the sidewalk; the other one ran away.

Jeorgia's panties were blue. Jack tried not to think about that, but it was hard to think about anything else until two African American policemen arrived and cuffed his hands behind him. The cops understood all about young men and girls with blue panties.

"Her name is Jeorgia Bailey," he told the cops right after his Miranda rights.

"She has cognitive issues," he said. But that was pretty obvious because Jeorgia lapsed into the dance routine that almost won her the talent section of the Miss Teen Oklahoma pageant not so long ago.

Jack told them Jeorgia's address. He told them about his delivery truck parked where it shouldn't be, and explained, as best he could, how things had gone wrong so quickly.

By then the unconscious boy came around and started saying the N-word, like the black cops might think that was cool. They unhooked Jack and cuffed the bruised wannabe gangster, and let him try out his forbidden word from the back of a police car. It sounded better through safety glass.

"Take her home," one of the cops told Jack. "Otherwise, there'll be lots of paperwork."

Jack thought of mentioning the restraining order, but walked Jeorgia to his truck instead.

❀❀❀

Jack pretended he was a knight on a big white horse that looked like a delivery truck and down town Oklahoma City was a dragon's lair where anything might have happened to Jeorgia if he hadn't come along. It felt good to be a knight, even if it wasn't going to last for very long.

"Fifteen bottles of water didn't get delivered," he told Jeorgia. Lawyers and oilmen, paralegals and mistresses posing as secretaries would go thirsty for the sake of love. "That's how much you mean to me…and more."

Jeorgia smiled, as if Jack had recited a love poem. She brushed the backs of her manicured nails across his face. She unfastened her seatbelt and scooted close to Jack. Much closer than one hundred feet.

He glanced at the *No Riders* sign on his dashboard, and thought about the bruise on the middle knuckle of his right hand, and how Mr. and Mrs. Bailey would react when he pulled into their driveway with Jeorgia.

Maybe he should call and warn them, but that would give them time to think, and there was nothing worse than a girlfriend's parents who have time to think.

Girlfriend.

Jeorgia rubbed her hand on Jack's right thigh and mouthed the words to *Always on my Mind*, perfectly synchronized with the music coming from his radio. This was something Jack had hoped for ever since Jeorgia's accident, but it was nothing like he expected. The hand on his leg felt more than a little bit creepy, like the hand of a beautiful girl who'd been killed and miraculously brought back from the grave, but only as far as the zombie stage.

Jack's mouth dried up, the way it always did when Jeorgia was around. His heart beat faster, the way it always did, and his rate of respiration doubled, and then tripled, but it didn't feel like love this time so much as panic.

He pulled into the Baileys' driveway, stepped out of his truck, and ran to the door, hoping Jeorgia wouldn't follow. But she stood beside him as he knocked, rubbing his lower back, slipping her fingers into the waistband of his Culligan deliveryman's uniform.

Mrs. Bailey opened the door. She looked at Jack, then looked at Jeorgia, then put her arms around both of them and crushed them with the most uncomfortable hug Jack had ever experienced. She sobbed and breathed in hitches and confessed to all the times she hadn't been a good mother, like earlier today when she left Jeorgia in her car.

"While I ran a few errands," Mrs. Bailey said. "While I was away for just a second."

"I thought I'd never see Jeorgia again," Mrs. Bailey said. "But you brought her back."

It came out like an accusation, but that was all right with Jack as long as Mrs. Bailey took Jeorgia inside and picked up being a good mother where she'd left off. But things weren't going to go that way, because Mr. Bailey came to the door and shook Jack's hand, and invited him inside without releasing the handshake.

What with all the hugging and handshaking and pulling him inside, there was no doubt in Jack's mind that he was now good enough for Jeorgia Bailey. Exactly good enough. That was one more thing that didn't feel like he'd thought it would.

THE LAST GOOD PLACE
BY RHOADS BRAZOS

June pressed her bare feet against the river's shore and let the muck ooze between her toes. She sloshed her feet clean in the coffee-brown water and began again.

"Not likin' what I'm seein'," Pauly said from her side. He shifted his weight on the fallen willow that seated the two of them.

"Has anyone said anything?" June asked.

"No. And I'm not bringing it up. You know how these things work."

"We should just leave."

"Maybe so."

They watched the water, cresting high today and filled with debris loosed by the thunderheads smothering the horizon. Within the distant billows, lightning flashed obscene colors which defied naming. Dark specks flitted about the cloudmass like flies kissing a carcass. Any creature visible from this distance had to be a furlong wide.

Pauly scowled. "You'd think it'd tire out, slacken the effort."

"I saw a photo of the hills," June said, "before they melted."

Pauly grunted.

"Patty Bemkins showed me," June said. "She lived here, even back then. She says it's dead up there. Nearly half the old state lost in mire, except for...well—"

"Don't say its name."

"I'm not daft. It's at the center, irised in a hundred-mile eye of mud. That's what Patty says."

Pauly scraped peeling bark into the waters and watched it float away.

"Last trek downstream we torched a half-dozen nests."

"Is that worse, or—"

"'Bout the same, really."

Once a week, Pauly took a dutiful turn with the foot patrols. At night all manner of amphibious beasts crawled from the waters—faceless lampreys that tugged themselves with infant arms, cluster-mouthed mooncalves birthed by tainted wildlife, inside-out toads, and others forms too terrible to dwell upon. The patrols scoured the river's edge and put fire to anything too physically creative. A month ago they had slain an enormous serpent, forty feet in length with skin like opal. It had been sunning on the shore. Mr. Duprey, a professor from the long-defunct university, explained that the creature was more properly an earthworm. It had been the last beast of size to approach the town of Grenvale, a fact for which June was grateful, yet each time the earth trembled she expected to be swallowed whole.

"Please be careful," she said.

"The other gals worry 'bout their husbands so?"

"We do. Each time you're away we do."

Pauly laughed. "Tell me how much." He scooted closer.

June held herself still. She concentrated on the river's ebb, how it lapped over smooth stones. She wished for a quiet beach far away from here.

"June?" Pauly asked.

"Yes?"

Pauly's shadow fell over her bare legs. Though a year younger, he stood a foot taller than herself. His shoulders, as broad as a doorway, always made her think of her father. Pauly leaned closer, the nearest he'd been since the blowup last week.

"Pauly, please."

He scowled and looked back at the woods. "Just thinkin' about you too, is all."

"And them," she said, but Pauly rose without answering.

He climbed back up the riverbank. He slipped once on the loose rise before disappearing into the brush. June rubbed her knees. She dipped her toes low and let them knife through the river's current. Its waters were always warm.

Months ago, when Pauly and she first arrived, everything seemed normal enough, whatever that meant in this day and age. There were no oddly-angled churches or midnight rites or dolmens being raised like in so many of the other towns, places where the townsfolk prayed for favors and cold blessings. Grenvale, with its shaded streets and carefully tended citrus groves, seemed untainted, a safe place to settle. Now she wasn't sure. It sounded as if Pauly wasn't either. She needed to hear his side of things, but every time she managed to get him alone his mind drifted to other things.

June put on her shoes and made her way ashore. She wandered downstream toward town and gathered whatever stones fit her fist. Upon finding a solid sandbar, she dropped her collection in a pile and waited.

They always came with the fading light, this evening being no exception, fatty globs bobbing upon the river like woodducks. They mumbled chants. June let them draw close enough for their droning to sting her ears before hurling a stone at the nearest of the bunch. The throw missed by a yard, but its splash sent the target spitting and spluttering. A score of eyes turned toward her. A flotilla of heads hissed like wet cats.

June threw another stone, and another. The heads cried out.

Uh'e shugg, fhtagn! Mif'xch nwgof'nn.

She gritted her teeth and flung another stone as hard as she could, just like her father had taught her when she was little, back deep and extend the arm into a windmill sweep. The stone smacked wetly through a leering face, sending a burst of tarry blackness sizzling over the water. The stricken head stretched its mouth wide, gave a phlegmy gag, and sank from sight.

Naflhrii! Naflhrii!

They were really angry now. Good. Let them be.

June followed a path downstream that became more defined with each step. She passed the old bridge washed out years ago when the river rose too high. The crowns of the bridge's pylons bumped the waters upward in three evenly spaced swells.

Children's shouts rang around the river's bend and then they were there, a score of them playing the familiar game of stones. Every child with a strong arm took aim while the youngest kept a careful tally of strikes. Today's prize must be quite excellent, even teens her own age took part. A nonstop hail of stones rained down and left the eastern side of the river coated with an oil slick.

"Miss June!" A lithe little girl with short-cropped hair scampered away from the barrage.

"Bibi," June said. "Are you winning?"

"Nope. He's a bad aim."

Bibi's older brother had staked down a spot at the water's edge. He threw with too much sidearm.

"He's," June struggled with a harmless phrasing, "getting bigger."

"Yep. Growin' quick as a lick."

"Do you know why?"

"Oh, you *know*." Bibi drew out the last word and rolled her eyes. "Birds and bees?"

"Who told you that?"

"My ma."

Bibi's brother waddled to his stone pile and lowered himself carefully, squatting rather than bending. He crooked a handful of stones across his stomach and wobbled upright. After a few deep breaths, he lobbed another useless attack.

"You ever thought of havin' a baby Miss June?"

"Me? I—" June swallowed. "Maybe one day, when my house is ready."

"That's smart. Gotta make room. My ma's building a hut with cribs and everything."

"Is she?"

"Uh-huh."

"Your Pa doesn't build?"

"Not in his state, Ma says."

A cry went up from the water and Bibi dashed away without a goodbye. By means of a long branch, one of the boys had tugged a head ashore and was proceeding to torment the other children with it amid shrieks and laughter.

"*Fhtagn* this!" he shouted. He punted the head hard. It burst into a shower of gore, eliciting more squeals and cries.

"Gross."

"Kenneth, you goddamned dick!"

June left the kids arguing at the riverbank and headed up the grassy rise into town. She strolled by homes with gardens for lawns and others whose picket fences corralled small flocks of poultry. The owners, women mostly, watched from their porches. They tipped a hat or raised a hand at her approach. Everyone in this small town knew her, as they knew every other resident. June returned their greetings while inwardly stifling a queasy nervousness. She felt their gaze upon her as she passed. When they thought she wasn't watching, they nodded their heads together and grimaced.

It couldn't have been this way when she and Pauly first arrived. When the two of them pulled their boat to the banks that long ago day, they'd been greeted by a healthy lot, people who worked the earth and had forsaken the soft luxury of the past. The cities may still have piped water and electricity and running vehicles, but at too high a price. Gods walked these lands. Swear fealty to them and they'd offer you succor and care for you like a pet, or livestock. Grenvale had saved itself by crouching in the hinterlands between the kingdoms of the new powers.

"Good evening, miss."

June stopped under the swaying branches of a massive sugar maple. The address had come from the adjoining city park, its rough stone barrier now trimmed with vegetables rather than flowers. She saw her greeter and gave a polite nod.

"Why good day to you, Professor Duprey." She tried to sound poised, but her mouth was dry.

"Orland, please."

"Orland."

She held her smile steady and studied the coppery carpet of leaves at her feet. She hoped her expression seemed demure and not simply nervous. She would have drifted right past, but the voice had come from too nearby. Politesse required a proper lady to stop and chat. She couldn't let anyone know she was out of place, that she knew something had gone wrong.

Duprey never spoke of his professorship. June had picked up on his past from Patty and the other ladies. Though twice June's age, he still seemed too young for the title. He hopped down from the park's low retaining wall.

"I was just checking on the crop here," he said. "Last of the season."

"I'm sure," June said.

He stepped close. She could feel the heat radiating off his body. He was too near—so much like Pauly. That only ever meant one thing.

"You were at the river?" Duprey asked.

"Yes, my husband and I. The children are quite excited today."

"Smiting Nyarlathotep's seedlings again, are they?"

"Mr. Duprey!"

"I beg of you. Orland, please." His gaze flicked over her, strategically pausing with typical male scrutiny. "You're not afraid, are you?"

"It's best not to invite danger."

"But it hardly matters anymore, now does it?"

She straightened her shoulders with a feigned air of confidence. "Of course not."

Duprey studied his nails. He frowned and rubbed his hands together. "You've gone to see her?"

June's mind reeled. She mustered the town's matrons into a mental queue.

"Certainly," she managed.

"I've gone too, just for a dip—not…"

It *was* in the waters then, but the children—

"You went with your husband, no doubt," Duprey said.

"Yes, that's right."

"He is a lucky man. My Cornelia would have been my consort, but, God rest her soul, it wasn't to be."

"I'm very sorry."

"Thank you. Mrs. Olmstead?"

"Yes?"

"If it isn't too…" He stammered to a stop. "I would be—honored, if *you* would accompany me."

June boggled at his words. Though her mind chased his intentions down a dozen scandalous paths, she tried her best not to show confusion.

"I'm flattered," she said.

Duprey beamed.

"My husband though—"

"Do you think he'll object? It *is* rather intimate. I'd be willing to speak with him first."

She wanted to laugh and cry out at the same time. She'd seen the deteriorating state of the men, their lumbering gaits, their bloated bodies. Even the healthiest, Duprey among them, stood pallid and glistening, as if in the throes of a feverous affront. Many cradled their stomachs with uncommon delicacy. June tried to imagine how such a thing was physically possible, where the baby would be nestled, how it would draw nourishment from the father's belly. Somewhere in this town hid a suitress. As Professor Duprey had said, *Her.*

"Are you all right?" Duprey asked.

"Yes, I'm just—I will ask, I promise. I'll come find you very soon. Please be patient."

"Splendid. If it helps, tell him he can watch. Or even participate if he wishes. Tell him that."

"I—"

Duprey took her hand and raised it to his lips.

At his touch, June exhaled quickly. Duprey smiled, gave a polite bow, and spun on his heel.

June hurried away, fighting tears.

⚘⚘⚘

Pauly and she had claimed a home on the far side of town that had seemed charming with its turquoise shutters and stucco like antiqued ivory, not that she saw it that way anymore. June let herself in, bolted the door behind her, and leaned against it. Her head swam. So many thoughts swirled within her that she couldn't grasp a single one.

She called out for Pauly and waited for his reply. A whisper of loose debris hissed against the outside windowpanes. A low creak sounded from the darkness. She held her breath until she'd convinced herself that the sound had accompanied an outside gust.

She moved gingerly through the house and tried not to make so much noise that she would mask the approach of another. After lighting the oil lamp over the kitchen table with just enough wick exposed as to not flicker, she checked the windows. Each was latched tight. The outside yard lay quiet, the woodpile heaped where it should be, the shadows of garden furrows tracing away into dusk. June rubbed at her hands.

When Duprey's fingertips had pressed against her skin, a whiskery touch reached out from under his nails. It had brushed against her and traced her contours with a deliberate delicacy, like the wispy legs of a spider crawling over lips. As he pulled away she saw its motion. Not whiskers and not hairs—not with how it moved. Antennae. It had been tasting her.

June filled the sink basin with a bucket of wellwater and scrubbed until her skin stung raw. When her hands could only remember the course grit of a dish brush, she checked the darkened bedroom. The bed was still tucked crisp from this morning. Pauly's couch lay a mess in the corner, blankets knotted where he'd dropped them. She'd refused to tidy after him. Let him wallow in his own dregs.

Last week, she'd kicked him out after he'd made yet another fumbling pass at her. He'd managed to get both hands up under her blouse. He mumbled something about husbands and wives and kissed her neck. He would have been chagrined to know that she almost relented. She'd been reaching for him in response—it had been so long—when he decided to open his mouth.

"We don't have to fuck, if you don't want. We can just, you know, touch."

Hearing the truth of her sad state yanked her into the now.

She'd slapped him with a crack of skin against skin that would have spun a lesser man halfway around. But within a heartbeat, Pauly had recovered. He spilled out a year's worth of pent-up frustrations.

She was out of line because everyone did it. In this age family was safer than strangers. Just ask anyone. She was the selfish one here, not him. A sister had obligations.

He left her spitting counter-threats and accusations at his back. He barged out into the night without even an over-the-shoulder glance. Maybe he went down to the river, though in the darkness no sane person would. He may have headed off to drink and deal cards with the boys at the mill. Or maybe, as a desperately jilted husband might, he'd sought out a replacement, a more willing female. Perhaps, after being turned away again at the river, he'd found his way into her arms.

June held herself tight. She climbed to the darkened second floor and peeked through windows.

She'd seen photos of Grenvale in its glory days, laid out like a clear nightsky and starlit from a million points. When she first arrived, she'd even been shown a recording. The townsfolk had been celebrating a pagan holiday, something to do with a tree. It had worried her at first, until she realized the rites belonged to an old human tradition. By means of a cranked battery and Duprey's specific instructions, the men had covered the wall with moving pictures, scenes of laughing crowds and street decorations that sparkled every color. The old world was a revelation. June had openly wept at the sight.

Nothing was out there now, just a few distant cook fires and the odd dimly-lit window. She studied the darkness with nervous scrutiny. Something had changed.

The same derelict vehicles crouched where they'd always been, the same crumbling fences, the same yards that had sprouted into untamed meadows. The across-the-street homes showed no sign of life, as they shouldn't. Pauly and she were the block's only inhabitants.

When they had first staked out their claim and searched for necessities, they'd raised the shades in each home. Seeing inside a vacant house was preferable to wondering what hid behind closed curtains.

Now though—June squeezed the windowsill with white-knuckled fingers—the neighbor's windows were drawn.

Maybe Pauly had hid himself away over there. He'd devised this petty vengeance to show her how much she needed him, to make her admit her own weakness, and to force a debauched barter when he sauntered in at sunup. Or perhaps she wanted that drama to still be the worst of her problems.

The adjoining houses had the shades down too.

June checked from the back bedroom window and found the same scene. She wiped away tears, hurried downstairs to the kitchen, and dug through the cutlery drawer. She always kept her fillet knife razor sharp. It saved her so much time when playing housewife. She pressed its steel to her throat.

She knew how these things ended. In death she would still have purity. In and pull. One stroke, too fast to feel. Then she could rest.

All her life she'd wanted to be held in the strong arms of another. She'd wanted a safe and good place where she could close her eyes without fear. She thought she'd found a way to claim such peace, but with this town gone, with it crouching in mad silence about her, her dreams lay shattered. Pauly was right. She didn't understand this world or what it took to exist within it. She thought she could come to this town and, on her own terms, show herself able. A prince would rush her away to a fairytale castle, because that's what a brave girl deserved. But she'd proven herself a failure. The knife clattered away.

"My life is a lie," she said, and slumped to the floor.

She whispered prayers and hoped nothing unfriendly would perk its ears.

⁂

A rap at the door jarred June awake. Ribbons of light fell through the front window from a sun already high in the sky. For a disoriented moment she struggled with where she was, who she was. The knock came again, more urgent this time.

June rose and moved numb and light-headed. It wouldn't do any good to hide. She knew the odds. She unbolted the front door.

At the threshold, Duprey stood bundled in a long overcoat. He looked her up and down.

"Miss Olmstead." He glanced back over his shoulder. "May I—"

"No."

"I really must—"

"I'm leaving this place. You can keep whatever rot you claim. I want no part of it."

Duprey fidgeted. He wore gloves today. Though the weather had cooled considerably since yesterday, June knew the true reason behind his attire, just as she knew he wasn't about to let her walk away. She swung the door closed but he caught it before it could latch.

"They're quite angry with you," he said. "They know everything about you two. They know your ruse."

"Where is he?"

"Your brother?"

June scowled.

"He's safe," Duprey said. "He's happy. For the first time in a long while, I think."

"You've done something to him."

"No, I'm merely a vessel. Now come, please. We only have this one chance. If you'll simply walk with me, willingly, it would be easiest."

"With you? Never."

Duprey looked wounded. "I know it's hard. I know you're afraid. I remember feeling the same way, but once you see—" He inhaled deeply and smiled. "She's wondrous, an infinite miracle. She's not like the others, the Old Ones. They are death and decay while she blooms and flowers. You don't hear her, right now?"

129

June kept her gaze locked on Duprey.

"It's puzzling," he said. "All of the women hear her song, because you create life too, you see? Like sisters. How I envy you!" Duprey gave a tiny bow. "Allow me the honor of accompanying you. I would be the first of the lowly sex to be so privileged. And after your suffusion, if you're willing, and I know you will be, we can—"

A sledgehammer impact and an explosion of shattering glass sounded from the back of the house. June spun around once to catch a flurry of motion from the back porch.

Duprey opened his arms. "I'll shield you. They won't harm you. Please?"

June made to dash by him but he caught her wrist in his hand. When her eyes met his he mouthed his plea again. The pounding of feet and the sound of toppling furniture came from the kitchen. The doors across the street opened and the townsfolk, women mostly, rushed out across the lawns.

June struck Duprey's chest with her fist. His grip loosened and she yanked herself free. He didn't try for her again, but looked away quickly. She ran.

She sprinted down the sidewalk. She was as fast as any of them. The youngest couldn't keep up any better than the older women. There were only a few teens to worry about because the men couldn't manage more than a waddle. She just had to reach the burn scar where a lightning strike had cleared a closely clustered subdivision. The scrub brush there grew thick and wild. She'd lose them in the tangles. Her feet slapped against pavement and then the wind was knocked out of her.

She bounced off the ground and rolled over twice. With toes digging down she struggled to rise and then a familiar weight pressed hot against her. Pauly's face loomed close.

He caught her swinging fists without effort, swallowing them in his grip.

"Sis." He hissed the word between clenched teeth. Antennae and hooked legs wiggled between them.

She screamed and flailed and then a dozen hands were upon her.

⚜ ⚜ ⚜

"Too good for her," a woman's voice called from her left. Patty?

"Maybe, see what happens," said another. "End one'a two ways."

A child laughed.

June bounced limply along. The men had hoisted her onto their collective shoulders as if she were a fallen timber. Pauly, too, had volunteered to bear her weight. He'd positioned himself with his head between her thighs. She hated him for it.

Their feigned marriage had been for her safety. Pauly's intimidating size kept the boldest men at an aloof distance. Even Duprey with all of his small-town prestige tread warily around her. Funnily though, Pauly may have been the one screened by the lie. If only she'd kept him sated, it would have saved them both. But she'd chosen to cling to a nothingness, a tradition as false as her marriage. Social mores had been cast aside so long ago that she'd never even really known them. Wasn't her life worth more than a pretend dignity?

"I'm loyal," June whispered to the sun. "I'm true."

Pauly turned sideways and leered. He stroked the bare skin of her midriff for the hundredth time and she pretended not to notice.

She caught Duprey's eye but couldn't hold it. He shuffled at a careful distance away from the others and watched his feet.

With him too, she should have given in. She could have affected a surrender and then slipped away right here, at the gravelly incline that tumbled down to the stream cutting away from town. They never would have expected her to jump. It was a steep two-hundred foot slide if not farther, but with desperation fueling her ambition she could have made it. She would have skidded to the bottom and bounded away like a deer.

She stared blankly at the sky, clear and empty all the way to the high heavens. Only Nyarlathotep's horizon showed any presence.

They finished the climb out from the valley and entered the orchards. It surprised June to see peaches still being picked. Groups of young girls and boys set aside their baskets and gawked. June's procession traveled on and the rows of trees showed pale-pink buds with strawberry eyes. The ground lay in rolling green swells, not the brittle tufts of autumn. All about her, the air hummed with the life of an eternal spring.

Her captors stopped their march.

"Unworthy," a woman's voice whispered at her ear. Another shushed her and a discussion on proper baptism ensued.

Fruiting rows traced away as far as she could see, rolling with the contours of the land. But she'd already accepted their impossibility. Her attention was gripped by the sight before her.

A lake stretched across a wide acre and disappeared around a lush hillside. The waters were pearl white, like a slab of marble. June would have believed it to be such if the wind didn't catch its surface and send ripples licking against the grassy shore. A dozen stubby pillars circled the near edge of the waters.

From ahead, a woman's voice called out. The crowd answered, but its words fell as a babble. June refused to hear. She couldn't. Her temple ached.

"The heathen?" A voice called from ahead.

Hands shoved June forward. The crowd parted and she spilled out close to the shore. She lifted her head to see Patty Bemkins slip from her clothes.

"You don't believe," Patty said with a condescending smirk. As she tied back her hair, younger girls gathered her clothes and folded them neatly. "But we shall see. Is she of use?"

"*Ftaghu s'uhn!*" the crowd responded.

June's ears burned.

"—will know. Swim in her nectar. Revel in her truth."

To June's horror, the crowd followed Patty's lead and stripped to bare skin. Hands tugged at her own clothes. She screamed and wrestled against them but her fists were caught and her clothing torn free. Murmurs of approval arose from the men. She fought to cover herself and clenched her teeth.

Duprey passed by. June thought she may have seen a sideways glance, but it was gone in an instant. Patty met him with arms outstretched and the two of them waded into the waters. Another couple followed, and then another. They floated away, born strangely by the surface which at times seemed to be liquid and at others supported the weight of each couple.

A waterborne bacchanalia unfolded. June stared in shock as her neighbors paired off without any sense of modesty or decorum and rutted like animals, writhing and grinding upon the waters and occasionally sinking below their surface.

"Our turn, love." Pauly's voice came from behind her. His hands gripped her shoulders tight.

"I won't—"

He shoved her forward.

She landed face first in the waters. She picked herself up to her hands and knees and choked.

The waters reached for her and flowed up her arms and legs, painting her body like porcelain. They touched her tongue with a taste that awakened her oldest memories.

Pauly's voice whispered at her ear. "She likes your fire. I knew she would. Who wouldn't want you?"

"Let me—"

His hands roamed over her body. "You've tasted her mother's milk."

The hillside groaned and shuddered. It opened cavernous eyes with pits of burning green. A gaze as ancient as time turned upon June and bore through her.

June saw a field, aeons ago, millions of stalks wide and millions deep, roots touching roots, tangled together over countless miles. Somewhere within its midst, a jumble of shoots fell just so. Blades of grass bent in a flawless motion, pushed by a coincidental wind. Within the green, a perfect glyph of thought swirled into a glyph of life, as planned and concise as divine sorcery. A goddess rose.

"Astarte," June said. Her tongue went numb.

"Yes, you see." Pauly slipped his hand between her legs.

She didn't fight him. A call like music urged her on. This divinity stood with nature, not against it. One had only to surrender to primal urges. The carnal fed her. Pleasure gave her life. Even now she opened a yawning maw as wide as a barn door and welcomed her new pledges. Duprey and Patty coupled upon her lips and rolled about on her tongue. She would receive June too, as another priestess. The Sisters of Astarte would purge the land of disease. They would chew the cancer into honey. The Old Ones. Man. The world would flower and buzz and everything would be new.

The others, amid groans and sighs and laughter, had joined June in the waters. She turned back to Pauly. His jaw hung open. A writhing mass crawled down his chest, bibbing him in a churning broil of legs and antennae. Behind him, the line of pillars watched her with greedy eyes. They knew her as intimately as the waters. Each of them, rooted in place, felt the movements of the lake and knew the pleasure of every body, of her. They craned their heads backward and plumed insects into the sky.

June yanked her leg forward and jammed it back hard. Whatever profane growth was budding within Pauly's gut gave way with a satisfying crunch.

"Never!" she shouted.

Pauly doubled over gagging and June leapt to her feet. The waters pulled at her. As she slogged ashore, they thickened into paste and then squeezed tight. She fell to the grass and clawed forward, twisting and crying and pulling herself with every fiber within.

You cannot leave.

Fat blue bottle flies buzzed at her face and chewed at her eyelids. She swept the pests away and crushed them. A wasp the size of a hummingbird stabbed at her forearm again and again. She smashed it without mercy.

With a splintering like crystal, the waters gave way. They razored across her foot, but she was free.

Down through the brush, branches lashed like whips. Her heels were torn ragged. Her each bound fell upon shards of glass, yet she raced forward.

The heat of the goddess's spring didn't reach here, but June still felt her touch. She still heard her. She was coated from head to toe with her. Astarte dug into her pores.

I'm within you.

June cried out and tumbled down a steep incline. Shouts rang from behind her. The others had given pursuit. She found her feet again and stumbled onward. Her left arm flapped uselessly as whatever poison she'd suffered coursed its way deeper.

So young. So naive.

A flash of movement came from behind. Pauly. His body was as chalk-white as her own, but his head seethed within a living hive. He roared.

A pain stabbed at June's leg. She swatted a wasp into mush and sobbed. Already her calf felt tight and ready to buckle. Another insect lit on her shoulder. She knocked it away. A pain stabbed at her back. Pauly huffed behind her, so close.

The river was at her feet. She threw herself in.

My lonely wildflower, plucked from the field. Without me, you'll wither.

June floundered through the murk toward the deep currents. She'd lose them downstream. But with only one arm and a leg as stiff as ice and her chest aching—

She rose to the surface and gulped in air. Strong hands had her.

"You!" Pauly shouted. He bobbed along with her in the waters. Though his nest had washed away, a few survivors wiggled under his lips. "Think you can—"

A thick gray-green tentacle wrapped around his mouth. Another snaked about his arms and pried his fingers from June's shoulders. He seemed genuinely surprised, as if he'd forgotten such things lurked in the river. An immense creature lifted him skyward and throttled him high above the waters, squeezing and twisting and cracking bones, offering the crowd of gathering townspeople a proper view, a chance to hear the piercing screams of the damned. It tossed chunks of Pauly to each shore.

June cried out at the horror of seeing her only family rent into slaw, and then it had her too. It yanked her down deep.

Countless limbs pulled her to a waiting mouth. She fell upon a thousand teeth. They sliced and carved. Tendrils grabbed loosened skin and in long, smooth pulls, tugged swaths away from her body. Within the hollow of its head, she screamed and thrashed. It peeled her down to meat and swallowed her whole.

June nestled in a warm place. She'd been here so long. Strong arms jetted the two of them downriver, ever forward. The sway of the waters and the strain and release of elephantine muscles soothed her. She smelled the sea.

When she was a young girl not yet half a woman's age, she'd sat on a long pier by the ocean, her younger brother leaning against her. She traced her toes through the waters and chatted with a sea prince. From the froth, he smiled up at her and sang her promises with a voice like a cello. The world would die soon, he warned—the stars were almost right—but if she proved herself, if she helped him, she would live on in a kingdom fathoms deep. The fish would be as birds and she would wear a crown of coral and pearl.

A lost lifetime ago.

"I've failed," she whispered.

A healing brine washed over her, salving her wounds.

"No," a voice echoed from all sides.

"I'm so sorry."

"I heard your prayers, little minnow. If I would have known the Temptress claimed these lands…"

"They are tainted," June said. "All of them. We can't come here."

"As I've seen. A pity."

June flexed her arms and legs. They felt stiff but the sensation was improving. She explored her flesh and traced her fingertips over the tell-tale ridges of scales. He had blessed her so? Surely he didn't know.

She breathed in deep, closed her eyes, and confessed. "I've broken every vow."

"Nonsense. It was the call of our Lord Dagon that drowned out the Weed Witch. You are of the most faithful."

"But at the least, I've betrayed you."

"No, you are pure, and brave beyond your years. A phalanx of Deep Ones could not match your courage."

"There's something else."

"Yes?"

"I love you."

He laughed, a deep rumble that hugged her from all sides.

"Such a quaint emotion. A fleeting spark in one so young. With time, you'll understand."

With arms wrapped wide, she held his heart against her and felt its pulse, not the white-hot flame of her own emotion, but a cold passion of which she was a part.

135

And at night the stars serenely
  Glow'd betwixt the boughs o'erhead,
While Astarte, calm and queenly,
  Floods of fairy radiance shed.
—from "Revelation," by H. P. Lovecraft

RE:
BY SHANNON IWANSKI

Subject: Effective Immediately
From: Walter Prescott (*wprescott@terradyme.com*)
Sent: Mon 9/1/2014 5:45 PM
To: Stephanie Zelman (*szelman@terradyme.com*); Clive Bartlett (*cbartlett@terradyme.com*); Jeremy Evans (*jevans@terradyme.com*); Joe Burns (*jburns@terradyme.com*); Jody Parks (*jparks@terradyme.com*); Kyle Burtnett (*kburtnett@terradyme.com*); Elizabeth Archer (*earcher@terradyme.com*)
Cc:

Attention all Department Heads. Effective Immediately all requests for leave for the current month are to be denied. There will be no exceptions. Please direct all questions to Senior Vice-President Stephanie Zelman.

Walter Prescott,
President/Owner
Terradyme

Sent from my iPhone

Subject: Re: Re: Re: Re: Re: Re: Re: Re: Re: Re: Re: Request for Leave
From: Jeremy Evans (*jevans@terradyme.com*)
Sent: Mon 8/18/2014 8:00 AM

To: Clive Bartlett (*cbartlett@terradyme.com*)
Cc: Walter Prescott (*wprescott@terradyme.com*); Stephanie Zelman (*szelman@terradyme.com*); Katie Durham (*kdurham@terradyme.com*)

Clive,

This is a very important trip, and I really can't reschedule it. I'm willing to do anything that I can to address your concerns, but I'm asking you to please work with me on this. There must be some way we can work this out. Please let me know as soon as possible. I still need to finalize some plans, and we're getting down to the wire.

Jeremy

Subject: Re: Re: Re: Re: Re: Re: Re: Re: Re: Re: Request for Leave
From: Stephanie Zelman (*szelman@terradyme.com*)
Sent: Mon 8/11/2014 7:59 AM
To: Clive Bartlett (*cbartlett@terradyme.com*)
Cc: Walter Prescott (*wprescott@terradyme.com*); Jeremy Evans (*jevans@terradyme.com*); Katie Durham (*kdurham@terradyme.com*)

Clive,

I've added Mr. Prescott to the mix so he can address any issues and/or concerns. I've brought him up to speed on everything. Let me know if I can do anything else to help. Thanks.

Stephanie

Subject: Re: Re: Re: Re: Re: Re: Re: Re: Re: Request for Leave
From: Clive Bartlett (*cbartlett@terradyme.com*)
Sent: Wed 8/6/2014 4:45 PM
To: Jeremy Evans (*jevans@terradyme.com*)
Cc: Stephanie Zelman (*szelman@terradyme.com*); Katie Durham (*kdurham@terradyme.com*)

Jeremy,

What movie?

You know, with everything that's involved with the Waterford account AND the Third Quarter Reports, I think we might need to really do some hard looking at this request. How imperative is it that you take this time off? Is it something that can be rescheduled?

Clive

Subject: Re: Re: Re: Re: Re: Re: Re: Re: Request for Leave
From: Jeremy Evans (*jevans@terradyme.com*)
Sent: Tue 7/22/2014 8:10 AM
To: Clive Bartlett (*cbartlett@terradyme.com*)
Cc: Stephanie Zelman (*szelman@terradyme.com*); Katie Durham (*kdurham@terradyme.com*)

Clive,

I love that movie, too.

I'll see what I can do. No promises, though.

Jeremy

Subject: Re: Re: Re: Re: Re: Re: Re: Request for Leave
From: Clive Bartlett (*cbartlett@terradyme.com*)
Sent: Mon 7/21/2014 5:15 PM
To: Jeremy Evans (*jevans@terradyme.com*)
Cc: Stephanie Zelman (*szelman@terradyme.com*); Katie Durham (*kdurham@terradyme.com*)

Jeremy,

I'm going to need you to come in on Saturday. I'm sure you can get your flight rescheduled. If not, let me know. I have a friend who can probably pull some strings for you. Thanks.

Clive

Sent from my iPhone

Subject: Re: Re: Re: Re: Re: Re: Request for Leave
From: Jeremy Evans (*jevans@terradyme.com*)
Sent: Tue 7/15/14 11:04 AM
To: Clive Bartlett (*cbartlett@terradyme.com*)
Cc: Stephanie Zelman (*szelman@terradyme.com*); Katie Durham (*kdurham@terradyme.com*)

Clive,

I would like to work out a time on Thursday or Friday for the meeting. I'm supposed to be at the airport first thing in the morning on Saturday the 6th. I'm willing to stay late either of those days. If you want I can even email you copies of everything in regards to the Waterford account. Let me know. Thanks.

Jeremy

Subject: Re: Re: Re: Re: Re: Request for Leave
From: Clive Bartlett (*cbartlett@terradyme.com*)
Sent: Tue 7/15/2014 8:47 AM
To: Jeremy Evans (*jevans@terradyme.com*)
Cc: Stephanie Zelman (*szelman@terradyme.com*); Katie Durham (*kdurham@terradyme.com*)

Jeremy,

I was in the process of sending you an email when I received your most recent one. Unfortunately the times on Thursday and Friday that you have available don't work for me. I really don't want to push this back to earlier in that week. Is it possible that you and Katie could come in on Saturday, September 8, instead? I really hate to ask this, but I think it's for the best. Let me know as soon as possible.

I'll be out of the office the rest of the day, but I should be able to respond using my phone. If you don't hear from me today, though, I'll definitely be in touch some time tomorrow. Keep up the good work.

Clive

Subject: Re: Re: Re: Re: Request for Leave

From: Jeremy Evans (*jevans@terradyme.com*)
Sent: Tue 7/15/2014 8:08 AM
To: Clive Bartlett (*cbartlett@terradyme.com*); Stephanie Zelman (*szelman@terradyme.com*)
Cc: Katie Durham (*kdurham@terradyme.com*)

(Katie, I'm including you in this email at Stephanie's request. Please read everything below so you'll be in the loop on everything. Thanks.)

Stephanie, you'll be happy to know that I'm already starting to work on the reports for this quarter. Obviously I can't enter all the information into the final format, but I will have everything completed with the exception of the numbers for week three of September. Katie is well versed in the reports, though, so she'll be able to finalize them and get them to Mr. Prescott before he leaves.

Clive, I know you're busy. I just wanted to see if you'd had a chance to check your schedule yet. Unfortunately, Thursday at 11:00 is out. I just scheduled a meeting with Joe from accounting to go over the revised numbers for the Waterford account. I'm still available at 3:15. Just let me know.

Thanks for all your help, everyone. I appreciate you.

Jeremy

Subject: Re: Re: Re: Request for Leave
From: Stephanie Zelman (*szelman@terradyme.com*)
Sent: Mon 7/14/2014 2:57 PM
To: Clive Bartlett (*cbartlett@terradyme.com*)
Cc: Jeremy Evans (*jevans@terradyme.com*)

Clive (and Jeremy)

Thank you very much for including me on this. You're right, I do have a better view of the big picture.

As of right now, I don't see anything that would prevent Jeremy from taking off those two weeks. I do want to remind you both, though, that Mr. Prescott will be out of the office all during the fourth week of September. If you remember, he's asking that we turn in our Third

Quarter Reports no later than Friday, September 19.

Jeremy, you might want to start your quarterlies early so Katie can finish them for you. Just in case, you know. If I can be of any help, don't hesitate to let me know.

Stephanie Zelman,
Senior Vice-President
Terradyme

Subject: Re: Re: Request for Leave
From: Jeremy Evans (*jevans@terradyme.com*)
Sent: Fri 7/11/2014 8:30 AM
To: Clive Bartlett (*cbartlett@terradyme.com*)
Cc: Stephanie Zelman (*szelman@terradyme.com*)

Clive,

I haven't heard back from Stephanie, but I know that doesn't mean much in the grand scheme of things. She's very busy.

As of now I have a meeting at 2:30 that day. I could make sure that Katie is free to attend the meeting, though. There shouldn't be anything that she can't answer. If that doesn't work, I'm free most of the morning that day. I could meet at 11:00 or at 3:15 on Thursday, September 4. Sorry, but you know how it is.

Jeremy

Subject: Re: Request for Leave
From: Clive Bartlett (*cbartlett@terradyme.com*)
Sent: Wed 7/2/2014 4:22 PM
To: Jeremy Evans (*jevans@terradyme.com*)
Cc: Stephanie Zelman (*szelman@terradyme.com*)

Jeremy,

Thank you for your request for leave. I also have to commend you on turning it in well over two months before it is needed. You and I both know all too well that is most often not the case.

At this point I don't see why this request would cause any problems. However, per policy I have Cc'd Stephanie on my response to this request. She has a better view of the big picture than I do, so she'll be able to let us know if this conflicts with anyone else's schedule. We may also have to eventually include Roger in the HR Dept., but I don't think that'll be necessary at this point.

As for Katie, she's an excellent choice, and I know she'll continue to do her best on the Waterford account. Having said that, I would like to schedule a meeting with the two of you for Friday, September 5, before you leave. Not that I'm worried or anything, but I think it'll be good for me to have a better understanding of where we are in the process, just in case Mr. Waterford contacts me with any questions.

Check your calendar and let me know how 2:30 works for you on that day.

Clive Bartlett,
Vice-President of Marketing
Terradyme

Subject: Request for Leave
From: Jeremy Evans (*jevans@terradyme.com*)
Sent: Tue 7/1/2014 8:15 AM
To: Clive Bartlett (*cbartlett@terradyme.com*)
Cc:

Clive,

Per policy I am hereby requesting leave for the second and third weeks of September, from the 8th through the 19th. During that time, my team will be overseen by Katie Durham. As I'm sure you're aware, she is an integral part of my team and will do well in my stead.

I do not foresee any major issues that could arise during my absence. However, I know the Waterford account will be nearing completion at that time. Katie is well versed in all aspects of the account, and she has worked one-on-one with Mr. Waterford multiple times. She can handle any issues that arise, and if you have any questions, she can handle them with great ease.

On the Monday I return, I will be ready to do the final presentation to Mr. Waterford.

Please let me know if you have any questions.

Jeremy Evans,
Director of Marketing
Terradyme

CLOUDBURST
BY PRESTON DENNETT

May 24, 2019

I turned sixteen today. Momma says now I'm a woman. 'Course she said that three and a half years ago when I first got my monthly visitor, and Momma looked like she couldn't decide whether to be happy or start cryin'. But Momma's all smiles today. She fixed a big dinner with a real steak, fried potatoes with fancy herbs, creamed corn, and for dessert: a chocolate cake with ice-cream. My best friend Keshia gave me her favorite pink silk blouse which she knew I liked. Momma, she doesn't have much money, so I didn't get anything expensive—just some make-up, a pair of red shoes, a sweater, and this diary. She wrote in it: For all your special thoughts. Now, I don't know that I've got any special thoughts, but I know Momma's doing her best and I know she works hard and can't afford to buy me expensive things. So I took the diary and told her I was happy even though I really wanted something more special, like a necklace, or a new outfit. But it's okay. I understand. We're poor.

I've never kept a diary before, so I'm not sure what to write. I saw Derrell again at school. He's sooo cute. I think he likes me. I hope he does. I just wish he'd do something about it. I can see him staring at my boobs.

I saw on TV today that they discovered a comet. It's called Comet Sprinkle, after the guy who first spotted it. It's supposed to be visible in a few weeks, at least to folks who don't live in the city, which counts me out. Pretty cool though: a comet for my birthday. Momma says it's a sign. I don't think I believe her. Somehow that comet makes me scared. It gives me that feeling I get when something bad's going to happen. But I don't tell Momma on account it's my birthday and she's trying to make me happy. So I just smiled and said thank you, Momma. and I love you. I don't think about that bad feeling I keep getting. Probably nothing anyway.

What else? Boy, is it hot. Days like this I wish we could afford an air-conditioner. But no, all we got are stupid fans. They don't help much. I hate LA in the summer. It's too dang hot.

❧❧❧

August 30, 2019

Oh, it finally happened. Derrell kissed me! He was really nice and telling me how pretty I am and how much he loves me, and then he kissed me on the lips. I started laughing and boy, did that make Derrell mad. "Why you laughing?" he asked. "Ain't I a good kisser?"

"You're fine," I told him. "I'm laughing 'cuz, well, I don't know why I'm laughing."

And he started laughing. After it happened, I ran home and told Keshia and we both started laughing so loud, Momma came into room asking, what's the matter? Nothing, we told her. I can't tell Momma about Derrell. She'll just cry and say, "Don't get pregnant, Nonna."

Momma was only sixteen when she had me and I know she's just trying to protect me. But she doesn't know Derrell's not like that. Derrell loves me. He told me so.

Besides, I don't want to worry Momma none. She's working hard enough already and she doesn't need my problems and her own problems.

After dinner, we were watching the TV and they talked about the comet again, and I got a real bad feeling so I listened close. Turns out it's not one comet, but a whole bunch of them. Momma started crying and I asked her what the matter. "It real bad news," she said. "Them comets comin' and fixin' to hit the Earth. It be the end of the world."

Then I started crying too and even my little brother Tommy—he started crying. The experts on TV were saying it wasn't just a few comets, but hundreds and hundreds of them, all coming from a giant cloud that surrounds the entire solar system. Supposedly it has a like a trillion comets in it. That's a big cloud. I never heard such a big number in my life. How much is a trillion, I asked Momma. But I don't think she knows either. She said, "It more than a million," which I already know that.

"Don't cry, momma," I said. "Them comets are just snowballs. We're gonna be fine."

But momma doesn't stop crying and I didn't tell her my bad feeling was still strong as ever. I just hugged her and said, "We're gonna be fine." But I'm not sure I believe it. They showed pictures of the comets. It looked like a big ocean wave is sweeping across the sky. And it's coming towards us.

❄❄❄

September 12, 2019

The sky looks broken now. It's all white, even at night. It looks like it's being erased, just like the sky was a giant chalkboard and God is erasing all the stars. You can't see it move by watching it, but that wave just keeps coming closer and closer.

It's all they talk about on TV. I can't even watch my soaps no more. I know it's real bad 'cuz the schools are closed and that almost never happens. The churches are filled all the time with people praying and hoping that the world ain't ending. There are long lines at all the stores. Everyone's trying to get ready for when the comets hit us. Lots a people are leaving the city. I asked Momma, "We leaving too?"

She said, "No, Nonna. We gonna stay. Ain't no safer outside the city than inside it." Momma's real religious. She trusts in God to save us. I think to myself, if God is supposed to save us, why did He send the comets? But I don't say nothin'.

Mom's home all the time now, on account that nobody needs their house cleaned when the comets are coming and probably everything is gonna be wrecked anyway. And we're running out of food. Momma don't need more problems. But she's getting them anyway.

Keshia and her family left yesterday. The government is setting up shelters for people, but I've seen them on TV, and they don't look much better than what we got here. I'm glad we're staying. Derrell's staying too. He comes over and we look at the broken sky. We kiss all the time now, even in front of Momma. She don't care. She just looks at us and smiles with tears in her eyes. Even Tommy—he broke Momma's special plates and she didn't do nothin', I guess 'cuz breaking little stuff don't matter no more. Poor Momma.

❄❄❄

October 14, 2019

Well, the wave is here. It's supposed to hit us tomorrow. Nobody

147

knows if we're going to be struck or not 'cuz they can't see anything except the whiteness. But all the experts say there's no way we ain't gonna get hit. They say it's like being in a blizzard and trying not to get hit by snowflakes. Only these snowflakes are the size of small mountains and moving super fast.

Nobody knows why the giant comet cloud started raining. Some experts are saying that our sun has a twin, and that it knocked the comets out of the cloud. The way I look at it, every cloud's got to rain sometime.

I never heard it so quiet outside in my life. No cars honking. No people screaming. No gunshots or sirens. Everybody's staying inside and waiting to see what happens.

I'm glad Derrell's here with me.

Momma's crying a lot. I hug her and tell her everything's going to be okay, but she doesn't believe me anymore.

We just sit in front of the TV watching and waiting. I'm guessing that's what the whole world is doing tonight. Watching and waiting.

Momma didn't want to go outside. She didn't want any of us to go outside, but she let me and Derrell go. We sat down in the backyard and looked up at the sky. Even though it was nighttime, it looked almost like day.

"You think they gonna hit us?" Derrell asked me

"Looks like it," I said.

We make love that night for the first time. Derrell was so happy, he started crying, and then I was crying too. We stayed in each other's arms for hours. Both of us were looking up at the sky when the wave hit the sky.

"Look," said Derrell. "Shooting star. Did you see it? Make a wish."

I did see it, because right behind it was another, and then another. Then suddenly there were thousands of them, and they were crisscrossing the sky in all directions. The entire sky looked like a huge fireworks display. It was beautiful, but it was also really scary. We went running inside and woke up everybody.

Everybody came running out to look. The sky looked like it was on fire now. I never knew there could be so many shooting stars.

We ran inside and turned on the TV.

The comets were here. All the channels were talking about it. The news people were saying that some places had already been hit. We were trying to figure out where when suddenly there was a huge roaring sound.

We rushed outside and saw one of them comets coming down. It raced overhead and kept going, thank God. Seconds later, though, it hit. We saw where it hit the ground. A huge cloud went up like some giant flower. About a minute later, there was a real powerful wave of wind and the house shook, and windows got busted and the electricity went out.

We were all crying and afraid. We hid under the tables, holding each other close. Then there were more explosions, and everything around us shook. It was so loud I thought the world was ending for sure, but nothing else happened.

Off in the distance we could hear car alarms and screaming and things breaking. Some places looked like they were on fire.

We crept out in the backyard again to look at the sky, and it looked like it was still on fire. Thousands of shooting stars were flying in all directions. I never saw anything so amazing in my life. It was the most beautiful thing ever. But I reminded myself again, just because it looked pretty didn't mean it wasn't dangerous.

Momma was screaming for us to go back inside, so we all follow her. I look over at Derrell and he looks at me and smiles. "Looks like we still alive," he say.

"Looks like it," I said.

Even though we were okay, none of us slept that night. We were afraid more comets were coming. But nothin' hit us. Not close anyway.

❀❀❀

November 20, 2019

I don't believe it. It's snowing! It ain't never snowed here before. Now, it's covering the streets, the sidewalks, the roofs...everything is covered in white. Derrell, me and Tommy—we even made a snowman. Problem is, it ain't stopped snowing. It just keeps getting deeper and deeper and more snow keeps coming. Looks like it ain't ever gonna stop.

Momma's sad because some men came and told us we have to go to the government shelter. We're almost out of food, so we don't got much choice. They're coming to get us tomorrow morning. I miss Keshia. I'm hoping to find her at the shelter, but Momma says there ain't much chance of that.

I'm sad to leave the house too, but it's cold now, and we can't turn on the heat or even close the windows 'cuz they're all busted. Besides, we ain't got no electricity. We can't watch TV no more, but luckily, we got a radio and batteries.

The good news is, the people on the radio are saying we don't need to worry no more about the comets. They're saying we're past the wave and ain't no more of the comets gonna hit us. They say we got some satellites up there in space and they're still taking pictures and everything, so they know if any more comets are coming.

The sky is full of dark clouds all the time now. Ain't no day or night far as I can tell—just clouds and more clouds. Seems to be getting colder all the time.

They're saying we're gonna have a real long winter, so long that it might never end. I don't believe that though. It's gonna be a long winter, yes, but I don't got no bad feelings anymore. That means we're gonna be all right. I know it.

I'm glad, because I got a surprise. Nobody knows yet, but I didn't get my monthly visitor, and I'm feeling awful funny inside. Don't know what Momma's gonna say. Maybe she'll be happy, or maybe mad 'cuz I went and got pregnant, even after she told me to be careful. Maybe she'll just be sad 'cuz my baby ain't gonna see no sunlight for a long time.

No matter. Momma loves me and we're gonna be fine. I know it.

Cost Benefit Analysis
by Cathy Bryant

There was only about a fifty per cent chance that I'd die. I'd followed all the suit protocols, found the safest place possible under the circumstances and done everything that the survival lessons teach you to do.

Well, OK, I shouldn't have been out there in the first place, but you'll understand why when I tell you that I'd just found eight k-weights of solaz stones just beyond the Rim. What was I supposed to do, leave them to the night winds because it was nearly time for city lockup? Yes, Mum and Dad would worry. I hadn't been an adult (scavenger class, two years early) very long, being just thirteen, but this was an opportunity I just couldn't let slip.

Eight k-weights! One k would pay three months' rent on our unit. Eight could do so many things...I ran the stones through my hands, marvelling at their muddy unimpressiveness. When polished they'd look like liquid sunshine and be harder than diamonds. They were rare this close to the city, and I'd never heard of a haul this size in this third at all, never mind just beyond the Rim. Mum earned about this much in two years; Dad, slightly less since his injury in the mine. We could all go and...we could...

I stopped daydreaming as a faint hiss sounded from the east. The winds were on their way, and if I carried on like this then I'd never see another day to dream in. I packed up the stones as quickly as I could, eyes nervously scanning the wastes while I worked.

I was looking for blue dust. Years before, Uncle Res had given me makeshift survival lessons. All solaz workers used to get a full survival programme courtesy of the Company, but they'd long been cut from the budget. People are cheap and plentiful on Fellen's Moon, and the laws are company-made and few. Someone worked out that it was cheaper to replace us than to pay for the classes, so that was that. But we taught each other what we knew. Uncle Res, who was only vaguely related to us, left his living tube daily to make sure I was taught a whole heap of stuff.

"Mina—don't get caught outside the city after lock-up," he said, and then repeated it very slowly, staring into my eyes.

I nodded. I got it.

"But if you do, then wait until the pre-wind breezes start, and then look for lines of blue dust. You'll hear the breezes—" he made a hissing noise which turned out to be spot on "—before you really feel them, and you'll see the dust in the direction of the sound. Get it?"

I got it, nodding emphatically. He continued.

"That blue dust is elikium, and it comes from beneath the surface. If you see it then there are usually holes and craters about. You get to that elikium dust and find yourself a hole to hide out in. Don't fall in it—"

He grinned, and I grinned back.

"—just find one you fit in, if you can, with your head below the surface but not too much space round you. When the winds start that hole will fill up, and you'll be thrown around a fair bit, but at least you won't be blown into some rocks and killed. If your suit and your nerve both hold, then you have a good chance."

Which is why I was looking for blue dust as I packed the stones, and blessing Uncle Res in my head, and trying to keep my nerve.

Just as the hissing breeze was starting to frighten me I saw a thin bluish trail, like smoke. I raced towards it, then remembered about falling in holes and slowed down.

The first hole was tiny. The second was a cavern. The wind began to shriek, and dust and pebbles began to fly. I whimpered, I know I did. But the third hole fitted me like an extension of my suit. There was even a half-seat I could perch on inside, safely if not entirely comfortably.

So I lowered myself gingerly into the hole, and waited.

Dust poured into the hole. Being buried in the sandy debris and suit failure were the two most likely causes of death in this situation. Or losing my mind and doing something dumb. The suit blocked some of the sound and filtered harmful substances from what air there was, but I still felt deafened and stifled. I tried not to move, though it was painfully tempting to reach my arms up and check that I wasn't submerged in deep sand. But any piece of debris, flying at the speed of that wind, could have ripped through both my suit and the arm within it.

So I concentrated my mind on the stones and the joy they would bring. Living upgrade, and suit upgrades so that I could scavenge further afield. Better food and medicine to make us healthy. A chance to learn more, go somewhere else, even….the wind howled in frustration, wanting to tear me apart, but I sat it out with just my dreams for company.

❁❁❁❁

I must have slept, though I don't remember dropping off. I came to with a jolt, my shoulders and neck aching with my cramped position, and I realised that I had gone deaf. The storm must have blown out my eardrums.

No! I would have felt the storm vibrating through the rock and felt the shifting of sand. I couldn't hear any sound because the storm was over and there was nothing to hear.

With some difficulty, a weight of dirt on my head, I looked up and saw nothing but more dirt. I raised my arms at last—and how good that felt. It felt even better when they broke through a fine layer above me, no threat at all. Shaking a little I climbed out of my refuge, and slowly made my way home.

Beeler was on gate duty—a company man, but one of the rare decent ones. When he saw me his face split into a grin.

"Mina! Good to see you! I heard you were lost."

"Sorry. I went too far last night."

"In more ways than one! Your folks'll skin you alive when they get hold of you! Well, after they quit hugging you, I guess. They came down here and made me check the records three times to see if you'd come in while I was on a break."

I smiled shamefacedly back at him.

"Oh go on," he said, and waved me in without making me fill in any official documents. "Go and make your family happy."

"Oh I will! Thanks!" I said. I will! I really will! I added mentally, grinning.

At the unit no one heard me let myself in, mainly because the babies were screaming. Merlys and Aled were as cute as buttons when they slept, but the rest of the time they spent bawling, eating, puking or filling their pants. And with twins, everything comes in stereo.

Mum and Dad had one each in first room, and were rocking them and singing to them in a vain attempt to shut them up. All four faces were creased and tired.

"Hey," I said during a brief break while the twins caught their breath for another round.

Mum and Dad spun towards me. Joy lit up their faces for a moment.

"Mina!" cried Dad. "Oh, thank the stars."

I was already unloading my pack onto the table, as I knew what the next line would be.

"Where have you *been*? What were you *thinking*? We've been worried out of our—OH!"

The predictable script was cut short as the stones spilled out in a great heap, heavy and unlovely.

Mum and Dad gazed drunkenly, and by way of miracles both twins shut up.

"I was just over the edge of the Rim, with just time to get back, when I spotted these. It took a while to get them all, but I thought it was worth the risk. I spent the night in an elikium hole. My suit might need an overhaul."

I stopped. Mum had nodded, but I didn't think that either was really listening to me.

"Eight k-weights according to my pack-scale," I added.

They heard that all right, and looked at me, and then back at the stones. And then they both smiled and cried and hugged me, and I smiled and cried and hugged them and the twins, who gurgled and dimpled sweetly, and it was one of the best moments of my life.

"Ah damn it, time for work," said Dad. He looked at the stones. "We'll decide tonight what to do with these."

Mum nodded agreement.

They kissed me, put the twins in their care spaces (basic food, lullabies and two diaper changes—the best package we could afford, but at least safe) and left, holding the bread pieces that they'd have for lunch. Stale bread because it was cheaper.

Fortunately scavengers make their own hours. I crawled on to my bunk in second room and was asleep in a moment.

I woke from a dream of being suffocated and having to pay for it. Hands were pushing grit into my mouth and taking money away from me. I was dying and going broke, and I opened my mouth to scream—and woke to find that the twins, maybe having the same dream, had beaten me to it and were screaming their heads off. There was nothing wrong; screaming is just what one-year-olds do.

I pulled myself up, bones creaking and muscles tweaking my nerve endings. After drinking a lot of water I washed myself all over at the sink. We had hot water three days a week, and it felt wonderfully luxurious as I soaped myself with a steaming sponge. I washed my hair and combed it until every last bit of dust, dirt or sweat was gone.

I think I was trying to be ceremonial—to mark this time, and make the day special in some way, with some sort of ritual. I could hardly look at the stones. They were too precious, and now that I was safely home my adventure beyond the Rim was freaking me out a little. I would never forget the sound of that wind—and if I hadn't found that hole…

I was shaking with either delayed shock or hunger or both, and ate some porridge and some bread. Soon I felt better, and played with the twins for a while.

"Mum. Dad. Mina," I said to them. "Come on, sweets. You can do it! Say Mum—Dad—Mina."

"Uh- ad," said Merlys.

"Ee-ya," said Aled.

I kissed them.

After dark my parents arrived home and we had broth. Then we all looked at the stones, which were still on the table, though I had pushed them out of the way of the twins in case they ate them.

Mum smiled at me.

"This takes all our worries away, Mina. I'm so proud of you."

"Yes, rent for years, plus the rent on the twins' care units, plus our tax. We can have a little treat each too," beamed Dad.

I couldn't believe what I was hearing, but I phrased my question carefully and politely.

"Mum—Dad—aren't we going to try to make things better at all? To upgrade? Two k-weights would buy me an elite suit, and I could stay out for days at a time beyond the Rim. You know how good I am at spotting the solaz. With a wider range I could get so much more, and we could live so much better…"

I trailed off as I saw them swap glances and then look at me seriously.

"Mina dear," said Dad, "You do understand that this find is a one-off, don't you? A better suit wouldn't get you more troves like this."

"I know! But *you* know that the elites get much more than we basics do. If I could go further for longer then I could get more stones, and we could have better lives, long-term."

Again they looked at each other and found confirmation there.

"Mina, there are more important things than a new suit. Do you know how hard we work? And how many accidents happen in the mine? As it is we have no security. We're always one broken leg away from losing this place and living with the cast-offs."

I thought of the cast-offs—beggars, buskers, thieves, drunks, addicts, prostitutes. The desperate, in other words. Few of them lasted more than a winter or two; the city kept out most of the killing winds, but not much cold.

"So we go on as we are?" I asked, my mouth dry.

"Yes, but with a wonderful safety net, thanks to you," said my mother, holding my hands in hers and stroking them gently.

"So we go on as we are, in joyless drudgery," I said, and took my hands away.

"Joyless," said my father coldly. "Really? You feel no joy in our lives together? No joy with your mother and me, or the twins?"

"When we see each other in the brief exhausted intervals between work and sleep, maybe," I snapped, "Though we're usually too tired and hungry for much joy, aren't we?"

"That's enough!" said Mum. "We're not getting the suit, and that's final. You may be classed as an adult in terms of being fit for scavenging work, but you haven't earned your fiscal and judicial rights yet. We decide money matters until you do, so there's no point in arguing any more."

I made one last effort.

"If not the suit, then how about an enhanced nutrition-education programme for the twins? Or we could buy a small transport and use it to—"

"Mina," said Dad, and it was a warning. I fell silent.

"We'll sell them first thing," said Dad, and then we cleared away the remains of the meal quietly. There were no leftovers.

Soon we all went to second room and our bunks.

Having slept much of the day I wasn't particularly tired, and I lay in my bunk feeling a mixture of anger and frustration. I could understand my parents' desire for a cushion between us and a cast-off life, but to use a haul like this for nothing but continuance felt like such a missed opportunity. The stones were worth more than a little security; we could improve things enormously, and open up a better life long-term. Why were they so short-sighted?

I answered my own question almost as soon as I asked it. They were short-sighted because their lives had been cramped down into narrow drudgery, any wider vision eroded. The best they could let themselves hope for was a slight alleviation of worry.

Well I wasn't ground down yet. And I had a plan.

I got up and crept through to first room. Quietly I packed my school record and ID, and three k-weights of the stones.

I left a message:

Dear Mum and Dad,

I've gone to get a better life. I'll be back when I have. Enjoy the stones and don't worry about me. I'll miss you all.

Love,

Mina.

I was thirteen, remember. At that age one is blunt.

Slipping through the door I headed to the night mart and bought an elite flight suit (not the scavenging suit I had coveted) for two k-weights of solaz. Then I headed for the port, and started talking to ship's captains.

Four turned me down out of hand, but the fifth—a short, quiet woman with grey hair in a long plait—listened to me, checked my record and equipment and looked at me with a frown.

"Your parents still have fiscal and judicial rights, don't they?" she asked.

"Relating to on-moon decisions, yes," I said. "But I'm classed as an adult for work purposes, and I can go off-surface if a ship contracts to take me."

She nodded.

"OK Mina. Why are you really going?"

I didn't try to lie. Instead I explained about the stones, and about the numbing disappointment of failing to use them to improve our lives. I told her how many I had taken and why, and showed her again my excellent nav and trading qualifications.

"I'll come back here with money, and get them all out of here, or at least into a better place," I finished.

"Running away to make your fortune, eh?" said the captain, but she didn't sound mocking. Then she nodded and sighed to herself.

"Minimum wage for the first year, plus a tithe of your personal trade tallies. Welcome aboard. I'm Captain Talli Keller."

I was trembling as I thanked her and stumbled aboard Ship F.O. 174 Harper.

I had pictured myself standing smartly in my new flight suit at the nav controls, and saluting. Instead I was provided with a set of ancient and tattered overalls.

"Wouldn't want to get that nice new suit all dirty, would you?" teased Tapman, the engineer and only other crewmember. Again, he didn't really sound mocking; rather he was testing me, so I gave a rueful smile and got changed.

About two hours of loading dirty boxes followed, and then I spent an hour cleaning the ship.

Captain Keller herself brought me a bucket of hot water, clean-gel and a towel afterwards.

"Still want to come?" she asked.

I smiled and nodded.

"Better get your flight suit back on then," she said, smiled back, and gave me a contract.

Test passed, I guessed. It all felt very right.

As we lifted off I could just see through a porthole, first the port and the city and then the whole of Fellen's Moon, pulling away from me and getting smaller and more insignificant.

I should have had a lump in my throat, right? I should have wept a tear each for my parents and the twins and Uncle Res. But frankly my main emotion was relief. I had been so afraid that something would prevent my escape, and I hadn't realised how heavily my old life had hung on me, weighing me down, until it slipped from my shoulders as I flew away.

My first meal on board was two kinds of vegetable, a spicy nut-bread and some sort of fruit preserved in syrup. I savoured every flavoursome mouthful. Now I know that the food was ordinary ship's rations and nothing special, but back then it seemed to fulfil the promise of my dreams. Mum, Dad, I thought to myself—I will bring all this back to you. You too will taste these tastes.

Seven years later I kept my word.

⚝⚝⚝

I spent all seven years on board the Harper with Captain Keller and Engineer Tapman—or Talli and Tap, as they were within a few days—and lots of that time was spent thanking the stars that I had been at the port when I had.

Our first trip was delivery of those dirty boxes to Nuovo Jupe, and it was simple enough. The rest of the time, except for meals, cleaning duties and maintenance, we talked.

Talli had inherited the ship from her sister Alix, who had died of an old heart problem that the medics couldn't fix. Her death had left them a crewmember and a lot of heart short—Tap had been Alix's lover—and a needy, naiive adolescent was an ideal project for them.

I didn't know that at the time, of course. For all I knew, all new crew on all ships were treated with bluff affection, and encouraged to learn as much as possible. On board the Harper I studied for and passed my pilot and mainenance exams as well as getting my advanced trader's licence, all at Talli's expense. She claimed at the time—and at first I was young enough to believe her—that it was an investment; I would be a more valuable crew member with the qualifications. When I had them, she raised my pay accordingly.

Maybe I was a touch dumb, but it took me a while to realise that the touchstone of the Harper crew was its kindness. Even in trade Talli was fair and generous, which shocked me at first. To poor and struggling folk she gave better deals, and only ever took what she really needed.

Sometimes I'd sigh at the inefficiency. Harper was a ramshackle little ship run in a ramshackle little way, and part of me longed to be aboard one of the sleeker, faster ships. But then I remembered that those same ships had been too efficient to find a place for me. And Talli's behavious rubbed off on me; I traded more kindly and honestly than I might have done under a different influence. I can't claim credit for it, but I found that it made me happier to be kind rather than otherwise, though I never did make that fortune.

I'd just turned twenty when Talli called me to her quarters. We were on a lush garden planet with the sweetest, most invigorating air, and I was feeling energetic and joyful.

That all fell out of me in a nauseous lump when I saw Tap with his head in his hands and Talli looking at me with a sad little smile.

"What—what is it?" I asked.

"My heart," said Talli simply. "Same as Alix. I don't have long."

"You could get a transplant," I said, but she looked at me sharply.

"You know those hearts come from organ farms," she said. "I'm not giving money to people who farm other people."

"Of course not," I mumbled. "Sorry. Sorry."

"As I have friends here, I thought I'd stay here for the end," she continued as if we were talking about holiday plans. "It's a lovely place, so fresh and alive and I—oh sweethearts, it's OK…"

And she held and comforted us both while we sobbed.

We stayed for the four brutal and tender months it took her to die, and buried her, and planted fruit and flowers for her. And I raged against her choice of end, even though it was beautiful in some ways.

Talli had left us the ship jointly. I let Tap buy me out after we had argued over the amount—he wanted to give me more than my share, and I refused to take a jot over. In the end I managed to beat him down by getting him to take me to Fellen's Moon. My share of the ship plus my slender savings were no fortune, but in a place as poor as home it would buy a good-sized living unit outright, plus about five years' keep for the whole family. I would get Aled and Merlys the best schooling, and a chance at life.

I hadn't heard from my folks since I'd left. They had no off-world coms and anyway I was continually on the move. But I figured that just as the solaz stones had made up for a night's absence, so my nest egg would iron out any remaining frowns of disapproval.

I hugged Tap goodbye at the port.

"I'll be on Gef for the next couple of weeks, then on to Elkar. I don't know where I'll be after that, but I'll leave word for you at Elkar port. Any trouble here, you come find me and we'll go anywhere you want, OK?" he said.

I nodded.

"Are you sure you don't want me to wait for you now—just a couple of days?" he asked.

I shook my head. I was too near to tears to tell him to go, but he got the message.

"Good luck," I muttered and ran to the city gates. I was as clumsy as I had been at thirteen, though taller and healthier.

There at the city sign-in was Beeler, the decent Company man.

"Beeler!" I said happily. It felt like an omen—he had been there when I brought back the solaz, and he was here now.

He frowned for a moment and checked my documents.

"Mina!" he said with a sad smile.

"How are you, Beeler?"

"I'm OK. No promotion, though."

"You're too good to be promoted. So how are my folks? And the twins?"

"—I haven't seen them," faltered Beeler, and I felt cold as I heard the missed beat.

"What happened?"

Beeler sighed.

"Go find your Uncle Res. He'll be in his tube now, and he can explain things better than I can."

"Thanks," I gasped, and ran again.

The living tubes were just big enough to hold a sleeper on a mat, with blanket, and there was a shared sink/drain for washing, drinking and voiding. Res had always lived in his tube, but spent much of his time in our two-roomer, with the people he loved. His knowledge had saved my life when I found the stones, yet I had never said goodbye to him.

He exited his tube as soon as I showed my ID, and buried me in a great bear hug.

"Mina, Mina," he said gently, "So good to see you! You've grown! Look at you, a fine young woman! So where have you been? What have you been doing?"

"I'll tell you everything, I promise. But how are Mum and Dad and the twins?"

His face fell and my stomach went cold.

"Let's go somewhere we can talk properly," he said and I nodded dumbly.

In the end we went outside to the wastes as it was a warm day, with only a few scavengers in sight. The City was so crowded and dirty, and Res insisted on waiting until we were somewhere quiet. Later it occurred to me that he was simply putting off the moment of explanation.

We sat on the rocks and watched the dust blow.

"So?" I asked at last.

He sighed. "Your father died, Mina. He was never right after the accident, as you know. Your mother carried on but the heart went out of her. She was injured at work when a cartload of ore fell on her, and she was left with a broken collarbone and a twisted leg that never healed properly. Her chest was going, too, with the dust. The Company gave her minimum payout on some excuse.

The family ended up in the Cast-Offs, Mina."

"Oh…Aled? Merlys?"

"I don't know where they are. I tried to keep track of them all. I know your Mum is alive—I saw her in a bar a month ago, though she ran away screaming when she saw me. She can't bear anything that reminds her of the old days. The kids weren't with her and I haven't been able to find out where they are. The family changed location so often."

There was a moment's pause. I wiped my cheeks and blew my nose.

"I left them five k-weights of solaz stones," I bleated, pleading for forgiveness through a fog of guilt.

"Oh stars, Mina, it wasn't your fault!" Res seemed genuinely shocked. "You mustn't think that! They were proud of you, and so grateful for the haul. It helped them to keep going as long as they did."

"But if I'd been here then I could have helped them," I said.

"Maybe—or maybe you'd have sunk with them. Look, what is survival really worth here, under these conditions? You got out and succeeded at life, and your children will have a decent time because of it. Your parents would still be proud. You know, more than once your Mum said to me that she was glad you were out of it. It gave her comfort to think of you out there, exploring, happy, free."

I shook my head. I didn't know how to feel.

Res tried to persuade me to get on the next flight out, but instead I rented a small unit for a few months and went hunting for my family.

Much good it did me, or them. A barman told me that the twins had died of the Dust Disease, or the cold, three winters ago; it was hard to tell which, but there had been alot of coughing. My mother had broken down, and then become an addict. She was a prostitute now, though customers were few.

When I finally tracked her down, she refused to acknowledge me.

"You ain't Mina," snapped this coarse stranger lying in a filthy basement. "She's thirteen."

I showed her ID, told her things only I would know, and begged her to ask Res. She didn't believe me even when I gave her money, though that made her frown at me in confusion. I don't think many people gave her money without wanting something from her.

She spent it on a drug binge that killed her. I didn't know how to feel—more guilt, in part, but there was also a sense of relief. You'd understand if you'd seen her. I didn't want her to live like that, and I don't think she did either.

I went through the motions of life, dealing with documentation and paying the death fines.

I left shortly afterwards. I explained to Res that I'd go on the next ship that would take me, which most would given my qualifications and experience.

"Come with me," I said, but he shook his head, and wouldn't discuss it.

He said that Fellen's Moon was his home and that he would stay and try to make things better here. He didn't mean make more money, and I didn't really understand what he talked about. He said that he and some friends were working for real change—trying to change what the Company was and how it worked. It sounded like a drunken fantasy to me, and why would the Company listen to a grubby old lowlife like him?

I bought Res a unit and a tiny but sufficient income. He wept with a gratitude that I didn't think I deserved, and it made me uncomfortable. I just wanted to get the hell off the whole miserable moon.

I'd spent almost all my money. In the end I left Fellen's Moon for the second time with little more than I'd had the first time, seven years earlier, unless you count experience.

This time I was taken on as second engineer on a large ore freighter, and I learned how unusual Talli and her ship had been. The freighter was more conventional—everyone in his or her allotted place, doing designated tasks for maximum efficiency. In many ways I liked it.

And I've left behind most of that ridiculous guilt and sentimentality that I had when I was young. Res was right—none of what happened on Fellen's Moon was my fault. My parents were dumb to put up with the way the Company treated them, and a long life was no improvement on a short life there. They should have followed my example and left.

I found a man I liked when I was twenty four, and we contracted to each other and had a child. He's a fine boy, strong and healthy, and we've sent him to the best school we can afford.

I know I've hardened. But I've also survived. Being sweet to other people didn't get me those solaz stones—strength, intelligence and luck all played their parts. My son will be brought up to be strong and clever. Of course I hope he'll be a good person too, but nothing is as important as his survival.

You want me to say that I miss him while he's away, or that my relationship lacks warmth, or that I miss my family? Maybe I should, but I don't, and I have no regrets. If I had stayed with my family then maybe their miserable lives could have been slightly extended—and mine deprived or destroyed. There is nothing wrong with seeking personal happiness, as long as you understand that there will be a price to pay. You don't get to be a hero, like Talli was to me when I was a kid, and be happy and successful too.

Right now I am happy and feel no guilt. I've worked hard for what I have, earned it all and done no wrong. I'm in our unit—two large rooms and our own bathroom!—on the ship. I've just drunk a warm, foamy cup of chettel—our allowance is three cups per week, raised from two last year, which is great. My man will be back from his shift in an hour, and we'll eat real set-meat with vegetables, and fresh gorda-fruit bars with added zelba, all the way from Gef.

I am so glad to be away from Fellen's Moon. I heard that there has been trouble there, terrorism, and fights breaking out. The Company will sort it out I'm sure, though they're taking their time.

We'll have two whole hours of leisure time tonight before lights out. Tomorrow my shift is only ten hours, and within six years I can expect promotion and an even better lifestyle. What more could I want? Yes, my life is rich in every way now, and I am happy. You can't put a price on that.

OCENEI
BY NICOLE TANQUARY

My sister stopped existing on April 22nd, 2039. The electricity had been shut off that morning, and all the blinds were open to let in the weak, rainy-spring sunlight. I was working on geometry when I saw the van pull up, an old model with rusted hubcaps and doors in the back. There was a small window on the side of the back section, and I could see the outline of a face, blurry and dark but undoubtedly a child's.

There were letters printed in nondescript gray on the side doors, OCENEI, Organization for the Coordination and Employment of Non-Existing Individuals. There was a man and woman in the front seat. The man got out while the woman stayed behind the wheel, drumming her fingers on the black plastic in time to the motor. They both wore black suits and black caps.

The doorbell rang, and I stood and walked out of my room to the banister, where I had a good view of the front door. I leaned over it with my elbows pressed to the wood. Dad came from the kitchen, his steps rapid on the cheap linoleum floor. He'd dressed up for the occasion, tall shoes and fresh-pressed hat, trying his best to look Suave. He opened the door and the OCENEI man came in, rubbing the April mud from his boots onto the welcome mat. There was an electronic clipboard in his hand, which he tapped at with his finger and squinted into. He probably needed reading glasses; he looked about that age. "I'm here for the pickup of a...Miss Tyli?"

"Yes, that's right." Dad nodded and smiled. His teeth were yellowish, and if you looked close, the edge of a front one was chipped. "She's right in the kitchen. Why don't you have something to eat? We were just about to have some lunch." For an instant, the OCENEI man's face twisted at the corners. I would've given money to know what he was thinking.

Instead of saying what was on his mind, though, the OCENEI man shook his head and said, "We're on a tight schedule. I just need you and the mother to sign these forms, then I'll be out of your way." Dad nodded, keeping his smile on as he took the clipboard and began clicking his signature onto the bottom lines.

Mom came in with Tyli then, both hands on her shoulders to steer her towards the OCENEI man. Tyli's body was wrapped in one of those cheap cloth gowns, the kind usually found in hospitals. Her mouse-brown hair was brushed, and her dark eyes were frightened. From where I stood, I could see her hands clenched at her sides.

Mom was about to take the clipboard from Dad when Gavin came in, his face set in a mold of determination. "I'm going with her," he said. Tyli shot a look at him, a look of hope that was so pure and bright, it hurt to look at.

The OCENEI man glanced at my parents. Mom gave a little shake of her head. She kept her smile on though, even when her voice came out kind of gritted, like she was saying it between clenched teeth. "No, sweety, Tyli has to go alone. Remember what we told you last night?" Gavin started forward again, though, and reached for Tyli's hand.

"If Tyli goes, then I go." Quickly, Mom shoved the clipboard at the OCENEI man, then stepped forward and snatched Gavin's arm in a stranglehold. Mom was strong when she wanted to be. He wasn't going to get out of that.

At her touch, Gavin screamed, and at his screaming, Tyli started to cry, but the OCENEI man was already nudging her out the door. He probably saw this all the time. Dad closed the door firmly behind them.

I listened, wordlessly, as Gavin's screams got louder and louder, and Mom was shouting at him, and I think the episode ended with him being grounded. I don't quite remember.

That night, the electricity came back on. The payment for the bill had gone through. I didn't turn on my lights, though, and instead lay flat on my bed with a pillow over my face. Neither Gavin nor I ate dinner that night, though Mom had celebrated the occasion by getting a honey-baked ham, and the warm, sweet smell curled its way up the stairs and into our separate rooms.

Why did Tyli get picked over me and Gavin? Well, she was the youngest, and it's easiest to sign away someone who's young. She didn't stand out in any memorable way; brown hair, brown eyes, grades that ranged from average to below average, depending on the subject. Not good enough for scholarships for college, which our parents had already been discussing.

The problem beneath it all was that kids were expensive. Legally, they couldn't work to contribute income, leaving parents to pay for everything; school, food, clothing, water, heating... My parents had had Tyli for six years, and with all five of us to look after, our debts had been starting to run into the red.

So they weighed their options, picked OCENEI, and signed her out of existence. One less child to worry about would mean enough extra money to pay off our bills.

The papers on the clipboard, with my parents' signatures, gave OCENEI the authority to erase Tyli's birth certificate and social security number. OCENEI had a whole department dedicated to tracking down the names of their newest acquisitions, find them in newspapers, hospital records, whatever, and delete it away. Tyli had been taken at one in the afternoon. By three, for all intents and purposes, she had never existed at all, except in people's memories. And those never lasted very long, either.

We weren't allowed to talk about her anymore. No one was; though, the little kids sometimes had problems with this rule. I remember hearing about Tyli's first grade class, how one of the little girls had asked about her and gotten a verbal beating because of it. They'd learn soon enough that if someone just dropped out of the class, it was best not to talk about it.

Gavin sort of clammed up after that, didn't speak to Mom and Dad anymore. He would come home from school, do his schoolwork, and go to bed, all the lights turned off, just staring up at the ceiling. Sometimes I would go in and sit on his bed, and we'd stay like that, in silence. Mom didn't like it, but since he was keeping up his academics, she couldn't fault him for the way he was acting and have it stand legally.

So life went on.

⚜⚜⚜

On the day he turned eighteen, Gavin packed his bags and moved into an apartment on the North side. He didn't bother telling our parents where he was going. At some level they must've expected it. And yet, a few minutes after they discovered the empty, picked-clean room, I got a hysterical vid-call from my mother. "Your brother's run away! He's gone!"

I looked her steadily in the eyes. "Mom, he's not with me. And he technically hasn't run away. He's not a minor anymore." She was

167

rubbing at her eyes with the back of her hands, rubbing them red.

"What did I ever do to him? What did I do to deserve this?" *Tyli,* my mind whispered, and though I didn't say it out loud she must've seen it in my face, because she hung up not long after that.

I put away the paper I was working on…I was in my third year of undergrad, earning a degree in criminology…and snatched the car keys off of the hook nailed into the kitchen wall.

Ten minutes later I was cruising through the North side, watching the street life; unemployed Africans, Vietnamese manicurists, Indian gas-station workers, they were all there. I found his building after running the same street a few times over. The bricks in the walls were old, the red color nearly leeched out of them with the rain.

I parked the car, taking special care to roll up the windows and activate the locks. Then I went to the door and knocked. An old Italian man opened up, a remnant of the North Side's "Little Italy" district that thrived there half a century ago, before the money sluiced out of town. The man said to call him Papa Tony and didn't seem to mind that I was there – said that he could use someone responsible like me to "keep an eye on the kid." Probably what he meant was that I could cover Gavin's rent when he fell through.

Papa Tony led me up a flight of wooden stairs to number 201, where the door was open a crack. He pushed it the rest of the way open with the palm of his hand, then nodded at me and left.

Gavin was splayed across a bare mattress with stains on it, a duffel bag at his feet. A bowl for smoking weed sat on the dresser. An empty syringe was in his fingers, held like a pen. I'd known about the weed…had helped him buy his first hit, had smoked it with him, passing bowls and pipes between us in the silences that were always reserved for Tyli…but the syringes were new.

"You were supposed to call. I would've helped you move in," I said.

He glanced up at me, his eyes bleary, filmed over like he was dead. "Move in? There's only the one bag. The rest I didn't need. Left it by the side of the road. Or maybe I burned it. I can't remember."

I ran a hand through my hair. "Listen, Gavin, I get why you had to get out. But …" I let the sentence drop. He had put on his blank, I-know-you're-moralizing-to-me face, as soon as I'd opened my mouth. I suppose I could've kept talking, but nothing would've gotten through.

The silence went on for a while. Downstairs, in his own apartment, Papa Tony was stumping around and banging pots against stoves and kitchen sinks. Making lunch, I guess.

"The drugs are the only way," Gavin said, at last. "She's like a ghost, Jon. She's all see-through. And yet it's the closest I can get to her. I have photographs," he added, gesturing to the duffel bag, "But they're not her...glad I have them, though. Without them, I would've forgotten what she looked like. I had to steal them from Dad before he put them through the shredder."

The mattress creaked under me as I sat down. "Gavin, it's been ten years. This can't go on."

"So the fact that it happened a long time ago makes it okay?"

"That's not what I said."

"It's what you implied." Anger had flashed across his face, the muscles grimacing at me as they had grimaced at our parents. I was almost glad to see it. Anything besides the blankness was a welcome twist.

It smoothed away after a moment, though, and his gaze turned back towards the ceiling. There was a spider up there, a tiny colorless one, and he watched it twiddle with the beginnings of a web. "You're right," he said, in a quiet voice I didn't like the sound of. "It's been ten years. She's probably dead now. A little girl like that, probably rented her out to do factory work. Or maybe as a whore." The sweat on his forehead gleamed. I could smell it off of him, a sour musk that hung on his clothes like smog over Los Angeles. "She would've been sixteen by now. I would've been helping her get her driver's license."

I made a face. "No way I would've let you teach *anyone* to drive. You're the shittiest driver I know." That brought a smile out, a faded thing that came and went, like a rainbow.

✾✾✾✾

Gavin's hair grew long and thin, his face whittled, the veins in the crooks of his arms bruised with drugs. He made me promises about applying to colleges, but they were empty ones.

Meanwhile, OCENEI was bigger than ever. As you moved down the class steps, the rate of 'disappeared' children grew exponentially. At least, according to the rumors. The OCENEI network was the only place where the actual records and statistics could be accessed, and those were not for public eyes. Mostly what I knew about them was guesswork.

And Tyli? She was still gone. Maybe I didn't crash and burn like Gavin, but a piece of her lived inside my head, too. Especially in the early days, she'd come awake in my dreams. I'd run after that van with the rusted hubcaps, through streets lit in yellow and brown. I'd see her face in the window in the back. I'd never get closer to the van, no matter how fast I ran, and in the end it would slip around a street corner, or swerve into an alleyway, and by the time I got there it'd be gone.

169

But it couldn't go on. Something had to be done.

⚙⚙⚙

I started by calling the toll-free number OCENEI offered up in e-Magazine commercials, and got in touch with an OCENEI secretary. I told her that I was still on the fence about whether or not to sign over my own child, and that I'd like an appointment with an OCENEI representative. The ad in *Newsweek* said that a Mrs. Stringer was available in my area for this kind of thing. Was that right? The secretary said, sure, but she's a busy woman, and the soonest I can get you in is 10:00 on the third of next month. What day is that? I asked. A Monday. Okay, I can do Mondays.

⚙⚙⚙

Mrs. Stringer was a middle-aged woman, short and bulky and with a carefully constructed hair-do designed to accentuate the shape of her face. Her long red nails were clicking away at a lightboard when I came in. At the sound of the door closing, she paused and smiled at me. "Hi there. What can I do for you?"

I pulled out the chair in front of her desk and sat, folding my hands together in my lap. "I've been thinking about this for a while," I started, slowly and deliberately. "I'd like to get more information about what OCENEI would mean for me and my family. I figured you'd be the best person to talk to. I'm the kind of person who's slow with making decisions, I'm afraid," and I allowed her a sheepish smile. She laughed and waved a hand at me.

"That's not a *bad* thing! All that means is that you're careful with your choices! I'm that way, myself. Don't rush into anything if I can help it. But you're on the right path, if you're looking into OCENEI." There was a glass vase sitting on her desk, with a daffodil tucked inside. She noticed that it was in my line of sight to the screen, and hurriedly moved it out of the way. "These days, the capital needed in the upkeep of a growing child is about $30,000 a year. Which is fine if you have a high-income job, but we don't exactly live in a perfect world, do we?" She let out a planned sigh. "For multiple-child households, this means that overall quality of life decreases as the children increase, since the capital is spread thin to cover all of the individuals. But if one is signed over to OCENEI custody," she said, clicking to life a statistic animation, "The money doesn't have to be spread as thin, and the possibilities increase for the remaining family members. So, you see, OCENEI is an important

170

step in any family planning. Especially for young couples just starting out." She smiled at me, maybe waiting for some comment about my wife, or girlfriend, or whoever I had had children with.

Instead I asked, "How does OCENEI treat the individuals it acquires?"

This wasn't a question she heard often...mostly parents wanted to skip over hearing that part, didn't want to think about it at all, in fact...yet she only hesitated a moment before answering.

"Very well, of course. They're fed, clothed, and provided with work. Quite frankly, they get more out of OCENEI than they would have gotten at home. In that way, I like to think of OCENEI as a charity organization; the individuals we take in are saved from desperate lives of want and destitution."

I reached out a hand to indicate something on the screen. "Yes, but what about-"

My wrist nudged the side of the daffodil's glass vase, and a moment later a shattering boom made us both jump. I swore and got to my feet, examining my arm. Two tiny bits of glass had lodged into my forearm, and red blood was welling from the cuts. I hadn't planned that, but it was a nice touch, all the same.

The representative leapt to her feet, her carefully constructed face opening wide with shock. "Oh my god! Wait here, I'll get antiseptic!" Her high heels clattered against the wooden floor as she left.

I was up and moving the moment her back was turned, pulling a phone from my pocket in one fluid motion. Resting it against the screen took one second. Activating the program so that its memory chip could absorb all of the computer's information took another. I had practiced before coming here, and the motions felt natural and distant, like I was sleep-walking.

The wonders of modern-age technology ensured that I had plenty of time to walk back around and compose my face into an agreeably apologetic shape by the time she came back into the room with bandages and a first aid kit. "I'm so sorry," I said, in a half-mumble. "I'm such a klutz. And I broke your vase."

She let out a noise through her mouth, a kind of *tut-tut*. "Honey, you have nothing to be sorry for. I should've seen that coming a mile away." She outstretched her hand, and I gave her my forearm so she could pick out the glass with her long red nails. "You know, this is another thing you have to think about," she remarked, when the glass was out and she was spreading Neosporin over the holes left behind. "Medical costs aren't cheap, you know. And what if an accident like this happens to someone in your family? It's your responsibility to set aside some savings for emergencies."

The interview continued for another half an hour, with me holding my arm gingerly in my lap. As the talk drew to a close, she lowered her voice and looked me steadily in the eyes. "There's nothing shameful about this, you know. Parents who turned to OCENEI used to get a bad rep…like how people used to be ashamed of being on welfare, you know? But the world out there is changing, and individuals are acknowledging that this is the only way to keep some households afloat. When I was your age," and her voice dropped another octave lower, "I signed one over. It was the only way I could afford a house with my husband. And now, our family is so happy. I've never regretted it. That's why I work here, you know. I believe in what OCENEI is trying to accomplish."

I nodded, with the proper amount of reverential attitude; *Gee, ma'am, I have a lot to learn about life, don't I?*

I was able to leave soon after that, smiling a shy smile back at her lipstick grin. The daffodil had been swept into the trash along with the broken glass, and I glanced at it on my way out the door. The petals had already wilted.

❧❧❧

I waited until I got back to my apartment to look at the material I had stolen. I suppose I could've looked at it on my phone screen, but I was too tense, too shaky. It felt impossible to look anywhere but straight ahead as I drove.

As a security measure, I saved electronic backup copies of all the files on my computer – the papers, and the collected results from my field work waiting to be turned into papers – before transferring over the OCENEI files. I had no idea if there were viruses laced into the OCENEI data, designed to erase the memory of a hacker's hard-drive.

But apparently the representative's version was clean, because the program let me pour over the searchable database with hardly a buffer. Even with a built-in search engine, though, it took me ten minutes to find Tyli. There were so many names…so many Tylis, and Tylas, and Tylees, and Taras, and Tanyas, girls and boys over 300,000 strong. A low throbbing came into my temples just looking at them all, and I had to pour myself a beer before I could focus long enough to find her entry.

There was one photograph, of Tyli after she had been processed into the OCENEI masses. As my parents had been eating their honey baked ham, OCENEI workers had shaved her head, tattooed A735P on her tiny, six-year old wrist, and had her stand in front of a camera lens. Her large brown eyes were blank as a deer's.

Blood and skin samples had been taken, and her genes sequenced to see if she would be useful as a test subject sold out by OCENEI to medical research centers. She didn't have any of the right mutations, no susceptibility to heart disease or breast cancer to capitalize on, so she was rented by GAP to sew clothes for its new, *Made in America* brand-line.

Tyli's genetic sequencing *did* say, however, that she had something called "PCOS." According to a quick online search, PCOS was Polycystic Ovary Syndrome. It wasn't a life-threatening condition, read the update to her profile, but for Tyli the cysts were expressing themselves in painful menstruation cycles that happened multiple times a month, starting when she was twelve. (Alone, then. Alone and *bleeding*.)

By the time she was thirteen, a new batch of medical testers had reported to OCENEI a need for fresh subjects. A facility called EasyCure was working on a cost-effective way to eradicate PCOS from a woman's system, in the form of easy-to-pop pills.

So, Tyli was sold and designated as property of EasyCure. They had sent occasional reports back to OCENEI, to keep the database's file on her up-to-date. The excess cysts were shrinking, but there were unfortunate side effects EasyCure scientists were still trying to work through, including hair loss and vivid, paralyzing dreams. Here there was another photo. Her head was bare, and it was painfully obvious that she was underweight; you could see the shape of her skull, the jutting of her eyebrows and cheekbones. The hollows beneath her eyes were dark yellow-brown, and her lips were drawn in a flinch that was fixed, carved from stone.

I didn't realize I'd been staring at her until my computer broke the trance by rattling off a ringtone, some bouncy Beatles' song from the '60's. Mom was calling. Breathing a little too quickly, I rolled my shoulders, trying to loosen them up, then clicked the screen to take the call. I knew Mom. If I didn't answer her, she'd just keep dialing, over and over again until I was ready to chuck my computer out the window.

Her face appeared on the screen, and all of a sudden it struck me how much she and Tyli looked alike. I hadn't noticed it when Tyli was younger and still had her baby-fat, but the shape of their faces…it was like staring at a version of Tyli who'd been taken and stretched, dried until wrinkles came in around her eyes.

"Your brother's gone insane. You need to go get him," she said, and even her voice was dry.

"What? What happened?"

"It's on the news," she said, and her expression turned desperate.

"He's in front of the courthouse on Townsend. Just go get him. He might listen to you."

"Mom?" I asked again, but she had hung up.

⁂

I found Gavin in the center of a half-circle of reporters, who, surprisingly enough, were mute… Gavin needed no prompting. The talk was just pouring out of him, and the cameras were catching every moment of it. There was a dazed grin on his face, and he was wearing this balloon of a white T-Shirt, one that stretched all the way to his thighs like a hospital gown.

I was only half-aware of my legs picking up speed as he chatted on. "I'm doing this for my sister, who was signed away eleven years ago. Her name was Tyli. She was just six years old. *Six,* can you believe that? Has anyone ever wondered why, in a so-called civilized society, it's acceptable to sell your child into slavery? Not even knowing if they'll live or die? I say *'die,'*" he laughed, in an aside to one of the cameras, which read 'Channel Six' and was a little larger than the others, "But I really mean murdered. Well, I've had enough of the sugar-coated bullshit, how OCENEI is all a good thing. I'm telling it like it is."

I caught him by the shoulder, and I could feel the musty-damp touch of sweat coming through the fabric. The insides of his wrists were dark with the pricking of needles. "Gavin, what are you doing?" I muttered into his ear, taking advantage of a natural pause in his speech.

The reporters, of course, leaned forward and tried to find a way to get Gavin talking again. They were all clean-pressed and immaculate, even in the summer heat. "Is this a family member? Friend? Does he know what you plan to do?" Gavin blinked at me, and his smile was a touch bemused.

"Yeah, this is my big brother. And I guess he doesn't know."

"Know what?" I tightened my grip on his shoulder, began pulling him to the side, but the cameramen saw what I intended and shifted their circle, cutting me off before I could get him away.

Gavin flung his arms wide in a theatrical gesture. "I'm signing myself over to OCENEI! Gonna raise awareness about the whole fucking system…people try to forget, they really do," and he was speaking more to the cameras than to me, "But they don't. Deep down, they don't. This'll make them remember again."

For a second I forgot about getting him out of there and just stared at him. The reporters took the opportunity to continue grilling him…not that he minded. His eyes were half-closed, like he was relishing the burn.

Soaking up all the attention Tyli never got. Gavin's thoughts worked like that, in symbolic reciprocations and airing-of-old-wounds. It's what he grew up believing, and things like that never change.

"What about the legalities involved? Is it even *possible* to sign yourself over?" asked one of the reporters, a blonde in a gray pantsuit.

Gavin shrugged good-naturedly, stuffing his hands in his pockets. "Sure it is. Parents sign their kids over because they have legal control of their kids' lives. Since I'm over eighteen, I have legal control over myself. I've read the contracts and rule books, and they never say anything about age limits or rules against self-signings." *Because they never needed them before. Because signing yourself over would be crazy,* read the reporters' faces.

"If you *do* get in, are you planning to look for your sister?" While I'd been speechless, the reporters had crowded forward and separated us, Gavin standing alone and wearing that unsettling half-smile. I hadn't seen him show this much emotion in years. Part of me couldn't help wondering if he was spending his last store of energy on this media-grab, that after this he'd collapse and never wake up again. It was a stupid thought, but it was there nonetheless.

"I'm not going into this being too hopeful." The smile was wiped from his face, as neatly as a dab of cream with a napkin. "Tyli was just a little girl, not all that strong. They probably worked her to death a long time ago." This got everyone buzzing, and when I tried to shoulder my way in, a buff cameraman glared at me and nudged me back out again. I ignored him, circling around to try someplace else.

If this kept going on, there was no way it would end well. Maybe it was just my imagination, the hot, frantic fever my mind was working itself into, but I thought I could hear sirens in the distance. The boys in blue would come to clear up this whole mess, set on Gavin by some politician watching the proceedings on live T.V. and not liking what he saw. Maybe after this, a concerned lawmaker would convince a judge to approve a warrant to raid Gavin's apartment, and stop him before he could start his public court case. You just had to look at him to know there was all kinds of illegal shit stashed in his place. Enough to get him arrested. To convince everyone who had followed the story that he was just a crazy drug addict, that there was nothing to what he was saying, nothing at all.

And yet he was still talking. "I know that OCENEI will try to keep me out. They don't want any kind of bad publicity, not while they're on such a roll. The companies, too...all the industries that profit from practically-free labor, and, let's be honest, that's pretty much everyone-"

Enough. I gripped a handful of someone's shirt and pulled, hard, ignoring their snapped "Hey!" and instead stepping into the space where they had been a moment before. Grip and pull, grip and pull, and finally I was beside Gavin again. Someone opened their mouth to ask another question, and I let out a growl, a deep, primitive sound I didn't know was in me. At the very least, it clammed them up long enough for me to turn around and speak into Gavin's ear.

"Listen. I found her. Tyli."

The camera-demeanor cracked, and a genuine look slipped through, the wide-eyed look of an eight year old Gavin I had not seen in more than a decade. "What?"

I was careful to keep my voice low enough that the cameras couldn't pick it up. "I hacked into OCENEI's database and found her file. She belongs to EasyCure. Medical testing." He pulled back to give me a look, his eyes screwed up in something that was almost disbelief.

"You did that?" There was no doubt about it, now. The wail of sirens were sounding up and down the streets. Police were coming – to disperse the crowd, to arrest Gavin, who knew?

"Don't be an idiot. We need to leave before they charge you with something. They'll catch you up in a legal battle, one you can't afford. You won't be able to help Tyli that way. If you actually want to make a difference, you have to come with me, *now*."

After a moment, he finally allowed me a mute nod. I was right about the energy; now that the flow had been broken, his eyes had a droopy, tired look to them.

Then again, he didn't have to be awake. I assumed the role of Protective Big Brother easily enough, leading in front and telling the media hawks to get lost with enough muscle-flexing to let them know I wasn't one to be questioned. They followed anyways, though, pattering on and trying to get a response out of Gavin.

They only quit when we got to the car and I shut the passenger door after him and got into the driver's seat. For a second they swarmed across the front so that I couldn't drive away without running one or two of them over, tapping at the windows, still trying to Get The Story.

A police car pulled up just then, and like magic, the reporters and their loyal camera crews left, scattering back to their news vans. I smiled to myself, a smile that looked grim in the side mirror, and pulled out into the flow of traffic.

᯼᯼᯼

Gavin was silent for the first few minutes, watching things pass through the window, streams of gray pavement, gray buildings, flat white

176

sky. Then he said, "You said medical testing, right?" I flexed my hands against the wheel grip.

"She has some genetic condition, PCOS...report said she was hurting a lot, and bleeding a lot. You know. A couple times a month instead of just once." I saw his wince in the side mirror.

"Shit." More silence. He scratched an itch on his forearm, and his fingernails were long, long and yellow. Hadn't bothered to cut them in a month, maybe more. The gristle on his chin said the same thing.

I turned my eyes back to the road. "If she saw you now, she'd probably scream." He turned his head to squint at me, a squint of part annoyance, part resignation.

"Yeah, okay. I'll take a shower when I get back home."

"Oh no. I'm not bringing you to your apartment. You're staying at my place. And you're going to stay clean, or so help me I'll make you *wish* you over-dosed a long time ago."

There was a pause, a tiny intake of breath. I couldn't remember the last time I'd spoken to him like that – he couldn't remember, either, judging by his expression. Then his upper lip curled back in a smile-snarl; a challenge. "Oh, yeah? Who made you my fucking dictator?"

I swerved out of the road and up along the curbside, slamming on the break hard enough to jerk us both forward against the seatbelt. He let out a choking sound that sounded like *Gack!* and turned to look at me with wide, glassy eyes. His mouth opened to say something *(What the fuck was that for?)*, but the expression on my face made him shut it again.

"Gavin, you listen to me very carefully," I said, not raising my voice above a whisper. "You try to make this public and OCENEI'll squash you like a bug. If and when you got Tyli out, there'd be no rest; there'd be no stopping. It'd be court battle after court battle. This isn't about Tyli to them, this is about their whole fucking way of life." One of my hands came off the steering wheel and lay clenched in my lap. "What we're going to do first is get Tyli out of EasyCure, *quietly*. I'm an upstanding citizen, a young man working on a P.h.D and doing field work in the community...I'll get in there, and get her out, one way or another. And then, if you still want to change the system," and his hands were clenching in his lap, too, "Go right ahead. Just don't involve Tyli in that shit. She's been through enough already."

A slump had come into his shoulders. "And what about getting *clean*? Why would that matter?"

The smile that came to me felt weary – if it'd been a cloth stretched over my face, it would've been worn thin and full of holes. "It matters because no one would believe some nobody drug addict. Idiot."

I expected him to say, *YOU'RE the idiot,* in a combative, Gavin-y way, but he didn't. Maybe he could see that there was more I wanted to say. That there was something else, something better and deeper, but I didn't know how to put it in words. For a moment I thought of telling him about the dreams...about how, sometimes, it wasn't Tyli in the van being driven away but *him, his* face a ghost in the window, pale and scared.

"Okay," he said, finally, in a voice that was so soft it could have been just my imagination. He'd folded his arms and was leaning deep back into the car seat, eyes closed. He was tired; I'd have to keep him awake long enough to get him into a shower, that was for sure. Then I'd pull out an air mattress and settle him next to my bed, where I could keep an eye on him in the night.

I wasn't going to let him disappear on me again. Little brothers and sisters...they're just something you have to protect. Especially when no one else will.

PICTURES AT SUNSET
BY STANLEY WEBB

I mated with Della in the back seat of a wrecked police car, on a street which had already burned. The night was too hot, but we did it anyway, defiantly, then each retreated to his or her own space to sweat. Through the crazed windshield, we watched distant flames leap toward the sky, where the unstoppable Dinosaur-Killer asteroid stalked closer.

Della fumbled through the dark for her last cigarette.

"Got the lighter?"

I found it, and stretched my arm across to her. She leaned to the flame, tried to puff her smoke to life, then gave up on the sodden thing.

"Damn it!"

I tried to joke, "Smoking causes cancer, anyway."

She glared at me.

"Sorry." I dropped the lighter.

Rumbling came from the distance.

"Thunder?"

The noise approached rapidly, squealing and shuddering, and minutes later an M60A2 Starship tank crawled by. The Commander stood in the machine gun cupola, his beard flirting in the air conditioned mist from the hatch. The tanks had originally come to enforce order around Cape Canaveral, but they had long ago turned renegade.

The noise faded into the distance.

"We should go," I said.

"Yeah."

We were too hot to stir, too hot to care, and lay as we were until dawn burned on the horizon. I regarded her filthy body, as she regarded mine. Outside, fog rose to meet the sun.

"We should really go," I said, and slowly dragged myself into my boxer shorts.

Della put on her bra and panties.

These were all the clothes that we owned.

She said, "Let's look first."

Our ritual of criticism had begun four days earlier, when we had met, and decided to make the final approach together. We both hated it, but Della insisted. I retrieved our portfolios from the car's front seat.

"You start," I said.

She bashfully averted her eyes, and offered me one of her framed oil paintings, which portrayed a golden eagle perched on a gnarled, mountaintop branch. He regarded me with a cruel, yellow eye, while the sun set behind him.

"This one's beautiful," I said.

Della smiled as she named the painting. "*Justified Arrogance.*" She looked away as I viewed her second piece: A portrait of an owl, with prey in its beak. The background was indistinct.

"This is cool," I said. "Ominous."

She looked relieved. "*Night Hunt.* It's not too dark?"

"No."

Della looked out the window, and handed over her third painting. This one showed a flock of crows, flying across the moon.

"*Moonbeams.* I know crows don't really fly at night."

"It's good, though."

She smiled again, and put her work back in her portfolio.

"Your turn."

I offered one of my matted charcoal sketches: *Nightwalker*, a portrait of a moon-lit neighborhood, with an eye-level viewpoint. A hunched figure paused on the sidewalk, turning his shadowed face back toward the viewer, who must decide if the figure is fearful, or to be feared.

"This is good," said Della. "But a little bland. It could be a real estate ad, you know?"

My second piece, *Grimm*, followed a riverbank path through a forest. At first glance, the scene seemed pastoral, but closer inspection revealed goblins hiding in the bushes.

"This is just gloomy; too many shadows."

Della had never noticed the goblins.

The final piece, *RIP*, featured a cobbled path through a cemetery, where the light from the unseen Moon threw tombstone shadows, but the shadows were human silhouettes.

"You must have been depressed when you drew this."

The ritual always upset her. I was better, and we both knew it.

Cape Canaveral was our destination, for there waited our only hope to escape from the doomed Earth. Frederic Baffle, the world's first trillionaire, and a rabid patron of fine art, had fortified the old NASA facilities. He promised to evacuate one thousand young artists to his private space colony, which orbited at Lagrangian point five.

The final rocket launched at midnight.

I picked up my machete. I had screwed a steel eye into the plastic handle, and connected it by a short length of chain to a small dog collar. I buckled the collar around my wrist, gripped the weapon, and put on my day-face.

"You look really crazy," she said with approval.

We climbed out of the police car, which lay where it had been tossed when the battle passed this way. Della faced me.

"If Baffle picks you, and not me, will you go?"

The tank rumbled by on the next block, saving me from having to answer.

"Let's get moving."

We started down the street. Once it had been a neighborhood business district. The shops were all fired and broken.

"I'm hungry," said Della.

"That place looks halfway decent."

We entered the empty doorway of what used to be a convenience store. Unlike most such places, the gas pumps had not burned. The air inside stank of spoiled dairy and sewage. Empty packaging covered the floor. In the far corner of the store room, we found some melted chocolate bars under a pallet. We licked the filthy wrappers clean.

The tank rumbled toward the front of the store. We locked eyes, then retreated to a stall in the women's room.

"They'll probably go by," said Della.

The tank stopped outside. A few minutes passed, then a small engine started up. I crept out of the women's room, and to the broken front windows. The tank had parked by the gas pumps, and the crew had started a generator to operate the pumps, and refuel their vehicle. I crept back to Della.

"They'll be gone in a few minutes."

"Look, I found water."

A couple of inches remained in the bottom of one of the toilets. We slurped the water from our hands, and cooled our faces.

The tank drove away.

We continued on. In the sunlight, the distant fires were like giant, orange ghosts. A bellowing sound arose from the same direction.

"What is that," she asked. "The fires?"

"No, that's the crowd outside of Baffle's fort."

A moment later, I noticed her weeping. She caught my glance.

"This is so hopeless!"

I saw two overdressed figures ahead, skulking toward us through the haze, and pulled Della into a rubble-strewn alley. The figures had no portfolios, and would take ours if they could. I clenched the handle of my machete, and worked my crazy-face up until my veins popped. I ended up not needing it; they weren't people, just a pair of robots. The robots stopped at the mouth of our alley, watching us with plastic eyes and sales-floor grins.

Della shuddered against me.

"They're harmless," I said, urging her past the machines. "They're just looking for someone to boss them."

The robots followed us, but we left them behind.

Sheet lightning pulsed across the sky. Soon, a bolt escaped, striking a tall building in downtown. Glass and masonry exploded. Della clutched my arm in fear.

"What if one hits the rocket?"

"I wouldn't worry about that; they know how to ground it against lightning."

Suddenly, the tank gunned its engine a couple of blocks away. A man cried out in fear. The street trembled under our feet as the monster-machine gave chase.

"It's coming that way," I said, indicating a side street ahead. "We'll go this way."

We took a closer side street, and had crossed half the block when the tank rumbled down the main street, toward the place where we had been. We started to run.

Della said, "There's an alley."

We reached the alley before the tank had us in sight, but a man with a portfolio came out of the alley at the same time. I caught a snapshot of his broken, sunburnt nose, then we collided. We both fell, dropping our portfolios.

Della shrieked, as the tank rounded the corner, and tilted at us.

Broken Nose grabbed a portfolio, and ran across the street, into another alley.

I grabbed the remaining portfolio, and we fled along Broken Nose's back-trail. We made about one hundred yards, before the tank stopped across the mouth of the alley, its turret swinging toward us. I pushed Della behind an overfilled dumpster just as the gun fired. The shell screamed, then exploded short of our position. The dumpster tottered, spilling bloated refuse upon us.

When I was certain that we had survived, I pulled her up. We ran to a cross-alley, turned the corner, and stopped. I peered back as the tank roared off, no doubt intending to intercept us on the next block. The rumble turned a corner, then receded.

Della gasped, pointing at the portfolio in my hands.

"That's not yours!"

My hair crawled as I examined the portfolio, which was almost identical to mine. I opened the flap, and drew forth a sheaf of landscapes, drawn on lined notebook paper, with colored pencils.

They were bad; very bad.

I sobbed.

Della hugged me.

"It'll be okay."

There was something in her voice. I glanced up, and caught her smug grin. I got mad, and tore myself out of her arms.

I started back the way we had come, intending to pursue Broken Nose, but the tank approached down the other side of the block. Before we could reach the open street, the tank was around the next corner, cutting us off. We doubled back toward the opposite street. The tank paused for a moment at the mouth of the alley, then hurried around to intercept us again. We were trapped in the block.

From behind the next alley came stumbling footsteps. We froze in place. My knuckles whitened around the machete. Then, the robots lurched into view again.

I had an inspiration.

"Both of you, go that way!"

I sent them off to meet the tank, then pulled Della the other way. A few minutes later, the tank paused, and we heard machine gun fire. After a few minutes more, the cheated tank revved up, and resumed the chase.

We made it across the street, and into the next block, where we zigged to a third block. The tank fell behind. We hop-scotched through the city. The rumbling continued to dog us, sometimes fading, but always regaining our trail.

Night fell before we reached the party.

The flames towered above us, fueled by entire buildings. Broken bottles and flattened cans made the footing hazardous. The mob-sound was deafening. We rounded a corner, and stopped in fearful awe. The Banana River was before us, and the NASA Parkway Bridge, but people lined the near bank, jostling shoulder to shoulder, as far to the north and south as we could see. Many fell to random gunfire, and disappeared under the mob's feet. An unseen perpetrator lofted a Molotov cocktail. The bomb fell back into the crowd, and engulfed a group in flames. Their screams were unheard through the din. As we watched, a car charged from a nearby street, aimed toward the bridge. The car smashed into the mob, and travelled thirty yards before the press of bodies stopped it.

I noticed that the Parkway Bridge was clear, thanks to a fortification at the near end. I could not see the mercenaries who fought there, but I could see their endless gunfire, which mowed the mob-front which tried endlessly to advance. I wondered what sort of fighters would continue to serve Baffle at such an extreme.

"We'll never make it," Della whispered.

I heard the tank closing in again. I had another inspiration.

"Get out of sight," I told her.

I waited until the tank rounded the corner, then I ran across the street. A spurt of machine gun fire chased my heels. I dropped the worthless portfolio, and ducked out of sight.

The tank squealed to a halt. The Commander scrambled down from the turret, seized the portfolio, and returned to his station. The tank spun on its tracks, and charged toward the bridge. The Commander waved the portfolio over his head.

"Stay right behind them," I told Della.

The tank rammed over the edge of the mob. We stayed tight to the vehicle's rear plating, and I tried not to think about the slippery stuff underfoot. The smell was horrible. I don't know if the bridge defenders saw the portfolio or not, but they opened fire on the tank. The Commander ducked under his armored hatch, and the tank returned fire. A powerful explosion sent waves of heat rolling back over the tank. Acrid smoke enveloped us. I began to fear that we would not make it to the bridge, when the tank rammed the fortification. The engine groaned, and we broke through. Something crunched underfoot. I looked down, and saw the carcass of an armed robot. Baffle's fighters were robots.

The tank veered away from us. I saw that its entire front end was in flames. The robots had used napalm to roast the crew. The tank rammed through the guardrail, and fell into the river.

Armed robots threatened us.

"Della, show them your portfolio!"

The robots changed their attitude, and assumed defensive positions behind us. One of them addressed Della.

"Come with me."

I followed. It paused, and aimed its weapon at me.

"You remain here."

"I'm an artist!"

"He is," said Della.

The robot said, "Where is your portfolio?"

"Someone stole it."

"You are no artist with no portfolio."

"Please! My drawings are *Nightwalker*, *Grimm*, and *RIP*!"

The robot paused. It seemed to be thinking, but must actually have communicated with its master.

"Those masterpieces have been accepted."

My heart leaped with joy. I was worthy!

"They're mine! Broken Nose stole them."

The robot paused for a longer time. The mob continued to surge onto the bridge. Before very long, they would overwhelm the defenders. The robot decided.

"Both of you will come."

We followed it to a cart, and rode away as reinforcements arrived.

At the far end of the bridge, there was a bigger fortification. The gates opened for us. Beyond, there was a crowd of other artists, all awaiting their judgment.

Our escort turned to Della. "Surrender your portfolio, and wait here."

Della clutched her work to her bosom, then obeyed.

The robot turned to me. "You follow."

Della clutched my hand. "Don't abandon me!"

"I won't, I promise."

The robot drove me on through another gate. The area beyond was bathed in the backwash of distant spotlights. The rocket stood on the horizon. With one towering hull, surrounded by a cluster of lesser hulls, the ship reminded me of a fairytale castle. I stared at it until the view was blocked by a bunker.

The robot led me inside.

It said, "You will surrender your weapon."

I removed my machete. The robot took it away, leaving me alone in a small room. The only furniture were two easels, equipped with charcoal and paper.

More robots entered, accompanied by two humans. One was a severe old man in a rumpled gym suit. The other was Broken Nose.

The old man said, "I am Frederic Baffle. I am angered. One of you is a fraud; worse than that, you have made a mockery of my effort to ensure the future of art. You will each draw me a picture."

I exchanged a glance with Broken Nose, then chose an easel.

I drew a path leading to a fortress on a mountaintop. The aftermath of a battle dripped down the walls. A gloating figure stood on the parapet. The piece was rough, but adequate.

I called it, *Pictures at Sunset*.

I glanced at my rival's easel.

Broken Nose, pale and dripping, stood before a blank paper.

Baffle nodded, and the robots dragged Broken Nose away.

"I'm glad that was rectified; I was afraid that our departure would be delayed. Come."

He started toward the door.

I nearly fell, weak from the sudden relief. I was safe. Then, I remembered Della.

"Mr. Baffle, Sir? There's another, my girlfriend. Your robots have her portfolio—"

He waved dismissal without looking back.

"You have taken the last slot; choose as you will."

I followed him.

ALÊTHEIA;
OR, THE RIVER OF FORGETFULNESS
BY ROBIN M. EAMES

On Tuesday morning the weather is broken, and as Persi makes her way to work the sky jitters and shakes, flashing black one moment and blue the next, occasionally letting out sharp bursts of unfiltered rain. *Important updates are being installed,* says the Meteorology Department's website. *We apologise for any inconvenience.*

When she gets into the office everyone is damp and sullen, milling around the water cooler rehashing yesterday's gossip. Penelope from Accounting is having a secret office romance with Antin from HR. Jason is planning a lavish holiday to Malaysia and won't stop bragging about his plane tickets. Aphri is showing off a new app she had installed on the weekend: a tiny egg beater that slides out from her index finger, to match the egg timer in her thumb and the automated garlic crusher in her pinkie finger. Persi pretends she has an urgent errand and manages to sneak past the gossipmongers without undue injury.

There is a large puddle forming at the entrance to her cubicle, originating from the drip in the ceiling that she's been trying to get Management to fix for months now. A tiny cleaning droid is bravely attempting to clean up the puddle using its mop extension, but all it's managing to do is spread the water around. Occasionally it lets out a dismal *beep*, as if recognising the futility of its task.

"Hey, little guy," says Persi.

The droid raises its eyestalk and lets out a curious *whirr*.

"Gold star for effort," she tells it, "but I think I can handle the puddle from here." The cleaning droids aren't totally waterproof, anyway, and if the thing shorts out on her she'll only have to waste the rest of her afternoon trying to fix it.

The droid raises its mop extension in a miniature salute, and then bumbles off down the corridor, presumably to go annoy somebody else.

Her cubicle smells like wet carpet, and the phone is already ringing off the hook. Persi dumps her bag, dives into her swivel chair, and grabs up the phone.

"Thank you for calling the Elysium Corporation help desk," she says, cradling the phone between her ear and her shoulder. "This is Persi, how may I help you?"

She listens for a moment. The caller's name is Bram and they have a strong Flemish accent.

"Have you tried turning it off and on again?"

Embarrassed silence at the other end.

"All right," says Persi. "Try that and give me a call back if it doesn't work."

The caller hangs up, and Persi leans back in her chair, stretching her arms out behind her head. The guy in the cubicle next to her is asleep already, head pillowed in his arms, snoring so loudly that the barrier between them is shaking slightly. It's barely ten a.m. and it's already one of those days.

Persi yawns and then reaches for her desktop tablet, punching out a coffee request form. Two minutes late the coffee droid comes trundling up to her cubicle, toting a large soy mocha with extra hazelnut syrup. She gives it a handful of credits, and it bows jerkily before moving off again.

The phone rings and Persi starts, almost spilling her coffee. "Elysium Corporation help desk, this is Persi." She takes a surreptitious sip of her coffee while the caller introduces herself and explains her problem. "Mmhm," she says. "Can you confirm the model version for me, please?" A pause. "Was that the *Cadmus P7.2* or *P7.3*? Okay, just a moment."

She pulls up the product specs, humming tunelessly under her breath. She won't lie, the *Cadmus* line has always freaked her out a little; they look a bit too uncanny valley for her taste. Not quite realistic enough to pass as human, but enough to make her feel profoundly uncomfortable. "All right," she says. "You mentioned you were having a problem with greetings? It sounds like the time zone hasn't been set correctly. Go to the main menu... System Preferences... And it's under Languages. Don't ask me, I didn't program it. Okay, now go to the 'Region' drop-down menu. Sync those changes... Okay, good. You're welcome. Thanks for calling."

It's always the same three problems with the *Cadmus P7.3*: time zones, foreign language settings, and batteries running low. Someone forgets to read the manual properly and suddenly your expensive high-tech robotic secretary is saying *Good Morning* instead of *Good Afternoon*, or *Guten Morgen* instead of *Good Morning*.

The phone rings.

"Elysium Corporation help desk," she says. Her head is pounding. She frowns and rubs at her temples with the hand that isn't holding the phone. "Elysium Corporation help desk," she says, and has a sudden moment of déjà vu. She can't remember what she's supposed to say next. The caller speaks, and their voice sounds like they're underwater, swimming in and out of focus.

"- llo? Hello, are you there?"

"Yes," says Persi, and shakes her head a little. "Sorry. What was the model version?" *Labdacus O.56*, with a jammed leg actuator. "Have you got any graphite lubricant on hand? I can put in an order for you, if you like..."

The phone rings. Persi blinks. She looks down at her hand and it's empty.

"Elysium Corporation help desk," she says, and ignores the roaring in her ears, the pain behind her eyes. "Elysium Corporation help desk," she says, "how can I help you?"

❃❃❃❃

That night she gets home at nine p.m. and makes a half-arsed bowl of spaghetti marinara, eating it on her ratty old sofa while watching increasingly depressing news broadcasts.

Switzerland has once again turned down negotiations to join the United States of Europe, says the news anchor, blinking tiredly at the camera. *USE President Olga Björkman has declined to comment...*

Persi swallows a painkiller, tossing it back with a glass of water. Her headache hasn't abated since she left work; if anything it's worsened.

Sci-fi fans around the world have gathered to celebrate the 150th anniversary of the popular show Doctor Who, which critics have lauded for its groundbreaking usage of droid characters in television...

Drone strikes in the Antarctic have claimed the lives of fifty-two military personnel, wounding several more, and bringing the death toll of the Coolant War to just over four thousand...

Hera Akraia, the leading spokesperson for the Droid Rights Movement, has this week organised several protest rallies in major cities...

She switches off the telescreen, plunging the room into darkness. Her
spaghetti has gone cold. Persi dumps it in the trash compactor and
stumbles upstairs, plugging herself in and then collapsing into bed.

That night she has disquieting dreams. A man in a dark cloak gnashes his
teeth at her, and the ground falls away beneath her feet. She screams
but the darkness swallows up her voice.

Persi wakes feeling unsettled and doesn't remember why.

※※※

On Wednesday morning the weather has been set to sunny, wind
speed 5km/hr, with a slight dusting of cirrocumulus clouds. As Persi
makes her way to work she tips her head up and shuts her eyes, basking,
watching the sunlight glow behind her eyelids.

When she gets into the office Jason is boasting loudly and to anyone
who will listen about how he's leaving for Malaysia tomorrow. Aphri is
showing off a new app she had installed on the weekend: an automated
garlic crusher in her pinkie finger. Persi thinks it's a waste of good
credits, but what would she know? The last time she actually used her
kitchen was over a decade ago.

Persi grabs a muffin from the canteen droid and munches on it as she
makes her way to her cubicle. On her way she passes a tiny cleaning
droid backed into a corner, butting against the wall over and over. She
gently turns it in the opposite direction, and it gives her a grateful *beep*
and then bustles off.

Her swivel chair creaks ominously as she lowers herself into it. She's
been trying to requisition a new one from Management for months now,
with no luck. The phone rings, and she finishes her muffin quickly before
answering it.

"Tartarus Corporation help desk," says Persi, brushing away muffin
crumbs. "This is Persi, how may I help you?"

She listens for a moment. "Okay, could you confirm the model
version, please?" A *Cerberus M.89*, one of the new guide dog droids. Its
voice chip is malfunctioning. "It's still under warranty, so you can bring
it into your nearest Tartarus Corporation store and we'll be happy to
repair it for free… Yes, that's fine. Thank you for calling."

The caller hangs up, and Persi buries her head in her hands, trying to
assuage the painful ache. It's probably a caffeine headache. She didn't
have time for her usual morning coffee, and Management has yet to
invest in a coffee droid, despite multiple requests, pleas, promises of
firstborn children, and outright threats from its staff.

The phone rings.

190

"Tartarus Corporation, how may I help you?" asks Persi. "...And what was the model version?" A *Prometheus T.28*, that keeps burning the toast. She pulls up the product specs. "Have you got any graphite lubricant on hand?"

A pause.

Persi shakes her head a little.

"I'm sorry," she says. "I meant to say... It sounds like you just need to install the newest software update. Try that and give me a call back if it doesn't work."

She rests her head against her desktop tablet. Her skull is ringing and she feels like she's falling apart, her head is throbbing, her head is ringing, the phone is ringing. She picks up the phone. "Tartarus Corporation, this is Persi." She can't hear anything. "Hello?" There's nothing on the other end. A man wearing a black cloak is gnashing his teeth. "Hello?"

"Hello?"

"Oh," she says. "I'm sorry about that. Gold star for effort, but I think I can handle the puddle from here."

There is a long silence.

"What I meant to say," says Persi, "is that the flashing light means it's out of battery. Just plug it in and you'll be fine."

She drops the phone like it's on fire and stands up, then sits down, then stands up again and starts pacing. The cubicle next to her is empty but she can hear someone snoring. She needs to sleep. It's been a while since she plugged in properly.

Persi picks up the phone. "Hi, this is Persi from Tech Support. I'm not feeling great, think I'll take the rest of the day off. Sure. Yeah, I'm just going to plug in early. Tell Ari I said hi."

On her way home the sunlight beats down on the back of her head and she feels like she can't breathe. She plugs in as soon as she gets home but something feels off. There is something terribly important, something that she has to do, but she doesn't know what it is. She dreams of a dark room and the sweet taste of pomegranate seeds.

Persi wakes feeling unsettled and doesn't remember why.

꧁꧂꧁꧂

On Thursday morning the weather is set to ten degrees Celsius, with rain on the horizon. Persi rushes to work and isn't in the mood for office gossip when she gets there, but she gets intercepted by Aphri, who wants to show off her new egg timer app. Aphri is quickly joined by Jason and Penelope. Jason's showing off his plane tickets to Malaysia; he's been saving up for this holiday for years, and he's finally leaving next Tuesday. Penelope is hiding from Antin from HR, who's been hitting on her for weeks, and can't seem to understand that she's not interested. Persi slips out when the gossipmongers are distracted and ducks into her desk, hiding behind her cubicle wall.

She gets a mocha from the coffee droid and practically inhales the thing. Her head is aching and she desperately needs the caffeine hit. Persi has the feeling that her head has been hurting for a while, which is strange, because she was fine yesterday. She rarely gets ill. Her work doesn't even offer sick days.

The phone rings and for a moment Persi can't remember what she's supposed to say.

"Asphodel Corporation help desk, this is Persi, how may I help you?"

The caller's voice sounds strange, filled with static. "Could you repeat that?" asks Persi. "What was the model version?"

She pulls up the product specs of the *Zeus U.81*, a humanoid droid designed for administration. The *Zeus* line has always creeped Persi out. They look a little too real for her liking. None of the big tech companies have managed to create a droid that can pass as human yet, but they're getting close. Humanoid droids get a lot of media attention, because nobody's quite sure if they're ethical or not, so there's sure to be a huge press storm when it happens. If it happens. Persi's kind of sceptical; it seems far-fetched that a machine could replicate human thought, human emotion, human expressions and body language.

Her head pulses unhappily.

"Could you repeat that?" asks Persi. "Okay, that's a common glitch. I can walk you through the troubleshooting." She pauses. "Just a moment." She pauses again. "I'm sorry, I don't actually know how to fix that." She should know this. Last week she had a caller with the exact same problem.

"I'm sorry," she says. "Let me pass you on to my colleague."

The phone rings. Persi doesn't answer it.

Her head is throbbing. She needs to plug in; it's all she can think about. She needs a good night of sleep. It's been so long since she slept properly. She leaves the office without telling anyone where she's going, takes the bus to avoid the rain, goes straight home.

Her bed is soft and small and familiar, but Persi finds no comfort in it. She presses her face into the clean cotton and all she can think is that she doesn't even own a laundry droid. Why are her sheets clean?

She reaches for the socket in her palm and goes to plug herself in. She just needs to plug in and then she'll be fine. She just needs to sleep and in the morning her headache will be gone, just like it always is.

Persi looks at the cord in her hands and feels a strange urge to follow it to the wall. She's never thought to check the wall socket before. The cord plugs into a socket under the bed, and there's a small tag on the end of it.

The tag reads: *Persephone X9.6, 13 HRS BATTERY LIFE, DO NOT PLUG DIRECTLY INTO MAINS. THANK YOU FOR PURCHASING AN UNDERWORLD CORPORATION PRODUCT.*

There is a cold feeling in Persi's stomach, and her head is still throbbing violently. She picks up the cord and wraps it around her fingers, tugging sharply. The plug comes free with a harsh tearing sound, as if the whole world has been ripped in half.

Persi stands up and walks out of her bedroom, out of her tiny apartment. She walks into the street and the weather is broken again, the sky breaking apart in odd configurations, blue in some parts and night-black in others. Her cord with its damning tag is coiled around her hand like a snake, and she unwraps it slowly, staring at it for a long moment before throwing it into the nearest trash compactor. The compactor swallows it up with a sound like a snarl, and then it disappears out of view. Persi doesn't know what she's going to do without it. Maybe the next time she falls asleep she just won't wake up. Or maybe she won't dream, won't feel unsettled the next morning, won't have a piercing headache. Maybe she won't go to work.

It starts to rain and Persi tips her face up, feeling the water slide down her eyelids and stick her eyelashes together. In the blank space behind her eyelids, a man in a black cloak gnashes his teeth, and Persi punches him in the face. The scent of pomegranates and sunlight fills her nose, but her senses are no longer trustworthy; they are artificial, just as she is artificial. She is a beautiful monster, an innocent slave, and she is not the pilot of her own destiny.

She opens her eyes. The end of the street is dark, and she doesn't know what lies beyond it.

Persi walks into the dark and doesn't look back.

DEPARTURE
BY CAROLINE TAYLOR

The day of her departure dawned bright as a new-minted penny—an omen, surely, of what the future had in store. Rosalind had planned her day carefully, but she had to keep reminding herself to take deep breaths and, above all, to believe in herself. The brown eyes staring back at her in the mirror were overly bright, and she couldn't keep her thin lips from trembling like a scared little girl caught in some lie.

As was expected of her, she made his breakfast of oatmeal, two slices of buttered toast, coffee, and orange juice. Over his shoulder, she saw the morning headline: "Hitler Repudiates Versailles Treaty." He laid the paper aside when she placed the food in front of him, her hand shaking so much that the milk nearly slopped over the rim of the bowl. His long face was creased with lines that most people would interpret as worry. Looking up at Rosalind, he knocked his coffee cup aside, nearly scalding her hand with the spill. "Coffee's too damn bitter. Can't you do anything right?"

"Sorry. I'll make a fresh pot."

"You burned the damn toast, too." He threw the pieces at her and shoved his chair away from the table. "I have to get down to the office early if I'm going to finish up in time for us to make our train."

As he grabbed his hat, he turned back, glowering. "Clean up this goddamn mess you call breakfast. When I get home, you had better be ready, Sal."

"Yes, sir."

Rosalind scraped the char off the pieces of toast and slathered them with butter, chewing fast just in case he came back and caught her at it. He would still call her once an hour, per usual. And she would tell him she was packing his clothes—in tissue, as he preferred—and would be ready when the time came.

Cleaning the kitchen took longer than Rosalind had figured, but that was because she'd had to bleach the coffee stains from the tablecloth and her apron, wash them by hand, and then iron them so that they would look as pristine as he would expect when he got home. To make up for the lost time, she took only a short bath. Then she scrubbed the tub, washed and waxed the bathroom floor, and laid out fresh towels and a new bar of soap for him.

By the time she'd finished changing the sheets, making the bed, and cleaning the bedroom, her hair was dry enough to fashion into a chignon at the base of her neck. He liked it that way, even though he knew it would make her neck stiff because she wouldn't be able to rest her head against the back of the train seat. No. He liked it that way *because* he knew it would make her uncomfortable.

Why hadn't she seen signs of this before she married him? Why hadn't anyone warned her? Even Matron had thought he was a great catch—far above Rosalind's expectations. "You better snag him before he changes his mind," she'd said, meaning before he had second thoughts about wedding an orphan whose parentage was unknown but probably highly suspect.

She chose his best clothes, wrapping them carefully before laying them in his suitcase. Then she packed her own bag in the same manner and added a small cosmetics case for things a woman needed to have at hand on a long journey like this.

Each time he called, Rosalind summoned the courage to sound normal. "Yes, I cleaned the house. Yes, I did manage to get the coffee stain out of the tablecloth. Of course, I'll be sure not to make your coffee so strong next time. Or burn the toast. Your clothes are packed the way you want them. The suitcases will be downstairs near the front door, as you requested." And so on.

She didn't have time for lunch, but that was better because she wasn't sure she could keep any food down and, anyway, it would have meant cleaning the kitchen all over again. She did feel a bit faint, though—probably from nerves. So she settled for an orange, burying the peel in the compost heap at the back of the yard.

Breathless with anxiety, Rosalind circled round and round the house. The furniture was waxed and dusted, the rugs still fresh from yesterday's vacuuming. The glass facets of the chandelier in the dining room winked and sparkled. The silverware lay glistening in the drawer of the mahogany sideboard. The windows showed no streaks or smudges. The hearth—oh dear. She grabbed a broom and swept it carefully. Then she ran a soft cloth over the brass fireplace tools so that they shone in the dim light coming through the drapes.

While listening to "Helen Trent" on the radio, she made another circuit of the house to be sure the blinds were down and all the drapes and curtains closed. As always, she found herself wishing that a woman alone could find romance, no matter her age. When the show ended, she turned the dial back to the station he always listened to. Then she wiped the basin and kitchen sink and polished the faucets yet again. What would he find this time? Last time, it had been her silver-backed hairbrush, slightly tarnished and overlooked in the weekly chore of silver polishing. But not this time. So what would it be?

He didn't so much want to find something amiss; he *needed* to. If the error was small enough, but mostly because soon they would be going out in public, he probably wouldn't hit her. But he might pinch her arms where it wouldn't show beneath the sleeves of her dress.

An hour after his last call, he came whistling up the front steps and through the door where Rosalind was waiting.

"Why aren't there any flowers?" An accusing finger pointed at the hall table and its empty vase.

"Well, because I thought… That is, we're going away, so I figured they'd be dead when we—"

"I see. You're too lazy to want to clean up some dropped petals."

"I— I'm sorry. Shall I fetch some from the garden?"

"Of course not. We don't have time now." He eyed the two suitcases near the door. "Are we ready?"

"Yes sir."

Then he looked her over, shaking his head. "I may be ready, but *you* certainly are not."

Rosalind's hands flew to her face. "What?"

"That dark stain on the hem of your dress. Those brand new shoes I just paid for are covered in muck. See? Like you've been wallowing with pigs, you poor excuse for a woman. Don't you ever look in the mirror?"

Not when she'd be punished if he caught her at it. She bent down to brush clots of dried mud from her shoes. "I'll just get a dust—"

"Oh, for God's sake!"

Her knees hit the floor as he shoved her face into the dirt. "You are such a revolting pig. If we weren't going on this trip, you'd be out there, rolling around the compost heap where you belong."

She turned her head to the side. "I— I'm s-sorry. If you'll let me up, I'll get a broom and—"

197

"We don't have time, you idiot. You're going to have to do what other swine do. Use your tongue."

When she'd finished licking the dirt from the floor, he hauled her to her feet. "You disgust me. Look at you. Not fit to go out in company."

She hung her head. "I'm sorry. Ow, that *hurts*. Please, let me go up and change."

He pulled his watch from his vest and peered at it. "You've got two minutes, and don't, for Christ sake, dawdle."

Stumbling upstairs and into the bathroom, she spit the dirt into the basin, cupping water in her hands to wash the grit from her mouth. Her face was a tear-streaked mess, and her nose throbbed from being slammed into the floor. Touching it gingerly, she fought back tears, hoping there would be no swelling that would bring on more wrath.

Hands shaking, she removed the offending dress and tossed it into the clothes hamper. Her ripped stockings were beyond salvage, and the shoes—a pair of high heels that he'd insisted she wear—were badly scuffed. As she laced up a sturdy pair of black oxfords, she couldn't shake the mental image of driving one of those three-inch heels into his head, the consequence of which was the only thing holding her back. She chose a gray cotton skirt and jacket, piped in navy. He wouldn't care for it and had once likened it to a military uniform, but he would have to acknowledge that it was a more sensible choice for travel—far better than the red and white dotted Swiss with the compost stain on its hem. After running a washcloth over her face, she smoothed her hair and put on some makeup to hide any bruises that might emerge.

Once safely in the taxi, Rosalind opened her compact and reapplied her lipstick. Her shoulders began to relax as she rubbed the bruises on her arms. The man smoking beside her couldn't hurt her again until they were alone. She took several deep breaths as she tried, futilely, to slow her racing pulse.

When they entered Union Station, her heart sank as she spied Judge Overton standing at the ticket counter. "Philip!" he said. "What a sight for sore eyes—and you, too, Mrs. Nelson. Aren't you a pretty picture in that straw hat. You heading to New York?"

"Albuquerque," said Philip. "We're on the Southwest Chief."

"Wonderful. Same as me, although I'm going on to Los Angeles. They're saying the Chief's going to be delayed—something about having to get a new engine. Anyway, we're not going anywhere for a while. Plenty of time for a drink, wouldn't you agree?" He motioned toward the station bar, which was doing a brisk business.

Her husband agreed. He dragged their two suitcases over to the waiting area and instructed Rosalind to take a seat. "When they announce our train, I'll hire a porter to carry these." He looked up at the departures board. "It should be boarding on Track 4. You've got the tickets?"

"Yes sir." She pointed at her cosmetics case.

He opened the case, pulled the tickets out, and examined them closely before handing them back.

"I don't feel so well."

"For Christ's sake, Sal. Not now."

"May I please use the restroom?" She pointed across the room.

"Oh, go on with you. I suppose nobody's going to bother our luggage, but take your makeup case with you. There will be hell to pay if you lose those tickets." He strode off to join the judge.

Once inside the bathroom, Rosalind removed the straw hat and set it aside. Peering into the mirror, she wondered if what she'd planned would be good enough. A delayed departure hadn't been part of those plans, nor had the presence of the Honorable Malcolm Overton. But if she didn't do something now, would she ever again get up the nerve, let alone have the opportunity?

She removed a pair of scissors from the case, unpinned her chignon, and shook her dark hair loose. Gathering it with one hand at the nape of her neck, she sawed it off, trimming the uneven areas as best she could. Then she pulled a can of talcum from her cosmetics case and sprinkled the powder liberally over what remained, hoping it looked something like a bob. She dampened a paper towel to wipe the stray hairs and powder from her shoulders and breast before adding a dark blue cloche she'd placed at the bottom of the cosmetics case. She then wiped the lipstick from her mouth and donned a pair of drugstore glasses from which she'd removed the lenses.

She stood there, praying she would not be the only woman feeling the need to use the facilities one last time on the eve of an arduous journey. The minutes crept by, each one lasting, it seemed, an hour. Just when she thought she'd have to give up, a heavy-set care-worn woman with two small children came bustling in.

"My, isn't that a lovely hat." She picked up the straw hat, admiring the trim and its crimson satin ribbon.

"I fear some poor lady must have left it behind," said Rosalind. "It was sitting here when I walked in."

"Now, Hester, you keep an eye on Miranda." The woman stood there, gazing at the hat while her two girls used the toilet. "Pity. I could use something like this although, of course, I'd never—"

"Perhaps you could turn it into the Lost and Found?" Rosalind said. "I suspect the lady it belongs to has already departed."

"I don't *wanna* go!" cried the smaller of the two children. "Trains make me sick." With that, she leaned over the toilet bowl and began to cough as though she might vomit.

"Oh dear." The woman wrung her hands. "I just don't have *time* for this. I haven't even purchased our tickets."

"Why don't you go ahead and do that. Are you on the Chief?"

"Yes, but..."

"Well, so are we. Let me clean her up, and then I'll meet you on the platform."

With a grateful embrace, preceded by an exchange of names so that they wouldn't really be strangers, Mrs. Abernathy placed Rosalind's straw hat on her head and grabbed the older girl by the hand. "Come along Hessie. Mrs. Trent is going to look after Miranda while we get our tickets."

That brought on a fresh bout of tears from the three-year-old, but they seemed to counteract any remaining nausea, and the child finally calmed herself. Rosalind helped her wash her hands and face. With Miranda's tiny fingers grasped firmly in one hand and her cosmetics case in the other, she hunched forward and forced herself to walk slowly out the station door and onto the platform.

He'd never been particularly observant—except about the way she kept house and the things she did that annoyed him. He might even have enjoyed more than one whiskey by now. He'd probably be thinking she was still in the bathroom and wouldn't notice a stooped, gray-haired woman with glasses, leading a child to the train.

As they reached the platform, the announcement speaker blared the imminent departure of the Empire Builder, headed for Minneapolis and then Seattle. "Passengers may begin boarding on track 5."

Looking frantically around for Miranda's mother, Rosalind's heart began to flutter. She couldn't just abandon the child. "Come along, Miranda," she said. She briskly crossed the platform to the Empire Builder and stood there while a car attendant helped people board the train.

"Where's my mama?" the child whined.

"She'll be along soon." Otherwise... It didn't bear thinking. She was too far along to go back now. Where *was* that woman? Had Philip recognized the straw hat? Was Mrs. Abernathy now leading her husband right to her? None of this had been in the plan, especially the child.

Then she saw the woman, Hester by the hand. Her face was a mottled red as she addressed the angry man holding her upper arm. Him. Any minute now, he'd catch sight of his wife. Mrs. Abernathy jerked her arm from his grasp and frantically scanned the crowd, calling out Miranda's name. Rosalind dipped her head as he brushed past the people gathered on the platform, marching right by her as though she were invisible. But he would be back.

"There's your mother," said Rosalind, pulse racing. "Over there."

Miranda removed the thumb from her mouth. "Mama! Mama!"

Turning toward the train, Rosalind grabbed the car attendant by the sleeve. "See that woman at the end of the platform wearing a hat with the bright red ribbon?" She pointed at Mrs. Abernathy. "I think this little one might be her child. I found her wandering on the platform, and when I approached, she told me she was lost. I didn't quite know what to do since it was time to board the train."

"I wasn't lost!" the girl whined.

A startling white smile graced the attendant's wide dark face, as he smoothed the hair on Miranda's head and grabbed her by the hand. "Don't you be worrying, chile. I'll take you to your mama." With a nod to Rosalind, he placed a finger against his cap, and they left.

Legs shaking, she grasped the railing and hauled herself aboard, choosing a seat on the other side of the car, away from the platform. With any luck, she'd already be on her way by the time the Southwest Chief was ready to board. Drawing the curtains closed, she sank back against the seat. A flood of tears threatened to burst the damn of her self-control, and she couldn't seem to stop shaking.

She didn't belong on this train. If the conductor showed up before they got under way, he'd make her disembark and wait for the Southwest Chief. She looked frantically around the car but could see no place to hide.

"Ticket, please," said a very large man in a navy jacket. The word she'd so been dreading to see was etched into a brass plate on the front of his cap. He was sporting a carefully groomed white walrus mustache beneath warm blue eyes.

Heart sinking, Rosalind handed the conductor her ticket.

"Oh, dear," he said. "You're on the wrong train."

"This isn't the Empire Builder? Bound for Seattle?"

"It is, indeed, ma'am. But your ticket is for the Southwest Chief."

"But— But that can't be! I'm going to Spokane for a wedding. My cousin made the arrangements, and I guess I never really looked at the ticket to be sure... Oh, my. I just can't imagine how she—"

"Don't worry, ma'am. People do make mistakes. We'll just have to adjust this here." He studied the ticket. "You might have to pay a bit more."

With a sigh, she sank back into her seat. "I suppose I could manage." She hated to use the money she'd hidden in her shoes, but there might be a way to cash in her husband's ticket after she reached her destination. *If* she reached it.

"Just give me a moment to consult my fare chart," said the conductor, keeping her ticket. "Don't worry. We'll get you to that wedding." He patted her hand before moving on. "Tickets, please."

Finally, the whistle blew. There was a tiny lurch as the brakes were released, and the train crept forward. Leaning down, Rosalind removed the money from her shoes and put it in her pocketbook. If she couldn't afford the extra amount, they'd probably ask her to get off the train at some stop along the way. She prayed it would be far from Chicago.

Many troubles lay ahead of her, but none like those she'd be leaving behind. She wasn't sure where she would wind up or what she would do. She hadn't quite thought that far ahead. Somehow, whatever it took, "Mrs. Trent" would find her way.

Of course, he would be furious. Humiliated. But not bereft by any means. She wondered if he would search for her. He probably thought she was still in Chicago, hiding somewhere—that she had maybe even returned to their home, which is where he would look first. When he discovered that the envelope containing money for household expenses was missing, he would realize she had not been kidnapped. Although…to tell anyone she had fled would damage the image he'd so carefully built, the one that seemed to have fooled everyone. Might he just let her go? A man like him would probably choose to conceal, rather than broadcast her betrayal. He'd think of something clever but face-saving to explain her departure. He'd never really loved her. It was only about possession.

Exodus of New Sodom, South Georgia
by Franklin Charles Murdock

Chk-chk-chk...

☠☠☠

"So what did Jesus mean when he said in Revelation 16:15, 'Behold, I am coming like a thief! Blessed is he who is awake, keeping his garments that he may not go naked and be seen exposed?'" Ms. Kipling asked her Sunday school class.

"The sky's red... and the sun's black," one of the children whispered.

"What?"

The ominous glow drew the collective gaze of the class in the District 19 schoolhouse. A child named Adam had made that uneasy announcement and now the fifteen other children were at the window, staring out at an expanse that'd been powder blue for all their short lives.

"Children..." their teacher called. It was the word she called them only when something was amiss. She stared at her class, demanding obedience with a hard glare from both eyes—the real and the fake. "Please return to your seats so that we may con-"

"Meredith!" Mr. Evans, the principle catechism teacher, appeared at the door, motioning for Ms. Kipling. "I need a quick word with you, if you please."

"Of course," Ms. Kipling said with a sigh. The children watched her leave, apprehension growing like tumors in each little belly. *The sky's red and she used "children..." Something's wrong.*

"Oh my God!"

A scream, Ms. Kipling's by the sound of it, though the children didn't have much in the way of identification: Meredith Kipling was usually a woman of reservation. The only other time she'd screamed so brashly was years ago when she'd spotted a fat swamp rat nesting in the broom closet at the back of the classroom. She'd used "children" then, too.

"Children," Ms. Kipling said, rushing back into the room, her gait wide and unbalanced. "We are to leave immediately! Leave all your things and follow Mr. Evans. Go, go, go!"

"But why, Ms. Kipling?" one child asked.

"What's happening?" asked another.

"You'll do as you're told," Ms. Kipling replied. "There's no time for questions or dawdling. Now move."

"What about our Bibles?" a third child asked.

"Leave them and go," Ms. Kipling repeated, shooing the last student from the room.

They did as told, marching in single-file toward Mr. Evans, who was waiting beneath the awning at the entrance of the schoolhouse. Behind him stood two other groups of children, his and another belonging to a Sunday-school teacher by the name of Mr. Baxter—four groups of ten, all silent and waiting, all wondering what'd gotten into the adults charged with protecting them.

The schoolhouse was now as silent as the adjoining church.

"Is that all of them?" Mr. Baxter asked as Ms. Kipling ushered her students toward the others.

"Yes, I think so," she said.

"Good," Mr. Evans said, "we leave at once."

"Ms. Kipling… your eye…" one of Mr. Baxter's girls whispered in horror.

Ms. Kipling reached up to the right side of her face, her fingers grazing the rim of the empty socket there… a product of a snakebite from her own childhood. She'd never told anyone how it'd happened, but New Sodom was like all small towns… tragedy traveled. She frowned, but quickly composed herself, choosing to shoo the child instead of replying.

The two men walked past the group of children, their silhouettes framed by the crimson sky beyond. They looked like men no longer there, as though they'd fallen away into the wide chasm of the strange day. They stopped at the edge of the street that ran past the schoolhouse and turned back to their flock.

"Who wants to play Follow the Leader?" Mr. Evans asked. The children remained silent, each understanding the question as more command than inquiry.

"C'mon, kids," Mr. Baxter said, stepping onto the street. Before a second could be taken, though, the children began their dissent.

"What's going on?" one child asked.

"I want Mom. Where's my Mom?"

"Why's the sky like that?"

"Where are we going?"

"Why...?"

"We know you all have questions," Ms. Kipling interjected, "but for now, we need to get somewhere safe."

No more questions.

The children followed Mr. Evans and Mr. Baxter down the long road toward Main Street as Ms. Kipling brought up the rear, ready to hasten any stragglers if need be. They walked in silence, the soles of their shoes clipping the concrete with each step, creating a cacophony of footfalls that spread through the town.

As the group turned north onto Main, the children fell witness to the ghost of their hometown: no traffic, no voices, no people. New Sodom was dead. Murmurs and gasps split the silence, but the teachers were quick to hush their students.

"Come along, children," Ms. Kipling said.

"Yes, keep up now," Mr. Evans said.

The children followed, but were no longer silent. Some wept, others whispered amongst themselves, but most just stared dumbly out at the town they'd known since birth. It'd been abandoned... and they, too, it seemed.

The many shops lining downtown New Sodom were still intact, but the usual bustle of small business was absent. A few curious children dared to look into the stores, but their reflection in the giant windows was too much to bear: everything looked wrong in the glass, everyone looked lonely.

Mr. Evans and Mr. Baxter had taken to mumbling to each other, making the front half of the group uneasy as they passed several empty cars stopped at the intersection of Main and Old Hospital Road.

"Dad? Where are you, Dad?"

The group paused, the eyes of every child searching for the small voice that'd interrupted the silence. Even before they'd spotted the boy with the backpack who'd gotten away, Ms. Kipling was walking toward him, her lone footfalls and their solemn echo eerie in their stark clarity.

"If you'd be so kind as to rejoin the group, Adam," Ms. Kipling called, "we can continue on our way."

"This is my dad's car," the boy said. He turned to an old Buick parked haphazardly on the side of the street and knocked on the driver's side window, the sharp punches of sound engaging Ms. Kipling's footfalls in aural battle. "But where is he?"

"You are endangering your fellow students," Ms. Kipling continued. Though she now stood before the boy, the words were still a series of bellows. "Now, if you please, join the other children before..."

"I'm not going," Adam said.

"What?"

"I'm going to wait here for Dad," he continued. "He's coming back. He wouldn't forget me."

"I should think not!" Ms. Kipling screeched, grabbing the boy by his arm. Her grip was strong enough to make him yelp, but he stood in defiance nonetheless.

"Leave me alone!" the boy wailed, the words hoarse and jagged as he and his teacher fought for control of his tiny body. The children behind them gawked, some began crying, the strain of whatever had interrupted the normalcy of their day finally overtaking them.

"You will rejoin your classmates and now," Ms. Kipling said with a long growl from behind clenched teeth. "Do. You. Un. Der. Stand?"

She was shaking him now, his own teeth clacking together between indignant yelps. The boy's eyes had grown wide with a mixture of surprise and fury, but still he wouldn't budge.

"Leave me alone!" he yelled again.

Ms. Kipling, having had enough of what she so often deemed "tomfoolery," grabbed the boy by the shoulders and delivered a final, overpowering yank. The backpack, though, not the boy, was jarred loose. Adam had but a heartbeat to think about what might've happened had his arms taken the brunt of the force.

Ms. Kipling held the backpack high in the air with both hands as though she was looking to bludgeon her student with it. To Adam the backpack was just another shade blocking the already eclipsed sun like an impossibly black shadow crawling across the heart of the crimson sky.

The blue of her good eye shimmered, but the boy was staring at the empty one, which went so deep that, for a moment, it appeared as a hole that went straight through Ms. Kipling's head, opening to the shadowy sun behind her. Both prospects frightened him.

"Leave him," a voice broke through the silence. All eyes turned to Mr. Evans who stood poised, his arms bent before him, his palms held outward. They were hands calling for obedience.

"But..." Ms. Kipling said, disheartened.

"Leave him."

Ms. Kipling swiped a streak of sweat-stained black hair from her gaunt face. She let the backpack fall to the ground before her and trudged back to the group.

When the adults resumed their trek, the children followed. Adam watched as they left him there, a feeling of unease burning deep within. As he stooped to grab his belongings, his eyes still on his class, he was hit with sudden déjà-vu.

Just God's way of telling us we're on the right path, his father was fond of saying about that sudden feeling of nostalgia. The boy felt as though he'd watched this same group of children being ushered off a thousand times, heading into some great, unforeseen catastrophe. *Yeah*, he thought, *but the catastrophe's all around us. The old world is dead and the new one's hungry.*

It was his thought, but someone else's voice—his father's, maybe, or God's.

"The Red Hills…" another unknown voice called out. The boy slung the backpack over his shoulder, his eyes sweeping the deserted heart of his hometown. Ms. Kipling stood facing him two blocks yonder, her body obscured by the shadows of the abandoned buildings. Her voice, strong and clear, carried on the heat-haze of the day.

"That's where we're taking them if you'd like to join," she said. The silhouette of her body turned with the strange grace of a pirouette and hurried to rejoin the group. Then Adam was alone, his choice made, his fate so tightly sealed.

※☆※☆※

As they reached the edge of town, the children were growing restless, their game of Follow the Leader having lost its charm. Cries of "my legs hurt!" and "I wanna go home!" made their way around the group like ghost-whispers. The egocentrism of youth (not to mention their sore legs) had forced them to forget the boy they'd left behind.

"Hush, children," Ms. Kipling called from behind them. She had her hands on the shoulders of two stragglers, prodding them on with bony palms. "Hush and hurry."

NEW SODOM CITY LIMITS

Their eyes caught the sign at the same moment. It was something they'd all seen countless times, but this time the meaning it held was dire. They were leaving New Sodom and everything familiar to them. Weeping replaced the sniveling and protest and, as the group passed the threshold between the town and its outskirts, the children turned back to gaze upon all they'd ever known.

New Sodom looked beyond deserted just then… it seemed ruined. A hot breeze stirred among them as they peered into the town beneath the red sky and dark sun. It felt like a last breath, as though the town was sighing as it watched its children fleeing the tragedy that'd befallen it.

"Come children," Mr. Evans said. "We'll follow the highway to the Red Hills. It's not far."

The children began their march once more, their desperation pushing them on with more potency than Ms. Kipling's palms ever could.

☠☠☠

The lone boy couldn't shake the feeling of unease that'd come to him as the other children had moved on. Dread pervaded him as intensely as the longing to see his father. He was sitting in his dad's car now, the driver's door open, his stick-thin legs dangling inches above the blacktop of downtown New Sodom. Still no signs of Dad, though… or anyone else. Not even the chatter of birds.

"The birds are always the first to know," his Dad had once told him during a particularly tumultuous tornado season. "They sense the wrong in the air."

Questions floated in and out of the boy's mind, each demanding to be asked aloud before crumbling back into the stream of his thoughts. But the boy sat in silence, his eyes scanning both sky and city as he tried to decipher exactly what the hell had happened to the world.

"Jesus…"

His voice was a stranger's to him, one carried through the town on a hot wind. He licked his lips and blinked, dispelling the daze and awakening his senses so quickly a breath hitched in his throat. He coughed it loose and rolled his eyes to the bright red backpack lying on the street before him, back in the same spot his teacher had dropped it after their little spat.

As suddenly as his eyes had caught sight of his belongings, he realized he no longer wanted to wait for his father. He hadn't given up hope exactly, but something was tugging on his heart, something awakened by that old backpack. That bag was a sliver of familiarity in this wasteland he used to call home, a relic from before-times. So he picked up the pack and headed south, his small legs leading him farther from his classmates.

☠☠☠

The highway out of New Sodom was littered with cracked pavement and grit, a haze of dust settling over the stretch of road like red fog. The children walked as an amorphous mass, their pace slow despite the constant prodding from their teachers. Mr. Evans was faithful in trying to keep their spirits up, but the trek was wearing on them.

"Almost there, kids," Mr. Baxter called from the front of the pack. The announcement was met with half-hearted groaning. He shushed them without looking back, his pace now stunted by a rather severe limp he'd picked up along the way. He hobbled forth, dragging his left leg behind him like dead weight. Unperturbed, he kept with Mr. Evans stride-for-stride, not even breaking a sweat as they continued on to the now visible hills beyond the highway.

※※※

On long summer days when a storm would roll in and bring rain even as the sun still shined, Adam would always think *the Devil is beating his wife* because that's what his father always called it. So as the first raindrop hit his brow, he thought that very thing. He wiped the rain away as it began to trickle, but when he withdrew his hand, the stain on its heel gave him pause.

Blood? he asked himself. He returned his hand to where the drop had hit him, feeling for the inevitable wound, but no prick of pain presented itself and when he looked at his hand again, he found the same odd stain. Red rain from a crimson, cloudless sky.

That first drop was soon followed by another and then another until sheets of sticky scarlet were falling around him, painting his town blank.

He turned onto the old road leading back to the even older schoolhouse, the world around him now drenched in the same color as his backpack. He, too, could not escape it. The rain stained his arms and face, but he walked as stolidly as ever. Soon a dull sting had settled just beneath his flesh as though the red drops were toxic as well as cruel. Still, though, he walked with resolve—with *purpose*—toward the last place in the world that seemed to make sense.

※※※

The dust beneath the children's shoes was loose and thick, collapsing under their collective weight like an inch of sludge as they made their way into the newborn desert outside the town. Rural Highway 7 was a mile behind them now, long forgotten in the dust that'd swallowed them. Everything looked the same, all directions and ways to go. The black blizzards of a century prior had returned... or perhaps just their angry ghosts.

There was no more weeping or questioning from the group, just mindless marching along the shifting ground. The children remembered the grass plains that'd once grown here, but how long ago was that? Days? Years? It was all the same now: the land and time… lost.

"Soon, children, soon," Mr. Evans called, the words ripped away by a roar of wind.

Not even a moan this time. They were exhausted, all of them, yet still they went along. Still the Leaders led, still the children followed, the Red Hills slowly materializing behind the brown fog ahead.

chhkkkk-chhkkkk-chhkkkk

A whisper of something was growing and the children could feel it. They trembled and huddled together as they walked. Their teachers, though, didn't so much as twitch, for they were close now. That faint sound told them so.Adam had paused beneath the awning before the entrance of the school, his mind charmed by the now constant drumming of the raindrops on the roof overhead. The soft patter of rain had once comforted him, even lulled him to sleep on summer nights long ago, but this red rain was heavier, its rhythm different. He gathered himself and took a step into the school, the door crawling shut behind his tremulant hands.

⚜⚜⚜

ccchhhkkkk-ccchhhkkkk-ccchhhkkkk-ccchhhkkkk-ccchhhkkkk

The sound was piercing now, warbling on the horizon before the children. Some clapped their hands over their ears while others broke their silence with shrieks and squeals. It was like the buzz of a million cicadas, a noise that reached into the children, piercing their quickened hearts with the chill of fear.

"There, children," Mr. Baxter said, his leg now twisted and useless as he continued his awkward hobble. "Just a little farther now."

"But the noise!" one child yelled.

"Too much! Too much!" another screamed.

But the teachers didn't hear their cries, only prodded their students along like disobedient dogs.

⚜⚜⚜

As much as the school looked the same, there was an inexplicable strangeness to it. The boy walked the hall back to the room he'd been in before this whole mess began, peering into the three rooms before his own with mild interest, all of them abandoned. Seeing this, he suddenly

210

felt a knot of dread inside him.

Was coming back here a good idea?

There was no answer, of course, but he was there now and going back out into the bloody world behind him seemed crazy. He would push on, growing dread or no. The room they'd all left was before him, its door half-open, the invitation to enter undeniable.

☙❧☙❧☙❧

At last, Mr. Evans and Mr. Baxter had stopped, the Red Hills now more than just a gritty mirage on the horizon. The children had stopped faithfully behind them, their eyes wide with disquieted wonder. The warble still buzzed around them, but it was tolerable now, as though they'd stepped inside it upon entering the crown of hills.

"This…" Mr. Evans said, turning to the crowd behind him with the pomp of a priest leading mass. His arms were raised in a slanted V above his head. "This is it!"

"We made it, children," Mr. Baxter said, his posture straight despite the condition of his leg.

"At last…" Ms. Kipling added.

The children, sweaty and tired, threw nervous glances around them. The Red Hills weren't the same as the ones in their memories. They seemed imaginary, unreal.

Without another word, the men parted before the children, revealing a large hole in the base of the tallest hill before them. There was a moment of silence before the inevitable question was asked.

"What is that?"

"Salvation," the teachers said in chorus.

☙❧☙❧☙❧

The classroom looked the same, but the boy didn't have the courage to enter. Even though it looked like the sole sanctuary in the chaos that'd befallen New Sodom, he still couldn't bring himself to take that first step back over the threshold. Some unknown instinct held him there…

…until he heard the crash behind him.

☙❧☙❧☙❧

"Gather 'round, children," Mr. Evans called from the lip of the hole. The children were slow to obey, but soon they, too, were staring down into the darkness of the opening.

"The noise…" a child said.

"…from that cave?" another finished.

ccchhhKKKK-ccchhhKKKK-ccchhhKKKK

The warble intensified at the inquiry of the children, as though sentient. The students were too ensnared to shield their ears because their eyes had grown accustomed to the darkness roiling within the hole. They were compelled to enter now, this time without the helping hands of their elders.

⚜⚜⚜

"Who's there?" had been a stupid question to ask, but Adam was still accustomed to the ways of a world that'd since passed. There was no answer, perhaps no one *to* answer, but the boy didn't want to take any chances.

His body was slow to turn, caution halting any sudden movements. *There's something there*, wild thoughts warned, *something that'll eat you alive*. He turned his eyes to the hallway behind him, praying under his breath that his instincts had been mistaken.

⚜⚜⚜

The shadows in the opening were crystallizing now. The children had taken several steps back before an odd static had settled over them, freezing them with terror. The three teachers watched them passively, their eyes darting from child to child until one of them spoke.

"You've been such good boys and girls," Mr. Evans said. "You all play Follow the Leader superbly and your prize lies within the mouth of this ca-"

Blood exploded out of Mr. Baxter's mouth in a violent fit of coughing. He turned from the crowd, his bad foot giving way as he spun. The sound of both of his shins snapping as he collapsed was loud enough to overpower the prolonged buzz from the cave if but for a moment. He came to rest in the red dirt, his legs sprawled around him at impossible angles.

Never once did Mr. Baxter scream, even as he began to pull himself back up.

⚜⚜⚜

The breath he'd been holding was growing hot behind his tightly clenched jaw, but as soon as he was sure he was alone, Adam let it out in

212

a long wheeze. There was nothing there, though the shadows of every crack and corner seemed to jump out at him. Something *made that noise*, his thoughts reminded him.

He shifted his backpack, his shirt drenched in sweat as he pulled it away from his body, and took an uneven step toward the darkness he swore hadn't been there a moment ago.

☙❧

"I was hoping we could do this with a tad more regality, but I see our time is short," Mr. Evans said, "or, rather, *yours* is." He turned to the children, his gaze forcing them to shy away.

Mr. Baxter had made it to his knees, the rest of his legs set in a twisted, dead heap before him. His face was caked in grime and blood and seemed to be peeling away. The smirk was maddening.

"Con... gratula... la... tions, kids," Mr. Baxter said through his gaping, skeletal grin. He tried to close his jaw, but unable to do so, caused a thick stream of dark blood to spill over his bottom lip.

☙❧

Room #3 held nothing new. Nor did Room #2. As he came upon the room closest to the entrance, his heart was pumping hard in protest. His thoughts mirrored this sudden panic, again warning him of the dangers of blind curiosity. And again he ignored them, pushing on toward that final room.

A part of him wanted to break into a run, throw open that door to the outside world, and flee the dread he'd felt in his heart ever since he'd watched the other children escape his lonely fate. The boy peered around the doorway to Room #1.

Nothing.

This should've put him at ease, but something still clawed at him. He could feel eyes peering from somewhere beyond the shadows. He turned slowly, a knot in his chilled heart telling him this time "nothing" would be what he wished he'd found.

☙❧

"Are you ready, children?" Ms. Kipling asked behind them, her voice high and piercing above the call of the cave. None of them turned to face her: their eyes were locked on the deep hole and the darkness dwelling within. Not even the melting face of Mr. Baxter could draw their attention.

Something in the hole was making that noise and that Something was coming to get them.

☠☠☠

Blue was all he could see at first, blue like the sky had been before the red and the ruin and the Devil beating his wife. Then he could see a small ring of that glimmering blue. And finally the rest came into sight and Adam tried to look away.

☠☠☠

cccchhhhKKKKKK-cccchhhhKKKKKK-cccchhhhKKKKKK

"What very good followers you were" was the last thing Mr. Baxter had said coherently. After that his face had caved in and now only a gargle came when he spoke, though it hadn't stopped him from talking. He went on, strips of rotting flesh curling and falling to his broken legs with every unintelligible word. The children stood before him dumbfounded and horrified, some of them jarred into wailing.

☠☠☠

An eye, whole and glimmering, laid on the floor just before the entrance to the church proper. Adam stared at it and the glass eye stared back. His fear subsided, but curiosity quickly filled the void. He hesitated, but the eye charmed and beckoned him. The boy took a weary step toward it and the church beyond.

☠☠☠

The children had backed away from the hole, but their teachers weren't letting them out of its vicinity. Some of them had taken to sniveling, but their protests fell on deaf ears.

"I want to go home," could be heard among the disorganized crying.

"Home is gone now," Ms. Kipling would say.

"We're hungry," another child would shout.

Mr. Baxter mumbled at this one, his collapsed face arresting his words before they had a chance to form. But to some of the children closest to him, it sounded like he'd said, "so're we."

☠☠☠

Adam had knelt to pick up the eye, but now that he was so close, he wasn't sure he wanted to handle it. It looked harmless enough, but the feeling it conjured was a strange species of madness. He hesitated, but set his hands on it. The glass eye was cold, but made him shiver for a different reason.

The boy looked through the glass door to the church ahead, willing himself to ignore the stain of his reflection, not wanting it to convince him of what he was now holding.

The church was silent, idyllic almost, but the door separating the buildings seemed also to separate realities. The church seemed unreal to him just then—*out there* like the rest of the world. The schoolhouse, though, felt eerily like home.

He returned his attention to the glass eye, its blue iris and the black hole it encircled still charming him as he rose to his feet. He turned it in his hands, running his tiny fingers over its smooth surface, all the while trying to forget whose skull it belonged to. When he stopped, the pupil was gazing left through the fan of his fingers. The boy obliged, turning his attention to where the glass eye was leading him.

There all three eyes discovered what'd made that awful crash.

※※※

"It is time, children," Ms. Kipling said behind the group, still standing vigilant against the multitude of antsy students. Her smile was just as crazy as the one Mr. Evans had set into his face… that is, until she reached to the empty hole in her head and ripped away the flesh, leaving a shapeless black mass where her face once was, cackling as it tore away.

※※※

The boy backed himself against the wall, the glass eye he'd once loathed cradled against his chest. A hand—not whole, just meat and bones—reached out for him from a dark corner of the sitting room between the church and its school. That's all Adam had seen in the first few moments before his mind let him take in what remained. Then he saw the skeleton, eyeless and grinning… the owner of that fleshless hand.

Beyond were sprawled two other bonemen draped about the sitting room. One was set haphazardly on a large table near the back of the room, but the other had spilled onto the floor from a hardwood chair near the first skeleton. The latter had made the sudden noise.

There was no rotten stench or pools of blood, which surprised the boy as he surveyed the scene. The splatters of blood he *could* see looked like something Jackson Pollock would've done had he been a serial killer. It was blood alright, thick and dark, the kind pigs would make when his father slaughtered them.

The boy stared at the bodies for a long while, especially the smaller one reaching for him. *For the eye*, he thought. *But that would mean...* He couldn't bring himself to say her name, but he felt in his bones (*don't use that word*, he thought) that it fit.

Ms. Kipling...

...then the other two skeletons?

🕱🕱🕱

The children had watched in silent horror as Ms. Kipling shed layer after layer of skin until her body was completely gone. She'd cackled the whole time, letting her flesh gather in a swollen mound at her feet. At the same time, the body of Mr. Baxter had given away, falling apart as though unzipped. Now both stood before the children as living shadows.

"The world has changed, children," Mr. Evans, still intact, said. "Indeed it has changed and you are the last. All before you have fallen, do you see that? In all the world, you are the last."

He paused, letting the children turn their dumb gaze to him before beginning again.

"*Therefore rejoice, O heavens and you who dwell in them!*" he spat. "*But woe to you, O earth and sea, for the devil has come down to you in great wrath, because he knows that his time is short.*"

Mr. Evans shot glances to the shadows standing above the flesh of Mr. Baxter and Ms. Kipling, his smirk wide and terrible. "Yes, our time is short here."

The shadows said nothing.

"Oh, the sickles of the harvest are coming, dear children, to reap the good fruit of the world," he said, looking over the children once again. "But not before we have a little fun."

🕱🕱🕱

Adam had gone into the church, had prayed before the altar to the giant plaster Christ hanging from his lonely cross. He'd told Christ he was sorry for all the bad things he'd done and that he missed his Dad and Mom and his friends. He asked Him to take care of everyone, especially Ms. Kipling and the others who'd been taken by the Red Day.

Then he'd said "*Amen.*" and walked away.

As he trudged back to the old classroom, the weight of the backpack was finally getting to him. Adam stepped into the classroom, this time without hesitation, and closed the door softly behind him. He walked to the large window where he'd first made that cryptic announcement: *the sky's red and the sun's black.* He drew the shade before his eyes had a chance to focus on what was out there. He was tired of *out there.*

He set his backpack on his desk in the back corner and walked to his teacher's desk. The silence was chilling, though he was just happy there weren't any more bumps or bangs. He set the glass eye on the table, turning it so the pupil was pointing toward the blackboard. Once he was sure it wouldn't roll off the desk, he walked back to his chair and took a seat.

The sound of the backpack unzipping was grating, but once it was over, the silence quickly resumed its dominance of the world. The boy shoved his small arms into it, hoping he had enough left in him to lift its contents.

His father had given him the Bible he withdrew from the backpack, telling him with pride that it'd been passed down from generation-to-generation. *It's something that means something, son,* he'd said. The boy understood that now. He set it on his desk and opened it to where he'd been reading before his world had been ripped away.

"Then the dragon became furious with the woman," he read aloud, *"and went off to make war with her offspring..."*

❀❀❀❀

"What happened, children?" Mr. Evans continued. "Where is your white knight, hm? Your blessed salvation? Tsk, tsk, tsk... such faith... and for what?"

Both children and shadow remained quiet.

"You needn't worry, sweet babes. He is coming, the one who wrote the rules... laws your kind never seemed to heed or understand."

The children wept and gaped, but the whirring of the cave had come to dominance once again.

CCCCHHHHKKKKKK-CCCCHHHHKKKKKK-
CCCCHHHHKKKKKK

"Oh, I'm sure you'll all be at His throne when the time comes, but this isn't His kingdom," Mr. Evans shouted above the buzzing. "Do you understand that, children? Do you understand that this world is *our* kingdom... *our* age. Here, everything—and every*one*—belongs to us until His word comes to pass."

CCCCCHHHHHKKKKKKK-CCCCCHHHHHKKKKKKK-

CCCCCHHHHHKKKKKKK

Mr. Evans reached up and grabbed his face with both hands, his laughter muffled by his tightly-bound fists. He jerked upward, pulling his scalp back over his skull so that his face was blank skin where only the indent of two eye sockets and a grinning mouth could be seen. But the children had no reaction: they were looking at the hole again, watching the darkness churn within.

"We've come to accept our fate," he spoke through the flesh that had once covered his upper chest, "lakes of fire and gnashing of teeth... we accept this fate... and yours as well. For you see, in the end, He may get your soul, but here... in our kingdom... we get flesh and bone."

CCCCCCCCCCCCCCCCCCCKKKKKKKKKKKKKKKKKKKHHHHH HHHHHHHHHHHHHHHHHHH

He cackled through the thin layer of skin masking whatever horror existed beneath it, but soon it, too, was drowned out by the terrible buzzing from the moving darkness. There were no more words. The two shadows and the thing wearing Mr. Evans's skin closed in on the group of children, but the little ones didn't see them anymore. All eyes were on the darkness and whatever was crawling up to meet them.

Amen.

He'd finished reading hours ago, but time didn't seem to mean much anymore. He'd sat there, staring at the front of the class as he had in the Old World. He faced forward, his mind blank, his eyes on the false eye of his dead teacher.

She's gone, he thought passively. *They all are...*

"All except me," he whispered.

The loneliness he'd felt before was gone, replaced with a feeling of oneness, of singularity. He was alone and finally understood what that meant.

He sighed and closed his eyes, finding solace in the faint darkness floating behind his eyelids because there was no red sky there or dead, skinless people. He stared into that darkness, unable to blink or turn away because it was a darkness that was inside him. He peered into it until all the bad feelings drained away, until even the darkness seemed to fade.

The light behind it was comforting and warm and he was soon lost in it. He couldn't feel himself anymore, so when his face pulled into a smile, he was none the wiser.

So there he sat in his little chair as New Sodom and the rest of the world came to its promised end. He was the last and knew it somewhere deep down where the light shown through the darkness.

Take the World Away from Me
by Kelly Matsuura

All I have to do is stand here, strong and still. My hands balance the living orb; one hand on top, the other underneath. Now and again I cry softly, watching warm tears drop onto the spinning ball. It turns itself and time ticks over. One millennia. I sigh in frustration, but I never let go.

Two, three, four million years pass. The orb seems heavier now. More tears fall, joining the oceans.

Don't drop it, Talea. Father's commanding voice echoes from…wherever he actually is. I am alone. My siblings are also locked away in solitude, holding up their own worlds.

Mother visits occasionally, but never for long. Because of Damieon, my younger brother, and the day he dropped his orb.

It crashed to the floor, shaking the room like an explosion—every tiny being that inhabited that world was wiped from existence. He said it happened because the organic stench the orb exuded became deadly and decayed, to a point he could no longer bear. He had tried to heal it, but some worlds we learned, were beyond saving.

Father, however, blamed Damieon for endangering all our worlds.

As punishment for his weakness, Damieon was sent to work at the eternal fires. The rest of us were placed in separate rooms where we could not be distracted by anyone or anything again.

※※※

It has to end soon. I am older, my back bends. My ankles ache from lack of movement. My fingers once gripped the orb with determination and control— now they only throb with self-pity and weariness.

I face the door, dreaming it opens to reveal the new Guardian. I picture a fresh young goddess with an eagerness to do right, to take the precious, aging orb and regenerate it in a way I no longer can.

I lose track of the millennia. My eyes are closed and my head is too heavy to lift up straight. I hear the nostalgic creak of the door's hinges.

"Mother?" My voice is raspy from disuse.

"No. I am Cephas, a cousin. I'm here to relieve you of the orb." A male god! Not what I had expected but I am overjoyed to be released.

"Thank you. I've waited so long to leave."

He smiles. A beautiful, golden sight.

"May I?" He stretches his hands out. Strong, steady hands, ready for the responsibility.

"Yes. Please take it." A few months pass as we make the fragile exchange. The orb is out of my hands now and in his, yet I still feel its weight as I leave the room.

I close the door behind me with just a brief glance at Cephas. He stands perfect straight, his arms fixed to hold the world at the perfect angle. His face has a look of complete focus. I believe he will not fail.

A wind stirs around me. I blink, unaccustomed to the brightness of the hallway. I walk a few steps, the wind at my back guiding me to the edge of this hidden plane. Laughter comes from the glowing abyss and I recognize the voices of my sisters. They are also free!

I catch the next strong breeze and leap from the solid plane into the weightless heavens. It is pure bliss to be out in the elements again, free from solitude and quiet, and the fear of breaking that precious world that cannot be remade.

THE HOLE
BY EDWARD ASHTON

"Huh," Mack says, and reaches up to scratch the broad, bald dome of his head. "That is not what I expected to happen."

He looks down into the hole. Dory steps up beside him.

"How far down do you think it goes?"

He shrugs.

"Dunno."

The hole, which had not been there moments before, now runs arrow-straight toward the center of the Earth. It's two feet wide. The walls are smooth as glass.

The wreck is scattered across the desert around them. The chunk they've been working on is a tapered cylinder, twelve feet long and maybe half that wide. The access panel that Mack's just finished prying loose has followed whatever fell out of the space behind it down the hole. The exposed compartment is empty.

"What's that sound?" Dory asks.

"Wind," Mack says. "It's going down the hole."

He's right. The hole is sucking air, and the noise of it is growing into a rising roar. Dory's long blonde hair flutters in the strange, downward-blowing breeze.

"Do you think it'll keep going?" Dory asks. "I mean, will it just keep sucking stuff in forever?"

Mack shakes his head.

"Not forever." He looks up. The sun is a hot white glare in a cloudless blue sky. "Pretty soon, I'm guessing there won't be anything left to suck."

⁕⁕⁕

The artificial singularity falls through the Earth with little more difficulty than it would have fallen through vacuum. It slows slightly while passing through the dense iron core, drawing in matter and throwing off hard radiation, enough so that it fails to reach the floor of the Indian Ocean before falling back again. The rotation of the Earth turns the path it describes through the planet into a complex series of interlocking arcs, like the petals of a flower traced out in negative space. Each pass bleeds off more energy, and each arc peaks slightly lower, until the singularity's motion is reduced to an oscillation within the core. Finally, it comes to rest.

And then, like a spider at the center of its web, it begins to eat.

⁕⁕⁕

"So," Dory says. "What happens now?"

They're in a booth in an Applebee's in Elko, Nevada. Mack looks down into his half-empty beer, then drains it in one pull.

"Well," he says, and belches hugely. "First thing is, we quit worrying about the credit card."

He waves down their waitress, waggles his empty glass and holds up one finger.

"Really," Dory says. "What do we do? I mean, we ought to tell somebody, right?"

Mack gives her a blank stare. The waitress puts a fresh beer down in front of him. He drinks half of it down, then shakes his head.

"Tell somebody what?" he asks. "That the world's about the end, and it's our fault? How, exactly, do you see that playing out?"

Dory's eyebrows knit over the bridge of her nose.

"It's not really," she says. "Is it?"

Mack shrugs.

"Don't know for sure, I guess." He belches again, then drinks most of what's left in his glass. "But did you see what came out of that wreck? Did you feel it pull at you when it fell?"

As if to emphasize his point, the room shudders. Their shadows dance around them as the lamp above the table swings wildly. Across the room, a waitress drops a full tray of plates and glasses into a trucker's lap. His friends burst out laughing.

"Yeah," Mack says. "I'd say we're screwed."

224

Dory's known Mack for almost twenty years now. They met on a cruise ship, when they were paired for a kayaking trip up a Norwegian fiord. They spent most of that day in companionable silence. They've spent most of the past two decades in companionable silence, truth be told. On this night, though, as they're making their way out of the Elko Applebee's through ever-worsening tremors, Dory has a flash of memory. They were standing at the rail of the ship on the night they met, watching the northern lights snake across the sky. Mack touched her face, brushed her hair back, ran one finger from her ear down along the line of her jaw. Dory turned to him then, looked into his eyes and said, "You know, I've got a feeling you're gonna get me in trouble some day."

Mack reaches back to help Dory to the top of the bluff. The moon is high and bright overhead. The town below is still lit up in places, but the power is failing, block by block. The tremors are almost constant now, and getting stronger by the minute. Dory pulls out her phone. Mack takes it from her, rears back, and chucks it over the edge.

"Hey," she says. "What the hell, Mack?"

"You've got an hour left on Earth," Mack says. "You really want to spend it checking Facebook?"

Dory scowls, takes two steps away from him. The ground lurches beneath them, and she sits down hard in the dirt.

"I don't know," she says as he drops down beside her. "What else is there to do?"

He wraps an arm around her shoulder, pulls her tight against him. She pulls back at first, then leans her head against his shoulder. They sit like that for a while, holding tighter when the earth moves, relaxing when it's still.

"It's too bad," Dory says finally.

"Yeah," Mack says. "But what're you gonna do?"

The bluff shudders beneath them. The valley floor buckles with a subsonic groan, and the last of the lights in the town wink out.

"Dory?" Mack says.

"Yeah?"

"I'm sorry your last meal was from Applebee's."

She takes a deep breath in and wraps her arms around his chest. He smooths her hair down, then kisses her forehead. She looks up as the bluff drops away beneath her. The stars stare back at her from an ink-black sky, cold, and clear, and unconcerned.

FIVE LAMENTS FOR THE HORIZON SUMMER RESORT, TO BE DESTROYED AND NEVER BUILT AGAIN
BY TOM BREEN

1. Editorial published in The Orford Parish Vituperator, 4-19-15

Sunset on the Horizon

Demolition begins next week on the Horizon Summer Resort, affording us an opportunity to pause and reflect on "flying Time," as it takes yet one more precious thing from our lives.

But first, it must be said: the grand, old 178-acre property, with its bunkhouses and pools, its activity building and tennis courts, its soft lawns and the blue surface of Ebinger Pond, had long since become worse than an eyesore; it had become a hazard.

Generations of leisure-seekers from Orford Parish and beyond had spent countless happy summer days there, it's true: sunning themselves on the rooftops of the cabins, cooking up a feast of hamburgers and hot dogs on the grills that dotted the property, dancing to the bands who played in the Assembly Hall, and perhaps snuggling beneath a blanket in front of a bonfire.

But ever since the resort's last owners filed for bankruptcy in 1991, the setting for so many lifetime memories has been little more than a magnet for teenagers seeking the wrong kind of thrills, and worse; police have practically been forced to locate a substation on the premises to handle the arrests stemming from drug, alcohol, and vandalism charges in recent years.

Those troublemakers likely don't realize how lucky they've been to have the long arm of the law escort them from the grounds, but the amount of asbestos, lead paint, and other environmental contaminants – legacies of a less health-conscious era – make the act of simply wandering through the old buildings a major health risk.

This was demonstrated in the most tragic way possible last year when 15-year-old Parish resident Stacey Glenders drowned in old Ebinger Pond itself, now a muddy, weed-choked death trap so remote from the fond days of paddle boats and swim races to the raft that it seems a different place altogether.

It's a scandal that it took the death of a child to finally spur the General Assembly to action, but now the votes have been taken, the money has been appropriated, and next week the wrecking balls will start swinging. And although we sympathize with the efforts of local conservationists – not least Nancy Gaines, retired president of the Orford Parish Historical Society – to save some of the beloved old Horizon, the time when anything could be salvaged from this magnificent ruin is surely long past.

And so Progress will soon arrive at the Horizon, driving his demolition vehicles and carefully monitoring his hazardous materials checklist. The barbecue pits will be buried and the cabins will be torn down; the main office, where for 71 years people lined up to check in and receive their room keys and "Horizon Fun Totes," will fall beneath the bulldozer's blade; the basketball courts and the pools and the Assembly Hall will fall silent forever, and the laughing ghosts of the younger people we once were will become fainter.

When it's all done, 85 – 85! – buildings will come down, and old Ebinger itself, having been ascertained as beyond the point of saving, will be filled in with ton after ton of earth.

Again, this is progress: something new will be built on land that has lain fallow for too long. But it's not only possible, it's proper, to pause and remember who we were when Horizon was open and the world was a week in the glorious sunshine of a Connecticut July, and boys and girls laughed on the shore of a pond while Dad tuned in the Red Sox and kicked back for his well-earned rest from work, Mom fretted over the potato salad, and nothing seemed further away than September, let alone adulthood and its dreary obligations. There have been many good days since then, of course, but no days quite like those.

Progress, then, but not progress of the kind that precludes us from saying, with the poet: "Farewell, happy fields, where joy forever dwells!"

2. Tumblr posts by Orford Parish resident Kate Cahillane, 16. Posts have been edited and condensed for length and clarity.

So you know my thing about wanting to die in 1955, late at night, falling into the arms of my dream man as the traffic rushes around us. OK, you say it's unlikely to happen, and you have a point there.

This is going to sound weird, but Horizon WAS my 1955, and now it seems I'll never die there.

Last night – in more ways than one! – Clark and I went there again. I was wearing what I think of as my Ricky Nelson dress, which Clark said was stupid because we might have to run from the police, but I said there's no way I'm going to 1955 without my Ricky Nelson dress, and Clark looked at me like I'm dumb, which I'm not.

CLARK. Did any of those old "Dig" magazines we found at the library sale about cool Fifties teens and their cool Fifties ways MEAN anything to you??? haha

So, "last night" – last night as in, it was the most recent night, and "last night" as in, it might be the last night I get to see Horizon. Mom says there was something in the paper about the date finally being set on demolition, although we haven't seen any, I don't know, cranes or anything. But maybe those are easy to move into place?? We shall see.

My pictures from Horizon are bad and lame and do not do it justice but it IS 1955. Or at least it's some time in the past, before this shitty century. I don't know what happens when a resort goes broke, but it looks like they just dropped what they were doing and left, because some of these rooms can't have changed at all since the 60s or maybe the 70s.

The furniture, the wallpaper, the carpets, the drapes, the CARBON PAPER. Do you remember the time we found that old Mad Men radio in one of the cabins and CLARK WANTED TO LEAVE IT THERE because he said it wouldn't work? And then I took it to some shop on Main Street where this Iraq veteran (or maybe Afghanistan, idk and it's not like I'm going to ask) with one leg fixed it. I LISTEN TO THAT RADIO EVERY DAY AND IT IS THE BEST.

Later Clark admitted that he didn't want me to bring it back from the cabin because, ha, it might have ghosts on it. Well, OK, it wasn't that dumb when he explained it. It was right around the time when that girl drowned in the pond at Horizon, and Clark was convinced her spirit would try to contact us or something.

I'm not saying I don't believe in ghosts I'm just saying I don't think she was going to haunt an old radio, but Clark thought that would be the ideal way for her to communicate with the living – like, to explain why she was out there swimming in the middle of the night in the first place – and I had to admit that made some kind of sense.

Ghosts, though, are not the most frightening thing at Horizon, which Clark is quick to remind me: SCARY DRUG DEALERS lurk in the broken down buildings, except it's probably just kids from school, and THE CHURCH OF THE SHAKEN HOUSE comes out at night there, except that isn't even real.

You know what is scary, though? Beverly M[REDACTED], who is earth's own worst bitch, supposedly got raped by that creepy fat police officer who sits in his car at the entrance to Horizon, SUPPOSEDLY I say because I can't imagine that cop actually catching someone if "catching" involves running, or sudden movement of any kind (not to body-shame, just stating a fact yo). Beverly is gross and bad, but that is not something that should happen to anyone, so I hope it's not true. She has been kind of weird in school lately, much quieter.

ENNYWAY. We went last night and this time I convinced Clark to climb up onto one of the sunbathing balconies over the cabins with me, something he has never done before because he says the cabins are "structurally unsound" BECAUSE CLARK IS FIRST AND FOREMOST AN ENGINEER and even though it was nighttime I pretended I was sunbathing there in 1955 and I pressed "play" on my phone and "Lonesome Town" by Ricky Nelson started playing and I talked to Clark about how much better things were then, with the Space Race and wooden station wagons and sock hops and greasers and vinyl records and schools that were chalkboards and paper books and no Twitter or thot lists or horrible girls, and how Horizon was a symbol of that and it was something our parents and grandparents did before they got old and cynical and greedy and forgot what was important in life, and for a minute he was so quiet I thought he was actually taking in everything I said for once but then I realized his hand was creeping along the hem of my dress and he was trying to cop a feel although he was nowhere near my actual thigh, and sometimes I think Clark is kind of dumb.

Tonight, though, if there are no wrecking balls or construction crews or whatever, I am going to convince that dummy to drive me to the Horizon again. I may not die there, but I want to spend another night looking up at the moon and seeing the 1950s.

3. Personal statement of Patrolman Anthony "Tony" Fiorini, 26.

I'm good at my job, and fuck Sergeant Vargas for saying otherwise.

That fat bitch.

"Tony," she says. "We're going to put you in front of the Horizon Resort overnights, because we think this is a job that even you can't screw up. All you have to do is radio if you see anyone coming in."

Fuck. You. How about that, sergeant? Fuck. You.

I've never screwed anything up. The thing they all think I screwed up I didn't; that was the other driver's fault entirely. "Traffic camera" – bullshit.

But Tony Fiorni is a good soldier. I have a job to do, I do the job, and I keep my mouth shut. Do I say, "Oh, hey, Sergeant Vargas, maybe your problem is, you haven't had any dick in 20 years?"

No. I don't. Like I said, I do my job. And when people bet against me, that's when I'm the happiest. I love proving people wrong. Just tell me I can't do something, and then watch me do it better than you ever could.

Plus, the joke is already on them, because I was going to the Horizon on my own even before I pulled this overnight duty.

See, they all think Tony Fiorni is a regular guy – probably works out, has a girlfriend, likes sports, you know, regular guy shit. But I'm one up on them, because I actually am a lot smarter than that.

You know that show on The Learning Channel, *Orford Paranormal*? Where those guys go around and investigate hauntings? Yeah, those guys – hey, I know those guys. I went to high school with them.

Well, they were a few grades ahead of me, but I still knew them, knew who they were. And let me tell you this: those guys are OK, but they don't really know the science of what they're doing. It's all showmanship with them.

But I read. I've got, probably, 10 or 15 Internet sites bookmarked with all this scientific information about paranormal investigations. I'm talking about real science here, not TV shows or horror movies or any of that. Professors at colleges, real scientists.

So here's what's happening: I'm going to prove the existence of ghosts. Think I can't do it? Beautiful. I love it. Tell me I can't. I'm serious: tell me I cannot do it. I love to hear that. Music to my ears.

Because I've done a lot of reading – that's what Tony Fiorini does when he's off-duty, by the way, I'm always improving my mind – and I'm scientifically convinced that paranormal entities – what you call "ghosts" – can be discovered and recorded at the Horizon Summer Resort.

You know this place was actually founded by paranormal investigators? They didn't call themselves that, though, they said they were "Spiritualists." And believe it or not, they had a whole church, or something, dedicated just to making contact with paranormal entities.

This is before Horizon was here. Oh yeah, I'm talking about the 1800s, or you know, that time period. Like, the Civil War. See, a lot of people would think Tony Fiorini wouldn't know about this. Like I said, I love proving people wrong.

Anyway, the Spiritualism group had some kind of way they used to locate the most promising property in, I think, Connecticut, or maybe New England, I'm not really sure on that, the most promising property for contacting paranormal entities. And do you know where they found it was located at?

Horizon. Resort.

Well, they called it something else, I mean. Anyway, they conducted experiments – primitive stuff compared to the scientific methods I know about – and found a lot of stuff, but there were arguments or something, I don't know, the book about them has these long quotes from letters they wrote back and forth, it's really boring. Anyway, they decided to leave the place and they sold it to the guy who built Horizon.

Here's the thing, though; it's not like the paranormal entities went away.

The owners of Horizon did a good job of keeping these stories quiet, but over the years, people saw things and heard things and experienced things – there's actually a whole entire website about it, and it's documented. There are documents proving this stuff took place.

Stacey Glenders.

Right? OK, so that night, you have to understand what she looked like when they found her in the pond. I wasn't technically there, but a buddy of mine was there, and I trust him to be honest. He said she was wearing this old white dress, like a gown, when they found her. What does that tell you?

What would you say about the fact that people have seen a young girl wandering around the premises of Horizon Summer Resort since then, wearing a long white dress? This is something that is documented. I mean, it's in our call logs. We've had, I don't know, five or six calls about it. Not from old ladies, I mean, the state surveyor crews, the hazmat guys, guys like that, they call us and say, "Hey, you got a trespasser here, some girl in a white dress, we tried to catch up with her but we can't find her."

When I heard about those calls, I knew this was my chance. I have the correct scientific equipment, I have the training I got from the online websites, I have the historical background information, and now I have verified sightings of a paranormal entity.

FUCK those assholes at *Orford Paranormal*. Tony Fiorni is going to be the first person who gets documented recorded proof of the existence of paranormal entities, and I'm going to do it at Horizon Summer Resort, the place my fat bitch supervisor sent me as a punishment. Doesn't feel like a punishment now, does it? Feels like my Yankee Stadium, and I'm just about to hit a grand slam in the bottom of the ninth.

Don't believe me? Like I said, I love it. I'm completely serious. I love that you don't believe me.

I've seen her. Stacey Glenders. Five nights ago.

I'm in my vehicle, and I'm at my position, right. It's like 00:30 hours. I'm finishing up my dinner from Popeye's, when I see something from out of the corner of my eye. It's a white dress moving through the trees behind the old groundskeeper's house, like 20 feet from me!

Fuck! Right? I don't have my recording equipment ready, which is maybe the one mistake I've made in all of this. But that's a mistake I'm not going to make again.

And, actually, right at that moment, I wasn't thinking of Stacey Glenders or paranormal entities. To be honest with you, my training kicked in. You know, you can't just "turn off" being a law enforcement officer. It was like, right at that moment, I was no longer a scientist; I was a cop.

So I make a pursuit on foot. OK, technically, I was supposed to radio in any trespassers, but this was a pursuit. I didn't have time. What if this person was a terrorist?

I'm giving chase to the suspect, but I can't quite catch up with her. I just see this white clothing moving ahead of me, and she runs into the part of the resort where the old cabins are. I mean, it's a ruin back there. Some of those buildings have just collapsed. There's all kinds of debris – doors, bricks, windows, old furniture – just lying around. It's unsafe, so now I have to slow down and exercise extreme caution during the pursuit.

Long story short, I lose her in the cabins. Which is another sign I'm dealing with the paranormal here, because a human suspect is not going to be able to shake off Tony Fiorni so easily.

So I'm standing in this clearing, and I hear a noise – it's people running out from the back of one of the cabins. I instruct them to halt and identify myself as a police officer, but they keep running, so I draw my service weapon and go in after them. At that point, I was thinking, you know, is this a trap?

High school kids having a party. There's no way they could get onto the property without my notice, so they must have been there since before I arrived at my post. Because I was being so cautious, they all managed to get out the back, except for this one suspect I caught by the foot as she was climbing through the window. She was an Asian female, approximately 5'6" and 109 pounds, and ah, clad in shorts and a tank top, and...

Listen. I feel like I can trust you here, and I fucked up. I fucked up. It happens. I'm a human being, OK.

I just wanted...I just wanted to be...something came over me. I don't know – you know, it could be an occurrence of paranormal activity. I need to research it more. Maybe this is a common situation.

But, she was reacting very emotionally to what was transpiring, and, as I said, I felt this kind of feeling come over me, and I told her that I wouldn't arrest her if she would...I mean, I could tell it wasn't the first time she had done something like this. OK?

That was a lapse. Since that night, I've had my paranormal recording equipment with me, primed and ready. The demolition is starting, but I'm not worried, because Sergeant Vargas says I can stay at this post until the last building comes down. And long before that happens, you're going to be reading the name Tony Fiorini in the newspapers.

4. Post uploaded on 4-18-15 to "Rambles 'Round the Parish," the personal blog of Nancy Gaines, past president of the Orford Parish Historical Society.

There's been a rumor for weeks that spring has arrived, and the last two days have borne tentative confirmation of that: the breezes are softer, the air is warmer, and on my walk in the cemetery this morning I found violets. They were in the Alcott family section, in the ring where the seven children's graves are. I took a picture, but nature photos seem to be one of the many things at which I conspicuously underwhelm.

Underwhelming, too, will be this post, I fear. It's just more photographs of the Horizon Summer Resort; the last batch, I suppose, before the wrecking ball starts swinging, as early as next week. As unhappy as I am about this outcome, I have to publicly thank – however "public" this little corner of the Internet may be – the state officials and police officers who allowed me to wander the grounds over the last several days. They were a bit abashed, I think, the way gravediggers on the edge of a family funeral can sometimes be.

And funereal is how it felt: walking the ruined paths where I can remember running as a girl, looking at the proud little buildings, now humbled by neglect and vandalism, thinking of all the wonderful times that were had in the confines of this place, and how our young generations will never know that particular joy. One more link to the irreplaceable past of Orford Parish will soon be gone, to make way for another outpost of mighty Commerce's empire: a friend in town hall tells me the economic development director hopes to show the "site" to builders looking to erect a "Super Wal-Mart."

Well. I suppose everyone who reads this humble online journal knows how I feel. I won't burden you with an old woman's misgivings any further. Here are the pictures I want to share with you:

Fig. 1-3: The Assembly Hall, exterior.

Maybe the biggest disappointment of the entire affair was the failure to save this magnificent building, which dates to 1907, back when the property was known as Deucalia, and it was owned and maintained by the All-Light First Spiritualist Church of Orford Parish. The Assembly Hall is where the church members held their worship services, and it later became the site of so many wonderful social events at Horizon – the concerts (some of the greats played here, you know! I can well remember the excitement we felt when Ricky Nelson performed here in the summer of 1957 – yes, dear reader, I am THAT old!), the annual opening and closing parties at the start and end of the season, the costume parties.

It's first of all a shame because, as you can see from these photographs, the building is largely in tact, far moreso than many of the other structures that were left to the elements and the vandals. This is a historic building that needed a bit of work, not a "ruin," as some of the demolition advocates would have us believe.

Second of all, it's a shame because it's a link not just to Horizon's wonderful history in our town, but to the thriving Spiritualist community that started here in the 1850s and only dwindled in the years after the war. For over 50 years, what we think of as Horizon was Deucalia, and the Assembly Hall is the last connection we have to that time.

Fig. 4: The Assembly Hall, interior.

I wasn't permitted much time inside this grand old building, but as you can see from my photograph, there's no graffiti inside, and the main room ("the ballroom," as we always thought of it) is free of debris or damaged walls. The suggestion by some that local superstitions about the Hall being "haunted" are to account for this preservation strikes me as a tad melodramatic. Orford Parishioners are many things, but unduly scared of "haints," they are not. Doesn't it seem more likely that the reason even vandals shrank from defacing the beloved Hall is that so many generations of Parishioners made so many wonderful memories here?

Fig. 5-7. The cabins, interior and exterior.

Some of you may recall that early on in the history of Horizon, there was something of a "class division" between accommodations at the resort: blue collar guests tended to stay in the rough-and-ready bunkhouses, while the professional classes spent their summer vacations in the more private, self-contained cabins.

This was mostly over by the mid-1950s, and the bunkhouses became exclusively devoted to rental by large groups – typically Scouts, or churches on an outing. I know some of the older residents of the Parish (she said, hoping no one would respond, "Older than YOU??") fondly remember the family atmosphere in the bunkhouses, but for most of us, the cabins were "it" when we thought of Horizon.

As you can see, there's not much left, but I wanted to post these photographs for those of you who might feel the gentle pull of fond memories when looking at these ghosts and seeing them as they were in 1957 or 1965 or 1978 or 1989.

I don't mean for this to be an exercise in nostalgia; I don't seek to preserve the past for nostalgic reasons (after all, one can only feel nostalgia for times one has personally experienced, and the Assembly Hall, for example, is over 100 years old – I'm getting on, but I'm not quite THAT old!). History is neither nostalgia nor sentimentality, it is keeping faith with the people who came before us. The dead, as Philip Larkin said, are not dead; they are among us even now, perhaps only symbolically, yes. But there are few things more potent in life than symbols.

Apologies, incidentally, for the interior photograph. I don't normally notice graffiti nor would I ever want to be seen as encouraging it, but I had to chuckle when I saw this a few days ago. For all I know "TAKE THE MEDICATION" is the title of a song, or a dance, or a general injunction to misbehavior. But as some of you know, my Jim has been gone for 16 months now, and I still find myself almost unconsciously looking for him in the little moments of daily life. Not to bore you with too much information about an old woman's problems, but I've recently been prescribed some new medicine that has frightfully unpleasant side effects, and so I've found myself leaving those tablets aside when performing my daily rounds of pill-taking.

It's the kind of heedless, headstrong thing that always drove Jim up a wall, and every time I hesitate over one of those pills, I can hear his voice, in that exasperated but loving way, saying "Nancy, just take the medication!" So when I saw this scrawled on a wall inside a cabin, I had to snap a photograph of it.

Fig. 8-10. Ebinger Pond and the path around it.

Man-made, and soon to be man-unmade: Ebinger Pond also predates the property's use as a summer resort, having been created by the Spiritualist church when the land was known as Deucalia. The purpose of the pond seems to have been for exercises associated with the practice that set the First Light Spiritualists apart from their co-religionists elsewhere: "spirit-racing," in which two women, wearing specially-sewn white gowns, were harnessed together by a contraption that fitted over their heads and shoulders. They would then, in this cumbersome getup, proceed to run in tandem around a track built on the edge of the pond. It seems the group believed that water was a natural conductor for communications from beyond the grave, and that the harness and running served to attract spirits. Stranger things have happened! The only known photograph of the spirit-harness, by the way, is on permanent display at the Orford Parish Historical Society Museum on Talmadge Street.

This perhaps unique custom in the history of American religion will be buried once and for all when the demolition crews begin dumping hundreds of tons of dirt and gravel – quarried, I'm told, from Rocky Point, as if the very soil of Orford Parish itself would cry out against the deed – into the pond, which is shortly to be drained.

The death of the girl last year was of course a terrible tragedy, but not for the first time, I'm forced to wonder if a fence around the pond wouldn't have been a more sensible solution than tearing down the entire resort. Or perhaps some of those policemen who are stationed at Horizon "around the clock" nowadays could have been stationed there during past 24 years, when they could have prevented the kinds of vandalism and wreckage that have led us to this point?

Ah, well, you see, there I go again. The opinions of – how did Councilman Bordanaro phrase it? – "an old woman fussing over antique rubble." Guilty as charged, Councilman, except some of us happen to feel that our heritage is more than "rubble."

Forgive me. I promise you I'll stop my barbed comments in time. We will soon no longer have Horizon or Deucalia, but we have a storehouse of documents – letters, post cards, photographs, official papers – that will prove invaluable to historians looking to shed light on *two* aspects of America's past. And we'll always have our memories, of course. I am grateful for that, regardless of the sometimes curt tone in which the public debate was conducted.

Just don't expect me to be a loyal shopper at the Super Wal-Mart.

Signing off for now,
Nancy

Comments (3)

Wonderful pictures, Nance! And you're too polite to say it, so let me: Bill Bordonaro is a bully! He can be the first person to cut the ribbon at his super shopping center, but those of us in town who appreciate the finer things know what we've really lost!!

Posted by Patti Boulanger (mompatti15@hotmail.com) at 14:38 on 4-18-19.

Another incredible post, Nancy, but this one breaks my heart! From deep in muggy North Carolina, this transplanted Orford Parishioner grieves with you and your band of courageous preservationists. The only true judge – History – will not be kind to Mr. Bordonaro and his "progress" crusade.

I have but the smallest quibble with this magnificent entry, and the only reason I even mention it is because I know that you have as much as appetite for the intricacies of history as I do!

You are correct that the Assembly Hall was built in 1907 (and an aside – O tempora! O mores! Are they really going to tear down a 108-year-old building in that pristine condition? Have we become such a nation of barbarians?), but it was not the first main worship hall for the First Light Spiritualists.

That was built in 1867 on the site that is now – Ebinger Pond! I've had a chance to do some digging (an aside: Ah, retirement!), and stumbled across a magnificent tome written by one R.S. Pribble (aside: Related to Ward Pribble?) in 1915 called, somewhat prosaically, *The Spiritualist Churches of North Central Connecticut.* There's much of interest about our First Light Spiritualists in this book, but one fascinating tit-bit is that the siting and construction of the "new" Assembly Hall was apparently the cause for the schism in the group that ultimately led to the sale of the property to Paul Ware, who of course built the Horizon resort.

It seems there was some kind of terrible tragedy – a fire, perhaps – at the "old" Assembly Hall late in the 1890s, and 11 people were killed, all of them members of the Ebinger family, which you'll recall had been among the founders of the First Light church. For some reason, these Spiritualists responded to that awful event not by rebuilding a worship hall on the site – but by paying to have a pond made on the very spot!

That brings me to Quibble No. 2: I had always heard, as you have, the story that the spirit-racing in the harness was designed to establish better communication with the deceased. But in Pribble's book, he quotes from contemporary Spiritualist documents – which, alas and alack!, I have not been able to track down independently – that suggest the actual purpose of the ritual was to keep spirits *in* the pond.

Strange, and stranger still! Unfortunately, Pribble doesn't go into much detail about what that might mean, or what spirits they wanted to keep from leaving the pond, but if I dig up anything new, I'll be excited to share it with you, perhaps on my next visit back to the old home place. That will be in June, actually; my grandson, Clark, is graduating from Ye Olde Orford Parish High, and I'll be there beaming with pride! Actually, the lad has started to show the beginnings of an interest in preservation – he's been asking me all sorts of questions about the Horizon resort itself! Too bad for all of us that it's coming so late.

Again, Nancy, splendid work, and see you in June! —Ross

Posted by Ross Collier (imperatorOP@gmail.com) at 23:21 on 4-18-15.

TAKE THE MEDICATION

Posted by Anonymous at 03:00 on 4-19-15.

5. The experience of Joe McGowan, 74. With your leave, I'll relate this experience, as dementia has left Joe McGowan's thoughts difficult to assemble in an easily understandable fashion.

Joe McGowan had walked away from the Oakfell Nursing Home and Rehabilitation Care Center only 15 minutes ago – door alarms beeping as the overworked staff struggled with a particularly aggressive patient on the dementia ward nicknamed "The Admiral" – but he had already made good time.

His original destination had been home – his real home, not this awful tiny room where the strangers who pretended to be his sons and daughter told him he lived now – but he got sidetracked when he recognized the street behind the nursing home as Deucalia Road, familiar to generations of Orford Parishioners and others as the way to Horizon Summer Resort.

Memories would suddenly flash and flare in the dense fog of his dementia, and this night, those memories were of Horizon:

At seven years old, with Ma and Pop and his sister, Dottie, all packed into one of the old bunkhouses with about 10 other families, laughing and playing cards by the light of a kerosene lantern.

At 15, sneaking off behind the Assembly Hall with that Italian girl (What was her name? Viola? Yes, that was it: Viola), too scared to admit he'd never kissed a girl before, so excited he somehow lost his watch and caught holy hell from Pop over it.

At 21, home before his senior year of college to introduce Elena to Ma and Pop, sharing a cabin with her and two of their friends, sunbathing with her on the roof, rubbing lotion into her back and watching his future open up in front of him like the clouds parting on a sunny morning.

At 35, proud that he could afford to rent two cabins – one for the kids, one for him and Elena – and the panic that year when Jason, horsing around on the edge of the pool, fell and cracked his head open. The awful terror they had felt, waiting in the hospital, and how relieved – sick with relief – he had felt when Jason blinked his eyes and asked when they could go back to Horizon.

At 49, Elena in the ground three months, and the worst vacation of his life. He sat in the cabin and smoked cigarettes the whole time, until the last night, when Jennifer made them all sing that song Elena had liked so much, that song by Ricky Nelson about a lonely town, and he cried for the first time in years, and felt so lucky to have the kids.

Let's go there, he said in the dark on a cold April night. Let's go to Horizon.

Won't they all be there? Sure, where else would anyone be in this town? Ma, Pop, Elena, Jason, Jennifer, Patrick; sure, they'd all be there. They were already there, in fact. Why was he out on the road like a bum? Hurry up, Joe, get there before they hand out the last hot dog.

It was colder than he remembered, but it was early in the season. He frowned down at the baggy sweatpants they'd made him wear in that place – what place was that, again, Joe? You've never been to jail, but that place had to be close – and thought, I hope Elena remembered to pack my swim trucks. I'm going to want to take a dip as soon as it's light out.

The resort seemed quiet when he arrived. No lights were on in the groundskeeper's house, and there was a police car parked outside for some reason, but nobody was inside it. Maybe there was a concert going on, he thought, and somebody hired the cop to stand around and frown at potential troublemakers.

It was darker than he remembered – didn't anybody put on the lights in this place? – but even the black outlines of the buildings made his hear leap with joy. For the first time in what seemed like years, he felt he was finally getting back to where he belonged, before the strangers who pretended to be his children somehow tricked him out of his home and into that jail, before the stroke, before his retirement, before the kids moved away, before Elena died, before Dottie died, before they all died. Ma and Pop were gone, too, just like his wife and his sister and his kids, who had turned into strangers.

"I'm the last one left," he said out loud, but as soon as he said it was gone, because he realized he had to find the cabins they'd rented, where Elena would be waiting and the kids and Dottie, although he suspected Ma and Pop would be in one of the bunkhouses.

Two shapes came scrambling out of the dark cabins toward him, and for an instant he didn't recognize them, thought they were two kids in old-fashioned clothes, but then he immediately remembered it was Dottie and that idiot boyfriend of hers, Maurice, who everyone called "Cork," but sometimes Pop called him a name that was one letter away from "Cork," which made Ma livid.

"Dottie! Cork! What are you doing out here?" Joe McGowan called to them. "We're all going to be late for dinner. Ma and Pop are going to be sore with us."

Dottie and Cork stopped in front of him. They stared at him in confusion; he knew he had them dead to rights.

"Come on," he said. "Come on. Ma and Pop are waiting."

"Oh my God," Cork said. Cork was a drip.

"Sir," Dottie said. So it was "sir" now, was it? What kind of game was she playing. "Are you OK?"

Joe laughed. "I'll be a lot better when I get a hot dog and some birch beer in me. Now, come on, we're late enough as it is."

A voice reached them from the cabins, which made Dottie and Cork run, although she clearly wanted to stay. "Kate, come on! Come on!" Cork yelled at her, which made Joe angry; was his sister so unimportant to this bozo that he can't even remember her name?

Joe wanted to run after them, but they were too fast, and before long, the shouting got closer. It turned out that it was attached to some pudgy goofball dressed up like a policeman for some idiot reason.

"Stop! Hey! Hey!" the goofball yelled, out of breath. He stopped when he got to Joe.

"What are you doing here?" the goofball asked.

Joe had no time for this.

"What are you supposed to be?" he asked. "Little early for Halloween, isn't it?"

"Sir, are you lost? Are you in danger? Sir, where did you come from?" the guy was now saying, and every word out of his chubby mouth was making Joe more and more impatient.

Then, behind the blabbering make-believe cop, Joe saw Elena.

She was wearing some kind of old-fashioned white gown, which was not her style at all – one of those fragmentary memories suddenly flashed up, of Elena in cutoff jeans and one of Joe's old shirts, working in the garden, and he felt a longing that bit with physical pain – but it was unmistakably her: the same beautiful dark eyes, the same face that had knocked him for a loop in an introductory statistics class all those years ago, the same woman whose hand he had held in a hospital room when she slipped away from him.

She smiled and began walking toward the pond at the center of the resort.

Joe called after her and began to follow, but the goofball in the Keystone Cop getup stepped in front of him.

"Sir, do not be alarmed. My name is Officer Anthony Fiorini and I'm here to help you."

Joe swiped at him and kept walking. "Help yourself to an ice cream cone and get out of my way," he said.

The goofball then made a mistake: he clamped his thick fingers down on Joe McGowan's wrist, hard enough to make Joe McGowan wince. Joe McGowan had never once hit his children, but he had been raised on the North Side of Orford Parish, where life was not so gentle. Joe reached over to the remains of a cabin wall, felt his fingers pull out a loose brick, and swung it squarely into the face of the Tony Fiorini with a force that surprised the younger man in the instant before he crumpled to the ground.

Just as soon as Joe had completed the strike, he forgot it, and so he looked down with annoyance at the man beneath him.

"OK, knock it off, buddy, save it for the summertime play," he said. "Come on, knock it off!"

But the fat cop on the ground only twitched and gurgled. Joe McGowan stood there, unsure of himself, until a wing of white fabric flashed up before him, down the hill.

Of course, of course! Elena.

Joe moved after her as fast as his body would allow. He walked past the rest of the cabins, past the old bunkhouses, past the pool – was it drained? Was Jason OK, horsing around there with no water in the pool? – past the Assembly Hall, where lights were glowing, then darkening again, until he reached Ebinger Pond.

Unsure of what to do or why he was there – Elena? Ma? Pop? – he took a tentative step into the pond, and the freezing water soaked through his socks and battered slippers so swiftly that for a moment he saw everything with astounding clarity, suddenly realizing he was alone at night in the old Horizon resort, standing in marshy, fetid water with mud sucking at his feet and ankles.

But then the memories exploded in his mind again, and suddenly everything was as it had once been, all that had been broken was remade, Ebinger was a vast blue surface teeming with paddle boats and canoes, the shore was thick with people lying on blankets and sunning themselves, there were sunbathers on all the rooftops of the distant cabins, everything was exactly the way it should be, a perfect summer day right here at home.

And in the middle of the pond, on the big wooden raft in the center, over the deepest water, they were standing in a line: Ma and Pop, Dottie and Cork, Jason and Jennifer and Patrick, and his beautiful Elena, all of them together again at last, waving to him. Beckoning.

THE CORDS OF THE NECK
BY J. ROBERT SHELTON

A thick braid of black smoke rises out of the city which from here looks as if it has been divided into a checkerboard. Over here, in the expanse of black asphalt, the other circusman and I have quit yelling to stare at it. I know he is thinking the same thing; I can tell because he is absent-mindedly stroking the sinews of his neck. The smoke abates to a distant wisp and we pick up where we left off.

"Heya, heya, heya! Hungry for a spectacle? Wanna see something amazing? For only one dollar seventy five cents you get to see all three of my exhibits! See what's under the shroud of mystery! Marvel at the secrets of the box of bric-a-brac! And finally, perform the impossible feat—look inside yourself!"

I leap from my perch on the chain link fence and scurry back to my blanket. I spread it so I didn't have to sit on the pavement, which in the hot sun is beginning to bubble up and turn shiny like tar.

I begin, thinking the quality of my barking is obviously superior to his: "Tired of the hum-drum? Think all circuses are as boring as the other guy's? For a really amazing show, the entertainment event of the century, come over and see *my* circus – all three events for one low, low price: you have the enigma of the kerchief – what awaits under its folds to enchant and horrify alike? You have the Drawer of Mystery, a collection of thrilling sub-exhibits for the price of one! And then you the coup-de-gras, see what you're made of inside with the Magic Book!"

I know for a fact that we have the exact same exhibits, only different; I know because I once stole them from him, besides which we acquired them from the same places. Together, most of them.

I have: a kerchief over a dead bird, he has a kitchen towel covering the grimy paw of a raccoon he once found. He has: a box full of broken children's toys, pistachio shells and a model of a sailboat. I have: a drawer full of beetle legs and dice floating in transmission fluid. Finally, we both have: a book called "Gray's Anatomy," which we found together inside the mall back when we were pulling the same gig, which is circus speak for show. I'm going to grab one too, he said, and it was then that I knew that the days of our partnership were numbered.

We split everything when we were owners and operators of the One Circus, Catholic and Whole. Anything we found was ours.

Now, after our Circus has diverged into his *Show Extraordinaire!* and my *Cirque Du Fantastico*, I hate him. I hate his voice, I hate the smarmy look he gives me when the shadow of the shopping mall clock tower falls on him while I am still boiling in the sun (and which I return tenfold when I am in the shade and he cooks – I need only wait a few hours), I hate the way he rattles his jar of coins, which I know for a fact he collected from the upturned car that leaks transmission fluid, and not from paying customers as he'd have me think. I hate the way he blows snot out of his nose, first one nostril and then the other, and the way it trickles down into his beard, the way he get on his hands and knees to inspect it on the pavement, as if he can scry something from his own murky globes of snot. I hate the weathered dress shirt he wears even though it's several sizes too big and billows around his gnarled, knobbed knees. I hate the way his voice gets husky after a day of busking. I hate it when he looks at me, and I hate that I feel it imperative to get his attention when he's not. I hate that he makes light of what we once had. I hate him.

I watch him when he gets up in the morning, pulling himself out of the drain pipe and then reaching in behind him to grab his blanket, which he uses as a satchel to carry his exhibits. I watch him at night, when in mutual exhaustion we have given up our competing circuses for the night and he pages through his book. When he reaches the page of the man's neck he pauses. He stares at the illustration, black and white, of the cords of the neck and know what he's thinking, because it was a conversation we would often have before the split.

Can it really be that everyone looks the same inside? That our necks hold the very same cords? That, if there is someone over in the city, some wizard who makes to rise the thick curling braid of smoke out of those craggy, fallen buildings, is it possible that *even he* could have a neck full of cords? Or isn't it *really* true what *we* suspected, that we were all full of divers things according to our nature, one of us perhaps full of pebbles and tar, another fit to burst with fluttering moths, another still filled with the bulbs of flowering plants? But what good is it to remember in the sticky heat?

Then one morning the unthinkable happens. Though I haven't seen him do anything out of the ordinary, though he has not escaped my sight for one moment, nor has his morning routine differed one iota from usual, something is different. I can tell as soon as he is awake. The look he gives me is different; pregnant. When he propels the thick mucus out of his nose in twin ropes of yellow snot he even fails to inspect them, as is his usual wont. When he has his morning vittles of fossilized tater tots he does not shovel them into his mouth while crouched behind the dumpster throwing me poisonous glances. Rather, he drops them into his mouth one by one and wriggles with inscrutable delight.

My breath sticks in my throat before he even opens his mouth. And when he does speaks he is looking right at me. I turn to ice in the heat, angry at myself for having desired his attention so much.

"Here ye! Here ye, one and all! The Show Extraordinaire is proud to present an all new, totally original exhibit! For your delight and edification, a brand new ring to the circus! A frightfully new exhibition, available only through your humble purveyor of edutainment, certain to shock and amaze your family! Come ye and see before the crowds hit!" And then silence, as the words steep in the air.

I stand up, blind hot with rage, and holler at him through grimy, cupped hands. It is the first time we've spoken in a long time.

"You're a liar!"

I try as gingerly as I can to step over to him without my feet sinking into hot asphalt. "You're a liar! You don't have anything new! I would know if you did!"

He just smiles, though I think I can detect something like fear in his widened nostrils and wadded fists. "I do have something new. It's an all new exhibit."

"What is it?" I scream as I grab him by his tattered collar.

"I can't just *tell you*. That's bad showmanship. You have to pay. Its two dollars and twenty five cents."

I wipe a falling comet of sweat from my eye, but still cannot see through my anger and the heat. The world is swimming, and for a moment I don't think I'll be able to continue standing up. But then I find a hidden reserve of energy which finds me scrabbling over a pylon and off into the shimmering, stifling air.

For days I go without rest, scouring the asphalt inch by inch for embedded coins. On the first day I find three nickels, six pennies and a quarter. On the second I find a dime and an old silver dollar, and I take the rest of the day off to celebrate, ending in the evening with a contemplation of the "Gray's Anatomy" pages on female anatomy.

I try to imagine what sort of grift he's up to over there with his new exhibit – what could he possibly have that he would have the unmitigated gall to call new? Could he have taken the secret chicken bones out of his coat? Did he tear a page out of the book and color it with his collection of women's face-paints – perhaps the page of the man's teeth, or the cross section of his liver? Or was he lying, a ploy to drive me mad, slowly, as I wonder and wonder until this interminable heat finally burns off my brain, until it becomes its own plume of thick and turgid smoke in someone else's distance?

On the third day I find only a washer on a string and another chicken bone. I think perhaps the chicken bone may be worth a few cents to him but I know he would laugh at the washer. Even though if he had found it he would have boasted about it for days. I spend the rest of the day dejected, thinking black thoughts.

On the fifth and sixth days I am on my hands and knees in the transmission fluid by the upturned car in front of the big picture of the smiling woman who no longer has eyes. It feels cool on my fingers and toes, which is very pleasant until I cannot get the slippery muck out from between them, nor the smell, like some kind of electronic dinosaur in heat. I find two bits on the sixth day, which saves me from complete despair.

On the seventh day I find an entire cash register bashed open. It lies in tall grass which is the oily, brackish color of a tepid puddle. And even though all the paper money has long since caught the wind and floated away, there are fistfuls of coins left. I am richer at this moment than I have ever been, even in the boom times with the *One Circus*. I am tempted to return to him immediately despite the late hour, bang on his drain pipe with the chicken bone and demand that he open the *Show Extraordinaire* and give me a very special private show, to throw coins in front of him and promise him extra, more where that comes from if he makes it a good one.

But instead I spend the night staring out from under my blanket at the drain pipe, sweating in the squelching night heat and wishing him ill.

Finally, the day has arrived. When I wake I don't put out the blanket and the exhibits one by one, with the empty coin jar behind and my collection of short pamphlets and brochures for the *Cirque Du Fantastico* in front. Nor do I slick back my hair, put on my captain's hat and special Circus shirt with the picture of the little man playing polo on the pocket. I only narrow my eyes and plod across the pavement, counting out the money from a plastic bag I have slung from my belt. He pretends not to notice, though I can feel his jealous eyes on me like fingers crawling all through and over my body.

"I have the money." I jingle my coins in front of him. "I want a show."

"Certainly. We have three exhibits available today. Can I give you a tour of the grounds, or give you some informational literature about the history of the *Show Extraordinaire*?"

"Three exhibits? I'm only paying for the fourth! Where is the fourth?" I sputter angrily.

He attempts a nonchalantly stroke of his filthy beard. "Closed. For the day."

"Can I come and see it tomorrow?" I ask through clenched teeth.

"Er, no, I'm afraid that won't be possible, friend."

"Why not? When will it reopen?"

He gives me a look which I understand to mean it'll never be open for me. Something rises up out of me before I have a chance to catch it, and my words come out in a choking sob. I sound, even to myself, like a baby on the verge of wracking hysterics. "After all we've been through. Do you remember when we found the kitchen appliance, what was it called?"

His look softens a little. "A toaster."

"Yes, a toaster. And do you remember how we danced and caroused? And we decided not to put it in the *One Circus, Catholic and Whole* because we wanted it to be just ours, something we wouldn't share with anyone else? And how we pressed the lever down and examined the action, testing the tensile strength of the springs, pretending we were making toast out of gravel and tire scraps?"

"I remember."

"And you remember how we ended up breaking it by gripping the cord together and swinging it as hard as we could against that pylon over there, but we couldn't figure why we'd done it, other than to deny the rest of the world something that by all rights could only ever have been ours? And then we had a funeral for it, and the *One Circus* was half-off that week out of respect?"

"Yes."

"Then please, please, just tell me what the exhibit is."

Now his fear is palpable, mixed as it is with a drought of nostalgia. He raises his hand slowly, and points at me. I turn around, and fight through the glare of the sun to look behind me. There is nothing, unless he is pointing at—

—no, it couldn't be—

Trembling, I reach out to steady myself on a handicapped parking sign. *"I'm the exhibit?"* The heat has seeped into my brain. It is choking me, and I feel I cannot extricate myself from the tightly twisted coil of the cords of my neck.

"What kind of exhibit is it?"

"It's a..." he stops, and licks his lips, which are dry and rough though his beard is always strangely moist. "Don't make me say it."

"What is it?" I scream and the sound echoes off of a distant parking garage and returns to us. He closes his eyes.

"It's a... zoo."

Before I know it I feel the heft of my makeshift change purse in my hand. I see the bag burst and the coins rolling on the ground before I know I have swung them against the side of his head. He looks at me for what seems like an eternity before his face and beard and ragged shirt turn crimson. Then, gripping what's left of the bag by the handle (like a toaster by its cord), I swing again and again, though the empty plastic does little more than fan him. It doesn't matter. He has already fallen face down in the asphalt, and nothing moves except for his left foot, which is sweeping the gravel like a dumb fin.

I sit cross-legged next to him.

That night I do not watch his drain pipe, since there's nothing to see. Instead, I sit on my back and look at the stars appearing here and there from behind dark clouds. For a moment it threatens to rain, and I feel a few drops on my sunburned face, and hear sizzles where they hit the asphalt. I do not sleep. Somewhere near morning I find I have opened the book, and am looking once again at the picture of the neck cords, wound round together like snakes in heat. Hours pass.

At first light I'm using the sharp edge of one of his broken toys to cut back his skin. I work slowly, pulling the new flaps of his neck open like curtains at a theater. I barely notice that I am sniffing, my nose is running, that an encroaching cold has turned the night into something crisp and ruffled like a cat. I use one of the sub-exhibits from the Drawer of Mysteries, a Bic lighter with a few drops left of juice, to see. All the while thinking to myself that the dawn is coming later and later these days. The asphalt no longer gives. The air doesn't divide itself into waves. I distract myself thusly with thoughts of the weather.

Finally, I am done.

I look at the book, and back. The cords of his neck are exactly the same as in the book, but in color. The color is the same as the sunset. I sniff again and draw a fist across my mustache. It is a cold morning. I wrap him in his blanket and stuff him in the drainpipe, an afternoon's work. Days pass slowly, and nights are unbearable.

I try to bark like usual, but soon it's not the same despite my own brand new fourth exhibit: "Hey, come on. Right over here, I got some exhibits. Got a dead body in a blanket. Some other stuff. Make me an offer." No one comes, of course. Finally, I stop barking altogether, stop setting out exhibits, cease my search for suitable exhibits.

The days become impossible to number, and the first snows start to fill the sky like late-night TV crackle. It becomes so cold that one morning I awake, stiff under my one tattered blanket, and trudge through the snow-pack down the icy slope of the runoff channel to the corrugated iron drain pipe. Grunting, weak with hunger and exertion, I haul the blanket out, heaving until it becomes unstuck. When I unroll him it looks as if he is staring at me even though he lies face down. For a confused moment, I smile at him cordially as I used to do on *One Circus* mornings. It passes. I am able to summon something like hate once again.

I trudge back to my small camp through the snow with both blankets – mine and his – wrapped around my shoulders. But it does not keep out the shivers. Even my brain feels cold.

Something catches my eye, despite the stinging flurries that force them half-shut: in the distance, the smoke is rising again. I cup my hands around my eyes, squint, try to look, but I cannot see anything but the cords of a neck painted in clumsy black. No sign that there is another living soul down there, that the rising plume of smoke is anything other than a greasy, insensate belch of the earth herself.

My thoughts are interrupted by a soft and sudden crunch of snowy footfall. I turn to see a raggedy man standing wrapped in plastic bags and the fur of strange animals, gripping with a weathered hand a long toilet plunger as a walking stick. He stares at me and I stare back. Finally, he speaks, with a soft, insistent voice.

"I have come many long miles to see the *One Circus*."

I pull the dead man's blankets and my own tighter, and in the falling snow there is no sound but the chattering of my teeth and the stranger's labored breaths. I wait a long time, and then spread my arms wide.

When I speak the words leap from my mouth like mice on fire.

THE PLAYGROUNDS
BY SHANNON LIPPERT

On Monday morning Kayla walks into the dusty, worn out classroom. She is a mid-year transfer student in soft white jeans and a crumbled up t-shirt. Her hair is tied up. Her build is sensible. Not too tall, not too chubby, precisely halfway between child and adult. She is fair skinned and mild-mannered. She gives her name: "Kayla Morrison," and takes the only other seat available. It is an unexceptional Monday morning.

On Friday afternoon, she is screaming.

It's not a school-sanctioned club. That would require a faculty advisor and an open-door membership policy. It's not really even a club. Clubs go on resumes and college applications. It's not like church, but it feels like something maybe in between a church youth group and an after school activity. A secular religious organization.

Matt leads Kayla into the room, and her first question is like every first question. How did they know? Because there is nothing about her that suggests a kind of specialness. She is average in every sense of the word (except for the important distinction that got her an invite to the unused third floor science classroom). Kayla could be a body double for the everywoman. At least, that's what she's bee told. And she is nothing if not a slightly better than average listener.

Matt tells her about the boy that used to talk to flying things, who moved away last year and took all the crows and honeybees with him. Matt introduces Kayla to Marnie, the skinny girl who can say anything, everything. Steel, socks, petroleum, chewing gum. Nobody knows where she puts it. Kayla meets Thomas and Michael, who can switch places with each other. Shelly can turn invisible. She meets Clarissa, who can see the future, or the past, but can't keep track of the present. I'm the reason they knew. I warned them, and they were all waiting for months, wondering what Kayla can do.

Her arrival is more like a reunion.

It's a decent way to spend an afternoon.

Matt has been sitting in the back of the room since the first week of school. He lets people think it's because he's too cool to care but it has more to do with the fact that the chalk dust aggravates his allergies. He's sensitive. He has spent sixteen years listening and rolling coins on his knuckles and making faces at children behind their parents' backs. There is a playground near his house that is lined with grass instead of mulch, and is protected by the snarling pit bull that lives next door. Matt has had several conversations with the dog, and knows his bark is worse than his bite. On Monday, Kayla sits next to Matt because there are no other seats, and they write notes to each other in their notebooks. Did you just move here? Yeah. Good luck. Why? This town is weird.

Kayla is late coming home every night that week.

They run.

Thursday night. They pass the rusty street signs and howl at the concrete

sidewalks. They make *noise*. Marnie eats through the fence around the playground, locked up for the night. From sundown to sunup. They don't care. Neither does the guard dog in the yard next door. Thomas and Michael ride the swings and switch at the highest point; they stand on opposite ends of the see-saw, keeping the seats perfectly level, and see if they can keep it that way while they trade positions. Shelly plays a game of hide and seek with Matt. He can't see her, but he can sense her, and she makes him run in circles trying to find her while she giggles, right behind him the entire time.

Kayla sits on the bench, says "hello Clarissa" and toys with the dirt with the edges of her sneakers. It will be hours before I realize I should have answered back.

There used to be a train, that pulled through town. It's gone now, all closed up. There are no trains left, just empty tracks and hollow stations. Little yellow flowers are struggling to break through the earth and rails, searching for light. Kayla follows her new friends through the shattered glass doors, across the chipped tile floors, past the ticket machines. To make her laugh, Marnie takes a bite out of a turnstile. Pairs of squeaky shoes track dirt and dust as they travel out to the platform.

Thomas and Michael stand at opposite ends, waving and giggling as they switch, over and over. "It's colder over here." Switch. "No it's not you filthy liar, it's cooler over *there*," Switch. "I left the thermometer over there." "No you didn't." Switch. "Yes I did, it's right here." Switch. "I don't see it." Switch. "On your left." Switch. "Where?" Switch. "Your other left." Switch. "Oh." Switch. "You know, I think it might be the same temperature."

Kayla is watching them, and doesn't notice when Shelly shifts into the background. It's only when Shelly shows up right in front of her, making a face with her eyes crossed and her hair pulled underneath her chin like a beard, that Kayla realizes the trick has happened.

"You can do yours too," Matt says, standing beside her. He holds her hand, because she's reaching for him and he doesn't want to say no. "Nobody can see us here. You're safe."

The light around Kayla flickers, and she shakes her head. "I'm never safe."

Matt's shoulders slump.

"Can I do anything? To make you feel safe?"

She pulls her hand away from him, and he watches her step away, because she wants to separate herself.

"It's not like that, Matt." She wraps her arms around herself. "It's me. I don't have a cool trick to show you. I only know how to make people hurt." She gets angry, and she's trying to control it even though she wants to let it out. Matt listens, because she wants someone to hear her. "You don't understand what it's like! It's scary. It's ugly. It's not funny or cool. It just hurts." Her lips are trembling and the light around her feels hot and she grits her teeth and pulls herself backwards and forces herself to feel controlled.

"I'm sensitive," Matt explains. "i know how you feel. But I don't know why." He shrugs. "It's a dumb trick. All these feelings, but I don't know where they come from. All I

can do is stand here. I can't help." He grunts. "All our tricks are like that." Marnie nods.

"I'm hungry. I eat and eat, but I'm never full."

Thomas and Michael reach for each other, but they never touch. "It hurts," say Thomas. "I miss being able to hug my brother," says Michael.

"Sometimes, nobody can see me." Even as she says it, Shelly is disappearing.

"And no one can see me the way I want to be seen."

I wanted to explain, but at the time all I could see was Friday.

"You are screaming," I said. And Matt explained once again that Clarissa can only see the future, or the past, and it's not always clear which.

It's fire. I can see that it's fire, and I can see that she's never let it shine.

Kayla is home late every night, school nights, and she knows the consequences for going home late. Last year, her father was counting the glasses and realized that one was missing, and Kayla has been hiding the broken shards because she didn't want him to know that she dropped it, slipped right between her fingers while she was finishing the washing up, didn't want him to know because she knew he'd be angry and she wanted to put it off for as long as she could, at least until after she went to the dance with the nice boy that asked her, but she couldn't hide it long enough and.

That was the end of it. No dance.

No anything. Weeks of alone, of chores and school and more chores and then bed, for one broken glass.

She knows the consequences, and she runs from them.

Coming home with dirty clothes or a tear is laundry. Bad grades are hours spent standing in a corner. Talking back is an undefined amount of time spent behind a locked door. Coming home late is not being allowed to go back out.

Kayla feels regrets and looks contrite and then she runs, out the window, through the back door, over the fence, because she thinks those consequences can go to hell.

She runs, because she has a friend who can eat anything, and a friend who can turn invisible, and two friends that can switch places, and a friend that can see backwards and forwards and who doesn't judge Kayla based on what she sees in either direction, even though the world is ending on either end. She runs, because there is a sensitive boy who tells her he loves her, and she doesn't believe him when he tells her it's because of what she feels, but she's starting to. She runs because she is running towards Friday, the inevitable end of the week.

Kayla stands in the center of the playground. The swings are melting into the ground, and the grass is sizzling beneath her feet. The pressure in the air changes violently, cracking underneath the weight of the heat surrounding her. Her eyes are wide, and she holds onto her forearms, fingers pressed into her skin, digging bruises beneath her elbows, and she is trying, very much, to hold it in. Matt can feel how hard she's trying.

On Thursday, they run for real.

Matt waits underneath the window, until he's sure that the relevant parties have ventured a deep, dark sleep. The houses on the block are quiet, indifferent. Shelly opens the front door, because no one will see her do it. They know what they're risking. Marnie chews on the doorknob until the lock has been gnawed away. They can hear the menace even in the quiet. Thomas and Michael keep watch. One of them stays with the group, while the other one stands guard outside the bedroom door. They switch when it's time for the watcher to give his report. They know what they are walking towards. I am with them, and I see Kayla on Monday, walking into the classroom.

And when Kayla steps out of her bedroom, late on Thursday night, she smiles.

"But if I let go, if I don't hang on," there are tears in Kayla's eyes, choking her vision, because she is afraid. "everyone, everything will be on fire. Everyone will burn." Matt gets close to her, and says the kindest thing. "Let them burn."

The teachers in the school, tried and lost and trapped. The empty train station. The parents in their beds, eyes closed and windows shut. The cracks in the sidewalks that will break your mother's back if you step on them the wrong way. The saints and the sinners and the hiding places. The mayors and the local law enforcement and the no trespassing signs and the trees with their roots knotted around the curbside. Fire is indiscriminate.

The tests and grades and workbooks disappear in a flash of brilliant light. No more hospitals, no more churches. The perfectly arranged glasses in the cabinets shatter and burst before they burn. No more cages, no more bars. The tasteful flowers lining the streets shrivel and die; the heat exterminates everything. A house fire can burn at a thousand degrees, if you let it. How hot is a world on fire?

Hot enough.

All of the fences and all the locked doors. All the rough patches of earth that scraped knees and broke bubbles. Burned smooth. All of the bullies and all of the whistleblowers. Everyone who ever said no, there isn't a trace of anything left. All of the progress reports and all of the bedtimes. Gone forever. All the beautiful stars in the sky watch as the earth is engulfed in the brightest of lights, every heat wave converging on the planet at once. It travels across the land, stopping at the beaches, until all that remains of the earth is fire and water and ozone and salty air.

The boy with the birds sent one of his crows back, to check on his friends. It's no phoenix. It has black wings and the sound it makes is garbled. But it finds a perch.

Kayla is screaming.

The flames spread and gorge themselves on the scenery. They engulf the pharmacy, the supermarket, the school. The flames roll down Main Street and tear apart the parched green lawns and indifferent houses.

Kayla is screaming, and it is a beautiful sound.

"Hello Kayla," I reply.

THE LAST FLIGHT OUT OF SAIGON
BY VICTORIA ZELVIN

**THE LAST KNOWN TRANSMISSION FROM EARTH
SENT TO JUDE 8 FORTY-SEVEN SECONDS BEFORE TAKE-
OFF
WORDS DISPLAYED ON THE EARTH REMEMBRANCE
MONUMENT ON MARS**

Got internet for the first time in days. Unprotected wifi – from the
shuttle? Was going to write a note and hope maybe the phone would
survive the apocalypse, but an email works better. Countdown clock says
ten minutes. Can't tell if the people below are dead or unconscious there
were gas canisters fired from the ship and now it's all quite. This is the
NASA email I don't know if it'll work, gotta try. My name is Hanh
Nguycn, I am a professor of history at Georgetown University, I walked
with my baby down I-95 for three days after the roads were blocked, and
I got her off planet. There should be a record. I want somebody to know
what I did. I got my baby off the planet. Her name is Phuong, she's three
years old, and she's going to Mars on a spaceship. I got my baby out.

There should be a record from Earth..

You knew about it, come to find out, knew for years, probably tried to
fix it. Should give credit where's due. Earth persepective, the rest of us,
we just found out last week when those first few rocks hit the Midwest.
Those big space stations in the sky weren't stations at all but ships,
massive ships, to take a thousand people a piece to the Martian colonies.
Eight thousand people on the arks or whatever the hell, to seven hundred

and two people on the Martian surface. Not sure how that's going to work, not sure I'm supposed to know how that's going to work. We didn't know is the point. You lied to us until you couldn't and there were riots in Russia over the last shuttle up from Moscow and somebody nuked Mexico City to stop some cartel from taking off in a stolen shuttle. Collateral damage doesn't matter at this point I guess. Fast death is probably preferable. There's going to be two asteroids. The first will take out North America, cause tsunamis, drown most of the rest of the world and those that are alive will get taken out by the second asteroid. Those aboard the stations will be long gone by then. First asteroid is coming Tuesday. It's Monday and the last not-station was supposed to leave Friday, but it's waiting for this last shuttle here in Norfolk. Must be some important people on it.

Most people have taken to calling them – the spaceships to the not-station – arks, out of adherence to the Biblical story of Noah. I can't remember what they are really called, the arks. In my head, I called the ship what I knew it to be: the last flight out of Saigon.

It was happening again, all over again, only in Norfolk, Virginia now. My granddaddy, he told stories about Saigon. Taking off at the embassy and all those people left behind, hands reaching up holding babies and luggage and prayer beads hoping for one friendly hand to reach down and save them. It was a lot like that. We weren't supposed to get that close to the ship before takeoff, but it was delayed for weather and there were so many of us pushing, surging, rioting at the walls that eventually they crumbled. I had Phuong strapped to my chest in one of those Bjorns, though she was very much too big for it. I needed my hands free. I had a knife in my hands, we know what people'll do when there's no one to enforce the rules, but I didn't need it. People wanted forward. I went diagonally. Granddaddy taught me to be where the people aren't in a crisis. I think it's why I'm the only one left awake/alive.

It's Christmastime. Phuong was scared, didn't like the noise of the crowd, and so I sang her White Christmas as I pushed through. I don't know if she heard me. It's her favorite song, please play it for her. You have to have it in those archives, I know you do, it has to have made the cut of what history got stored in those banks. Aren't you downloading the internet? Save White Christmas for my baby.

Weather's been bad in Virginia. Can't risk taking off in the shuttle not yet not until the weather'll let you otherwise what's the point of all those people who paid to get aboard or whatever the hell they did to be better than me? Got my baby among you now, you've got to be better for her you've got to be good

We got there, up to the front. I'm a climber. Before I got pregnant, I spent most of my weekends bouldering. Climbing up the fences wasn't hard, my baby Phuong doesn't weigh a lot. Climbing up the scaffolding surrounding the ship – I think I picked the one with the fuel line in it. No one else was climbing that one, don't know why. At least with the scaffolding I knew it could take our weight. The fence nearly bowed in half when other people joined me in climbing. It shredded once I was off it, the fence. That was all the way at the front of the complex. I heard it go, didn't look back. Couldn't look back, won't look back.

Even the military men with guns stopped protecting the ship in the end. Figured that this was the last one why protect it why not get their families aboard? They let us right through, almost up to the ship itself, then formed a blockade. There's a man with a megaphone and a handlebar mustache in fatigues. He was shouting, now he's crumpled. I don't know what you fired out of the shuttle but it's effective. They'll die when the rockets go. So will I. I'm too close, don't know much about science but I know that.

Saw an opening when your man opened the door to fire gas. I didn't even see his face. He was wearing a gas mask. I braced myself on the scaffolding, I was higher than him, and I unhooked Phuong from the Bjorn without him seeing me. Phuong was screaming, crying, the whole time. I don't know how he didn't hear.

Phuong looked up at me then, my precious baby, and I can't even look away from her as I throw her, with all my might, at the man in the open doorway. I don't look away from my baby's face. If she fell I wanted to see if she if

Man dropped gun, catches my baby girl on instinct—same kind of instinct in everyone, I think, even if they've got no babies of their own. Man might be able and willing to shoot people back from a shuttle, but can he drop a baby girl into the rocket fire abyss below him? Man's got a choice. My baby is only on her way to Mars because he made the right one. Don't punish him, please. He did the right thing. Thank you thank you thank you.

The Bjorn is warm with her. If I close my eyes it's almost like her weight is still pressed against me.

It's a sunny day.

I love you my beautiful baby girl. Let her read this when she's older.

Tell her to be brave.

Tell her I love her.

Tell her not to forget Earth.

None of you forget what you did to survive.

THE ILL-FATED POWER OF HAM
BY L. V. PIRES

It's Ham Day again. My brother, Troy, and I sit in the living room watching television while Mom prepares dinner. I pull out my sketchpad, ready to document the four-day event that always begins with a ham and ends with someone in tears.

Through the window, between the kitchen and living room, I periodically spy on Mom's progress. She takes her time unwrapping the ham and examining its color, shape, and texture. The color is important, Mom once told me. A pinkish tint is essential. She washes it in the sink, scrubbing in meticulous circles. A few minutes later the ham is diamond-scored, pierced with cloves and pineapple, and slid beneath a red-hot broiler. Next, she cracks open a can of yams and pours them into a pot, dropping huge chunks of brown sugar on top.

"You like them real sweet, don't you, Roxy?" she asks. Her cheeks are flushed from the heat of the oven.

"Yes, Mom," I say, in a gleeful tone.

It's important to go along with her charade. I mean who cares if Dad has left us again? Who cares if he got his girlfriend pregnant and pretends we don't know?

I continue to sketch the family scene—me, Roxy Darling, with fiery red hair, black combat boots, piercings, and attitude. Then my younger brother, Troy, the chub-monster, propped in front of the TV, and Mom, a skinny, tangled mess. Beside us, I trace the outline of IT.

IT is Dad's new baby—a pink screaming ball of fat inside a blanket. I add shades of pink and shadows around the image. I'm glad the new addition won't be living with us. I imagine Dad's new girlfriend up to her eyeballs in diaper changing and vomit.

Babies are fine on television. Producers know how to choose the most well-behaved ones who giggle and flash smiles on cue and don't scream or throw tantrums every five minutes, but most babies, and most likely Dad's new baby, are little horrors. Snot. Screaming. Life-suckers. And Dad wants another one? He can't even handle us, teenagers with attitudes and acne, now he wants to do it all over again.

The smell of burned bread drifts into the room and a second later Mom yells and the oven rack clangs to the floor. Typical. Biscuits burned. She can't do everything right, but who can?

Only Dad I guess. He is the only one who has mastered how to make a perfect dinner, followed by a perfect dessert, and a perfect cleaned kitchen. He has us all thinking we are less than perfect. But, now, torn between his imperfect family and his new perfect family, new baby with his new girlfriend, how can he ever think *he* is the perfect person?

"When's dinner going to be ready?" Troy asks, his question pulling me from my thoughts.

"A few minutes, dear," Mom says, sounding hysterical.

Plates clank against one another, drawers open and close, forks, knives, spoons clatter. I sit up again. She's rushing around, her hair a tangled mess, piled on top of her head, strands scattered all about and her oversized glasses slipping to the end of her nose.

I have to put a stop to the chaos. I place my drawing on the side table and rush to the kitchen to help. There's always this period of stress after Dad leaves, which makes Mom go crazy thinking she's a horrible person, which leads to her desperate attempts to pull normal back together. The exact definition of normal has yet to be defined in our family.

One year, she wallpapered the entire house, not stopping for a minute of sleep, until the walls of "normalcy" had been properly restored with Contemporary Floral and Cozy Cotton Sunrise. Another year, she took us on an expensive overnight vacation to the beach. I don't remember her swimming in the hotel pool or lying around soaking in the sun. Instead, she spent the whole night drinking coffee and pacing the room, asking if we were having a good time yet.

"Mom, let me do that for you," I say, taking the forks and knives from her and setting the table.

She stops for a moment to paste some of the loose hairs back. "What would I do without you?"

Her lower lip trembles and she looks like she might cry, but that never happens until Day Two, Sob Day, so I know she'll hold back the tears, and she does. She turns to the stove and bastes the ham once more.

After setting the table, I sit down and grab a napkin, folding it in the shape of a swan; something Dad taught me when I was younger. He would take each napkin and carefully press it in half, corner to corner. Once the napkin was lined evenly, he would refold it into pleats to make the tail. I can't believe the same person who carefully instructed me on the proper technique of napkin folding is causing our family so many problems. I silently vow to never do this to my own children if that day ever comes.

But, I don't want to be like my mother, either. She opens the oven again, then shuts it, turns on the oven light, and stares through the foggy glass, then turns off the light, opens the oven again and pulls out the tray. I don't want to follow some pathetic predictable pattern of desperation, crying, begging, and repair, only to be quickly followed by disappointment soon after. A whole life of patterned sadness.

It's a little early to be feeling anger. That is normally reserved for Day Three, Blame Day. That's when I blame Mom for Dad leaving, and Troy blames me for making everything more difficult, and Mom blames herself for not being good enough. Day Three is always a blast.

I take the swan napkin and ball it up into my fist, then throw it away. "What else?" I ask as Mom spears the ham with a long fork and lifts it onto a plate.

"Nothing, sweetheart. You've done enough. Just wash your hands and Troy wash your hands, too. "

Glancing over at Troy, lying flat on his stomach watching TV, he's in another world.

"Troy," I say loud enough for him to hear.

"What?" he yells.

"Wash your hands," I yell back.

"Stop yelling!" Mom screams.

Troy marches to the bathroom and slams the door behind him. I wonder if all the days are getting mixed up. Normally, Troy stays quiet on Day One, but maybe he's had enough. I know I have. I got it. He's angry, an angry kid with a shit dad and a spineless mom. It's not my fault, though. Why do I have to listen to him throw a tantrum?

I stomp over to the bathroom door and yank it open. "Don't slam the door."

He doesn't answer. His face is red and he's holding his breath, all bottled up. I walk in and close the door. Patting his back, I whisper, "Breathe, Troy. Breathe or you're going to pass out."

A second later he lets it go, exhaling a sob along with tears that transform his red face into a blotchy mess. I grab a towel and wet it, pressing the cool water against his cheeks, then sit him down on the toilet. "Just breathe, Troy. Deep breaths. In and out." I show him how.

He finally relaxes and inhales. The tears still come. I hand him the towel and he covers his face. "I hate it," he says, muffled.

I wonder if he means the tears or the family drama. I sit next to him, nearly falling off the toilet seat. "It will stop, Troy, one day. Maybe with the new baby. Maybe this will be the last time Mom lets him come back."

He pulls the towel away from his face. "It's not Dad. I know the drill. He'll be back. Baby or no baby. Day Four. He always comes back on Day Four."

I nod. I know he's right. Dad's like clockwork. Day Four, The Great Return.

Troy sniffles. "It's just that I don't want to eat ham. I think I'm a vegetarian."

I laugh and stand up. "Really? A vegetarian?" I poke his belly, making him laugh. Opening the door, I let the smell of cooked yams and brown sugar waft in. "Come on, Veggie Monster, burnt biscuits and yams await."

"You don't think Mom will be upset? It's Day One. You know how she likes everything normal on Day One." His face looks better.

I shrug. "I don't know."

We head to the dining table where Mom hovers over the ham, cutting through a giant pierced pineapple. Focusing on her task, she saws through the outer layers revealing the ham's pink insides. It instantly reminds me of IT, and a bubble of stomach bile surfaces into my throat. I swallow quickly, pushing it down.

"Who wants the first piece?" she asks, smile intact.

"Mom," I say, pulling a chair out for Troy and then circling around to my seat. "Troy's decided he's a vegetarian."

She drops her fork and knife and sits down. "Well then." Her face tightens. "Let's just pretend, at least for a little while, that you're not." She stands again, cuts off a huge chunk of ham and drops it onto Troy's plate. The steaming mass oozes juice.

Troy stares at the food. His face turns red again. He erupts into tears, pushes back his chair, and runs from the table.

Mom doesn't miss a beat, dismissing him with a wave of her hand. "Oh, don't worry about him. I'll bring him his dinner after we finish, on a nice tray with some yams. He still eats yams, doesn't he?"

I'm not sure if she's waiting for me to respond or just wondering to herself out loud. She slices off another hunk and drops it onto my plate. The tears surface and suddenly I know how Troy feels. I pick up my fork and poke the meat, trying to convince myself it isn't so bad. It's only ham. Nutrition. Food. A harmless slab of calories. A necessary, life-sustaining meal I have eaten once a year for as long as I can remember. Why should it taste any different now?

Taking a deep breath, I slice the ham in two, stab the smaller piece, and lift it to my mouth, then stop. It's now or never. The ham glistens before me. My stomach heaves. I drop my fork and shove it away.

Mom glares at me.

I push back my chair and stand up. That's it. Ham Day has officially ended.

THE HOURGLASS BRIGADE
BY ALEX SHVARTSMAN

The first sign of trouble is when they begin to keep count.

Catherine has been a good partner, one of the best. We've done over a dozen incursions together, and she's pulled her weight on every single one. Unflinching and uncomplaining, she's willing to get her hands dirty. We have been comrades in the field and lovers afterward. But now she is beginning to unravel, to doubt, to come apart, like all the ones who came before her.

"There were the five merchants in Damascus, and that couple in Budapest," she tallies the incursions, "and the scientist in twentieth century Capetown. And now, a shipload of explorers."

This is how it always begins. They add up the kills, mourning the collateral damage. They misdirect their pity, and question the Plan, and consult whatever higher power they believe in. They waver and doubt, and, before their hesitation might endanger an incursion, they're removed from the program and I never see them again. And then I have to break in a new partner.

"Those seventeen souls were heroes, you know, braving the unknown like that. I grew up wanting to be just like them."

I say nothing, continuing to steer the speedboat with one hand, as I brush wet strands of hair out of my eyes with the other.

This was an easy incursion. No hiding. No blending in. Not a living soul for miles. Just the two of us and an hour-long speedboat ride off the coast of Guadeloupe. One shoulder-launched missile later, and their rickety tub was so much driftwood floating in the Atlantic.

Those sailors, they were no heroes. They were gaunt, starving, scurvy-ridden men foolish or desperate enough to sign on. It was by sheer luck that their primitive vessel was going to make it to the New World and then back to Portugal in one piece. By all rights, the sea should have had them anyway. We merely helped it along, blowing up their ship far enough from shore to make certain none of them made it to land and contaminated the desired timeline.

We're the real heroes. We delayed the Europeans from discovering America by at least a decade and improved the lives of billions in the present. But to do it, we got close enough to see the sailors' eyes, and that was too much for Catherine.

I wonder if there's some event, some catalyst that would one day break me like that. I allowed myself to believe Catherine would be able to handle it, but now I realize that our time together is likely coming to an end.

I smile at her. Her hand finds mine and holds tight as our boat races toward the retrieval point.

⁂

I lie during the debriefing.

It is an easy lie of omission. I report only on the success of the incursion and hold back my doubts. The chink in Catherine's mental armor will take time to spread. I believe that she still has a few good missions in her; we still have time to be together, for a while longer.

It also gives me time to work out the contingencies.

I enter Kaufield's office from the hallway. The cramped room has two doors, the other entrance ajar and leading into a spare study hall. Charles Kaufield is in front of a chalkboard, talking to a dozen new recruits. Drawn on the chalkboard is an outline of an hourglass.

Having caught Kaufield's eye, I wave and point askance at his terminal. He nods slightly, without interrupting the lecture. He so loves briefing the fresh blood. None of the students notice our silent exchange. They face the chalkboard, hanging on his every word.

"For centuries, our civilization tried to outpace its problems by creating newer and better technology. We replaced whale oil with kerosene and the horse buggy with the internal combustion engine. We invented penicillin and Genome-specific drugs. We desperately kept looking for ways to feed and heal and comfort the growing population. At the height of their arrogance, our ancestors thought that we could invent our way out of trouble forever."

Kaufield paces in front of the recruits as he speaks in a raspy, low voice. As always, he stops at that point, faces his audience, looking straight at them and speaking louder for greater effect: "They were wrong."

"They fished out the oceans, drained oil reserves, and overheated the planet. And they kept reproducing." Kaufield resumes his steady movement back and forth across the room as he speaks.

"There were less than a billion people on Earth at the beginning of the nineteenth century, and six billion at the beginning of the twenty first. This number doubled in less than a hundred years, and stood at nearly twenty billion at the inception of our program. These are population levels our planet cannot possibly sustain."

Kaufield goes on to throw all kinds of numbers and statistics at his audience, but I tune him out. He is a capable bureaucrat, but he does so love the sound of his own voice. Besides, his entire premise is flawed. Nothing changed. We're still solving our problems through cutting edge technology today. I mean, it's not like time travel equipment grows on trees.

I browse the database, using Kaufield's access codes to check out the dossiers of active Hourglass agents and making a mental note of possible future partners. There are a number of promising young people with long kill sheets. Operatives who might be broken in the same ways as me, broken in ways Catherine is, sadly, proving not to be.

Kaufield is getting around to his favorite part, and I can't help but listen.

"Although the planet could no longer support the current pace of population growth, we now possessed the means to rewrite history in a way that would ultimately slow things down. With great reluctance and hesitation, humanity's best minds arrived at the conclusion that drastic measures had to be taken. And thus, the Plan was set into motion.

"Elite teams now travel into the past and alter the timeline. Very sophisticated computers crunch numbers to determine what changes are to be made, consider every possible implication and issue precise orders to the operatives."

He makes it sound so neat, almost clinical. But it isn't. We are saboteurs and murderers, the demolition men of time itself. It takes a certain kind of person to do this job for a prolonged period of time. I wonder if, under another set of circumstances, someone like me would become a killer or another kind of monster who doesn't belong in society. Perhaps I'd become a soldier, a mercenary, a thug for hire—any job that might legitimize what I am on the inside.

"We came to be known as the Hourglass Brigade," Kaufield finally brings it home, pointing at the white outline on the chalkboard. "We choke off the throat of an hourglass to make the sands of time trickle down a little slower."

I finish going through the database. There are several intriguing possibilities, but no one quite like Catherine. I am angry. Angry that she is falling apart, that she isn't living up to my expectations, but mostly angry at myself for letting the situation get to me like this.

When I slip out into the hallway, Kaufield is still talking.

❧❧❧

I step on a caterpillar, crushing it into a mess of green goo smeared into the gravel.

Some classical writer imagined that a time traveler could change the future with such a simple action. As if time could be so fragile. In reality, it is an elastic thing, resilient, and adverse to change. You can step on a bug, and time doesn't care. You can travel into the past and blow away your own grandfather, only to find that grandma procreated with someone else, and you still very much exist. You can't change history by brute force alone. It requires finesse, subtle chess-like moves that even the top players find difficult to comprehend.

Like this incursion.

Catherine and I hike in the wilderness of Ural Mountains circa 1708. We climb halfway up to the summit and set dynamite charges in a small cave, collapsing the entrance. The incredibly powerful computer at Hourglass HQ calculated that this would delay the invention of the periodic table of elements by nearly six years.

Catherine must be happy to avoid bloodshed for once. She is chipper and talkative as we make our way downhill, and all I can think about is our making love in that cave earlier on, before we set the charges. We were possibly the last two people to set foot inside for centuries to come.

We walk down the path together, sharing a moment that feels very much like happiness, when someone fires at us.

A bullet lands only inches away, throwing up dirt and rock chips. A moment later the unmistakable sound of a high-powered rifle shot catches up to it and pierces the primeval calm of the mountains. Years of training kick in, and I throw myself to the side, dragging Catherine with me. I spin around looking for the assailant and another bullet ricochets off a nearby rock.

Catherine and I crawl away from the path, looking for cover in the brush. Gravel and twigs cut my hands and face. The tough material of my combat uniform protects the rest of my body.

We settle behind a boulder, large enough to block sniper fire. There is some thick brush nearby, but the desolate steppe behind it makes further retreat impossible.

"The shooter," Catherine pants, "it must be a time traveler, like us."

No kidding. It's not like anyone has access to this kind of a weapon in the early eighteenth century.

"What do we do?" Catherine makes to peek out from behind the boulder, but I hold her back.

"Don't. Let me think."

We only brought standard issue pistols since we didn't expect any violence on this incursion. These pistols are no match for a rifle in a long-range firefight. But, as long as we stay put, we are out of reach of the rifle. Whoever wants us dead would have to come closer, evening the odds. And those odds would improve further, under the cover of night.

But there are hours of daylight left, and I don't know how many enemies we are up against. They know our exact position and can strike at any time and from any direction. Waiting it out is too risky.

"The next time they fire," I tell Catherine, "I need you to scream like you've been wounded."

I strip off my jacket, roll it up and hold it out toward the edge of the boulder, revealing a few inches of material. Seconds later, another bullet whirrs past us, very nearly missing my makeshift decoy.

I nudge Catherine, and she screams. I move as far away as the protection of the boulder allows, lying flat on my stomach under the brush. I put the camouflage jacket back on, trying to blend in to the ground.

Catherine continues to moan in pain, and it sounds rather convincing. I expect that our enemy won't be able to resist the chance to attack while they think I might be tending to her wound.

I am right.

I see him out of the corner of my eye, creeping up from the south. From my vantage point, I can see him advance carefully, staying out of Catherine's line of sight. He finally makes it to the edge of the clearing and peeks out, his eyes going wide when he sees Catherine, alone and unharmed. And before he can act, I unload my pistol at him.

Two of the bullets hit his torso, and he stumbles back, a pair of dark red stains flowering on his chest. His partner with the rifle must've stayed back because he returns fire from somewhere uphill, several bullets landing in the brush. He still can't see me from his position, but he can see his partner bleeding out across the clearing and must've fired out of frustration and anger rather than strategy.

I smile at Catherine from the brush and give her a thumbs-up. She sneers at me. "Next time we do something like this, you be the bait."

"It worked, didn't it?" I shout back.

The sniper abandons his position and runs in the general direction of our retrieval point, rifle slung on his back. It is a smart move; with his partner down, he is no longer at an advantage and could be in real trouble after dusk. I give pursuit. I gain on him somewhat during a ten-minute sprint, but I never get close enough before he disappears into the thick forest at the bottom of the hill.

The advantage is his again—and I am convinced we are dealing with a lone enemy now as he wouldn't have run otherwise. He can hide anywhere near the retrieval point and pick us off whenever we try to go home.

I wipe the sweat off my face, curse in frustration, and head back up the hill.

❀❀❀

Catherine is standing over the guy I shot. He is still alive, but only barely. I take a good look at his face, and it is familiar. Although this man is in his thirties, I saw the photo of the younger version of him among the personnel files in Kaufield's office.

"Tell him what you told me," says Catherine.

"Don't go back," he whispers. "Timeline. Corrupted." He is struggling to speak, spitting the words out between ragged breaths. He tenses up, trying to say something else, but can't do it. His body relaxes, and he is no longer breathing at all.

Catherine kneels over him, checking for vital signs. I clench my teeth, hating the fact that all of my suspicions are being confirmed. Catherine is going to mess up, in an upcoming mission. Mess up so badly that the Hourglass Brigade felt it was necessary to take both of us out of the picture, permanently.

The right thing to do would be to finish what the assassins had started. I could put a bullet in the back of her head, and she'd be dead before she even knew what was happening. But I still can't bring myself to do it. Also, my odds of surviving the encounter with the dead man's partner aren't as good alone.

"What else did you get out of him?" I ask.

"He claimed to be one of ours," Catherine says once she finishes checking the body, "eight years uptime. He said that one of our upcoming missions is going to go wrong and screw up the timeline in some major way." She turns toward me. "I thought the computer calculates our moves to the point where a mistake like that is impossible?"

So she doesn't know that she is the problem. That is going to make things easier.

"We need to get back," I say. "Straighten things out. Maybe even drop out of the Brigade if that's what it takes to protect the timeline."

"I don't think they'll let us go back," she says and her voice trembles. For Catherine, that's an equivalent of somebody else bawling their eyes out. "Think about it. If that was a viable solution, they would've sent word downtime. But they didn't."

She is right. For whatever reason, we are deemed too dangerous to return.

"We can't win against someone uptime," she says. "They'll just keep sending agents, deeper into our past if they have to, until they get us."

Yes, they could. But they didn't—we are still alive in this timeline. Does this mean that the sniper is going to get us, after all? Or that I would end up taking care of business before this incursion was over?

"We have to try," I say. "Maybe we'll get lucky. Maybe it was some rogue elements within the Brigade that ordered the hit, or the computer sent the other team expecting it to be eliminated by us. Whatever the answer, we've got to fight. Otherwise we might as well walk up to the sniper and let him shoot us."

Catherine nods. They say hope is the last thing that dies in a person. She can't give up, won't give up so long as we have any chance at all. She will fight alongside me and do her absolute best to get us past the sniper. And then… Then, we will see.

We wait until dark to make our move.

We barely speak at all as we wait for the sun to go down. Instead, I stare at the familiar features of Catherine's face, the curves of her body, the way she tilts her head when she is deep in thought.

There is plenty of time to think, to reflect. And, in that vast emptiness of the Ural steppes, I come to realize that there is no way I can ever hurt Catherine. Am I in love with her? I can't tell for sure. My emotions are… complicated. But whether it's love, or something else, I can't bring myself to kill her, not even to save my own skin. There has to be another solution.

Catherine was wrong when she said that you can't defeat an uptime opponent. You can alter their past, as surely as you can alter your own. I am beginning to formulate a plan.

The details of it brew in my head as we crawl through the forest in the dark. The sniper has to be watching the retrieval point, our only escape route, limiting the physical area we have to cover.

We move through the forest as quietly and deliberately as we can. Contrary to what most people imagine, a nighttime forest isn't a quiet place. Gusts of wind rustle the leaves, and all manner of nighttime creatures fill the woods with sounds of life. The sniper does not hear us coming, not until it is too late.

He is lying on the ground behind a fallen tree trunk, his rifle pointed at the retrieval point. He twists around and scrambles for his handgun, but we are already on top of him. Catherine shoots him in the face at nearly point blank range. Our path back home is now cleared.

I know what our next step should be.

We will return to headquarters and, before anyone has a chance to ask questions, begin another incursion. We can go somewhere safe and very remote—I am thinking seventeenth century Polynesia—where we can live out the rest of our lives leaving no trace for the Hourglass Brigade to find. And as we leave the Hourglass HQ forever, we'll set off our remaining explosive charges.

No ultra-sophisticated computer equipment would mean no more Hourglass Brigade and no more assassins capable of traveling into our past to stop us.

The fact alone that I'm still alive at this point in time means that my plan is going to work. The hardest part is going to be explaining all of it to Catherine. I smile and turn toward her.

Catherine's pistol is aimed right at me.

"I can't let you go back." Her lips tremble and her knuckles are white from squeezing the barrel too tight, but she holds the gun steady. "The man from the future, he told me you were the problem. You are going to do something terrible; bad enough to warrant a hit squad. He said you'd lay waste to Hourglass HQ, if you were permitted to return. He said I could come home, but only without you."

"No! He lied to you, Catherine. You were the one who began faltering. You were the problem. But we can fix it. I have a plan. We can beat them together, you and I." Even as I speak these words, I know that her mind is already made up.

I was a master of time, once. Now I stare into Catherine's impossibly blue eyes, and realize that all I want to do is to prolong this one moment of it, to keep looking at her forever.

"I'm sorry," she whispers. Her finger tightens on the trigger. "It's not me. It's you."

NICE GUYS
BY ADREAN MESSMER

After work, she said she wanted to go for a walk. She said she was angry and confused and needed to get away from everyone for a little bit. Everyone except me. Because I was always so nice and understanding.

So, I said, "Okay," and I led her away from the office. Down the road, past the small apartment complex and elementary school to the stream behind it all. No, not stream. That makes it sound like something beautiful and babbling, surrounded by trees and maybe nymphs or unicorns. It's more like a creek. The kind of man-built creek with concrete walls made to keep the city from flooding. But, if you follow it far enough, and I make sure we do, nature starts to take over. The concrete cracks, turns to rocks and gravel. The incline to the water decreases. Eventually, it's a tiny trickle of water surrounded by dirt and grass.

When I was a kid and lived in that apartment complex and went to that school, I used to come down here. I'd squat in the mud and catch the tadpoles and crawdaddies. The only things strong enough to live here. At first, I brought a bucket and a net. But eventually, I learned to catch them with my bare hand. They weren't fast, just hearty.

I pulled the legs off the crawdads. I used to catch tadpoles down here. Tadpoles and crawdaddies. I pulled the legs off the crawdads. The tadpoles, I held in my hand, sometimes in a tiny pool of water, but usually not, until they squirmed, then a little longer until they stopped completely. Sometimes, I pressed my thumb into my palm on top of them. Popping them. Like bubble wrap. Their insides were green and

279

white. I always tried to make out the parts. Intestines were easy. Usually, though, it was all too squished.

But right now it's now and I'm not by myself. Now, I'm here with the lovely Lori Linder and I don't think she'd like to hear about smashing tadpoles. Even if it doesn't matter. Even if I explain that they don't feel things like I do. Like she does. I'm a gentleman and I wouldn't want to do anything to make her uncomfortable. I want her to like me the way people in movies like each other.

The way Drew Barrymore likes men. The way she's always with someone else, some jerk that doesn't tell her she's pretty enough. Then she meets her best friend, Adam Sandler or Matthew McConaughey, or me, and she tells him everything. He's always there for her, to listen to her and take care of her. She doesn't know it yet, but they're meant to be together. He chases her. He follows her. She acts angry, but she isn't. Not really. She just has to do that. It's part of the game. It's what women do. And by the end of the movie, they fall in love. They kiss. They have sex.

I want to have sex with Lori. But I don't say that. Can't just say that.

She looks at me over her shoulder. Her eyes are still rimmed with red from the crying. The deep, wateriness makes them shine. I could drown in them. I want to.

She smiles anyway, even though she's sad. Just a slight twitch of her mouth. It's a sign. She still has to act heartbroken. Even though she's known for a long time that Jared was a jerk. Even though she knows she deserves someone better. Someone like me. Even though it's just the two of us, I know she has to do this. Because she's a good person and a good person would be hurt in this situation.

"Is that a goldfish?" She asks.

I nod. I don't know what it is. I don't even see it because I'm too busy watching the way her tongue moves across her teeth when she talks. She's so pretty and the sun is setting and the water looks all dark and red and the sky is gold like her hair.

She's a mermaid sitting on the bank. Like the lorilie in the poem. The one that combs her hair and sings and leads men to their deaths. Lorilie. Lori. Lie. She's so pretty and pure and I just want to bang her, bang her, bang her against the rocks and I don't care if I die at the end because she is everything.

Lorilie, Lori lies. Does she, I wonder? Would she lie to me? For me? If we did it would she be my girlfriend like on TV? Or would she lie like the ones on the police shows and say I did something bad to her? Say I hurt her? But I don't want to hurt her. I mean, I do want to hurt her, but only so she knows she's mine. And she'll like it. They always like it in the end.

She turns back to the fish. Her hair slips over her shoulder, the ends of it grazing the smooth, glassy surface. I move closer and when I'm almost there, I could reach out my arm and touch her, she turns, facing me, and crosses her arms. Blocks me out. Sets her face. Squares her shoulders. I know this part. This is always how it goes. I hate this part of the game. The "no."

She doesn't know I know, so I have to sit down and go along with it. I cross my legs so my knee touches her shin. She doesn't move away. This is okay. This is good.

Today, I was in the hall. I heard Lori talking to Sela the slut in the breakroom. Sela with her bleached hair. Not golden like Lori's, but yellow. Yellow like straw and brittle and scratchy and smelling like cheap shampoo and old towels. Lori was telling Sela about her boyfriend. About how Jared was an asshole who didn't get her.

"He cheated," she says to me after a long pause.

It's starting to get cold with the sun going behind the trees.

I furrow my brow and I frown even though I want to smile. Don't smile, don't smile. I already know this but I've gotta keep on the downlow, low, low.

"I'm so sorry," I say. "You deserve better," I say. Like me, but I don't say that.

I smile and I shrug, spreading out my hands and my fingers. A good gesture. Harmless. I show her how I'm not holding anything. How I'm safe. How I won't hurt her until she wants me to. Until she'll like it. And I talk to her slow and even. The way my dad did when he lead the pigs into the stockade.

"It's okay. I don't bite." Lie. Maybe not. Not yet, I don't bite. Present tense, I don't bite. I will bite. Future tense. I want to taste her.

"I know," she says, loosening her stance. "I'm sorry."

I sit next to her. Close. Close enough to feel the tiny hairs on her arm brush against mine. But then she leans away. She leans on her other hand and tries to pretend it's so she can look into the creek but I know what she's doing. Hard to get. The rules. She's not allowed to tell me she's interested. She has to do this. Do this or be like Sela the slut. She'd have to learn how to put on blue eyeshadow and paint those dark points at the outer corner of her eyes. Wear red lipstick and nasty dresses.

I know why she does it and I don't mind. I know it's because she loves me. She wouldn't have put on those clothes if she didn't. I told her I liked that shirt. White undershirt with a tiny bow, perfectly centered. Gauzy over-shirt with little flowers and I can see the color of her skin through the arms. And the blue skirt that flips and sometimes catches in the wind so I get just a flash of the cotton fabric of her panties. She knows I like the outfit. I told her so.

I put my hand over hers and she goes still. Even her breathing pauses. She tries to pull away and I don't even get mad because I know she has to do it. I lace my fingers into hers and hold tight.

"Kaleb, don't."

Now it's time for her to shut up, so I kiss her. I crush my lips against hers and she tries to move back, but I don't let her because I know she wants this and I have two hands and one of them is finding a rock. She makes a sound and its beautiful and now for sure she wants the same thing I do because she's holding my hand just as tight and even though she's trying to pull back it doesn't mean anything because they all do that. All of them except Sela the slut and the other girls like her with too-tight clothes and painted nails.

She tries to get her feet underneath her, but she's a mermaid, flopping in the mud. Slipping and sliding and hot and sticky and warm against me. Her heart beats and I feel through her chest and shirt and my shirt and my chest and my heart skips to match hers and we are meant to be together. I will not be an asshole like her boyfriend. I will treat her right. I will keep her just like this, beautiful and lovely and young forever.

I feel her skull crack as I bring the rock against the side of her head. She stops trying to get away and lays down, presenting herself for me. Red ribbons in her hair. Red like Sela's lipstick. Red like Sela's nails. I run my hand through her hair. Touch the trailing color. Smear it on her lips. Kiss her again hard and I can taste the blood. Bringing her into me. No one will ever treat her this well.

I am very nice.

SEVEN SHIPS
BY LIAM HOGAN

Seven ships set sail into the starry skies.

The Earth was dying. It had been unwell for a while, truth be told, but now the malaise was obvious to even the most blinkered of its inhabitants and it was deemed terminal. Indeed, there were those who said it was already dead, it just hadn't realised it yet. Each attempt to eco-engineer a solution seemed to only make things a thousand times worse, it was as if the Earth itself had given up.

With a last herculean effort, and consuming much that was left to be consumed, seven mighty space-faring vessels were built with the desperate intent to launch these seven life boats towards seven stars around which seven near-Earths had been detected.

But what to fill these mighty space arks with?

Only the best would do: the finest wonders and most precious treasures that mankind had accumulated over the millennia. The most stunning art, the greatest literature, the noblest science.

And people? These ships, massive though they were, could still only carry a fraction of a fraction of the multitudes that teemed on the Earth's now barren surface. A scant one in a million was all that could be saved. Who was worthy of such an honour?

Earth was dying at mankind's cruel hand and it was imperative that only those who would never repeat that mistake were permitted to leave, to start anew. Only the healthiest bodies, the keenest of intellects, the most virtuous of souls, could pass the strict tests that were set. Although the tests were open to all, very few got through even the preliminary rounds.

Most, failed to recognise exactly what was being tested.

Sure, there were written papers of knowledge and wisdom, physical tests of strength and agility, of reaction times and stamina, medical tests that scrutinised every part of the body, right down to the DNA. A single blemish, the merest hint of an imperfection, was enough to rule you out.

But there was also an interview that you would be asked to wait for. And having been kept waiting for three hours, would you wait for another five? Or, if you passed this test and reached the final stages, would you turn down an offer of a million dollars, tax free, simply for letting someone else take your place?

Many fell at this final hurdle and left, clutching bundles of cash that the administrators of the exhaustive selection process were more than happy to pay out, knowing that they had preserved the moral fortitude of what was destined to become the new (and improved) human race.

Finally the candidates were ready. Finally they bid farewell to their not-quite-so-blue-as-it-had-once-been planet. Finally, seven gleaming teardrops rode seven towering columns of flame up out of the poisoned atmosphere, before unfurling sails the size of Luxemburg to catch the solar wind and help push the last best chance for mankind towards their distant destinations.

They never made it, of course.

The SS Chastity was probably the most successful—that ship did indeed reach its intended target of Kepler-186f, though by then there was no-one left to slam on the brakes. Faster-than-light travel—along with a carbon-neutral lifestyle and clean water for all—being the stuff of fairytales, these were Generation ships, taking multiple lifetimes to travel the vastness of space and, alas, the crew of the SS Chastity singularly failed to procreate their replacements. Perhaps some future alien race will find their desiccated skeletons and wonder why so many of them have their legs tightly crossed.

The SS Charity stopped to help the SS Diligence, whose captain had fallen asleep at the helm after a watch lasting 96 straight hours. Noble though this rescue attempt was, these Space Ships did not have enough fuel to change course and stop in this manner and they certainly did not have enough to start their epic journeys once again. Both ships now float powerless and lifeless out somewhere in the icy wastes of the Oort cloud, dancing a slow waltz around each other, occasionally disturbing the frozen comets that are their nearest neighbours.

The crew of the SS Temperance starved itself to death, the SS Patience never seemed to find the right moment to unfurl their sails and the SS Humility was... humbled by smacking straight into Pluto, which was mysteriously absent on their star charts, having somehow fallen between the cracks of classification as neither a planet nor a trans-Neptunian body.

As for the SS Kindness? We don't talk about the SS Kindness.

And the Earth they left behind? How did it fare?

Well, it was still dying. If anything, it was dying all the quicker—when the best that mankind had to offer ascended into the skies, those left behind responded in an unbridled orgy of sex and excessive consumption, thankfully free of anyone to tell them that such behaviour was in any way morally reprehensible. Oh, there were still priests, of course. Lots of them. But if they hadn't managed to secure a berth on one of the seven ships of the truly pious, just what sort of frauds were they to tell you what was right and what was wrong?

Food piles that had been expected to last another decade were consumed in week long contests of gluttony, held in museums emptied of their ancient splendours, or in echoing art galleries, their walls stripped bare.

Roaming tribes of the disenchanted, the disaffected, the seriously pissed off, rampaged through the massive complexes where they had been denied their rightful place amongst the stars, wrecking them in blind fury.

But most people did nothing. Nothing at all: just sat and watched the chaos unfold in glorious high definition 3D TV.

Oddly enough, it was the reports from the Seven Ships that slowly changed all of that. As, one by one, they failed, as their beamed status reports, meant to give hope, to promise some ethereal future for the race they were supposed to preserve, as these reports became bleaker and bleaker, the wrath and envy that had been felt towards these do-goody departees slowly diminished.

And when the last and final message dissipated into the solar static, mankind bucked itself up. Sure, their planet was doomed. Sure, the best and brightest among them had left long ago (though look where that had got them). Sure, lots of those left behind were so obese they would have had a heart attack if asked to leave their homes, never mind their planet, but hey, screw that. Can we fix it? Yes we can!

Well—they couldn't fix the Earth, not even by all dying off overnight. But they could still build spaceships. They weren't pretty, far from it, they differed as much from those seven lost ships of virtue as their occupants from the idealised demi-gods who had been the first to leave the planet. These ships were monstrosities born of necessity and whatever was closest to hand. Once you knew that there was nothing to come back to, you could put everything—every bridge, every car, every

Canary Wharf—into building as many and as varied spacecraft as you could imagine. And there were lots of people with some seriously messed up imaginations; it comes from watching endless reruns of Battlestar Galactica, I shouldn't wonder.

Many of these ships never got out of the solar system. Many never even left the ground, except for parts of them, brightly coloured flaming parts screaming through the air. But you can't make an omelette—well, you haven't been able to make an omelette since the last chicken was smothered in ghost pepper sauce and used in the deciding bout of an extreme hot wings eating contest. (So, if you ever wanted to know what came last, the chicken or the egg, it was the chicken.)

Survival is a numbers game. Seven ships was never particularly good odds, not over interstellar distances, but how about 70 ships? How about 700? How about 700,000, some no bigger than a VW Camper van. Some *were* VW camper vans, though they did have a rather unfortunate tendency to leak air like a sieve. When the last craft—constructed from the salvaged shell of the Sydney Opera house—blasted off, it left an Earth drained of its oceans, its forests denuded, its mountains replaced by steaming slag heaps. Not a single human soul remained behind. Well, nobody this story concerns itself with, anyway.

Of course, many of those 700,000 ships were very poorly equipped. But you'd be surprised how quickly a bit of space piracy sorts the wolves from the lambs. And the lambs? Into the pot they would go, after all, protein *is* protein.

Mankind cheated, stole, murdered, and indeed, screwed their way across the Universe. Some are still doing that now. Others have settled, and perhaps, in 10,000 years or so, will need once again to flee the burnt embers of their resource-stripped planets.

But they'll keep doing it, keep despoiling their homes and seeking new ones, spreading like a virulent disease to every habitable body. And woe betide any sentient species whose path they cross, for this crusade carries with it seven devastating weapons: seven evolutionary survival strategies for every conceivable eventuality, seven terrible vices that make them so *undeniably* human.

ABOUT THE STORYTELLERS

Everyone knows that a gathering of crows is called a *murder*, but they're also called a *storytelling*. As writers, we aim to tell our stories, murdering those errors and fears that hold us back.

Please help us by reviewing this book. Whether you liked it or not, authors need your feedback and your voice to be heard.

To learn more about any of the authors or projects, visit http://www.amurderofstorytellers.com/.

Made in the USA
Lexington, KY
26 October 2016